S0-BDP-119

"AS EXOTIC AS *DON QUIXOTE* . . . A SLOW—MOVING, FANTASTICALLY DETAILED QUEST."

The Kirkus Reviews

"A MESMERIZING STORYTELLER . . . A RICH, CONTROLLED PROSE THAT RIVETS THE IMAGINATION."

Library Journal

"The style here is polished without being mannered, and the enigmatic, ambiguous quality of this portrait of a man of notoriety falls comfortably and unaffectedly into the magical realism mode so often practiced by Latin American writers."

Booklist

"THE CHARACTERS AND EVENTS ARE NOT QUITE OF THIS WORLD; THEY ARE OUTSIZE, LEGENDARY, THE STUFF OF FOLKLORE."

Publishers Weekly

THE
TIGER

Lisa St Aubin de Terán

BALLANTINE BOOKS • NEW YORK

ISBN 0-345-33680-1

This edition published by arrangement with Franklin Watts, Inc.

Manufactured in the United States of America

First Ballantine Books Edition: October 1986

Contents

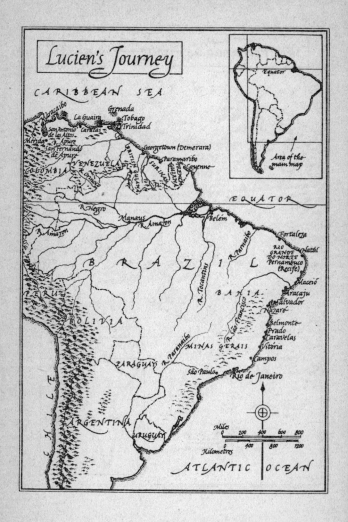

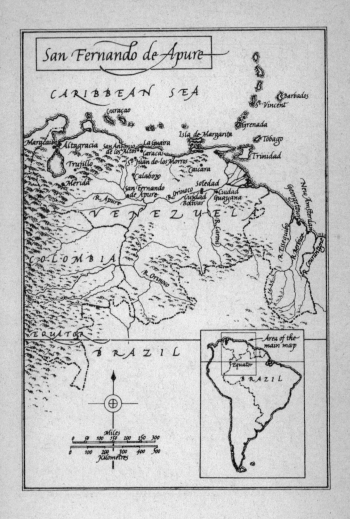

San Fernando de Apure

CARIBBEAN SEA

Barbados
St Vincent
Curaçao
Grenada
Isla de Margarita
Tobago
Maracaibo
Altagracia
San Antonio de los Altos
La Guaira
Trinidad
Caracas
Trujillo
St Juan de los Morros
Merida
Calabozo
Caicara
San Fernando de Apure
Soledad
R. Apure
Orinoco
Ciudad Bolivar
Ciudad Guayana
georgetown
VENEZUELA
New Amsterdam
R. Caroni
COLOMBIA
R. Essequibo
R. Berbice
Courantyne
EQUATOR
R. Orinoco
B R A Z I L

Miles
0 50 100 150 200 250 300
0   100 200 300 400 500
Kilometres

Area of the main map
Equator
B R A Z I L

I

The Empress of the Orinoco

Chapter 1

Lucien lived in a landscape of fear, on the dry lands known as los Llanos, 'the flatlands', whose name stretched over the plains with a resigned echo of their flatness and that only. And there, the sun never set, but sank and was buried in the hot dust and lay in a scratched grave with the remains of dead cows, crawling out each early morning to gloat in the sky. Lucien had been born in el Llano, and he and his brothers were the sons and heirs of these lands of frayed hessian, with their sleeping sickness and their diarrhoeas. They were the masters of the peasants' bloat, and of twenty thousand head of Ceibu cow that dropped dead in their tracks in the drought three years out of four, but on the fourth year they sold for bags of coins, and life was like that, like roulette.

Lucien lived in a household that lived in the dread of Misia Schmutter, whose Prussian spine had never touched the back of a chair. She wore whalebone stays, even, it was rumoured, in bed, and her voice was rarely raised above a whisper. The servants said that the waters of the Orinoco obeyed the whispers of Misia Schmutter, but then the servants were mesmerised with fear.

Haydn Lucien Schmutter had been denied the use of his full name by his grandmother, Misia Schmutter, and from his earliest childhood he was known by his first surname alone. No one ever dared to ask her why it should be so. Neither did anyone ever question why, at the age of seventy, Misia Schmutter, who was preparing to die, and had been setting her house in order accordingly, should have

3

discovered Haydn Lucien, aged three, in his nursery, and taken him to her wing of the house. And her heart, no longer of horsehair, became human, but not again, because no one could remember it having happened before.

So her frailty of the desiccating climate left her, and a shrillness returned to her quiet voice when she drilled the servants or pounced on their faults, or caught the man at the pump at the moment when he stopped pumping and ordered him to be whipped in the courtyard. And always four paces behind her came Lucien, her diminutive page in white linen, who had been freed from the boredom of the nursery to live with this white-haired old lady who treated the world like her slave.

In the evenings, when everything was done, and the maids were locked into the sheds where she kept them, and her son, el Patrón, who was Lucien's father, had been given his gun to go whoring, and the trays of dough had been set to rise for the night; after the boys had been beaten and the dogs unleashed, Misia Schmutter would tell Lucien stories until he fell asleep. Every night, when Lucien's eyes closed under his mosquito net, he culled his grandmother's whispers through the whirring of wings. She had such hopes for him. She told him stories about her native Prussia, and about her family there, and about her husband, Don Wilhelm Lucien, who had died of a snake bite, and who, she claimed, had lacked the will-power to live. Best of all, she told him about Der Altman, who had been the first of them all to come from Germany, and whose name had also been just Lucien, like him.

Lucien loved to hear how his family had begun with this Altman who had travelled from the Black Forest to La Guaira, crossing the Atlantic battened under the decks with the other survivors of the famine that had ruined them and their corn and potato crops, and that had stripped them of everything but their pig-headedness, and brought them penniless and half-starved to the Customs House of La Guaira with nothing to declare but their poverty and their determination to survive.

More than anything on his father's lands, Lucien loved the old gazebo on the raised ground over the eastern cattle pens, skirted by orchards and a thicket of honeysuckle. This delicate stone building was said to be older than the estate house itself. Later, as a man, he was to have many passions, but as a child he had just one, his gazebos. Nobody ever questioned his right to have them. Even the first one, the family one that had stood for so long before he was born, became 'his' by right of usage. Later, with the help of the estate carpenters, he built them himself, labouring over their design and decoration. Misia Schmutter imported and employed painters and carvers to finish his work on belvedere after belvedere. Evidence of these buildings was to be found for miles around the estate house where he lived. He built them with the singlemindedness of Der Altman, and gradually he grew familiar with the arts of plaster-moulding and gilding, and the way to his heart was through presents of panes of stained glass and ancient lintels, or of beams of black beechwood that were slow to burn, and poles of the primeval tirndí, the fern tree that made wooden pillars like stone. While one of his gazebos was under construction, Lucien had no thought for anything but the thing itself, and an ear for the subdued shrillness of his grandmother's calling. But once they were finished, and in the brief reign of each one, he would lie on a carved bench that he had carried from one to the next, and think about himself in the context of his history, of his father, and his grandmother, and Der Altman and the intermittent Luciens who had tyrannised the plains and Llanos of San Fernando de Apure with such rigidity for the past hundred and fifty years.

It was on this ornate bench that Lucien did his thinking. Misia Schmutter claimed it had been carved by the great Grinling Gibbons, and Lucien had never contradicted her, although he knew better. How could that foreigner have come into this wilderness of San Fernando? And how could the wood have survived the onslaughts of beetle and giant bee, and the steady boring of the woodworm? Not to mention the invisible breath of dry rot that the heat and the damp spored everywhere, so that no house in San Fernando could withstand more than a century of this natural warfare. But Misia Schmutter, in her wisdom, had her fantasies, and this was one of them. If anything, it pleased Lucien to see her ease the whalebones of her principles, if only in these minor details of woods and carvers. And although Lucien knew that the carved grape was the grape of their own orchard and not the sign of the master, and that the G.G. in the tally book was for Gregario Gonzalez,

5

carver, of Bogotá, and not the other, he kept his silence, and his grandmother kept her pride, in this relic of 'the superiority of European art'.

It was on this special seat, overhung with mangoes and cashew fruits, or bucare or guavas, depending on where it was, that Lucien mastered the rudiments of his philosophy. It was there that he came to believe that life was entirely a matter of chance and decision; in fact, just a game of roulette. It was chance that had led Der Altman to acquire the wealth he did, and decision that had enabled his heirs to keep it. All that was required of Lucien himself, from his release from the nursery at the age of three to the later days when he sat on his carved bench, aged nine and ten and eleven, was that he behave like a man, and attend to his meals with impeccable manners. Misia Schmutter insisted on this.

But men were not men in the usual sense of the word on those wastes of San Fernando, a man was an image on Misia Schmutter's mind, he must be a modern Altman with a love of art, he must have Der Altman's strength without his animality. There were few specimens, especially in that underpopulated place, with the clay worth moulding into this perfect man. Misia Schmutter had despaired, and prepared to die, and grown bitter in her disappointment, but she had found the makings of her Messiah, a man who would be one of a chosen few whose right and duty it was to control the earth, as she did. She had seen the glint of her own ruthlessness in Lucien's baby eye, and she had chosen him as the new high priest of her hopes. But she taught him only the outward order, and nothing inside. So Lucien grew harder and in places softer than other boys, but nobody really noticed that he was strange, in that landscape of eccentricity. If it hadn't been for his gazebos, he could still have fitted into the loose ritual of the estate.

'After all,' his brothers whispered, 'he spends so much time with Misia Schmutter: I wouldn't be Lucien for the world.'

Misia Schmutter wasn't all corsets, though. When they were alone in her wing of the house, and the double doors were closed that led to the hall, and Thor, her favourite bull mastiff, was patrolling the corridors, the two of them played for hours and hours on end, and there were always the stories. Misia Schmutter only ever played one game, roulette. She had a strange ability to shed her years around the lip of her ebony wheel. Lucien never felt her condescend to his age; she wasn't playing to amuse him, but to amuse herself, and he felt their age difference only when he lost heavily, and the time came for the forfeits, but mostly they played with counters and splinters of wood. Even when the forfeits did come, Misia Schmutter would grow drunk with her gain, and give Lucien cranberry glasses of chilled Rhine wine that was brought up from the cellar, and that not even his father was allowed to touch. Once, when he was five, Lucien had asked Misia Schmutter why this wheel game of hers was so much fun, and she had said,

'Because you can monitor chance, Lucien. And sometimes you can control it; only the great can ever master chance.'

Lucien was often aware that his father didn't like him, and he was hurt by the rejection. The last of Lucien's brothers had gone away to school: two to the Jesuits in Mérida, two to the military academy at La Grita, and two to Caracas. Of all the boys, only he was left to fend for himself and find his own education. And he was forbidden to play with his sisters. Sporadically, he had tried to feel something for the eighty-odd children of the estate, bunched into straggling groups of fours and fives, and even the ten brothers Sanchez, but he could only despise their poverty. For him, their apathy had nothing to do with the amoebae that they scrabbled up with the dirt in their food. He saw it only as a lack of decision, they refused to rise up out of their penury and their hovels, and he had no sympathy for these boys of the plains with the niguas tunnelling into the calloused skin of their bare feet, and their legs festering with thorn sores. These boys were unlucky, these sons of his father's peasants; even the fat sons of the servants, fed on scraps and squeezed into cast-off clothing, were weak to remain where they were. They were all unlucky in their lot, and bad luck was a crime in Misia Schmutter's Bible. All Lucien's respect was reserved for the men who could live up to his and Misia Schmutter's ideals: men such as Lope de Aguirre who had defied the King of Spain and declared himself the wrath of God, men like Boves, el Urugallo the military tyrant, and Bismarck, and Wagner, and their own Der Altman.

Der Altman had arrived, poorer even than the children whose friendship he spurned. He had worked day and night for six months to earn enough money to buy a mule and a few tools to take into the Interior. Then he had set out along the patches of cobble and dust that formed the King's Way, the Camino Real, from La Guaira to San Juan de los Morros, Calabozo and, finally, San Fernando. He had had no destination in mind, and no trade other than his former blunt skills as a farmer. He was just a German peasant in a foreign land with his mind set on making something of his life, and determined to let no one stop him.

The name 'San Fernando', so different from the guttural sounds from his own mouth, had caught his fancy, and he turned towards there, rather than anywhere else in that straggling Spanish colony, because it reminded him of an aria he had heard once as a boy at the street opera in Heidelberg, and he liked it. The first days of his journey had been uneventful. It was the end of the rainy season, and after six months of stopping leaks and nursing fevers, the people of this Venezuelan State, now called Miranda, were taking to the roads again. Government officials with their boxes of papers rode past him on their way between the Governors of the State of Guyana and the capital. Soldiers and prelates, noblemen and slaves all travelled the thin winding road with its uneven cobbles that wore down both shoes and hooves and kept only the blacksmiths happy.

Most of the travellers had too much haste of their own to notice Der Altman, on foot and alone at a time when a retinue, if only of family, was usual. But some, intrigued by his size, and his cropped blond hair, so different to any of their fashions, and his piercing blue eyes, stopped and asked him where he came from, and where he was going. But Der Altman had no mind to stop for anyone, and he feigned more ignorance of their language than he really had, so that he could keep moving, and not even pause for the peasant girls who came as near to the roadside as they dared, to stare and giggle at his height and colouring. Der Altman was going somewhere, he didn't know where, and he wanted to get there, so he plodded on with one hand on his mule, in case it should stray from him, or be stolen. And even the malandros, who lived by waylaying lonely travellers, instinctively let him pass, with his fat hands and his thin purse, because he had the shadow of murder in his eye, and he wasn't worth dying for. So he kept going, with his cropped head pointing stubbornly towards the Orinoco, until he reached the toll-gate of Calabozo.

Der Altman had a peasant's inbred dislike of surprises. In La Guaira he had slept under a tarpaulin on the docks, and he had eaten only gulls' food and drank no ale. He had scraped and denied himself so that he could save enough to carry him through all the toll-gates for as far as San Fernando. He hadn't been able to plan much of his journey, but he had learnt to decipher the names of the places he would travel through, and months of questioning had taught him that it would cost him one rial to travel through every toll-gate on his route. He had decided that, should he fall sick, he would keep going, and if his mule should fall sick, he would carry its load himself, and if it should die, he would skin it and cure the meat, and salt and lime the hide. He had sewn his money into thin bands of cloth in individual money-belts so that when he drew one rial it would always seem to be his last. Death alone would part him unbudgeted from his money.

Der Altman was not, therefore, prepared for the tollman of Calabozo, when the man took his rial as payment for himself and still barred his way through the gate.

'That will be another rial for the mule,' the tollman said while the German looked at him in stupefied silence.

'Pay for the mule,' the tollman said again.

Der Altman came slowly to his senses, and then drew himself up from his stoop to his full height, which so towered above other men and which had given him his name, and then he answered firmly, 'No.'

The tollman was not used to dealing with men of this stature, neither was his post a court of law. It was not his place to decide, but to gather the Viceroy's money, and the law was very clear, 'At Calabozo: one rial per head'. All luggage passed free if it could be carried across, but 'horses, donkeys and mules, one rial each'. So the tollman asked again, more angrily now, with a crowd beginning to block the road, 'Pay for the mule.'

Der Altman refused. The tollman was more upset than angry—toll was toll, either you paid, or you skirted the road and risked the snakes in the scrub that crossed the bumpy plains. The tollman had his musket by his side, but he was cowed by Der Altman's outrage.

Misia Schmutter told the story of Der Altman's journey to San Fernando more times than Lucien could recall, but he could remember the detail. It built up like brush strokes to a maximum of points, and then it would be told and retold, always in the same words, like a herbal recipe or a chemical formula. And there would be pauses during which he would be expected to comment and inquire. And this was one of them. Waiting deadlocked at the toll-gate, Misia Schmutter waited for Lucien to say, 'And then what happened, Misia Schmutter?' And he could sense the contours softening momentarily under her stays.

Lucien knew that she liked to be asked, and he recognised her pleasure which she showed by flurries of irritation, rearranging the lace of her gloves, or shaking imaginary creases from her hem, before she would say, in her special thin whisper, 'And then the Viceroy came.'

For Misia Schmutter, even these stories were part of the order of things. It was as essential to her that Lucien should keep asking his questions in wonder, as it was that the servants should scrub their hands with carbolic. She inspected their nails every morning only half for their cleanliness, and half as a referendum of her power. She always punished uncleanliness with stripes of her own knotted thong, given across the wrists directly before breakfast. And all of the servants were scarred the same. Even the ones whose nails were impeccable had worn her bracelets of welts. Even Lucien, who alone could control her displeasure, and whom, of all the household, she strove to please, would suffer if he missed a cue for a question when she was telling him about Der Altman. Only then, or if he made the slightest murmur from his mouth while he ate, or let a scrap fall from his plate. None of the children had much of an appetite, they would eat fruit in season in preference to the delicacies of their table, because never yet had a meal been finished when one or other of the assembled company had not mismanaged some aspect of the food. Then the younger children would be beaten and strapped into their beds for days on end, and the boys would be tied to the post in the courtyard and flogged or just left to the sun for an afternoon, and the girls would be locked in the meat cellar, where the smell made them sick, and then that made Misia Schmutter even worse.

Lucien alone was preserved from her scourges against

uncleanliness. For him, there was a private punishment. She spared him the humiliation she caused the others; even his father, el Patrón, could be confined to his quarters by Misia Schmutter. But, on the rare occasions when Lucien transgressed, she would wait until they were alone, and then stand him in the marble hall that led to her apartments, and beat him with her worn piece of knotted leather until she tired, or he collapsed. And Lucien couldn't help noticing as he grew older that she beat him less and less hard. And he knew things about Misia Schmutter that no one would have believed. He, of all the world, had seen her weep. She used to weep when she beat him. It was one of their many secrets. She would squeeze her aching grandson to her breast and beg him to understand, and he understood that certain things were unpardonable and that, in their house, lack of etiquette and lack of respect were the worst crimes. Lucien knew that he was different—Misia Schmutter would never punish him for herself, unlike the others; she beat him for Der Altman, and for his future, because one day he would be famous, and the order of things had to be part of him.

She would hold him to her, forcing his blond head into her stays, denting his cheeks against the sharp sticks of her clothing, and keeping him there with her spindly arms until he forgave her. In lieu of words, she accepted his relaxing in her grip as a sign of forgiveness. He always relaxed, eventually, although it was sometimes at the point where he felt that his neck would snap after one more second in the vice of her thin arms and her corsets.

None the less, Lucien loved his grandmother, with her terrible strength and her occasional weaknesses, and he loved to hear these stories about Der Altman, so he would ask, 'And what did the Viceroy do?'

And she would tell him, 'He sent a man to discover the cause of his delay. And then the man went back to his carriage and told him, "There is a giant with yellow hair who refuses to pay for his mule."

' "But that is absurd," the Viceroy said. "Tell him to come here." So Der Altman went to the carriage door, dragging his precious mule with him. "I could have you shot for this," the Viceroy told him. But Der Altman was unmoved, staring with his deep blue eyes into the carriage and through the gilded representative of His Majesty The

11

King of Spain, and through the Viceroy's companion, and out into the crowd of dwarfed faces on the other side.

' "Will you wager?" the Viceroy asked, brightening suddenly at the prospect. To which Der Altman neither answered nor moved. But the Viceroy was a gambling man, and he was bored with his journey, and determined to have some fun with this strange man who had already succeeded in delaying his carriage and who was proving to be the only real diversion in that whole dreary day of bumps and dust and changing horses, so he insisted, "Since you will not pay for your mule, and since you block and hinder His Majesty's business, you should be shot. I understand from the tollman that you claim that your mule is your baggage. Well here is our wager . . ." '

This was always the part that Lucien liked best, the moment of glory when the roulette wheel took over the world. Misia Schmutter would repeat the challenge, mimicking the drawled devilry of the Viceroy's voice, as he pointed to his silent companion hunched in a corner of his carriage.

' "My cousin here and I have come from San Fernando de Apure. I have inspected the garrison, and I have here the charts and deeds of lands that stretch down to the great Orinoco. Carry your mule across the toll, and they are yours. Fail, and you die."

'Der Altman had understood the gist of the wager, and he prepared to accept. The crowd was cleared back, and Der Altman reslung his flask and knife and pack. And then he put his arms under the taut belly of his bewildered beast and very, very slowly lifted her into the air and carried her through the toll-gate and along the widened track on the other side. His face had turned from its former blotchiness of pale skin and patches of raw sunburn to an overall porphyry colour, and, although he staggered under the weight, Der Altman kept the four legs of his burden off the ground, while the crowd cheered, and even the Viceroy's companion himself stepped down from his carriage, and followed the spectacle of man and beast reversed, and when the mule was finally restored to her own feet, and the veins in Der Altman's neck and forehead had subsided into their rightful places, he shook him by the hand, and tried to persuade him to return with them to Caracas, where he

12

could become famous as the strongest man in the garrison. But Der Altman only wanted to follow the road.

'The Viceroy honoured his bet, and gave away the lands with title and deed as he had agreed, and the documents were signed then and there, witnessed by the Viceroy's cousin and the tollman's illiterate cross, and the Viceroy added a pouch of gold and some fine tobacco to the prize, and thanked him for having provided the best entertainment since he had left Madrid. And all the time Der Altman was anxious to move on. Eventually, he returned to the dusty track with the papers that he could not read, bearing his signature, "Lucien", which was the only word that he knew how to write, and he never learned the extent of the wealth that he had gained at that toll-gate of Calabozo. It was his sons, who learnt to read and write, and who grew up under the dust shield of money and power, who discovered how much of San Fernando belonged to the Luciens'.

Chapter 2

LUCIEN HAD AGED WITH HIS INTRANSIGENT GRANDMOTHER from the years of deadlock to the years of defeat. The war in Europe ended when Lucien was seven, but the humiliation was never forgotten. No one, not even the batches of new maids herded in from the mud huts on the far side of the estate with their tangled hair and their horny toenails that turned claw-like into the ground, was allowed to forget. To them, war was something that happened every day, and deadlock was the compromise that they all had to come to in order to survive on those dust-streaked plains: scorpions and snakes were killed, but the maggots and flies and lizards were allowed to remain. None of them ever won at San Fernando, and what Misia Schmutter was trying to tell them about her broken nation was the same defeat that they knew from day to day under her own rule, and they were all right, so why should she fret? None of them understood what it was that she had lost in that place that she called Germany which was so many days away, travelling over the patchwork rivers that she called the sea.

Misia Schmutter had summoned the whole household to her, on that fateful day of November 18th, 1918. It was only much later that Lucien discovered that the real Armistice had come on November 11th of the week before, and then it was too late to supplant that first anniversary of the 18th, when a traveller had come to their home, to bring news of the war. All the family and their workers and servants had been summoned, and Germany's defeat had been announced. The news itself had made no impact on

14

anyone but Misia Schmutter and Lucien. To the others, the loss of a toy meant something, or the loss of a rope, or the death of a cow, or the loss of a cheese. But this new loss of dignity that had turned the old lady's face a dreadful grey and dulled her blue eyes to ash and stone was beyond them.

Nothing, it was claimed, would ever be the same. The house was to go into mourning, the sun-battered tricolour was to hang at half-mast over the front terrace, black ribbons were to be bought and draped over every door and window, and when the errand boy returned with all the black crépe and ribbon that the town could supply, it was not enough, and the black drapes and curtains from Lucien's mother's room that had lain at the mercy of moths and cockroaches for four years were to be torn into strips and shreds and draped over all the doorways in the long corridor. Lucien alone had asked what all the household had in mind, 'What would my mother have thought?'

'She would have agreed,' her grandmother told him and Lucien knew that it was true. She would never have dared to disagree, having lived her short life in dread of Misia Schmutter. There was to be a night of fasting and prayer, the boys were to burn their new toys and the girls their favourite dolls. Germany was beaten. Misia Schmutter saw that the word meant nothing in this land of drought, and she knew that it was up to her, one of the few survivors of the old regime, to brand the memory of it into everyone there that day. That transatlantic Armistice was to be a day of slaughter, when all that was most prized was destroyed.

Misia Schmutter came into the courtyard in her plainest black. She had worn nothing but black since her husband died, not so much as a sign of mourning for him as a mark of regret for what he might have been, had he wanted to, but now never would be. Lucien's grandfather had been a cross of ineptitude that she had had to bear, and she had mourned her own misjudgment in marrying him. Over the years, lace cuffs and collars, jet and black pearls had been added, the latter specially brought for her from the island of Margarita by the man who had tried in vain for fifteen years to marry her. This suitor had suffered himself to be insulted and slighted, despised and dismissed. But he had always returned, undeterred, with his carriage weighed down with gifts. Misia Schmutter would see him for minutes only, sometimes she would refuse to see him altogether. If his presents pleased her, she would take them without thanks; if they didn't, she would still take them, but have them destroyed then and there, in the courtyard.

Thor, her bull mastiff with his temper in his hackles and his teeth, had been a present from this man. Shipped at great expense and labour from Miami, the dog had travelled first-class the whole way and then by special carriage to San Fernando. He had arrived together with a lap-dog. The one had been taken, and the other spurned. So the little Pekinese, with her silken hair and pink silk ribbons, complete with the stamped and registered scroll of her pedigree, had been instantly dispatched to the head herdsman's hut, to rot and fester in the wattle and daub with the mange and ringworm to comb out her hair and only the slops of stale yucca to pamper her stomach. So, too, the black pearls had been gathered and brought in a chain-mail pouch of silver, and these had appealed to Misia Schmutter, and even received a nod of approval; she had sewn them on the bodice of her favourite dress, and as the climate rotted the cloth, she would transfer the pearls from one gown to another, but on that day in November 1918, she had stripped them away, leaving only the plain cloth and the stubble of the unpicked stitches. Her head was bound up in an extraordinary rag, and her hands, her immaculate hands, were powdery with ashes.

Misia Schmutter came on to the terrace like Savonarola, and ordered the bonfire to be lit. There was one huge fire built up on the lawn. El Patrón, who was the nominal head of the estate, had remonstrated feebly with his mother about the location of this fire. 'It took seven years to perfect that turf, mother, it's never looked so good. Please be reasonable.' But Misia Schmutter was never reasonable. She was consistent, but not reasonable, and seven years of a gardener's time were as nothing to the defeat of Germany. Everything would wear the mark of this downfall. If all the thousands of hectares on the far side of the garden wall already looked like the aftermath of a bonfire that was no reason to spare the lawns. This was to be a moment in history, a day that San Fernando would remember, a day when the glory of self-sacrifice would mix with the shame.

There was to be a procession, led by herself with Lucien following, and then all the other children, el Patrón, punished now, behind his offspring for his lack of patriotism and his lack of feeling, and his lack of will, and then the servants, and then the workers. The bonfire itself, made out of dead branches of araguaney, and added to with newly-cut limbs of guava and acacia, towered into the blurred afternoon. First one treasure and then another was added to fuel the blaze, and then the ritual developed into a fervour of self-sacrifice, with the girls leaping and yelling, for the only time in their lives when they met with their formidable grandmother's approval, racing to and from their nursery laden with toys and ribbons, smocks and hats, and throwing them in to be burnt, for the fatherland. They had learnt the phrase, they had picked it up in German, and they repeated it over and over again, flushed purple by the heat and the excitement, while they emptied out all that they owned and used. They even managed to smuggle on their blackboards and their slates, and their shoulder straps and the hated liberty-bodices with their rough linings and tight buttons.

El Patrón, and his two sons back from the Jesuits after an outbreak of the Black Vomit in Mérida, were not to be outdone, and they saw in this sudden burst of sacrifice a licence to be rid of all that irked and cluttered them. Misia Schmutter was a great believer in ritual. If she put a chair in the hall in 1870, that was a good enough reason for it to remain there, even though the woodworm had rendered it useless long ago. Tradition, she would explain, is tradition, and that would be that.

Thus the entire Lucien household was able to throw out all that they most detested in their mansion, and with every item that they burnt, they gained more and more of the dreaded Misia Schmutter's approval. The boys burnt their clothes, and even brought token offerings belonging to their absent brothers. Everything they wore was ridiculously outmoded, and at school, it was only their wealth, position and strength combined that kept the other boys from bullying them. All their old breeches went in the cause of shame on that belated Armistice, and their unfashionable jackets of best tweed as well, and their overrounded boots of rough hide, and their hated lederhosen.

El Patrón, who at the age of forty-seven had earned himself the meagre right to wear, with certain limits, what he wanted, was less anxious to unburden himself of his clothes, but he seized the opportunity to turn out all the decaying furniture on the ground floor at least, and the crumbling hangings from the walls which were little better than a breeding ground for cockroaches, and which his mother kept sprinkled with lime to collapse their insect lungs, and which exuded thin clouds of white powder, day and night, to settle on all his clothes and in his hair like a great crop of dandruff, and he knew that the girls laughed about it behind his back in the town. Nobody laughed at El Patrón to his face, though. His mother might be the terror of the Hacienda San Fernando, but he was the terror of the town. He never went there without his gun, and a month rarely went by without his using it.

Lucien was also wild that night, but he was wild with jealousy. For the first time since his reprieve from the boredom of the nursery, it was the other members of the family who were impressing Misia Schmutter. He had even tried to lure her away from the chanting party around the fire, but she had said, 'Not now, child.' Until then, he had been a child for every moment. There had never been a 'not now' in his life. It was always chance. Chance now that had brought a stranger to their door to spill the news of the German defeat and the Allied victory, to tell of the broken troops who had crawled out of their trenches, to tell of a country that had lost its pride. Earlier, alone with Lucien in their hall, Misia Schmutter had cried. She had not cried for these raving shouting people, or for his sisters, or for her son, she had cried with him, Lucien, alone and for Germany, and the race apart, of which he was one. The others were all gloating. They were glad of their chance to turn the old house upside down, they were glad to see the old woman weakened for once.

He had tried again, claiming Misia Schmutter's attention as was his right. But he had fared even worse. She paraded them, the others, the rest of his family whom he would never really forgive again for trying so to usurp him in her affection. He, Lucien, who had tried again and again to reduce their punishments, who had often taken the blame for things they had done because he could move under the sign of her favouritism while they could not. And now, his allies had all turned on him. He began to understand about war. This was what it did. It changed people, and it came between them and it cut out the good parts of them. It made people use each other, and it made them blind. His own Misia Schmutter had said to him, 'They are all doing this for the fatherland, what are you doing?'

So Lucien had gone away from the flickering crowd of them. Misia Schmutter was the law. She had said that nothing would ever be the same, and she had made it a day to remember. Her old suitor who had brought her the black pearls and the dogs and the caged birds and the fruit trees would have been proud of her. If he could have seen how she had set the whole house dancing around that fire, how she had drawn them all, even the ones who most hated her, to chant her service, he would have loved her the more. But the old man was dead now. He had died three years previously when Lucien was four, and he didn't remember him well, although he had seen him waiting, but then they had all seen him waiting. He remembered that some days the old courtier wasn't allowed to eat with them at the same table, and once, Lucien had found him weeping in the old gazebo in the heavy twilight. He had been tall and bald, and when he was in the presence of Misia Schmutter he sweated and stammered, and when he was in the yard under the scalding midday sun he was cool and shouted to the stable boys and his brothers; that was all Lucien could remember of the man. His brother Detlev said that Misia Schmutter had had him murdered, and it was true that the body had been found three days old and dug over by vultures right down to the bone, and some of the bones were shattered by gun shot, and Misia Schmutter had smiled when she heard. But even Lucien, cloistered by the hacienda, knew that you weren't called the Empress of the Orinoco for just scrubbing serving-girls' hands. People did disappear at San Fernando and sometimes a body was found and sometimes it wasn't, and a man wasn't a man until he had taken the life of another, or, at least, that was what his father said.

It was still light when Lucien left his grandmother and the rest of the household gathered on the lawn in front of the house, burning up all they could before the spell was broken. He walked on his own and unnoticed to the quiet of the summerhouse. And he sat and watched the twilight pierced with a thousand fireflies from the sparks below. He could feel the strange knot coming in his side and rising up

19

to his throat so that it choked him. It began slowly and then grew. He had compared the pain to that of his brothers and the boys on the hacienda. They said they all had similar pains, they blamed the worms and the water, green mangoes and guava seeds, and so many other things that Lucien grew confused. But he swallowed his purges and steered clear of the unripened fruit and the pips and drank all his water boiled and still the pain came, twisting through from his waist to his chest, holding him doubled like a great fist thrust in him. It impaled him for days on end, making him green and stooped and wheezing. Later, in prison, they would give it a name: some of the prison doctors called it tuberculosis, others disagreed and called it asthma. In el Llano, they called it el tigre—because it was like a tiger on his back mauling him so that he couldn't breathe. Lucien had grown to recognise the pain as tension; he could feel it coming, and he learnt to make it go; he never believed that his lungs were damaged, that was an excuse, and he didn't need excuses. They even said that he suffered from photophobia, those same prison doctors employed by his worthy brothers to exonerate his alleged crimes. If he turned purple in the sun, it was because his colouring was never designed for that vicious equatorial sun.

Perhaps, on that November evening, he would have welcomed a name for his pain. It was making him sweat, like his grandmother's dead suitor, from the upper lip. All around him the drought was settling in. It had begun in September with the grasses, making them rustle and yellow and brown. Then it had burnt them so that they would have blown in the wind, had there been any, and had not the famished Ceibu begun to roam all over the nearlands of their hacienda. Here the herdsman could keep a closer watch on them, and see when they fell from weakness, and take their meat before the turkey vultures claimed it, and the progress of the drought could be monitored through the thinning of the dry meat on their bones. Misia Schmutter would lift the great shins from the cauldron, and know whether the rest of the herd would follow or recover. Then the dry grass had been burnt to make way for new shoots when the rains should come. Then the brush had followed the grasses, scorching its furry leaves where they stood, hanging like stale decorations from their scrawny branches. And then the new trees followed, leaving ghostly trails of dead scions among the hosts of decaying stumps that remained like crumbling gibbets and whose thorny branches stood leafless against the vast horizon. The last specks of green left on the landscape were always the cactus and the araguaney. This last with its yellow blossom was the commonest of all the trees, but the cactus could outlast it and that one underplant, the 'cat's claw bush', as they called it, that kept going after all else had died, with its roots anchored so far underground that he had never managed to reach their pale tips. The vultures and the Luciens and a few other families were the only ones to thrive on the plaguelands that stretched from the River Orinoco to the River Apure with nothing to break the monotony but the occasional tale of a man's survival there.

When the drought was at its worst, and the lesser rivers dried, and the pools became too foetid even to bathe in, then Misia Schmutter would issue dynamite, and new wells would be blasted from under the caked surface, and the glee at the explosion, the contagious exultation, was the only other way that Lucien had seen his family so excited. It was the old game of chance and decision. Misia Schmutter had taught him very little. She had taught him to read, and given him the free run of her library, she had guided his tastes nowhere in particular, excepting that she had steered him towards Europe, and away from his home. It was he who had chosen the subject that he grew to delight in at random. It just happened to come first, after Agriculture, which, by its daily proximity, seemed uninteresting. So he studied Architecture, alone, and from the age of four, and his grandmother accepted this early choice as one of profession, and ordered as many books as she could on the subject, and let him neglect all the others. 'There is nothing wrong with having a vocation,' she said, 'as long as it is one that will do us both credit.' But she did insist on one other lesson: the roulette, the chance and decision. 'Never let anything get out of your control, Lucien,' she would say. 'If you feel a situation slipping, get it back.'

If the others chose to ignore him, if Misia Schmutter herself had done so, he would make them notice; if they had a fire, he would have an explosion. The girls might give up their toys and ribbons, and the boys their trains, but he would blow up his summerhouse. Nobody had made a bigger gesture, even Misia Schmutter had burnt only the books she didn't read and the gowns she didn't wear. When she saw her son offering up his furniture, she had burnt her own sofa but not her rocking-chair. They were all holding back, only he would burn the ultimate offering, the thing he loved best, better even, he didn't know, but maybe, than Misia Schmutter herself. At least, he liked to think so on that thick evening of his jealousy.

When he came back to the gazebo with his dynamite, seven sticks to be sure—he didn't know how many he would need to make his fire bigger than the one that was burning a hole in his father's precious lawn—he began to feel sorry for the carved bench. He persuaded himself that he needed to keep it as a token of what he was about to do, and he dragged it out and let it roll down the steep, man-made hill that was crowned by the condemned gazebo.

He had seen dynamite used often enough for fishing in the river, when lighted sticks were thrown, and the explosion brought up a mass of blasted flesh, like red dripping plankton, to be scooped into the nets. But that night it all seemed different. Once the sticks of dynamite were in place it became impossible to light all the fuses with one taper. In the evenings, in Misia Schmutter's rooms, he had always been allowed to light the candles in the great candelabra that sat on a special table of its own and lit up their private sitting-room. It was a point of honour to light every candle with the same taper. There were twenty-four candles in that holder and only seven sticks of dynamite, but the thick fuses were harder to light, and two of them refused and had to stay as they were. So it was with a sense of incompletion that Lucien ran down the hillock and into the eastern cattle pens. But at the first explosion he turned round and looked, and the whole hill lit up and the sparks and lights showered over the house, and Lucien himself felt the pain in his chest lift and leave him and in its place he felt a warm glow biting through his skin, and he saw the others coming, pushing their way through the sick cattle in the pens to where he was standing and the thin sparkle that had begun to come back into Misia Schmutter's eye flashed and grew. The dynamite was still exploding in his ears. He had made his own war with guns and mortar, and they were all standing, afraid, herded in behind barbed wire. But now there was no pleasure on their faces, only fear.

It was Lucien's day. He had managed to put an end to the burning of clothes and chairs. Misia Schmutter was his again, shouting at the servants, pushing at his sisters.

'Give him air,' Misia Schmutter ordered. 'Can't you see he's burnt?'

Chapter 3

WHEN THE GROUP GATHERED AROUND LUCIEN, HARDLY any of them had noticed that he was hurt, but by the time he emerged from his sick-room in Misia Schmutter's wing, his injuries had been drummed into every one of them. Lucien's condition and the frenzied Armistice pyre had grown into one strange mass for the rest of his family and all the retainers of San Fernando. It was four months until he was allowed to join them. Four months spent under padded rings and thin gauze bandages with different balms and lotions tipped over him. His favourite had been the cool coconut oil with its thick, rancid smell. The servants didn't know how they hated his grandmother most, as martinet or matron.

As though it were not enough to keep him caged those sixteen weeks in a darkened room at the mercy of every mosquito of the Orinoco, and to strap and bind him to the bed with linen thongs that cut into his chafed raw wrists, and to embalm him with every concoction that she could lay her hands on, bringing dozens of wizened peasant women to help diagnose his cure, Misia Schmutter starved him too. To Lucien, aged seven, reared as he had been in the midst of her cruelties, her refusal to feed him seemed like just one more whim of this woman whom he had trusted, but whom he would never quite trust again.

He didn't know how his grandmother suffered, he refused to accept her tears or grant his forgiveness. She could no longer squeeze him to her, he was too ill for that, but she stood or sat, hovering over his sick-bed, fidgeting with his mosquito net. She had begun now, in this sudden coming of her old age, to stroke her grandson's hair at the crown in the bristling whirlpool that grew perversely over his fringe; she had also taken to whispering to him, telling him her every thought. She felt guilt for his injuries, and she cursed herself for her lack of love and feeling for this child, who lay racked by fever. He was the only person that she ever wanted to be with, and now she could see by his refusal to open his eyes, by his refusal to speak, that he was irked by her. She had lost her magic in the blast that he made. The proudest woman in los Llanos was reduced to pleading.

'Lucien, speak to me, tell me that you're getting better.'

But Lucien lay like an old Carthusian, determined not to break his vow. He would not reply, wouldn't open his eyes until she looked away. He knew when that would be, for although the old lady had weakened, her power was still with her in a trampled form, and he could feel her eyes boring into him. She watched him, and her tenderness was like one of his brothers sitting on his stomach. When she thought that he was asleep, she would whisper, 'Lucien, I didn't leave you.'

But he would be waiting for her, he would shrug what little he could move away from her, or tense his every muscle to imply his disgust. He was thinking, 'Not now.' He had never known until the months that he spent in bed with his burns that he was capable of holding a grudge.

He knew that his sister, Katrina, sulked and stared, and would turn down the offer of a square of sugary white fudge or a sliver of guava cheese because she would still be grieving over some slight that had happened so many months before that Lucien couldn't even remember it. And Misia Schmutter never forgave things, but her grudges weren't drawn out, because her opponents, and there were hardly any who dared to oppose her, always disappeared or died. Misia Schmutter seemed to collect words and looks in the way that his brothers collected postage stamps and cigarette cards and penknives. For instance, if one of the kitchen girls dared so much as to look resentful when the thong came down before breakfast on what she knew to be her immaculate wrists, then the thong would fall daily, harder and harder, and her tasks would increase until she had no moment's rest from dawn until late into the evening.

Lucien had often wondered what it felt like to be called to service at the estate house. He supposed that it must be rather like being press-ganged into the army. There was the fleeting glory of their higher position, there was the brief pleasure of walking to church in the train of all the family, and of being able to look down on their former associates from the height of their new rope-soled alpargatas, with the tops woven in the family colours of red and black, and to turn up their noses at the dusty calloused feet of those who were still free to go hungry and scrabble a living and make a bundle of their aches and pains every night in their own worn hammocks. Lucien wondered if having black gowns of rough cotton and starched white aprons and their hair cropped short like convicts was really a pleasure, or just another cross that the poor girls had to bear. It hurt him that they put up with the treatment that they received— even the dogs were better treated than they—but Lucien had never a kind word for them.

He despised them as he had despised his mother, in the back of his mind, for not having dared to complain. But somehow, pressed against the damp linen of his sheets and the insufferable heat, they were all like his mother as they tiptoed in and out of his room. From behind, as they tended his candle or changed the bowls of water with which Misia Schmutter swabbed his head, or while they brought in new compresses of comfrey steaming from the range or bowls of St John's wort that had been carefully pounded and were to sit in their blobs of green slime on his wounds that no one would leave alone, they were just like his mother. But when they turned round, her face, weighed down by the loops of her braided hair, with her sad grey eyes and her apologetic smile, was not there. Instead there was only the bitter line of their mouths, tight with fear of Misia Schmutter behind them, and their dark eyes like the eyes of a Ceibu cow in that minute when it begins to feel the poison of a mapanare snake eating into it, the sudden seizure of the glands and lungs, that fixed look of hopelessness at the moment of death. Lucien definitely wanted his mother. He wouldn't cry for her, but he wanted her, and he felt the keen disappointment daily when the maids turned their toothless mouths to him, and the face that he wanted to bring back from under the marble slabs in the cemetery never came.

His father, el Patrón, visited him night and morning. At first, Misia Schmutter had refused, but by the third day of his fever, after Dr Rodriguez had told her that there was little hope of the boy's recovery, she had let him in, to sit with them while she said her rosary. This rosary and their monthly visits to the local church and the crucifix in the dining-room were the only concessions that the Luciens had made over the centuries to the native Catholic religion. But if their faith was deficient in the eyes of the Church, that Church had learnt to turn a blind eye to it. El Padre Tamayo was said to have ventured out to the Hacienda San Fernando in 1870 on the birth of Misia Schmutter's first-born son, to remind her and her husband of their duty to bring up the child within the strict confines of the Catholic Church. 'But I am not a Catholic,' she had told him. And he had the impudence, so she told Lucien years later, to tell her that she must waive her own principles to those of her husband's in this as in all things. 'But he is not a Catholic,' she had said.

'Don Wilhelm was born a Catholic, mi señora,' Padre Tamayo had said, 'and you must bow down to him.' But Padre Tamayo had been thrown from his horse and trampled so severely that it was only by his robes and ring that his corpse was recognisable.

'It serves him right,' Misia Schmutter was reported to have said, and everyone agreed, although nobody voiced their thoughts as to who it was who had served him, so near to her own boundaries, and so soon after his visit.

Then again, at the birth of the next generation of Luciens, an intrepid priest had once more ventured into their homeland, urging the same tenuous cause. This time Misia Schmutter was more restrained in her reaction. She waited a week, and then the priest's house was razed to the ground by a single explosion while he and his housekeeper were at Sunday mass. The point wasn't lost on the town, and there was no more interference. However, Misia Schmutter mellowed in her own time, and when her first son died a child, the peasants' rumours of the curse that had fallen on him came to her ears. With the general distress at his perpetual torment from that day of his diphtheria to the end of time, Misia Schmutter had taken to holding a rosary now and again, if only, as she claimed, to cool her hands. And her own faith, the faith of Calvin and a love of righteousness in which she alone was right, was also outwardly strengthened. And the big bible in the dining-room that always lay open under the crucifix, and that exuded a faint smell of paraffin from the days of her arrival from Prussia when she had baptised it by total immersion into its new life in the tropics to keep the marauding insects away from its words, shared its evangelism with a dozen smaller versions of itself that took up their positions all over the house.

The servants, who were all thoroughly Catholic in the way of los Llanos which combined the old Amerindian customs with the witchdoctory of the incoming slaves and the distilled rites of a neglected Church of Rome, saw Misia Schmutter as a kind of Anti-Christ. Her one redeeming feature, as far as religion went, and for them she had no others, was the crucifix in the dining-room. This great heirloom was carved out of a single piece of black beech, at the same time, it was said, as the bench in the summer-house, and the great bed in Lucien's mother's room. It hung, taller than Lucien himself, like a single crusader, and the cook and all the servants and even the children be-lieved it to be the one thing that kept the Wild One from the door of their house, and their only hope against the Evil Eye.

Lucien's father came into his son's sick-room at nine o'clock in the morning and at six at night, every day, without fail. There was a gaiety about him in those four months of sickness that his son suspected was pleasure at his absence, and that of Misia Schmutter in her new role as nurse. The entire household had relaxed, in the way that it relaxed after the flood, when even the walls subsided, and the beams creaked and assumed a new position. Lucien could imagine his brothers and sisters enjoying themselves, eating for the first time without their grandmother's retri-bution. They would probably eat too much, they might even have ordered dishes that Misia Schmutter forbade as unwholesome. They might even have cut down the number of black rolls served in the great earthenware bowl on the sideboard, and replaced them with the local arepas, rounds of ground and pounded corn slapped into shape and cooked on a hot plate over an open fire. He sensed that the whole house knew and was rejoicing, Misia Schmutter had lost the tip of her power, the beginning of the end had begun, and he himself had been the one to stab her in the back. Or rather, was the one, still, with his silence and his stiff limbs.

Misia Schmutter tried everything with him, everything, that is, except her old tyranny. She filled his room with bowls of powdery-green flowers with pretty pond-lily shaped leaves, she called it Wiesen-frauenmantel, and she told him that in the olden days, alchemists used to gather the dew from the silvery leaves, and they claimed that they could turn it into gold. Misia Schmutter, always a little more brutal than others, gathered not the dew from the leaves, but the leaves themselves, and she stewed them on her smoky paraffin stove and made a lotion that she said would turn his burns into healed skin. She bathed him every morning at eight-fifteen with swabs dipped into her potions of green gold and then she dabbed him with marigold lotion, 'to make scars,' she told him. And then, at nine, his father would come to visit him. He was el Patrón, the boss, who had never managed to graft away from his mother the power that was his by rights. But now, after all his years of submission to her, he could finally see his own time rising. Misia Schmutter had actually consulted with doctors and witchdoctors, she had doubted her own abilities, and had been afraid of a possible failure in his son Lucien's cure.

Of all Misia Schmutter's own children, only he and one younger brother survived. His eldest brother had succumbed to the diphtheria at the age of seven, Lucien's age. El Patrón had heard the wheezing and croaking through the floorboards, and he had heard him screaming while they scraped and cauterised his throat, making instruments of torture in the blacksmith's forge at the back of the stables. He had even heard that his mother had slit his brother's throat, and smiled when the blood came. When he himself was seven, the age now of his youngest son, he had knelt and prayed every night for half an hour at a time, with no heed of the mosquito bites that would fester the next day on his pale allergic skin. He just prayed and pleaded for God to remember him, and to allow him to suffer, albeit as much as his newly-dead brother, but to suffer for that limited number of days, and not have to bear the torture of Misia Schmutter's temper any longer. He had prayed to be released until he was fourteen, when he gave up praying and discovered the local brothel, and life became worth living again.

Misia Schmutter didn't really like him, just as he, el Patrón, didn't really like Lucien. The boy had too much of the old lady's wrath in him, he was at once too hard and too soft, and there was something about him, the way he sat mooning all day in the summerhouse, and the way he preferred to drag his great leather-bound volumes on architecture about with him, and sit and stare at a single page for hours on end, without even reading, just staring at the engraving instead of going riding or hunting or whoring like a man should. But worst and most damning of all Lucien's sins was the fact that Misia Schmutter liked him. Previously, she had only ever liked her own eldest son who had died of diphtheria, but she positively doted on Lucien. El Patrón secretly despised them both for it, his mother for weakening after her long years of unremitting harshness, and Lucien for being so perverse.

Despite all his reservations, el Patrón was drawn to Lucien's sick-room like a high priest to the altar. He could hardly bear to look at the burnt skin, blotched and creased and stretched across the frail body from the various effects of the blast. He was thankful that Lucien didn't cry. It was his own flesh and blood, after all, and although he was reluctant to own him or love him, he could not tolerate any signs of cowardice in the family. El Patrón was often surprised to find how like his mother he was growing in some things, almost reverting to type. He was growing more and more intolerant of minor irritations. He was irritated by increasingly more things. He found that he could no longer drift through his life with his eyes blinkered only towards the brothel. When there were gunfights in San Fernando they were no longer the casual affairs of his youth. His aim was still as good, his grip just as steady, but he actually minded about the things he quarrelled over, and the offences rankled and grated on him days after they had happened, days even after the funerals of his unhappy opponents.

Lucien's father was nearly fifty, and he thought that maybe this was what growing old was like, it crept into your ways and reason before the grey hairs and the sagging skin really took a hold. However, he was not a man to worry unduly or for long, and he succeeded in forgetting most things. He had, however, waited forty-seven years for his birthright, forty-seven years for what was his. He had outwaited even the vultures with the grey sags around their necks like the scrawny old men who herded the cows and were good for nothing else but to lean on their stripped sticks and hide from the sun. He had outwaited everything for the day when Misia Schmutter would give in and he watched her now, surrendering to his own seven-year-old son, and he gloated, inwardly; while outwardly, he came to visit the child and wish him well.

Even in the dim light that came through the cracks and hinges of the shuttered windows, Lucien knew that his father didn't really wish him well. When he felt most sad, when the knot in his side burnt and stung more even than the poultices on his skin, Lucien imagined that his father wished him dead. On the days when he felt less depressed and more realistic, it seemed that his father just wanted him to be gone. That it would have been convenient if he had died in the blast was undeniable. But since it had not happened so, el Patrón bore him no grudge about it. He just wasn't anxious for his son to recover, and he couldn't bear the sight of his half-healed wounds. He was a man with strong views on aesthetic beauty. Lucien had heard his brothers say that el Patrón put a cloth over the heads of the maids with whom he slept if they weren't pretty enough for him, and he imagined him thinking that, as he blessed him and wished him good morning. As he said, 'Dios le bendiga,' he was thinking, 'Cover your face.'

After four months Lucien was on his feet again, and the scars from his many burns were virtually healed. There were still some patches of reddened tissue, but on the whole, the daily baths of marigold, hypericum, ribwort and plantain had worked their cure. His only treatment now was the abominable tonics that his grandmother gave him, wormwood and the bitter Tausendguldkraut that Misia Schmutter swore by and that she had sent to her from Aachen. Then there was a positive witches' cauldron of unspeakable leaves and seeds that she brewed together and administered to him under the name of a 'restorative' tisane. As the weeks wore on, these restoratives became nastier and nastier, and much of Lucien's time was taken up with vomiting and retching. He had grown thin, and cadaverous, and when his embroidered nightgown was taken off him, and his grandmother heaved inside her stays to bend and anoint him with a white liquid that she made herself from mother-of-pearl buttons dissolved in lemon juice, he was always surprised to see how many bones he had, and how little flesh.

In his third month, he was allowed broths and gruels, but in the earlier ones he had been kept to a diet of various febrifuges. 'Starve a fever,' they said, and they had starved Lucien. Every food and drink and fruit was divided in Misia Schmutter's mind, as it was in the minds of every woman who lived in San Fernando, into two classes, hot and cold. Because of his fever, Lucien was denied everything reputed to be hot. All his favourite fruits and drinks, puddings and sweetmeats, meats and cordials turned out to be hot, while all that he most loathed happened to be cold.

No wonder he was on the bone, thinner even than the Ceibu who dropped in the drought. Lucien thought that if he were in the cauldron, and Misia Schmutter happened to pick out one of his shins from the stew, she would foretell ruin and death to the whole herd. Lucien had his books to read, including a pile of new ones recently arrived from Caracas and bound in grey cloth, and he had a jigsaw puzzle that he never even bothered to open, and a deck of cards that he also ignored, and there was Thor, the bull mastiff, and Amelia, the parakeet, to stare at him. And there was Misia Schmutter, with her roulette wheel, still trying desperately to engage his attention.

Lucien always had more time to reflect on his life and himself than most people. As a child, it had been on his carved bench, and then while he was strapped on to the canvas stretcher in Misia Schmutter's rooms, trapped in the heat and the unpleasant smell that exuded from his own burns like a half-blocked drain, like meat before the maggots hatched. And all through his early life his thoughts had been allowed to roam, and he brooded, as he was to brood later, in prison. Twenty-five years in prison is a long time to brood, especially when two of them are spent in solitary confinement, trussed and manacled like an old cow for slaughter. Of all the times and incidents that he came subsequently to tease and go over in his mind, those four months of his burns stood out significantly. Only the first betrayal is ever quite real. Misia Schmutter had kept asking him, 'Shall we play roulette?' and he had answered, 'Not now,' and watched her face fall into its new pattern of anxious old age. How it pleased him to taunt her with the words that she had used to him. She had abandoned him, and now her power had abandoned her, or rather she had mislaid it, and he didn't like her so well without it. He was stubborn, as stubborn as she was herself, so he wouldn't show her that he did still love her, and need her, not while he resented how she had gone against her own creed of chance and decision. Chance had stolen him from her, and decision alone could return him. But she was blind, more blind than the cataracts creeping across her pale-blue eyes could make her. Sometimes he wanted to tell her, as she had told him, 'If you feel a situation slipping, get it back.'

The room was still dimmed, and Lucien still shone under his lacquered flaky layer of mother-of-pearl. Misia Schmutter asked him, 'Shall we play?' and she spun the wheel with her unnaturally white finger.

'Not now,' he said.

But this time, Misia Schmutter didn't flinch, she rose, straightening her black gown angrily; always a bad sign in the old days. Then she snatched the bunches of wild flowers that she had used to heal her grandson, and she threw open her shutters, that had been closed for four months, and she tipped the jugs of tonics and lotions out of the window, and she sent his spare and no longer needed bandages and sheets of gauze after them. Then she half-closed the window and took down her whip of knotted leather, and she said, in a semblance of her old voice, 'We shall play, now!'

Lucien was surprised but not frightened as she stood over him, cracking the whip in her hand, and he didn't answer her.

'We will play now,' she repeated, striking the edge of the table where he sat.

'No, grandma*mma,* I don't want to.' His voice was firm, and his manner gentle, as though explaining something to a child or dog.

Misia Schmutter took his chin roughly in her hand, and jerked it towards her.

'*I* want to,' she said, 'and nobody calls me "grand-mamma". My name is Misia Schmutter and don't you forget it.'

Lucien had had too much freedom to submit, so he made a token compliance.

'I beg your pardon, Mi Señora Schmutter,' he said, giving her her full title.

'Play now, Lucien,' she whispered, and it was no longer the old wheedling whisper of his bedside, there was the threat there, only just behind her words. 'Play now, or you shall feel this across your skin, burns or no burns.'

Lucien didn't believe her. He was never sure whether it was a mistake of his not to have believed her at that moment. But at least it allowed her to regain her power, and he loved her best when she was powerful. He didn't move towards the wheel, and before he could think again, the thong came down across his bare arm with such force that he screamed. She had never hit him so hard, and now she wouldn't stop. He felt the pain of the burns all over again and worse, he threw himself under the table for cover, and Misia Schmutter threw down her whip, dragged him out with her wiry arms and sent him back to his room. He waited, sobbing, but she didn't ever come and ask for forgiveness. In fact, it was he who went to her room later that night and asked for her pardon, and now, it was her turn to be cool. She forgave him, but sent him back punished to his room, and the welts from her whip on his newly-healed scars left three red stripes where they broke the skin, three scars that stayed with him all his life, the three ribbons of his failed coup marked across his arm.

Chapter 4

IT TOOK LUCIEN A YEAR TO REGAIN HIS FORMER RANK OF captain, but the sergeant's stripes on his arm were enough to make him persevere. For the rest of the family, that year came like a reign of terror following the respite of his confinement. For Lucien, it was a year of diplomacy and reconciliation in which he was the eight-year-old go-between of the two warring camps. He felt that he had come so near to losing Misia Schmutter's favour that the same could happen again. Thus, for the first time, he cultivated the real friendship of his brothers, and he learnt always to find moments to be kind to his sisters, and he struggled even harder to win a place in his father's heart.

For the brief time while he waited in his room for Misia Schmutter to come and forgive him, Lucien had known what it felt like to be alone. He had looked from the inside through the frightened stares of the broken-mouthed servants. The edge had been sanded off his indifference. He could no longer watch Misia Schmutter terrorising his sisters without wanting to help them: not out of his old sense of chivalry, but out of a genuine wish to protect them. He still believed that everyone had the chance to alter his position, and he still couldn't admire those who failed to take it. But now he allowed for the moments of miscalculation in life, and he discovered that there were other, subtler means of getting his own way. They would never be as effective, but as a last resort, they were definitely respectable.

In his eighth year, his luck had temporarily deserted him,

and he survived from hand to mouth, gambling cautiously with the few stakes that he had left. These were: that Misia Schmutter still preferred him, despite her anger, and secondly, that this still made him the best mediator there was between her and the world. Thus he could suggest a day's hunting to his grandmother and the scheme would be approved, while if his brothers so much as dared to broach the subject, they would be confined to their rooms for a day and fed on stale black bread and water.

During the rains of 1918, and the subsequent drought of 1919, Misia Schmutter had to re-establish her government. At first, Lucien could hardly keep count of the casualties. Word had spread that she was 'chocha'—losing her grip, senile—and once a rumour broke loose, it never took long to spread around San Fernando. It was said by malicious outsiders that no one could drink coffee at anyone's house there without half the town knowing what had been discussed before the caller was safely back home. But the natives of the town knew this to be untrue. It was a well-known fact that what half the town knew, the other half knew too, and then, as I have said, news spread quickly, and there would rarely be any need to wait for the visitor's return. The servants might be ill-paid and ill-treated, but they had their pride, and their network could broadcast a conversation in a matter of minutes, blow by blow, even as it was taking place. So it came as no surprise that what was whispered in Misia Schmutter's kitchen and marvelled at in the nursery should have become common knowledge everywhere else. Besides which, she had more enemies than anyone else, and when the time came there was a concerted effort to undermine her authority.

Even while Lucien had been ill, travellers and tradesmen, and wandering Turks with their bales of cloth, and even the lovers of some of the maids, had found their way into the back courtyard that led off the kitchen at one end of the long verandah that stretched round the house. They would all come in on the slightest pretext and linger. Chucho Delgado, the foreman, knew better than that, nothing would have induced him in, even if the old lady were dead and her nose already green from the heat, and her arms stuck rigid around the crucifix on her chest in the coffin. No, he stayed in the cattle pens and warned off the workers.

'I wouldn't go in,' he said, 'not even if she had been

dead and buried a year. Misia Schmutter isn't human, believe me, she'd be capable of lifting up the vault-stone and catching you!'

But the younger boys who worked with the cattle were wilder than he, and they hadn't seen the things that Chucho Delgado had. They didn't know how many people got thrown into the lime pit late at night and were never heard of again, or who fell off their horses, or into the river, or whose own guns went off in their pockets. They didn't know, as Chucho Delgado did, how little life meant to Misia Schmutter. Neither did they remember to what lengths she would go to get her own way or to stop other people getting theirs.

'Don't do it,' Chucho Delgado warned them. 'Don't go near the house.' But they would laugh and twist their red scarves round their necks and pull down the long brims of their grass hats and say,

'We're not afraid, Señor Delgado.'

Then the old foreman stayed out in the pens, sitting on the fence, or sometimes on the eastern hillock among the ruins of the old summerhouse that the boy Lucien had blasted, and none of them knew why. And he saw what happened when the outsiders moved into the precincts of the estate house, and he bit his old purple lips and shook the hot rain out of his hair, and wondered what trick of fate had brought him there, to that particular estate, to drudge his life out under the ungrateful tyranny of the old woman with the poached blue eyes who didn't even fear God Himself. For it was well known across the length and breadth of los Llanos that Misia Schmutter was afraid of nothing, not snakes, not scorpions, not hardship, not death. When he was younger, Chucho Delgado and his fellow herdsmen had consoled themselves with the thought that Misia Schmutter was bound to die young. But it was her husband, the true master by rights, who had died, and she, the frail dowager, the foreigner who shouldn't be able to cope with the climate or deal with the ravages of the plains, who had lived on, from strength to strength. Now, Chucho Delgado consoled himself with the thought that it was he who would die soon, and be released from her torment.

From his viewpoint on the posts of the cattle fences, Chucho saw how Misia Schmutter came down one March morning and found fault with the entire household. She lined them up in the long corridor, servants at one end and

children at the other, with the men in the yard. She believed indefatigably in segregating the sexes. Contacts of
any kind were necessarily clandestine. Only el Patrón was
allowed his run of the maids, and if any of them dared to
get pregnant, Misia Schmutter had ways of making them
miscarry, so dire that few of them survived it. It was a day
for palms, and every one of them received stripes, more or
less vicious, depending on who they were rather than on
what they were supposed to have done. Even Lucien had
four smarting flicks across his fingers, and poor Katrina,
his eldest sister, was strapped until she fainted.

By eight o'clock the callers had begun to arrive. Mer-
cifully, the estate boys had heard that law and order was
being restored, and only el Tonto Salazar, who everyone
knew was deficient, was foolish enough to venture through
the gates. El Tonto was dealt with 'properly', as Misia
Schmutter called it. And Lucien always remembered him
kindly afterwards because it was through the poor halfwit's
misdemeanours that Lucien's own were momentarily forgotten. Thus Misia Schmutter engaged Lucien to help her
tie the protesting young man to the whipping post. Everyone else had been dismissed, but they saw through the bars
of the opened windows how an example was made of him.
And they heard, as they couldn't help but hear, because his
screams carried over the house and the pens and over the
parched fields right back to the mud hut where el Tonto
lived with his mother. She said later that it had curdled her
blood to hear him and that the turkey vultures and the
buzzards had flown away startled at the sound of his cries,
and then they had flapped and dropped and returned when
the screams grew weaker. And they had stayed there for
everyone to see, circling over the courtyard, waiting for
what they knew would soon be theirs.

The old foreman didn't know what it was about the
place, or indeed, about the plains in general, that these
birds knew when there was to be a death. Some people said
that the vultures could smell it in the air. But Chucho
Delgado had been born there on that stretch of land between the Orinoco and the Apure and had never gone
further afield, and he knew that death was always in the
air. It never left, so how could the vultures sense the
precise time, and the precise place, where every frazzled
blade of grass was identical to the next and where there

were scarcely no landmarks, just dry river-beds and abandoned carcasses?

But sure as life was hard, the vultures knew that day that Misia Schmutter had gone too far in the setting of her example. And el Tonto Salazar fell and broke his wrist on the thong that Lucien himself had tied so well and wouldn't give. And when he was down, Misia Schmutter ordered him to rise. She was renewing her power, she told him to stand up like a man, but he was down on the ground, a blubbering half-wit. And she kicked him with her tiny buttoned boots, kicked him and kicked him to make him stand, and went on kicking him until he ceased to move, and Lucien winced at the sight of the boy's suffering, but he was proud of Misia Schmutter.

On the whole, that year, of 1918—19, was one that Lucien chose to forget, and yet it was not a time that was easily forgotten. There were little details that stuck in his mind and wouldn't go away. Like the time it took him to untie the knot in the thong that bound el Tonto Salazar's broken wrist to the whipping post, and how he had to keep pulling at the wet body to take the weight off the knot. The vultures had blackened the sky above him, and Misia Schmutter was picking them off with her tiny inlaid revolver which she kept for the purpose, and they would crash and splatter on the cobbles beside him, until he felt smothered by their great black feather quilt composed of the dead and the impatient. Once he had untied the knot, however, and the ritual took over, the dead boy himself didn't bother him, but the idea of the knot remained, long after el Tonto's coffin had been measured and made and buried, and his grave had grown over with mottled escoba leaves.

Of all the faults of which Misia Schmutter was accused, meanness was never one. Men, women and children on the Hacienda San Fernando, no matter how they died, were provided with a fine funeral. El Tonto Salazar had been no exception. Even his mother was pleased at the splendour of the candelabra that were placed on her hearth and on every ledge of her tiny wattle and daub hut. And the oilskin cloth, stained black with generations of spilt black beans, was replaced by one of spotless white satin. Then the coffin came, made of she knew not what wood, but gleaming with its handles. All his tattered old rags had been taken from him, and instead he was wearing shiny white robes with gold embroidery and his hair that had always been so stark and unruly was cut now, professionally, as his mother proudly announced to her neighbours, and the few tufts of long baby hair which was all that he ever had by way of a beard had been shaved, and his face cleaned and whitened. In fact this slow-witted child who had been such a disappointment to his mother in his life, although he was always very affectionate, she remembered, did his old mother proud in his death. She was even given two black dresses that had hardly been worn by the housekeeper, and the rum and the guarapo for the funeral party were all sent up from the estate house, together with a side of salt beef.

Hunger in San Fernando was when the salt beef ripped the lining from your own stomach, and the blood of fresh meat took a matter of minutes to run from your mouth to dysentery; hunger was a grain hunger, and thirst. No one ever wanted for meat, just corn and water. And to the wealthy there came salt-fish as well. Lucien remembered the salt-fish wagon that came once a week to sell its goods. You could almost hear the fishman coming, such was the buzz of flies that fanfared his arrival. There was a convention that he came round to the back of the house and parleyed with the house boy through the iron railings of the courtyard. He had arrived on that day of Misia Schmutter's purge, as he always did, at ten o'clock. In the preceding months he had taken advantage of her absence to walk right into the forbidden yard and even drink coffee at the kitchen door, and he had grown very friendly with Rosa, one of the maids. That day, he should have noticed the vultures circling, and stayed away. But like so many of his fellow Llaneros, he found the sight of death irresistible. So he was undeterred by the tension and squabbling overhead, and too much off his guard to notice the milky creosote around the whipping post, and Misia Schmutter, lying in wait behind the heavy kitchen door, took him entirely by surprise.

Why she chose the great wooden washing dolly of bleached sycamore, nobody knew, but she did, and she beat his wares to a pulp with it, pounding the salt fish with her fanatical zeal. It was as though one excess deserved another, as though she had to prove that she had been right in killing the Salazar boy, as she always had to prove her supremacy, even to those who would no more dream of questioning it than they would of questioning why their world was flat when everyone else's was said to be round.

Again, they had all watched while the fishman cowered beside his cart as it cracked and splintered under the sudden blows, and they had watched how Misia Schmutter had tipped over his trays of salted merluza and mana-mana, batting his merchandise across the creosoted yard. But what Lucien remembered most was a detail, the snatch of his sister Katrina's laughter. Katrina hardly ever laughed, and was always in more trouble than the servants themselves. Katrina's pleasures were a mystery to her brother, and her penance was the iron-framed board that was strapped to her back as a symbol of the kind of life that she had to look forward to. Katrina had been standing at the window of the music room in her white muslin dress that was too short for her, and the strange contraption of Misia Schmutter's invention that made her arms hang too far back like a marionette's. If Lucien had been given the choice, he would have chosen this one sister for company above any other. She had something of his same look in her eyes. He had even wondered, occasionally, if they could not have shared their grandmother's favour. He had liked her, from a distance, but never more. It was when the fishman's cart was tipped over and he saw the look of terror in all the eyes that turned hurriedly away from the scene, that he noticed how Katrina stared, and laughed.

Nobody had ever dared to laugh at Misia Schmutter's anger, or wanted to for that matter. But Katrina had then, she laughed out loud, and when her grandmother called her to come out into the yard, Lucien watched her in wonder. She was not afraid, there was a recklessness in the way she swung her skirts clear of the doorway, and she looked into Lucien's eyes as she passed him. It was a strange mocking look, and he blushed and winced. He would have liked to have pulled her back and stopped her from being beaten. He would have liked her to rub his face in the warm braids of her hair. That was the beginning of his love for her. It would last, second only to his love for Misia Schmutter. When the image of his grandmother had faded until the exact length of her hemlines or the exact line of her mouth had blurred, a sense of Katrina's face would always remain

41

behind it, and every girl he ever knew would have to measure up to this hazy, soothing memory of his sister.

Misia Schmutter didn't usually like Katrina. She objected to precisely what Lucien liked best in her—the mocking smile. There was a teasing hint of superiority in Katrina's manner, but it was a gentler streak than her own. It lacked her savagery, and far from treating this grandchild as a kindred spirit of sorts, she tended to treat her as a half-caste. She was calling her again now, she had seen her coming, but she always called and went on calling right up until the moment that her victim replied, 'Yes, Misia Schmutter,' and bobbed or bowed.

'Ka . . . trina!'

'Yes, Misia Schmutter.'

'Why were you laughing?' she demanded.

'It was funny,' Katrina said, filled with a sudden daring that she herself would not have thought possible. Misia Schmutter touched her granddaughter's hair and face with her gloved hand, and she said, simply:

'You may laugh again, sometimes, child.'

Katrina curtseyed and said, 'Yes, Misia Schmutter,' and went away, leaving Lucien to weigh up the significance of what he had seen, and to draw his conclusions.

Firstly, he had seen his sister's face as the gloved hand patted her. She had frozen like someone under a snake, or waiting for the lace scales of a fat lizard to crawl off her skin. Lucien guessed, rightly, that Katrina would never laugh again to please their grandmother. If she had unconsciously found a way to be inside the circle of the old lady's anger, she would make sure never to use her power again. Any power she had she wanted to use against her. Katrina wanted to survive, not to please. She loathed Misia Schmutter too much for that. However, she began to view Lucien differently, for at eight, he might be insufferable at times, but he was still a child, and he had noticed her for the first time as a person, and she could sense that he liked her. Lucien was still innocent in the eyes of the Lord; if he had died of the blast he would have been an angel.

Even, she, Katrina, was still an angel, she had one more year of grace before her twelfth birthday, two more years before the threshold into guilt. The choirs of children with silk wings stitched to their clothes sang only for the twelves and under and innocence was reserved for them alone. If

42

Katrina were to die then and there, even Misia Schmutter with her love of ritual would be obliged to walk past her corpse and forbear to hit her, and repeat the words of all the other mourners, 'She was innocent.' She would have to say it, even though she felt her lip curl with rage, she would have to say it. And Lucien and she were still of that clan. Thus Katrina decided to do what she could to save Lucien from Misia Schmutter, and although she never understood his love for the cruel lady whom she herself so hated, they somehow managed to grow close.

Lucien had never seen Misia Schmutter laugh, she could grow very flushed and excited when they were playing roulette, and she had a way of straightening her lace that showed when she was angry, and a way of ruffling her cuffs that showed when she was not. After much thought he decided that when she talked about Der Altman that was her way of laughing, but the incident with Katrina puzzled him. Much later, he had asked her why she had been so pleased by his sister's laughter on that otherwise violent day, and she had told him, 'I used to laugh like that.' Lucien found it hard to believe that his grandmother's piercing voice could ever have held the melodious tones of Katrina's, and the doubt must have shown on his face, because she added, 'I used to laugh at accidents, Lucien; I was young once, you know. When I was nineteen, I could even dance the polka.'

Chapter 5

THE DAYS HUNG VERY HEAVILY ON LUCIEN'S HANDS. ALL through 1919 he remained an outcast from Misia Schmutter's wing. He was allowed to visit but not to sleep there. Neither was he allowed a place in the nursery. El Patrón and the other children regarded him as a spy. They gave him a room of his own wih an arched window looking over the cattle pens, and Lucien could never tell why they had chosen that one room in particular, with its view of the ruined summerhouse, but he suspected that it was to remind him of the means of his downfall. Only Katrina and his brother Detlev, on his rare visits home from school, showed him any kindness. The others were not beyond using him as a go-between, but they couldn't forgive him his five years of idolatry of Misia Schmutter.

After months of looking out over the desolate hillock where he had once spent so many happy hours, Lucien determined to build another gazebo; he would then, at least, he argued, have somewhere to hide his sorrows, and something to look at other than the jagged ruin he had made. He would need not only Misia Schmutter's permission, but her help in securing the materials and the necessary labour for the project. He waited for his plans to grow and shape in his head, and then, gradually, he drew them on the sheets of squared paper that Katrina smuggled out to him from the schoolroom. It was to be more of a temple than an ordinary summerhouse. It would be classical in the style of the one he had blown up, but in the west there would be a kind of altar to commemorate the first one.

Only Katrina knew about his plan, and Lucien didn't really know why he had told her, except that she took the trouble to seek him out, and talk to him. Then Lucien would secretly unstrap her backboard and she would talk and read to him while he worked, measuring and drawing his plans, elevation after elevation, until he felt that, if need be, he could build the thing himself. And sometimes, when the pain in his side and chest came with its old gnawing, and kept him in his room, Katrina would come and stroke his hair.

He waited carefully for the day when he would ask Misia Schmutter to accept his plan. But each day seemed worse than the last in its prospects of success. On several occasions he began to explain what he wanted, but he couldn't bring himself to come to the point. Finally, he met his grandmother on the terrace while she was walking there with the panting, ferocious Thor, and he approached her just as he had used to do, coming suddenly up in front of her and clicking his heels in such a way that she must either stop or trip over him. Her first instinct was one of anger, but then so was Lucien's, and she waited to hear what he had to say for himself. He began with such a poise and coldness of phrase that could not help but please Misia Schmutter, who was always delighted by signs of strength of character being grafted on to what she considered the degenerate stock of the Luciens. It was her own blood rising to the surface in the veins of her offspring, and it made all the years of her life, spent shut away from the world in that half-dead hacienda with a rabble of subjects so unsuitable to her rule that she scarcely cared whether they lived or died, seem more bearable. 'Misia Schmutter,' Lucien told her, 'I have drawn up a plan for a new summer-house. If the design seems feasible, perhaps you would approve it.'

Misia Schmutter knew as much about architecture as she did about Arabic, and Lucien was counting on her ignorance. Confronted, on the terrace, with a portfolio of designs, she had either to approve them outright or confiscate them altogether. She chose to approve them, and further delighted Lucien by going to the extreme of giving his project top priority on the hacienda, higher even than the rounding up of the stray cattle, and higher than the repairing of their pens, and higher than the bi-monthly search and kill of snakes, and higher than the redigging of the trenches that would keep the floodwater from the skirts of their house.

Lucien almost forgot about his fall from grace in the eight months that it took him to complete his new gazebo. He had matured far more in the past year than it would have seemed possible. Apart from his size, and he wasn't tall, no one would have thought that the boy who gave such energetic orders to his team of workmen, insisting that every angle be right to the minutest degree, and that the lead of the cupola be exactly the right thickness, and that the altar inside this new temple be built and rebuilt until it met with his requirements, was a mere eight-year-old. And the requirements were ones that no one else understood, only this strangely despotic child and his master builder who worked tirelessly to modify the difficulties involved in Lucien's infantile dream.

Even as the structure grew, Lucien began to be aware of its defects. These were largely of proportion. What seemed right from behind the window in his room seemed wrong from under the roof and on the steps of his new creation. But he quickly overlooked the faults and turned to the challenges. He wanted the floor to be made of slabs of marble, cut into diamonds of black and red; and he wanted to be able to hold the pillars with his own arms, so that only the very tips of his fingers met. He had wanted the pillars to be of stone, but the local masons were too clumsy to handle such large pieces, and he made do with stuccoed wood, carved and sculptured to his own design. Inside, there was the altar at the back, a place for his old bench, and a new, circular table to stand in the middle, at which he could study his books and draw up further plans. Through the open pillars that led on to the steps he could see the site of his new summerhouse's blitzed predecessor. Over the months of construction the new building came to resemble the old one more than Lucien had intended, for where the builders followed his design and found it failing they would secretly follow the size and shape of the old structure. Lucien was so pleased to see his new building rise from the undergrowth that he didn't notice the discrepancies between the actual measurements and his own—if they didn't tally, they didn't tally, and he didn't care, not even when the massive cupola shrank, or the proposed marble triangles grew. It was enough to feel his own ideas taking shape.

Anyone born under the same roof as Misia Schmutter needed an extra sense to survive. Lucien's immediate family had felt his fall from glory as surely as they felt the first heavy bouts of rain after a drought. They had left him then to his own devices, knowing that it was as safe to leave him as it was to leave the last stagnant puddles of the new wells, once the old ones had begun to refill. They had left him, with the exception of Katrina, like a glass of stale water for the more refreshing draughts of their own. But when his summerhouse began to rise in a recognisable shape out of the ground, and when Misia Schmutter began to go every day to the base of its great stone steps and nod her approval, the household sensed that it was time to prepare for a new regime. They could feel the second coming of Lucien sit heavy in the air, and instinct told them to beware.

El Patrón himself set the example, arriving one early morning on the site with the offer of a set of dollies for plastermoulding. He walked around the half-finished construction, and found himself looking at Lucien with new eyes. He had not credited his son with such a talent. He felt at once proud and disturbed to find himself the father of a genius. He felt rather the way that his daughter Katrina felt when Misia Schmutter had stroked her face. There was something unpleasantly reptilian about Lucien, the boy was precocious only in his mind and manner, but he was always the same pale runt. Of all the boys, he had the weakest frame.

Circumstance had robbed el Patrón of the satisfaction of bringing up his own sons, although sometimes he thought that he had the better bargain with his mother, and that he was saved from a great deal of bother by being rid of their supervision. None the less, he derived a meagre source of pleasure in seeing his person multiplied into youthful and increasingly more manly copies of himself. Just when his own hair had begun to grey on his sideburns and over his ears, it was reassuring to see so many crops of fine blond hair on the heads of his sons. Only Lucien had tufts and crowns, and hands like his grandmother's, hands that would wind better round a lady's pistol than one of his own shotguns. If el Patrón had his way, he would put Lucien on

47

a horse at six every morning and keep him there until nightfall, and make him hunt and swim and fight. No son of his needed books, there was money and land enough for all of them. If the other boys were at school, it was for their own protection. Misia Schmutter had grown so extreme in her old age, more extreme it seemed than when he himself had been a boy. She would destroy the older boys if they lived at home, pulp them like el Tonto Salazar; no school could ever be as treacherous as their own house, or as cruel. Not even the Jesuit school at San José in Mérida, where two of his sons slept on bare wooden boards with only a thin sheet to protect them from the mountain cold, and where the food was served stale and foul for the good of their souls, was worse than coming home. And he knew that the two boys at the military academy preferred their fatigues, and even volunteered to do the latrines rather than return to San Fernando.

El Patrón had swallowed his pride so many times that it gave him indigestion. He had enjoyed watching Lucien flounder, and he would have enjoyed seeing him continue to suffer. The boy belonged to the other camp. El Patrón refused, on principle, to like anyone who was liked by his mother. It was not a predicament in which he often found himself. Misia Schmutter had very few preferences. When el Patrón was a boy, she used to punish him with the green withes of the young fruit trees. She would make him go and cut them first, and she would send him back and back again to choose the right thickness and size, and then she would thrash him until the blood ran down his legs. He had so many scars and welts on him that the blood ran easily, and his mother would shout at him as she still did with her thin, hysterical voice, 'Have you nothing of Der Altman in you?' Well, el Patrón had inherited his pigheadedness. His mother might think that she was winning, but time was on his side. Misia Schmutter was growing old, there were knots of arthritis forming on her blue lizard's hands, and the third eyelid of oncoming blindness was edging its way across her once sharp eyes. El Patrón might not be stronger-willed than she, but he was waiting stubbornly for his turn, and he had stored up every grievance, every look and word. He was already dreaded in the town. There was hardly a man in San Fernando who wouldn't have leapt at the chance of an ambush. It wasn't much to boast of, he would tell himself, but it was something, and he, Domingo Lucien, was more hated in the town of San Fernando than even Misia Schmutter. There was a pettiness in his character that the locals didn't like, and a spitefulness too. 'At least,' they would say, 'you know where you stand with Misia Schmutter, you can rely on her. But el Patrón depends on his mood and his mood alone. One day he wants to make friends and the next day he'll kill you. Give me Misia Schmutter any day. Now there's a woman to respect!'

Perhaps it was the tragedy of el Patrón's life that although he was feared he was never respected. There was something ridiculous in his predicament. None of his children respected him, and of all the boys, only Lucien, whom he detested, really liked him. But Lucien's willingness to please only irked him the more. However, the boy was regaining his ascendancy, he was no longer to be ignored. The way to his heart was through this summerhouse, and el Patrón had to grit his teeth and smile at his youngest son, and praise his creation, and pay homage to his new prowess with offerings of wood and plastermoulding. For the last three months of the building work, and the final month of interior decoration, el Patrón would also come daily, following in his mother's footsteps up the well-worn track to the new gazebo, and he would clench his wide white teeth and smile. 'You're doing a fine job,' he would tell Lucien, and the boy would smile, not like himself with a mouthful of disgust, but with real pleasure.

In the last month, it seemed that Misia Schmutter climbed the slight slope to the site a little more slowly than she usually did, and she pulled on Thor's lead and allowed herself to be dragged and helped a little by his flexed muscles as he made his way through the charred grass and scrub. El Patrón hardly dared to hope that his mother was finally ailing. She had offered to die, years ago, and falsely raised his hopes, so he would not be tricked by what he saw, although he watched her carefully for the slightest pause or catch of breath.

There had been no rain for five months. The cattle were beginning their, by now, habitual droop. The outlying lands around the estate house had the sweet heavy smell of decaying flesh. Fruits and seeds had wizened on the trees. The family had their stocks of corn, both yellow and white, and their sacks of red and black beans, and there were

trays of salt fish and salt beef in the cellars, and baskets of
wizened fruits, but there was nothing succulent left to eat.
Lucien believed that it was no wonder, given the drought,
that Misia Schmutter was slowing down.

The workers on the building site had slowed down, and
the final month of work was dragging itself out needlessly
on details that would have been finished in days at any
other time. But the men moved slowly, and their hands
seemed to hang like lead, and their eyes no longer seemed
to co-ordinate as they used to. The horses in the stable
slept for most of the day, and when they went out into the
sun, they teetered and swayed, and had to be taken back
and exercised only at night, when the flies and the heat had
subsided enough to keep the less practised of them from
swooning. Even the hens hardly ran after their necks had
been wrung, they just staggered and fell and twitched in the
scalding yard, while the cook waited for them to be still
rather than have the effort of holding them so. Thor laid
himself on the stone flags of the inner hall, splayed out like
a zoological specimen with as much of his wiry belly in
contact with the cool floor as he could, hardly caring whether
Misia Schmutter came or went. Katrina and her younger
sisters buried themselves in their embroidered hammocks
in the lower nursery, swathed in mosquito netting, and
slept in fitful sweaty spells from meal to meal and punishment to punishment.

Their governess, Fräulein Fraenkel from the Colony Tovar,
contracted typhus and was locked into the quarantine shed
on the far side of the yard. The children could hear her
calling and scrabbling for help, as they had heard one of the
servants the year before. Chucho Delgado, the foreman,
said that nobody ever came out of the quarantine sheds
alive but that they were locked there for the common good,
so the girls put their heads deeper under the swathes of
netting and blocked their ears, and after four days Fräulein
Fraenkel was quiet again. Misia Schmutter hired a contrac-
tor from out of town to deal with her funeral, and none of
the children was allowed to attend, although they saw her
coffin being carried out and the tins of creosote that were
thrown all over the quarantine shed and in the yard around
it. Misia Schmutter doused the corrugated iron of the walls
and roof of this little hut with paraffin, as had been necessary before when her cures failed. Then Chucho Delgado

set fire to it, and it burned in a great rush of flame that charred the rusty metal entirely black, and the girls thought how their mousy governess, Fräulein Fraenkel, with her secret delusions of grandeur, might have liked to have left the hacienda where she had been so unhappy in that way, rather than in any other.

Misia Schmutter always secretly welcomed any outbreak of disease. She had a herb garden at the back of the house where she grew so many different roots and weeds that only she knew what they were and their different properties and uses. Anyone coming to the estate house, whether they were peasant women from the estate, or travellers or relations, could be sure of a good reception if they came armed with some new herbal remedy. Misia Schmutter lavished all the affection she could muster on her flourishing herb garden. When Lucien had been in favour she had shared its treasures with him. In 1919, the year of his disgrace, she enjoyed it alone. All through the drought the serving girls brought relays of fresh water to tend her delicate herbs. They came at sunrise and just after dark, and they stood in line, passing their jugs of water to her garden. The whole world could go thirsty, but Misia Schmutter's flowers never suffered, she gave them shade and climbing frames and she fed them with ground eggshells. They were individually mulched and dead-headed, she put wood ash down to discourage slugs, and planted a barricade of garlic to keep out snakes. The only insects allowed in her garden were butterflies and bees, anything else was systematically destroyed.

Beside her bedroom, Misia Schmutter had a kind of fitted pantry. This was a long thin room that had once been a dressing-room, lined now with narrowly spaced shelves. Lucien knew that she kept all her remedies in there. Under that one title of 'Remedios', there were jar upon jar and bottle upon bottle of syrups and powders, roots and teas, cures and poisons. An illness in the house gave her a chance to test and record the strength and efficiency of her drugs and potions. The peasants believed that she could cure everything except the Evil Eye. And there was no cure for the Evil Eye. When Fräulein Fraenkel died, they thought that her condition must have been complicated by the Evil Eye, or Misia Schmutter would never have put her in the shed in the first place.

51

There had been typhoid before on the hacienda. There had been the great outbreak of 1913, and then there had been cases of it, on and off, almost every year. Misia Schmutter said it was the water, and she used to dock the pay of any worker who drank it unboiled. When she docked their pay, they went hungry, but they had been drinking the same water since the Christians first came to los Llanos and it didn't get any better, and they didn't believe that it got any worse. So they went on drinking it as they found it, and they went on suffering from dysentery and worms and typhoid and cholera, and Misia Schmutter's rule didn't get any easier, and where was the point of living at all if a man couldn't run the risk of death and retribution?

The vultures knew when their prey was ready, and Misia Schmutter had an extra sense for hers. She could feel all the bodily upsets in her bones. She knew when the enteritis was coming, and she knew when a kidney was bad or a wound needed lancing. She didn't have to see the victims, she could sense them, and call them to her. The peasants respected her for that. She had seen Fräulein Fraenkel sickening. She had waited for her after dinner one night with a jug of Jamaica sorrel infused with rosemary and angelica. Fräulein Fraenkel had drunk it and been sick during the night. Lucien and the girls had heard her, they could hear her praying in her thick frightened German.

The next day she had asked Misia Schmutter to let her return to her home in the Colony Tovar. Fräulein Fraenkel must have been really ill, Lucien thought, to have imagined that she could ever get away. Nobody ever left the hacienda once they had worked there: Misia Schmutter didn't allow it.

'Why do you want to go back there?' Misia Schmutter had asked her kindly.

'I want to go home,' Fräulein Fraenkel had said.

'But this is your home now.'

'I am not from these parts, Misia Schmutter, I am German, I don't like los Llanos.'

Poor Fräulein Fraenkel, Lucien thought, as he dressed and went down to breakfast. She should have known better. No one was more German than Misia Schmutter. It didn't surprise him when the sick woman failed to appear at breakfast. In her place, the great family bible had come to sit where her plate would usually have been. It was opened at the passage in the Book of Kings about the Plagues of Egypt. It was always opened at the Book of Kings when there was a contagious disease in the house. Breakfast that day consisted of black coffee, and stewed Jamaica sorrel and angelica roots to chew. During the meal, Misia Schmutter prayed out loud for the soul of Fräulein Fraenkel, soon to depart, and they all said, 'Amen.'

After breakfast, Lucien went straight to his new gazebo; it was nearly finished, and the sight of it filled him with elation. Katrina, who was not allowed to do so, followed him there, and hidden from the house by a clump of acacia trees, she said, 'Don't you care about Fräulein Fraenkel?'

'No,' Lucien said. 'Do you?'

'But of course I do, Lucien, she's going to die. Our grandmother is going to let her die, don't you understand?'

'Fräulein Fraenkel has typhoid, Katrina, you know that.'

'Don't you care about anyone?'

'Of course I do,' Lucien told her.

'Would you care if I died?' she asked him.

'Of course I would, Katrina.'

'You might care, Lucien, but I bet you'd let Misia Schmutter do it.'

'Do what?'

'Kill me.'

'I would not,' Lucien said flatly.

'But you are!' Katrina shouted and ran off down the hill.

'I am not,' Lucien said out loud to himself, and then he smiled. Katrina was always teasing him, she was like Misia Schmutter, always teasing people.

Chapter 6

ONCE THE SUMMERHOUSE WAS COMPLETED, LUCIEN ENJOYED
it for a period of six weeks, and then he grew restless and
bored. Now that it was finished, Misia Schmutter stopped
coming to see how it was getting on. The drought was
beginning to work like a kind of suction. The naked sky
over the heat haze had been gradually dehydrating the land
and the people. Even the timbers of the great house itself
were creaking. El Patrón's special lawn had finally singed
under the tepid sprinkling from the cans, and even Misia
Schmutter's herb garden was wilting between its morning
and evening waterings. Chucho Delgado and the other
herdsmen had escorted a trail of bony haunches to the
market place, and the cattle had been knocked down at
auction for their pock-marked hides and their bones for
glue, and Lucien didn't know what their stringy meat could
be used for. But the cattle had gone, and now there was
virtually no work to do on the hacienda.

Misia Schmutter insisted on planting and replanting small
crops of Indian corn, but without any water it never came
up. The last crop of yucca had been in for months, and the
leaves had been fed to the cattle and the roots had been
stored, but they were tough and tasteless, and half of them
had turned woody underground. That was what the peasants ate, grey woody yucca and a zancocho of withered
bones. They didn't seem to care. After a few months of
drought nobody seemed to care about anything. Lucien
himself was bored and apathetic.

One day, he went to Misia Schmutter in her herb garden,

and found her sleeping in a bamboo chair under her wide straw hat. He was about to tiptoe away, when she said to him,

'Why are you here, Lucien?'

'I wanted to play with you, Misia Schmutter.'

'What will you wager, Lucien? Why should I play with you?'

'If I lose, Misia Schmutter, you can have my summer-house.'

'But I don't want it, child.'

'No, but you could blow it up.'

Whether it was the excessive heat of the afternoon that had worn out Misia Schmutter's grudge and resistance, or whether she was really keen on the bet, Lucien never knew. But she relented and together they took down her old roulette wheel, and they played for the first time in well over a year. Lucien had a lucky streak that day. With each win, his grandmother made him a concession, and by the end of the afternoon, he was installed back in her wing, with virtually all his old privileges. That night, they didn't go to dinner with the rest of the family, but they had a tray of their own sent up from the kitchen, and together they brought up a bottle of the old Rhine wine. By sundown, the entire house knew that Lucien was back on his throne, and they crossed themselves and thanked God and their own foresight that they hadn't offended him while he was with them.

That night, Misia Schmutter tucked him into his old bed with his old patchwork quilt turned down and redundant in the heat, and she kissed him good night and held his head close to her ribbed chest in a way that Lucien had nearly forgotten. He gasped and struggled against her rigid corsets and then he relaxed, and she kissed him again. As she blew out his candle, and swatted a green lizard with her glove, Lucien said, 'I shall make a new gazebo, Misia Schmutter, a new one for you, and when it is drawn I shall blow up the one I have made, because you won really, you always win.'

The wine and the heat didn't mix. It had been 38°C. in the shade that afternoon, and the night was so still and heavy it was like being wrapped in cobwebs. Misia Schmutter used to wrap his cut fingers in cobwebs. As he fell asleep, Lucien saw her outline in his doorway, like a great spider,

55

she had a bale of gossamer tied to her waist, and she was unreeling her corsets, winding the thread round and round him, it was sticky and he couldn't move. Misia Schmutter had caught him in her web, she would never let him go now, he was safe under the stickiness, she was saying something to him, she was talking to him in German, he couldn't remember the words. He was only a fly, only a little spider, he knew how to make a web, he could hear her now, calling through the palings of cut fingers, she was saying, 'When we are alone, Lucien, you can call me grandmamma.' That was what she was saying, she was the Großmutter, the spider with the thin, thin arms and the great fat body under her corset.

The months merged like a layer of loose dust across the land. Christmas came and went in its usual celebration of nochebuena preceded by a frenzied preparation of hayacas and sweetmeats and pan after panful of rich sickly foods that they ate through a strict sense of ritual with virtually no enjoyment that year. Any festival that centred around eating was always a trial. Misia Schmutter was so strict about what could and could not be done at the table, and the girls secretly complained that she varied her rules to suit herself. However, the workers enjoyed themselves and they, at least, seemed to enjoy the unprecedented quantities of food and rum. Chucho Delgado's eldest son drank himself to death, and one of the boys from the far side had a knife fight with the fishman on his way home from town, and it was not yet clear who was worse off. El Patrón spent three days in San Fernando proper without once coming home, and when he returned Misia Schmutter told him to stay in his rooms but he climbed out in the evening through his window and scaled the roof. Misia Schmutter was waiting for him with the slavering Thor, and she ordered her dog to attack, and it did, and ripped out a piece of el Patrón's leg, and he was in bed with a fever until the New Year.

By general agreement, they all liked the New Year better. There was more to drink and less to eat, and everyone was allowed to have new clothes. These were chosen by Misia Schmutter herself and although they contrived to suit each wearer as little as possible they were still new, and crisp with the tailor's tacks tickling through the seams, and the ribbons shone and the collars were stiff and untouched by moth or cockroaches. Everyone was expected to stay up until midnight, and then toasts were drunk, and Misia Schmutter played 'Deutschland über Alles' in cracked German on her graffonola. Then the children sang it to her again, followed by a song called 'Alma Llanera', which Misia Schmutter claimed would have made a much more sensible National Anthem for Venezuela, which was a country full of people who had never been slaves and never would so they didn't need to go chanting about chains and yokes like some banana republic.

Lucien would always remember his sister Katrina best as she looked that New Year's Eve of 1919, with her hair beautifully arranged by Fräulein Dorst, the new governess, also of the Colony Tovar, a breeding ground in Misia Schmutter's opinion of fine German girls cut out for service. New Year's Eve was the only time when Katrina was allowed downstairs without her backboard, and it transformed her to be rid of it. They all drank to Germany and San Fernando, and Misia Schmutter and the new year. Even the servants drank their hollowed coconut-cases of rough rum grinning hopefully. What had these servant girls with their scarred wrists and their bruises to look forward to? They must know that they could never escape from Misia Schmutter, they must know that their future held nothing but hardship, and yet there they were, drunkenly happy at the back of the dining-hall. Lucien's New Year resolutions were to stop his endless self-analysis, and to be kinder to Katrina. While Katrina's was to get away, come what may, from San Fernando.

Lucien didn't know whether his resolution to worry less, backwards and forwards, over what he did blurred his memory of what happened over the next four months, or whether it was the significance of what followed them that blocked it. Whatever the reason, his mind always skipped from the New Year to his birthday on April 23rd. It was to be his ninth birthday, and he had chosen the date as the right time to destroy his gazebo. He wanted to see it go, not just to honour his pact with Misia Schmutter, nor yet to be rid of its flaws and imperfections of design, but also for the challenge of building another, superior one. Only Misia Schmutter was invited to the ceremony, and Chucho Delgado, who had been chosen to light the fuses. The carved bench had once again been removed and the seven sticks of dynamite chosen. Seven seemed an appropriate number to Lucien, it was far more than was strictly needed but it had a precedent, and as a strict traditionalist, precedents appealed to him.

After the eight months of construction, Lucien had looked forward to untold pleasure inside his new gazebo, and he had been saddened to find that all his enjoyment had lain in the making. With his second, well planned and timed explosion, he discovered the even greater pleasure of destruction. All the structural faults that had niggled him over the past months were set to rights, the roughness of the plaster, the moulding set askew, the window sloping down, the dome too small for the whole, the pillars too mean. Lucien was not one to bear his own mistakes easily, there was an impatience of spirit about him that was to hinder him all his life. The blast inspired him, and the ruins gave him a chance to start again. Nothing would ever be quite perfect, but Lucien would strive to make it so.

None of his brothers understood about this, it was a secret between him and his grandmother. Not long after his birthday, Katrina told him a secret too. She was going to run away. She told him so that he might help her to get together the few things that she needed to escape. Lucien couldn't understand it.

'Misia Schmutter will know, whatever you do.

'Only if you tell her.'

'No, she knows everything, Katrina.'

'Good Lord, Lucien,' Katrina told him. 'She only looks like a witch, she isn't one you know. Why are you so afraid of her? She's just an old woman, old, do you hear me, and she's getting ill, you can see it on her, she's going to die soon, but I'm not waiting for her.'

Lucien was horrified, both by the blasphemy and by the thought of his sister even imagining that she could get away. However, it was impossible to dissuade her. When the day came for Katrina's flight, Lucien was relieved to find that she was prevented by Misia Schmutter spontaneously locking her into the upper nursery, and keeping her there between the barred window and the padlocked door for three days.

On the third day she was allowed out.

'Are you sorry?' Misia Schmutter demanded of her in the

dining-hall. Katrina looked hard at Lucien, and he saw the doubt on her face, but she said,

'Sorry for what, Misia Schmutter?'

'Sorry for being born.' The old lady stamped, and whipped her granddaughter's wrists until the girl fainted. Lucien knew that she had a knack of fainting when she was hit, but even so the welts were puffing under her cuffs.

'Go back to the nursery,' Misia Schmutter ordered when she came round, 'and stay there.'

Katrina went, and Lucien never saw her alive again. He guessed that she must have come down in the night. The door was no longer padlocked. Misia Schmutter had read her thoughts and kept her back on the planned day of her escape, but she had underestimated Katrina.

The rains had begun on the very day of her leaving. They had found her body less than a quarter of a mile from the house, floating in one of the ponds that formed when the rains began and grew unusually deep because of the inability of the caked ground to take in any water. She had been found with her backboard strapped to her back, floating face downwards on the water. Lucien couldn't understand why she would have been wearing the backboard at night. Surely, he felt, she wouldn't have put it back on to run away? Also in the new rain pool they found the things she had taken with her.

Lucien began to worry again, searching for a meaning to these events. Was it good or bad that Katrina had failed to leave the hacienda? What did it prove? What did it mean when Misia Schmutter brought him the things that he had given Katrina and slammed them down on the table beside him? How could she know? After he had put them all away, why did she gather them back into a bundle and put them under his pillow? What did she mean when the under-taker asked her if Katrina was an angel and she said 'No'? That was what mattered most of all to him. That Katrina, who was only just thirteen, was denied her place as an 'innocent'. The estate children would not sing for her. He, Lucien, who was only nine, and his other two sisters, would not sing for her. Poor Katrina. Lucien prayed for her for hours into the night after they found her. 'Please God,' he said, in his thoughts only, because Misia Schmutter could always hear him whisper. 'Please God, don't let Misia Schmutter bury her with her backboard.' Her coffin was closed though, except for a door for her face, such a lovely face that Lucien wept for her.

Lucien pinched himself during the night of his sister's wake, and he drank his hot chocolate with its thick rim of cocoa grease around it, and he ate his sandwiches, the quarters of filled corn bread for tradition, and the coarse black bread for Misia Schmutter, and he waited for the moment when the old lady would leave the room to relieve herself, and then he went close up to the coffin and whispered to his sister the words of the cracked mass he had heard so many times, and a scrap of the old tune was there in his croaking voice as he sang, 'Take this angel, Lord, to you, for she was innocent.' She did so much like music, and the singing at other children's funerals, and the graffonola on New Year's Eve.

Chapter 7

LUCIEN WAS NINE IN THE YEAR 1920. HE HEARD LATER HOW that year had arrived all over the modern world on a wave of manic arousal. Much later still, people would talk about the phenomenon of 'The Twenties' with its chain reaction of extravagance. Perhaps that was what had crawled into San Fernando that year. It was not hit by any spontaneous energy, or inspired by new ideas, or even kept awake on dancing, drink and drugs, through any grasping fear of death. But still a fear of death did creep into the house, and a general loosening of their lifestyle began to occur, and withal there was a kind of gaiety, a forced enthusiasm smeared over the lassitude.

Misia Schmutter was growing ill, and with the onset of her decline there was both glee and dread. Could their world exist without her? Would she take them with her? Who would dare dress her corpse if she ever came to die? And who would dare bury her? These were all thoughts to be continually put aside. Misia Schmutter herself was ignoring her infirmity, and the others tried to follow suit. She also ignored the absence of Katrina and again, the others did so too. All, that is, except Lucien, who refused to forget his drowned sister. So many pairs of hands had come and gone on that estate, and nobody but Misia Schmutter quite knew how or why that one more person gone, albeit their own sister, and for el Patrón, his daughter, seemed to make little difference.

Lucien watched them all with new eyes, with the eyes of the gecko camouflaged against the wood, the gecko who could see everything and who knew more than anyone would give him credit for, with his pale clammy hands and his dividing body. The peasants said that there was a curse on the gecko, they believed in killing them whenever they came and clung quietly to the roof, transparently warty and harmless to anything but flies and mosquitoes. Yes, the peasants hated them, they said that they raped young virgins, that they waited until they were off their guard and then fell on to their bodies and crawled inside and stayed there, scrabbling like the devil to be free, and that they made the girls go astray. Lucien liked the geckos. He didn't like it when they dropped bits of themselves on to his bed, but he liked them, in one piece. The maids and the children clubbed them to death in a way that made him feel sick. He just liked to lie in bed and watch the geckos watching him, and then to watch the others, drawing their innermost thoughts out with his gaze. If they had ever cared about Katrina they didn't now. Not even Franz, or Detlev, his eldest brother, who had seemed to have a soft spot for her. For, he had said, 'She was always a queer fish. She's probably better off as she is, poor thing, she would have only brought trouble on us all.'

As a result of his second explosion, Lucien was once again without a summerhouse, but he was well established in a process of building and demolition. His plans were already drawn up for a new creation. This time he had abandoned classicism in favour of a kind of fantasy that was, if anything, like the gothic castles in his sister's story books. He had begun on this ornate and pinnacled design when Katrina was still alive and there to keep him company and take care of him. She had liked its fairy-tale quality and it was she who had encouraged him to invent new patterns beyond the existing ones in his grandmother's books.

Secretly, he dedicated his new creation to her as a token of tribute and respect, a fairy palace for the fairy princess who had lived thirteen years in the prison of her backboard and who had borne her shackles with pride, and had drowned with her grey eyes in the wrath of Misia Schmutter. Lucien suspected that she had taken her torment to the grave, since, under the circumstances, it would be unlike his grandmother to have sanctioned her burial without it. Sometimes, as he sat morosely in the rubble of his second gazebo, waiting for the rains to stop so that he could start building anew, Lucien imagined that Misia Schmutter had tightened the screws that bound his sister to her board so tightly that her shoulder blades would have cracked in the coffin.

Poor Katrina, he thought, now he would never know what it was that had been wrong with her back. She was rumoured to have had a stoop when she left the Little Nursery, but it seemed more likely that she had fallen foul in some way of the ruling deity. Later, it was true, she could hardly keep straight without her wretched board, but ten years on the rack had deformed her spine. When they were alone, Lucien would take off the metal and wood contraption, with its rows of screws and its steel armbands, that tried her like some medieval torture and was specially made by the estate carpenter. Then, although she wouldn't admit it, it hurt her to stand up. Lucien tormented himself wondering if his grandmother felt any regret for his dead sister. He watched Misia Schmutter sitting stiffly in her rocking-chair while the damp and the mould gathered around the house, and he knew that she felt something, but for whom or for what he couldn't tell. There was, however, no mistaking it, Misia Schmutter was ill.

It rained all through April and May, falling steadily and heavily through June and July as well. Misia Schmutter's buried crops of Indian corn grew up in straggling lines across the near plains of the hacienda. They grew with giant heads and massive leaves, to exactly Lucien's own height, and then they began to rot. The yucca that had been planted as soon as the rains began had no sooner sprouted than its leaves unfurled into huge umbrella shapes that curled and twisted against each other in the fields. Lucien could walk under them, wending his way through the thick stalks, and hardly get wet at all except underfoot. It was like a doll's house Orinoco with a patchwork sky, and there were snakes under the yucca, and hairy caterpillars on their leaves.

Lucien knew that, nine times out of ten, when the metre-long tubers of yucca were dug out of the mud, there would be nothing but stranded slime. The leaves made passable fodder for the cattle, but there would be no boiled fluff with its firm white core to sit beside his meat. In 1920, the rains won again, and the flood waters came in before the yucca was even half-grown. A few sacks of baby roots were salvaged from under the débris, but it was never worth sending the men out to work in the floods, they sickened when it rained.

Despite the regularity with which their whole land became this swampy mess of muddy water, the Llaneros seemed to have hardened over the centuries to bear the sun and the hardships of drought and hunger. They were defenceless against these onslaughts of water, it was an inborn weakness. Misia Schmutter would weigh her business head against her dislike of weaknesses of any sort, and send the men out to plant rice and plantains and new groves of coconut, and then cut her losses and bury the dead and leave the crops to thrive or die as chance would have it.

Every day since the day of her arrival in 1869, apart from the forty days of each of her confinements when she stayed in her room and ate only white flesh to staunch her own flow of blood and drank enough potions to bloat a mule, Misia Schmutter had walked thrice around the terrace, at precisely eleven o'clock. All through April and May, with the first signs of her sickening, she had dragged herself round her ritual track, helped more and more by her stick and her bull mastiff. Lucien observed that it wasn't exactly that she limped in any way, but she was slow, so slow sometimes that it would be midday before she had finished her course. She was slow as though with a sense of impending disaster.

It was in June that things really began to change, for it was then that she cut her walk down from three rounds to one, thereby throwing the entire household into confusion, and it was also in June that her womb began to show signs of its swelling. As usual, it was the maids who were first to notice these changes, and it was they who alerted Lucien.

'Look at Misia Schmutter,' they told him, 'and tell me what you notice about her dress.' He did, and the seams had been altered at the waist and the dark lines of the inner cloth were clearly visible.

'What does it mean?' he asked the servants. But they wouldn't tell him for many weeks. Every day, while she was walking, he would ask them again, 'What does it mean?' It was common knowledge that if anyone knew the meaning of a thing, it was the servants, so Lucien persisted until they shared their news.

'Misia Schmutter is with child,' they said, 'but we'll poison your soup if you tell her we told you.'

'She can't be,' Lucien told them flatly. 'My grandfather has been dead for nearly forty years.'

'You're a child yourself,' they said, ruffling his hair, 'you don't understand these things, ask your father about it.' But Lucien didn't want to ask his father, he didn't even like to think of him dropping like a fat gecko on to the ageing body of his grandmother. He couldn't bear to think of Misia Schmutter without her shield of discipline being reduced to the helpless screams of the servants in his father's bed. Would his father wash her down with carbolic between the legs as he was said to do to the others? It seemed wrong whether he did or not.

That night Lucien slept, and woke wondering whether she would qualify for the cloth or paper bag over her head, or would her alabaster features and the thin line of her mouth be considered fit to stay uncovered while his father crawled over her? Lucien lay awake for the remainder of the night, and he heard, for the first time, the faint sighs from his grandmother's room. When he rose, it was to study, and he finally ventured past the A section of Misia Schmutter's library, and after three hours' research he returned triumphant to the kitchens.

'She's too old,' he said firmly. 'So you're wrong!'

'You don't understand,' they repeated. 'It's not the child of any man, not at her age, it's the child of the devil himself. Either that or a creature of pure guilt.'

Lucien went away again, with worse things to consider now than incest. He found Misia Schmutter resting in her old carved rocking-chair on the verandah, looking out through the streaks of rain at the barricaded paddy fields and the swamped remains of her yucca and Indian corn. He sat close by her and watched how she could hardly breathe for her corsets. Every ten days or so, her dresses widened. By mid-August they were way past the seam, with black gussets let into them. For the first time in his life, Lucien was aware of a shrillness that was not Misia Schmutter. The voice of the tree frogs was growing into his head more piercing than her own fading voice. Lucien stayed close to her and watched her face shrivel as her waistline grew. By now her walk consisted of getting to and from her chair on the verandah. Her herb garden, raised on its platform of rocks, was safe, but she had come to rely entirely on Lucien to tend it. Most of his day was spent thus, ferrying leaves and buds to Misia Schmutter as she sat in her chair, for identification and instructions.

At first, half of Lucien's task was to learn the names of and care for all of his grandmother's plants. But gradually, she came to demand that he know and bring her only a list of specific ones and Lucien recognised many of them as painkillers, pregnancy drugs and some that he knew to be poison. As the weeks went by, the list became shorter and shorter. It did not surprise the servants to see that Misia Schmutter was suffering from morning sickness, but it did surprise them, as the weeks wore on, that this customary complaint did not stop. They crossed themselves and burnt their stock of kitchen garlic and made what other preparations they could against this evidence of the presence of the Evil Eye. Despite her unwieldy size and her by now constant nausea, it was September before Misia Schmutter finally left her place on the verandah and retired to her rooms.

The rain had relaxed its ferocity, although it would not relent altogether. So there were odd bouts of drizzle and a dampness in the air that was so thick you could swallow it and it caught in your throat, but gradually the water around the house itself began to subside until all that was left of the pools and puddles was a smooth grey covering of slime and the various tidemarks. Within weeks the gardens and the surrounding fields would be rich with lush grass. There were plants that could spring to life in a matter of days as though by magic and cover the land with a rush of colour.

However, Misia Schmutter was not to see the coming of the Orinocan spring that year and nor would she witness any other. Instead, she dragged herself from the verandah that had been the second circle of her tyranny for so many years, and took herself to her bed, escorted by Lucien, while the fat drops of water were still falling intermittently from the trees. She had seen through the netting of her copious black hat the red shifts of new leaves on the mango and guava and cashew trees, and the acacia and bucare and araguaney were wheezing under their sap and new growth and the thousands of beetles scrabbling in and out of their bark. But her last look across the fields that she had governed for the best part of her life was across the desolate mud-streaked no man's land that came every time like a chrysalis between the drought and flood. She had sat with her pain and her encumbrance through the fat caterpillar stage, and she had lived in the débris of the dead butterflies' wings often enough, but for the first time she would miss the coloured wings themselves. There were only the leaking wattle huts, battered by five and a half months of rain, and the workmen sitting out on their squalid verandahs in a far circle of fellow sufferers.

All over the hacienda the peasants were nursing their fevers and fighting the paludismo that came as regularly as the new year itself, to rack and shake them and then trick them into a sense of freedom and then shake them again. The more gullible of them thought that Misia Schmutter was the paludismo, the great hand of malaria with its lifelong grip. Dying was the only way to escape it, and it was the only way to escape her. Through the bleary eyes of their torment, her distant tired figure at the big house didn't seem very different to life itself. She, too, had her cures and balms; she was the only one who could soothe their pains, the only one who could dispel their apathy. They lived through no desire to live, but through a dread of her. She gave them powdered water-hemlock seeds, still sent from Germany, or gathered in her luckier years from stagnant pools as the floods receded, and they ate them on their corn bread and dripping every morning, religiously like the sacrament after a twelve-hour fast, and then they drank water from the quinine cups that were a part of every home. It had been whispered that Misia Schmutter was taking this water-hemlock herself every morning on black bread and butter, and no other breakfast but her herbal teas. The knowledge that they might be sharing their malaria with Misia Schmutter herself was insufficient to rouse them from their annual stupor. After all, they had lived with it ever since they could remember—why shouldn't she, especially since she had all the cures?

Lucien did what he could to help his grandmother, but most of all, she seemed to want to sleep and talk. In the beginning she slept more, muzzy from the drops of laudanum and morphine that he himself counted into her tisanes. She vomited far less lying flat and soon the camomile and hops and the sage and marjoram were struck from her lists, and their places were taken by new and more sinister names such as spurge and the deadly Vallesia Glabra. These last Misia Schmutter prepared herself, bent almost double as she groped her way from jar to jar. And then she just wanted to talk. Lucien determined to stand by her whatever happened, and he even had visions of bringing up the deformed creature that Misia Schmutter was to bear, should she die in childbirth, but he was too afraid to ask her much about her condition or the forthcoming birth. So he just sat and watched her grow under the blankets like a great pumpkin in the middle of the bed while her arms grew daily thinner.

One day, he plucked up the courage to touch on the subject.

'Misia Schmutter,' he said, 'why do you take the oenanthe?'

'The what?' she asked him.

'The water-hemlock. I have seen people take it for malaria, but why do you take it?'

Misia Schmutter paused for a long time, and Lucien waited, suddenly afraid again that he had offended her. He prepared to jump back in case she should spring out of bed.

Finally she said, 'There is something growing inside me, Lucien, something I don't want. I am hoping that the hemlock and the ayapana and the marigold and heliotrope and the arnica and all the things you see here will get rid of it.'

'And will they?' Lucien asked.

'Not any more,' she said. 'It has taken my strength away, just when I needed it.'

Lucien sat in silence beside her bed with its folded patchwork counterpane matching his own, worn down and marauded from time to time by the moths but never used because of the heat. Even when it rained and when the rains passed it was still too hot. The seasons were a mere transition from a cracking to a stickiness on the skin, and an alternating of plagues, and a switch from thirst to a stagnant drunkenness. There was always one special time though, the coloured time that came when it came and was gone within eight weeks, sometimes in as little as three, but it was always worth waiting for. Lucien watched the counterpane that his grandmother had kept folded on her bed for fifty years in case it was ever cold enough to be able to crawl under it. It had never happened, and it never would, but she kept it there as a token of the Prussia she had left and the hope she kept with her. Lucien thought that if he could fill her with a new hope, she might stay alive. There was no fear of her as bad as the fear of being without her. So he sat in silence beside her, praying secretly that she would rally and live, and thinking very hard about the flowers that were to come and all the remedies that she could gather from amongst them and that it was only six weeks away from the Armistice day again, and he knew that nothing that grew inside Misia Schmutter, be it the devil's child or the whole world of guilt, could prevent her from living until that day, but he didn't know what would happen after, and down in the kitchens they were whispering that her time was nearly due.

Chapter 8

Ｎ*OVEMBER 18TH CAME, AND MISIA SCHMUTTER RALLIED A* little, as Lucien had prayed she would. The time had passed when she could manage alone the stairs that separated her from the rest of the house and the terrace where the ritual bonfire would be lit. Neither did she wish to let anyone but Lucien and the servants into her inner rooms, and she would not suffer any of the peasant men, not even Chucho Delgado, to carry her down.

'Lucien,' she whispered in the cracked remains of her former shrillness, '*you* must carry me downstairs.' They stared at each other for a long time, silenced by their mutual shame. Lucien, because he had neither the strength nor the size to lift her, and she, because she had needed to ask at all.

Finally, it was Lucien who voiced what they both knew. 'I can't, Misia Schmutter.'

His grandmother was again silent, chewing water in a gritted way that she seemed to do whenever she was off her guard. She looked at the nine-year-old boy from whom she expected so much, seeing him as though for the first time. He seemed suddenly threadbare, with great gaps in his education, and he was physically weak with a weakness to which she had been blind before. Then she rallied properly, not so much for the Armistice, for she knew that there was no real glory in celebrating defeat, but for a new aim. She would strengthen Lucien before she died, transform him into a proper man. This one boy was all that was left of her own family and Der Altman's; the others might come and go, but the spirit wasn't in them. She cleared her throat and said,

'Your grandfather didn't give me much, after I married him. The name, as you can see, I've never used, and the power I took for myself. He gave me his wealth, and he gave me a chance to bear the children of Germany. I don't think he ever much cared for the legend of Der Altman. It travelled with him, though. Everyone knew about it, and I married him because of it, in part. But of the things that came out of his head, there was never anything that I wouldn't have had buried with the latrines. He had a mind like a hummingbird, that man, and no sense of history. But, there was one thing, though, just the one, mind, but it may be enough for us.'

Lucien looked up, and something of Misia Schmutter's optimism spread to him, and he had the presence of mind to remember to prompt her in the way that she liked best.

'And what was that, Misia Schmutter?'

'He told me how Der Altman had the strength to carry his mule.'

Lucien felt a sudden sense of relief. If Der Altman, who had been such a giant, had gained his strength by some artificial means, then maybe he too could gain enough, not to carry a mule, but at least to lift that frail bundle of bones with hardly any flesh left on them except where the new being was growing.

'And how is it done?' he asked, bracing himself for the worst, and prepared by his recent humiliation to swallow even the most vile and slimy of Misia Schmutter's potions without vomiting so much as a drop into any of the baskets of ferns and cheese plants that hung all over the house and that alone seemed able to survive Misia Schmutter's more potent remedies.

'It is an old Black Forest custom,' Misia Schmutter began. 'You will remember that Der Altman came from the Black Forest.'

'Yes, Misia Schmutter,' Lucien replied.

'It seems that whenever a boy nears his manhood, he is given a calf to keep for his very own. This calf he must lift every day in his arms, and tend and feed it too. Gradually the calf grows heavier, but the difference in weight between one day and the next, one morning and an afternoon, is so slight, that the boy grows stronger, lifting its weight, until the calf has become a bullock, and the boy a man. A man who can carry a bull can carry a mule.' She smiled triumphantly. 'Now tell Chucho Delgado to give you the next male calf to be born, and tell your father to come here, he has never been anything but a trial to me, perhaps he can begin to make amends.'

Misia Schmutter was carried down the stairs in the arms of el Patrón, and she watched the bonfire blazing from her hooked position in her chair. Lucien was worried that she would notice that behind her back, work had begun on her next pavilion, but she was too busy trying to stay awake through the haze of opium to notice anything so far away. When it was all over, she didn't even seem to hear the servants' whisperings as she was carried away.

'Did you see that?' they were saying. 'She could have twins there, for the size of her.'

'She's shrinking all over with it,' another one said. And they all agreed that she couldn't have long to wait, one way or the other.

Lucien's calf was born on December 3rd, but he almost lost faith in the plan when he found that he could scarcely lift it. By nochebuena it had outgrown his strength, and at the New Year he was allowed to have another try with a new calf. This time, he cheated a little, stinting the calf of its milk to keep its weight down. The first calf had always seemed like a slippery dirty brute. He had never covered himself with dung, or even dirtied his boots around the cow sheds, let alone his hands. However, by the time he was given his second calf, he had begun to learn its ways, and he grew fond of it, and even gave it a name. He called it Niemen, after the river in East Prussia on the banks of which Misia Schmutter told him she had grown up.

The birth of the calf Niemen coincided with a more talkative stage in the sick-room. Misia Schmutter had seemed to feel a remission in her suffering. The kitchen maids assured him that this was always the case. 'She'll not be wanting you around in a bit,' they winked.

Meanwhile Lucien made the most of her company, dividing his time between her bedside, the site of his new gazebo, and Niemen, his spindly calf. There was a kind of peace in the household. For once, el Patrón and his mother had agreed on something: they both wanted Lucien to be strong. Strange new cereals appeared in his bowl as though by magic at breakfast time, and larger and larger steaks and plantains would be heaped on to his plate. Misia Schmutter gave him pills for his appetite, and his father drilled him to keep him from growing fat.

What exactly the reason was that caused him to grow and the pressure in his chest to ease up, and his voice to break in those first months of 1921 he didn't know, but he felt that everybody's effort contributed to it, and he was grateful. By short-feeding the calf, Lucien had managed to keep abreast of its growth and although he could go as many as five times a day and lift his calf without any fear of failure, the calf itself was growing daily more spindly and its fine Ceibu mother with Niemen's quarter of her udder left permanently unemptied began to grow ill. At first, Lucien had emptied this quarter out himself, copying the other milkers, and then surreptitiously tipped half the milk on the ground, but after the first month he grew lazy, and his hands were so stretched by the milking that he could hardly move his fingers even to hold his own dinner knife.

He kept Niemen in a stall of his own, and the mother cow in another. He didn't really like the mother, with her long horns and her vicious kick. It took him fruitless hours learning to hobble her back legs and to tie her forehead and horns round the milking pole to keep her quiet. He had seen Chucho Delgado do it, and there had seemed nothing to it, but on his own, even though he just had the one quarter to do, and even though the cow was usually already tethered, they didn't seem able to get along. Sometimes she would even withhold her milk.

Despite these technical problems, everyone seemed pleased with him for the first time he could remember. Perhaps that was why he had tried to conceal the hardness in the old cow's udder; so that nothing would change. It was when Niemen could no longer stand, not even when Lucien lifted him on to his feet, that he had to fetch Chucho. The old foreman examined both calf and mother, and then, stroking the fretful cow's neck, he pointed at her udder, spat his tobacco and said,

'It's mastitis.'

'What can I do?' Lucien asked.

'It's what you've done!' Chucho said sadly. None of *his* cows ever got mastitis. They died by the dozen when the epidemics came, and sometimes he could see them just jump in the air, almost skittish as they rose to fall down dead from a snake bite. There was a lot could go wrong with a cow in its few short years of life, but Chucho kept the worst of the worms dug out of their hides, and their lumps were lanced, and their soft feet were herded through baths of creosote, and if the poor beasts lived a life of torment from the flies that sat like astrakhan on them it was no worse than he himself went through, but they never got mastitis, not in *his* pens they didn't!

He massaged the udder himself and then gave Lucien a jar of iodine and pig grease to rub into it every two hours, and he cut back the cow's diet to keep her milk flow down.

'Will it work?' Lucien asked him.

'You can pray to God,' he said bitterly. 'But God's got more sense than to come sniffing round these parts. Misia Schmutter might have been able to save her. But seeing as how she can't save herself . . .' He shrugged, and left Lucien to his task, and his guilt. Two days later, the cow had milk fever, and Chucho shot her. Niemen was bottle-fed, and Lucien found an outlet for a tenderness that he never knew he had, in this pathetic creature, orphaned by his own neglect.

When his brothers returned home from school that Easter, they found Lucien quite unrecognisable. He had become both sunburnt and taller and although he was nowhere near their size, there was no longer anything freakish about him. Even the work on his new gazebo was taking place almost mechanically. Lucien would inspect the works rather as their father might inspect the ammunition room.

There was no outward rejoicing or excess on account of Misia Schmutter's illness. Her last period of retirement and its consequences were still remembered too well. But with Misia Schmutter being temporarily dormant, they all took advantage of the respite to spend their time quietly as they pleased, hunting or stalking birds so that the girls could make fans and plumes from the captured feathers. The mysterious malady that kept the old lady in her rooms didn't deeply concern them. Some of the household believed her to be with child by the devil, and the other half drew a blank. But they were unanimous in believing her sufficient to deal with whatever trials the Evil One had visited on her, and nobody seriously thought she would die. Nobody, that is, except for Lucien and el Patrón, and

Misia Schmutter herself, and they kept a kind of conspiratorial silence on the matter.

All through February and March, Misia Schmutter had confided in Lucien, unburdening herself of her history in order to give him his. Her frenzied preparations of tisanes and compresses had finally subsided into regular doses of opium and lythrum alatum and heliotrope with hot compresses brought in relays by the curious maids, of arnica and mustard. There was a new smell in the room that was not the smell of any of her plants or pills, and sometimes, as she told her story, Lucien felt it smothering him, just as she used to smother him herself in the vice of her own arms and her corsets. As the months wore on, certain objects began to gravitate towards her room. The great Lutheran bible left the dining-room, and was given a new place on the round table beside Misia Schmutter's washstand, and cups and vases and the old colonial basket that lived in the hall all found new places in her room. Thor took to moaning on the floor at the end of her bed, and was banished to outside her door where he whined continually. Misia Schmutter herself lay propped slightly on her horsehair bolsters—she didn't believe in pillows as such. 'A soft bed makes a soft man,' she claimed, but none of them had had the chance of putting this to the test. All through her illness she wore a kind of black drape with copious lace at the cuffs and plain cloth buttons at the neck.

'I was born', she told Lucien, 'in Tilsit on the banks of the River Niemen in north-eastern Prussia. I was born in 1843 in the reign of Friedrich Wilhelm IV. My father was a doctor and a botanist. He was a Burgher, and I was his only child. We were rich,' she said, and then she paused. Lucien listened avidly, aware of the privilege she was bestowing on him. Nobody knew who Misia Schmutter was, or from where she had come. It was known that she had come from the German Colony Tovar to San Fernando when she married her husband, Lucien's grandfather, Wilhelm Lucien, in 1868. Even then, Chucho Delgado said, she had been very thin, but she had inspired a kind of homage to her flaxen, vicious beauty, and nobody who saw the wedding at the old church in San Fernando town would forget the procession or the week of merrymaking and stabbings that had accompanied the event. Chucho himself had been nearly kicked to death by one of the other workers for criticising the straightness of Misia Schmutter's nose. Don Wilhelm Lucien had said that his new wife would come like a balm to his estates. Poor man, he soon knew better.

Don Wilhelm had been noted for his pride of bearing, and the cruel twinkle in his pale-blue eyes, and for his love of hunting. There was hardly a tuft of grass for three hundred miles around that he hadn't stalked or beaten in his time. He had shot tigers and chased peccaries, there were no creatures too small for the notice of his gun. All along the near bank of the River Apure, there was a litter of caymans, left to the vultures. Don Wilhelm Lucien hunted more than his porters could carry and more than he himself could count. He had once caught a monkey with a shot in the arm, and had taken it home as a pet. The monkey was terrified of him, and refused to be touched. When forced to put up with Don Wilhelm's teasing strokes, the monkey had bitten its captor, to the bone, on his finger. Then Don Wilhelm had extracted his attacker's teeth, one by one, with a pair of pliers. After that, whenever the mutilated monkey saw its master, it would hop around frantically on the end of its chain, clutching at its broken mouth with its two tiny hands, while Don Wilhelm stood by laughing.

When he married Misia Schmutter, then it was for others to laugh at him. Behind his back, for his gun was always to be feared. They said that Misia Schmutter had pulled out his teeth, and mockingly that the great hunter had been trapped by the very tiger he so often killed. Don Wilhelm's will was as nothing beside that of his slim, unforgiving wife. Inch by inch she took over his lands, and bit by bit she ruled his life, his thoughts, his very guns.

When the Llaneros of San Fernando came together to swap stories of Misia Schmutter, they could talk for days on end, vying with each other to recall her most extravagant deeds. But her past was shrouded in a kind of mystic silence. To Lucien, it seemed like sacrilege to hear that she had been born the daughter of any man, with dates and places to her name. It made her seem almost human, and Lucien was disconcerted.

'That first time, I could have married any man,' she continued, 'from Königsberg to Berlin. I didn't have to choose the man I did, but I took a gamble on him, I suppose. My father didn't like him, but he liked his aristocratic name and his title, and I liked the dash in him. We had moved from Tilsit to a small town outside Königsberg when I was still a child. Thousands of acres of loose sand and rocks and then thousands more of heath and stunted pines with nothing moving but pheasants and the odd rabbit. There was nothing to do but shoot and hunt, and despite our money, we had books and pictures but no land to hunt on. Besides, father didn't care for hunting, and although a gun means something to a woman here, Lucien, a woman was no good for anything there but to glitter or breed. I saw the choice, I had the benefit of a fine education to help me make up my mind. When a man, like my father, or Hieronymous Bock, or Otto Brunfels or Leonhard Fuchs understood about plants; ah, then he was a great botanist, a great man. But when a woman learned how to cure with flowers, she'd just be a witch or a charlatan, and they don't like witches in Prussia. You had to be a Saint Hildegard and be born in the Middle Ages to get away with that! That meant I couldn't be what I wanted to be, what my father had taught me to be, not then or there. So I married my captain from Berlin, and went with him to the great city and the glitter.' Misia Schmutter paused, gathering her whisper to give it strength to be heard over the inane croaking of the tree frogs.

'It was a mistake,' she said. 'I realised that almost as soon as I married him. You see, he was dirty, and despite his fine name he had no self-control. My father thought it was his gambling that I didn't like. But I liked gambling. It was roulette each evening and through every night. Roulette, Lucien, real roulette with everything at stake. Heinrich used to have winning streaks. Sometimes he'd win for days on end. Hundreds of thousands of Thalers. I bought diamonds, hundreds of diamonds. That was what I had gone for, after all, the glitter. But Heinrich didn't know when to stop. His luck changed and he went on gambling. I told him to stop, and he left me. He just went away. I didn't mind, I didn't like him, but he came back two months later without any money, without any castle or land, even the lodges had gone.

'Then my father died, it was the same year as old Friedrich Wilhelm stood down. They said that the king had been insane: the whole of Prussia seemed insane in those last years of the Fifties, and then Wilhelm I came, and Bismarck, and father was dead.

'Thank God you are not a girl, Lucien, to see your

77

father's property pass into the hands of a dissipated wretch. Centuries of Schmutter wealth took Heinrich six weeks to lose at the wheel. And then he went away again. This time it was three months before he returned, and then it was only hours before the bailiffs. They took him, and I was glad, but they took my diamonds and other jewels, and all our other things. Father's books, that was all they left. You see, even valuable books become worthless in the possession of a woman.

'The diamonds paid for most of his debts, but Heinrich was still six months in jail. He should never have come home to me, Lucien. I had married a fine rich man, not the beggarly dirty sot that he became. "We'll start again," he told me, "I've still got my name." You know, you can never start again. Everything has just the one time, the one chance.

'Looking back now, it was always my father who helped me. You see perhaps the other things would have been enough. I think they probably would, but the last was the real reason why he shouldn't have come home. Heinrich was like everyone else in believing that women didn't understand certain things, not even when they're doctors' daughters, not even when they've read their father's text books so often that the Latin comes back like rote to their heads when they're tired.'

Lucien waited for Misia Schmutter to make herself clear. She always did, eventually.

'Uncleanliness', she continued, 'must be punished by death. Heinrich never changed his inner linen except to replace it, it could fall from him and stink, and he wouldn't care. He told me that all the officers in his regiment were the same. They were all "noblemen", Lucien, the best in the land, steeping in their own filth.

'He came back from that debtors' prison with a pink mottling on his chest. He told me it was from the fleas; but I saw the scabs from his chancres where his underlinen stuck to his flesh, there was a smell then, Lucien, worse than the smell of death in this room now. Worse than any smell I'd ever known. He was frightened too. He used to cry like a child. He had syphilis, you see.

'They used to say that it came from here, you know, the New World; brought to Europe by Columbus's sailors. But it wasn't, it was bred in the groins of the unclean, the degenerate dregs of our own land. Father used to say that it was a shame how the soldiers came and infected healthy country girls and left them to spread the filthy eruptions over our poor waste lands. He used to say those soldiers should be shot on sight, like deserters in time of war.'

Lucien was getting lost in the threads of her story, but she was determined to go on. 'I have only ever told one lie, Lucien, and it was then. I doubt that you will often meet a lying Tilsit man or woman. I suppose it was the one thing we had to be proud of, a little pride to drape over our shame. I told you before of the treaty that was made there when the Emperor Napoleon signed away half of Prussia, and there was the shame of the witches they stoned there too, later, perhaps, than anywhere else. Tilsit was the place of shame where the poor men hunted witches, and the rich men hunted grouse. It wasn't much of a beginning, being born there, but we didn't lie.

'And nor did I, except, as I say, for that one time, to Heinrich. I told him that I was with child, to keep him away from me, even he was wary of an idiot son, and I told him what he already knew, about his pox, and I told him that father had had a cure for it.'

Lucien was growing tired of sitting still. His mind kept turning to Niemen in his stall, and the roof structure that the men were erecting that very day on his new gazebo.

Misia Schmutter shifted herself in bed and asked him, 'Are you tired, Lucien?'

'No, Misia Schmutter,' he said.

'Oh, Lucien, I do not like a lie, but I will not tolerate a lie that can be detected.'

'Forgive me, Misia Schmutter,' Lucien said, standing up and bowing slightly. 'I *am* tired, but I feared that you would stop your tale if I were to admit it.' He sat down again, and Misia Schmutter unruffled her lace.

'So much bother could have been avoided,' she said wearily, 'if only people would think far enough ahead to see the consequences of their words and actions. Give me my drops now,' she said, implying that Lucien's misconduct was directly responsible for her sudden pain. He passed her the laudanam and her medicine glass.

'I have no patience with the fools who use arsenic and cyanide fresh from the chemist to poison their friends,' she said, struggling with the lid of the treen case where she kept her glass safe from the unclean feet of flies. 'I made mine fresh from the summer flowers,' she continued. 'There were no traces, no suspicions, just squeezed drops in his mercury and in two months Heinrich was dead. He had misused my father's wealth, wasted poor papa's life. He was trying to drag me into the gutter with him, he had begun to eat like a pig. I can't tell you what a relief it was. Not just for me, for everyone, there was no place in Prussia for a man who wasted his chance. I could have stayed in Prussia, I had cousins in Königsberg, but I had no money left and I was never suited to be the poor relation. I wanted to continue my father's studies in plant cures, but no one was going to stone me for a witch. That's what it might have come to in the end.'

Misia Schmutter's eyes were glazing over with sleep. Lucien looked into her dilated pupils and hoped that she would not tell him all her life in such detail. He didn't want to hear how people disappeared or how his sister Katrina drowned. Misia Schmutter moved like an avenging angel, and Lucien didn't want the workings of that wrath explained. He was interrupted in his thoughts by the return of her drowsy whisper.

'I saw them stone a girl, Lucien, they followed her . . . all through the town, past the railway, past our door, I knew her. She was carrying plants to father. She couldn't see for blood, but I knew she was looking for us, with her basketful of seeds and flowers. They shovelled her on to the bier barrow with a spade.'

Misia Schmutter's voice had tailed off into a mere croak among the muffled croaks of the tree frogs and cicadas. 'I never let anyone throw stones at me,' she said. 'In the summer, when we went away, cousin Willi used to call me "butterfingers" . . . All these stones inside me, Lucien. Look,' she said, pointing savagely at her bursting waistline, 'all these stones and nowhere to throw them. That's all there was at Tilsit, sand and stones. I thought I had left them behind, but they're here with me.'

Chapter 9

I *T WAS FEBRUARY 1921, AND IF THE YEARS WERE REGULAR,* there would soon be rain, but Lucien knew better than to expect it. Nothing came easy on los Llanos, not life nor words nor water. The great lengths of brushed velvet crept into the horizon with their pile of sweet grasses weighed down with worms' eggs and fever ticks. For as far as the eye could see in every direction, the lands of San Fernando were peppered with grazing Ceibu. It was always so, in the interlude between the floods receding and the drought beginning, this time of plenty and apparent health; it had the depth of sleep that came between bouts of fever, and there was a suspension of bitterness. Lucien divided his time between his new gothic pavilion and Misia Schmutter's room. The roofers and masons had left him now and returned to the cattle, leaving only two workers to plaster and paint the interior. With every day that Misia Schmutter shrivelled a little nearer to her death, the new pavilion became inevitably more a place of prayer than a palace.

Lucien prayed alternately for her and for himself. He prayed for a miracle to save her and for an end to her suffering, and he prayed that all the others might learn to love her in these her last moments as he did himself. And he prayed for his own strength, and for the strength to live without her, and for the will to want to and for the power to comfort and hold her as she slipped from his grasp. She had told and retold him her story, repeating the details to pin them in his mind as she might pin a butterfly to a board. By the middle of March there were some things that he

81

would always remember, such as, 'Everything has a place, and everyone, and the place is aligned like the sights of a gun to its target, a place for itself and a place for others. It is often impossible to match the two perfectly, but they must be near.'

The initial shock of Misia Schmutter's whispered confession soon took second place to her doctrines. 'The only way to survive, Lucien, is in an ordered society: the Greeks and the Romans and the Prussians knew it, but they had a vast machinery to maintain it, we have none. We are the rear guard of civilisation. When you're on your own, Lucien, you'll have to live your life through the barrel of a gun, not as your father does, for pleasure, but for the common good. For the good of those who will never like you, but rather who will fear and hate you.

'My father left me a legacy of wealth and learning. The wealth is in your blood, boy, but instead of learning I leave you a mission, you shall be an inspector of humanity. In cold blood you must control the hot blood of chaos. And when you're lonely, Lucien, and you shall be, remember me and take for comfort the certainty that God smiles on the lone crusader.

'Yes, God gave me a long life to make people suffer, but that is the fate of a doctor: I have cauterised the inconsistencies, and I have brought order to this chaos and decay. Every man who has ever survived me is a better man for that. And you have Der Altman's blood in you, you can be free of the caprice I sometimes feel, you can live by your own law without anger, you can . . . ' and Misia Schmutter's voice trailed into the sultry afternoon. She would often fall asleep mid-sentence, and Lucien would wait for her to wake again, fiddling with the trinkets that were accumulating in ever-growing numbers around her bed. When she slept, she lay like a corpse and Lucien was fascinated by the changes in her. The flesh on her frail face had gone, and her greying skin stretched over her cheekbones. Her eyes were set daily further back in their sockets, surrounded by dark stains, her arms were like the bones of dead cattle. She was shrivelling up like a crushed spider with nothing but the huge unreal belly pushing out from under the linen counterpane. Lucien sat and waited for the Großmutter, the spider, to die. He had no hope left for her life, sometimes he was even impatient for her death, cloistered as he was with the stifling smell of her dying flesh. But then when he watched her closely, and no muscle twitched nor any breath seemed to scrape from her diminished chest, he would panic and jog her awake, and she would croak, 'I am not dead yet, Lucien, but leave me awhile and carry your calf.'

So he would go and wander around the house and grounds, and test his new strength on the long-suffering Niemen, who had grown fat but was slow to grow strong, and together they would watch the household making its surreptitious preparations for Misia Schmutter's death, since even the least observant knew by now that she could not survive the growth. The nine months of gestation had come and gone, and some of the maids still gossiped about the devil. 'And why shouldn't the devil's child be more than nine months in the womb I'd like to know? And how many suchlike have you known?' But most of the household adhered to the theory that it was Misia Schmutter's own conscience that was growing there, and that the old lady was dying of guilt. Gradually, as March turned into April, this produced a softening of the general attitude to the invalid and her suffering was taken as a proof of her humanity after all. The plains were singed again, and many of the migrant birds had moved down the dwindling rivers and away from the drying lands of San Fernando. The macaws and ospreys and feathery egrets all abandoned their nests, leaving only the nightjars and their loud discordant notes through the deserted plains, and the beber-humo birds, or smoke-drinkers, to fly ahead of the grass fires and pounce on the lizards and snakes who crawled out of the burning stalks. Chucho Delgado had once told Lucien that Misia Schmutter was like a beber-humo hawk, hovering over calamities with her hungry eyes and her claws forever drawn.

Chucho Delgado drove the young bulls and two-thirds of the herd away and sold them before a new drought set in, and the ones that were left were already beginning to thin. As the days dragged on and Misia Schmutter refused to die, people began to get impatient. Only the old lady herself remained oblivious to the urgency and the expectation. Delivering her history over and over again in her voice that had grown barely audible, so that Lucien had to crane over her face. That was how Lucien knew that whatever his grandmother carried inside her was no living being, but something dead: as she spoke, her breath conveyed her inner decomposition, and Lucien was amazed that a human being could live for so long in a state of such obvious decay. And although he had heard what she had to say, he didn't want to miss a single word, so he leaned over her foul breath and listened as she told him yet again of the witches at Tilsit and of the Colony Tovar.

'After Heinrich died,' she told him, 'I wanted power, and Königsberg didn't seem the place to get it. If you educate women, and they did there, then there will always be people like me who refuse to sit back in silence. My cousin Haydn was going to Venezuela and, for want of anything better to do, I said that I would go too . . . He was a fine man was Haydn Schmutter, very like my father to look at, I called you Haydn after him. Your father thinks I named you after the composer, but your father is a fool and always will be. Cousin Haydn never got further than Caracas, he died of the black vomit there in '69, he's buried in the German cemetery on the south side of the city.

'I believe that Venezuela would be German today but for that black vomit, that and the malaria and the dysentery, the only things that were ever worse than the Russians for us. A long time ago, the King of Spain mortgaged Venezuela to a German bank, and for twenty-three years that bank, owned by the Weslers, owned this whole country, but they couldn't deal with it and they gave it back to someone better able to bear the scourges of the climate and the bloody flux.

'It was very different after my cousin Haydn died. You could say that I had miscalculated then, but I never miscalculated again. I went to the Colony Tovar in the hills outside Caracas where the climate was fresh and everyone spoke German. It is true that they were mostly peasants but they had at least heard of Luther and their bread was black. I had either to marry, teach or whore there. There was no one I wanted to marry, not after filthy Heinrich. I decided to wait until someone special came, and there is no point in being courtesan to a colony of clodhoppers; so I taught at the school to keep myself fed while I waited for a means of escape. It was then that Wilhelm, your grandfather, came. I had heard of the legend of Der Altman—who hadn't, who was German and out here? Wilhelm was huge, and handsome, and he seemed to know what he wanted, and he seemed to want more than the average man. Perhaps I thought that because I was so sick of eating pumpernickel with the other worthy teachers at my school. But he was quite a man when I met him, and I was glad to marry him and be rich again and bear a son worthy of our race.

'I had flowers, Lucien, at the wedding, cream lilies lining either side of the drive from the main gates to the house. The smell of those lilies was even stronger than the cattle—imagine it! Of course all the local people were terrified and crossed themselves till their arms ached: they see the lily as the flower of death, and they thought I would die in my yards of cream silk (I didn't mention Heinrich to your grandfather, and a little alum and a razor nick served their purpose on our wedding night). They've been waiting ever since for me to die.

'Your grandfather was weak in spirit, Lucien, but he believed in order, and he kept his place at the head of society. He kept it by killing, and he was famous for that, but he never did anything else, except, perhaps, to die of a snake bite, and some said that he died so readily to get away from me, but I wouldn't give him such presence of mind.

'It wasn't all in vain, though, I had one son of whom I could feel proud; but he died of diphtheria, and I was left with your father and three more children, none of whom has survived me. They were all weaklings one way or another. Your father is a great disappointment to me. It's easy enough to kill, but it's virtually impossible to make someone worthy. I used violence to mould your father, I have used kindness with you. Don't let me down, Lucien, you are all that is left, just you in this wilderness.'

Through the slatted shutters Lucien could see bats weaving and slicing through the twilight, and their shrill squeaks came through the window like a mockery of Misia Schmutter's dwindling voice. He could scarcely hear what she said over their gloating.

'Go now, Lucien,' she said, 'and when you return, burn a little sulphur to ward off the bats.' Lucien left and the relatively fresh air of the hall made him dizzy.

That night, only Lucien and his sisters and their governess came to dinner. El Patrón had stayed in the house for weeks, waiting for his mother to die, resentfully careful to keep up appearances, to be present at the moment of death so that no one should call him undutiful. It was the old '¿Qué dirán?', the 'what would people think?', even though it was common knowledge that he loathed his mother. Finally, however, he had given in to his own impatience, and Chucho Delgado had saddled his horse for him and he had ridden into town with a bad grace and strict instructions to Chucho to call him if anything happened. He wouldn't be hard to find, he never was, he was always at the brothel called the Arco Iris.

Lucien ate his meal in silence, except to order the black bread that his grandmother always insisted on and that nowadays had a way of not appearing on the table. At first, leaning over Misia Schmutter's sick-bed had destroyed his appetite, but now, he found that the very fact of getting away from her room made him feel ravenously hungry, it was as though he needed to prove his own life to himself, so he ate shredded beef with onions and tomato and chicken boiled with rice reddened in the seeds of onoto, and he ate eggs scrambled with garlic and green cumin leaves, and mana-mana fish soaked and boiled, and he ate not one but three ripe plantains into which he mashed a small round of fresh soft cheese.

When he returned to his grandmother, he found that she was awake, and propped on her hard bolsters in a way that she had not been for weeks. She smiled when he came in, a strange ghostly smile that was hard to engineer on her tight wizened face. 'I have brought you some camomile,' he said. She drank a little and thanked him, and he was relieved, since the camomile was one of the few things that helped her breathe.

'Do you remember, Lucien,' she asked, reading his thoughts, 'how we used to drive to church, and always note the dead donkeys on the wayside, and count the days that they lay there, the weeks, and wager as to which would explode first, and give them points for the most sickly smell?' Lucien blushed. 'I know what they are thinking in the kitchen. I can hear them tote this decayed growth of mine. They want to know how many days it will be before I burst. Well it won't be long now.

'When I die, Lucien, bury my books with me, my father's books, or what the cockroaches have left of them. I should have left a book of my own, written down what I

86

know and what I have learned. There are plants here whose properties are unknown to anyone but myself. It will all go with me. Some of the peasants know a lot when it comes to herbal remedies. They have no choice, it is handed down from mother to daughter by word of mouth, but it only takes a deaf ear or a mouthful of fish bones at the wrong time for a word to be misheard, and then there is another dead child. Then they will tell you that it was the Evil Eye. It is a useful concept, like a great shawl to wrap your mistakes in. Some of them think that I am the Evil Eye, and I suppose I have been hard on them sometimes, but if you knew, Lucien, how I feel at times, you would see that my every move is one of self-restraint. I have given them fifty years of my life.

'There are no casual ties with los Llanos, you have to be born here to stay, or driven here by greed or lust or sheer insanity. Your mother came here for love, but love can't survive under four inches of flood slime with a layer as thick as your fingernail of pure infection. She came from the same Colony Tovar where I met your grandfather. I told your father to choose new blood, and he did, and the climate killed her. This is a stagnant place to be, but in fifty years there have been two real consolations: the rare plants, and you, Lucien.'

Misia Schmutter's voice had grown louder again, with even a hint of its old shrillness, that high pitch that could carry across miles of wasteland and that filled every peasant in the neighbourhood with dread. For once, Lucien no longer needed to lean over her bed, and he moved away from her terrible ulcered breath.

'You shall have power, Lucien. Sometimes I see you wonder about the power. But it is our birthright, our prize for holding this desolation together, for beating the parasites, for surviving the drought. It is always there, you just have to get up and take it. No one else will. People love to believe in supermen, they won't stop you if you show them that you mean business. All you'll ever need to show are tokens. Tokens of your will-power, tokens of your strength, but only if people get in your way. If they don't, you will have your power, and they'll have theirs. You see they'll find a use for you, make a legend of you, that is the weak man's strength, to incorporate extremes.'

Then Misia Schmutter paused for a long time, breaking

her silence eventually to say, 'I would like you to see Niemen for me.' This last was said in such a whisper that Lucien nearly missed it. He leant forward to hear more, but her eyes were ablaze with their old tyranny, and he rose instead and went out to see Niemen, his calf. He found him in his usual stall, and he stroked and combed him for a while, daubing his hide with paraffin and pulling out the bloated ticks. There were horse flies in the stall, so Lucien led the willing calf out into his grassed pen, then he stooped and lifted him off the ground, struggling as he always had to to keep a grip on the fat belly of the calf. When he had finished he felt proud to have raised the half-crippled beast.

From the house and the stables and the store-rooms and his distant pavilion Lucien could hear shrill voices calling. It was as though his grandmother had shattered into a thousand pieces, and the bats and cicadas and tree frogs and crickets were all piping his name, 'Lucien, Lucien, Lucien, Lucien.' And then through them all he heard one last appeal, not so much his name as a shriek from inside his head. He left Niemen were he stood, bewildered, and ran to the terrace, ran through the doors and the hall and up the great staircase to Misia Schmutter's room, and there he found her just as he had left her but with her mouth open now, and her chin hanging down. He touched her thin arms and found her fever gone. He tiptoed to the door as though she were still alive, and he closed and bolted it, then he pulled the frail, still remains of her body into her bed, and propped her chin as best he could. For the first time since she had come to los Llanos fifty years before, she was covered with the patchwork quilt that it had always been too hot to use but that now might warm her. And he sat by her bed and wept for her in the knowledge that no one else would weep a single tear of love for this woman whom they looked on as a witch but whom they had always feared too much to stone. And he checked, for his own curiosity, to see whether the sand and stones that she said she carried with the growth in her womb, dragged all the way from Prussia, had spilled, but they hadn't.

He lit the candles on the wall for her, and prayed for both of them. He would have liked to have waited until morning to announce the death, but you couldn't leave a body overnight in San Fernando, so he waited until the clock struck ten and then he rang the old bell that hung over the courtyard to assemble the household. When they had all come, he stood by the post where el Tonto Salazar had died, and he said very slowly and clearly so that no one would detect the catch in his voice, 'Misia Schmutter is dead.'

He might have said that the sky was made of corrugated iron, or that horses have three heads, for all they believed him. Despite the long illness and the months of waiting and the secret preparations, none of them had really believed that such a thing could happen. They stared at Lucien and he stared back, but it was only when he turned and vomited, sicking up every scrap of beef and fish and egg that he had eaten, that the others turned and flocked into the hidden chamber of the dreaded old lady, and even then it was some time before anyone would dare to approach the figure lying on the bed with the patchwork quilt draped over the great dome of her growth and the heavy crucifix that Lucien had taken from the wall and placed on her breast. Lucien had forgotten to close her eyes and they glared from deep inside their sockets at the crowd at the door.

By eleven o'clock dozens of people had gathered around the house and the road from the town was blocked with hundreds more who had come to see with their own eyes what they could not believe with their ears. All the outward signs of mourning had been hung and draped in the house, and the dining-room was already being cleared for the body to be laid out. But there were more than outward signs, the whole house was in a state of shock; he and a handful of peasants were mourning Misia Schmutter herself, but the others were also mourning. Their grief, however, was not for the passing of the woman but for the passing of an era. Nothing would ever be the same. The only world they had ever known had died that day with Misia Schmutter.

II

The
Casanova
of the
Wasted Plains

Chapter 10

AFTER THREE MONTHS, WHEN THE DRAPES WERE DOWN, AND the armbands returned to their camphor pellets, the house relaxed, easing itself down on to its joists and boards with an assurance that it had never dared show before. Although the changes that took place were gradual ones, for Lucien—shocked by his loss into a state of torpor—they seemed more significant. Whole days and weeks would pass by in a series of slow involuntary actions, and then Lucien would emerge from his day-dreaming like a new moth from its chrysalis and take stock.

Less water was pumped from the well each day, and less bread was baked in the kitchen. The great plants in the hall no longer had their leaves washed with egg white, and instead, they had been allowed to gather dust and a film of powdered lime. And the dry lime which was scattered in every corner and under every chair to choke the cockroaches and deter the ants lay unswept in ridged drifts of hardening wings and corpses. The long graces before every meal had been whittled down to a bare minimum, and the children's governess appeared to have either left or died. For a while, Lucien found the house littered with the laced rope hammocks that his sisters had unearthed and hung from every available pillar on the verandah. And they would lie, whispering things to each other in a strange language of their own. The starched cotton of their pinafores became criss-crossed by the greying strands of the hammocks. Had Misia Schmutter been alive, they would never have been allowed these hammocks, nor even to come downstairs during the day. They even lay the wrong way round, with their backs rounded by the curves of the strings. They had grown pasty and overweight, and Lucien watched them as they giggled and rolled like fat maggots on the memory of Katrina and Misia Schmutter and all that had been before. Cloistered as the girls had been in the utter seclusion of the nursery, it did not surprise him that they seemed hardly human, but their presence in the absence of his grandmother seemed to irk him more than the heat and the lethargy together. Sometimes, it irked him more even than the drought and the approaching decay. He had tried everything he could think of to keep them out of his sight. He had even tried beating them off with a raw hide switch. They had run screaming for shelter, but they always came back again like gnats to the cattle's eyes.

When the girls were finally sent to a convent school in Calabozo, Lucien was surprised to see that they seemed both glad to go and sorry to leave him. They even cried when the bow-topped cart arrived to take them. However, Lucien could not return their affection. Later on, he would relent and grow kinder to them, but then and there, they seemed no better than the boys who crept down to the house from the cattle pens to urinate on Misia Schmutter's herbs. Lucien looked at his sisters with their travelling frocks and their straw hats, and their pinafores and tears. But as they waved goodbye, he could see beyond their sad eyes: they too would go and pass water on their dead grandmother's herbs, if they dared.

After they had gone, the house still seemed to fill with whisperings at night. Lucien could hear them in his empty wing. He could lie awake under his festoons of netting and hear a kind of surreptitious rustling rising up from the area of the herb garden. It was more than the kitchen maids hushing their lovers, more than his father fumbling with his camouflaging cloths and paper bags in his room, and it was more than bats squabbling and cicadas voicing their unease. To Lucien's ear it sounded like the disguised trickling of children peeing, just as he used to do himself, when it seemed too dark to go down to the latrines, or when Misia Schmutter had locked herself into their earth closet and didn't emerge for so long that Lucien felt he would burst if he didn't empty his bladder in the ferns or the cheese plant on the landing. He had done that when he was very small, and at night he had lain awake with the guilt of his uncleanliness, in the sure knowledge that Misia Schmutter would despise and hurt him if she knew. The poor ferns and the long-suffering cheese plant had grown yellow on their intravenous feeds of uric acid, and Lucien had watched their mottling, and his grandmother's endeavours to correct it, with a kind of fascination. He had continued to relieve himself in this way from time to time until he was seven, and burnt, and fallen from grace. This passing water was the one thing for which he felt remorse. Even when he bound up el Tonto Salazar, it had been in the order of things, whereas the other was an aberration. It had been unpardonable, and now it was unpardonable that the estate children should come and empty their bladders on his grandmother's plants.

Each day Lucien examined the garden, monitoring the death of the more delicate of the herbs. In his mind, he allowed no part of it to the drought or to a gap in his own expertise. No, he believed that the sons of his father's workers were systematically destroying what Misia Schmutter had loved the most. They were causing her rare herbs to wilt, one by one and row by row. The marigolds and the leopard's bane, the thyme and the verdulaga still held themselves erect, unsinged and unwithered by the children's blight, but they were the sun-flowers and hardier than the rest. A few straggling stalks of some of the others managed to survive over the shrivelling tangle of the beds, but the rest were dying, unmistakably dying, and Lucien, for all his strength, was powerless to save them.

He made the servants bring drinking water, passing the cans of it from hand to hand as for a fire. But the water seemed only to speed the decay, causing the parched stalks to rot at their bases where it refused to seep into the caked sand and clay. It stood to reason: Lucien knew that it was poison, poison in and around the roots, that was making his heirlooms die. It was the unhealthy urine of the children with their accumulated toxins. He even tried transplanting some of the choicest plants to the rock-hard ground around Misia Schmutter's tomb, to see if the proximity to her could save them. But they died on the same day that he moved them, as Lucien must have secretly known they would, away from their carefully prepared beds and his own care, and the water. He had waited for the moon to wax so that its growth might draw some corresponding growth from the herbs, but it was no good, they died. Chucho Delgado could have told him they would, any of the children could have told him. No plant could bear a transplant at the oncoming of the drought. But Lucien would hear no advice.

As day followed day and the state of the herb garden deteriorated visibly, he switched from his policy of recruiting the servants and workers to help him save it, to excluding them altogether. He took to watering the plants himself, maniacally, and even flaunting the midday sun, when some of the water that fell on them would be so hot it scorched them. But even when he reflected and was calm, he still spent most of the day patrolling the precinct. Whenever his back was turned he imagined boys stretching their penises so as to project their steaming jets into the very centre beds where the heliotrope and the quimpí still grew fitfully. He imagined girls squatting in the lavender bushes, breaking down the already powdering branches with their bare backsides. He never caught them, but he could feel them there. It made his skin prickle all day, and at night, in bed, Lucien was aware of their presence outside. He could hear the dry leaves falling from their stalks as insensitive feet brushed past them. He could hear the rustle of knees dragged along the littered ground. He could hear the dry sound of stalks snapping, and most of all he could hear the gush and trickle that so offended him. He had tried hiding behind the high shrubs that stood, some alive and some dead and some dying, at the end of each narrow path that ran between the maze of beds that Misia Schmutter had planted. He had waited all night to pounce on the culprits, he had run out with lanterns to show them up, but he couldn't catch them, he couldn't even see them. He just heard the incessant trickle, and sensed the disrespect. Long after he had banished them from the house and gardens, Lucien still felt their presence, and his plants still died.

Each morning, after he had rung for his water and washed and dressed, and laced his high leather boots, Lucien ran down into the garden, taking the big stairs two by two in his eagerness to examine the damage. The red ants hadn't been in the night to carry away the leaves, neither had the red spiders crumpled bubbles in their undersides, nor the fungal candelilla swept through the rows and burnt them to ashes, but the garden was still dying slowly, as Misia Schmutter herself had died. On one morning Lucien found a huge human turd steaming in the heliotrope, and that was the morning that he ordered the whole area to be fenced in with barbed wire.

The wall was reinforced with cyclone netting, and over this wire, reaching up to a height of ten feet, came the barbed wire nailed into wooden posts. Lucien left one gate as the only means of access and to this he added chains and bolts with padlocks to which he alone had the keys. After the enclosure was finished, but before the week was out, another such turd appeared. This time it lay caked on one of the gravelled paths. Chucho Delgado, when consulted, claimed that it must have been catapulted in from behind the sheds. However, Lucien believed more in children so thin and parasitical that they could squeeze through the diamonds of his wire mesh and kill both the sweet and the bitter herbs with their own bitterness.

Every day, Lucien used to think, 'If only Katrina had survived, she would have helped me to protect the garden.' She might not have understood how rare and precious some of those strange plants were, but she would have helped him. And he couldn't help remembering how she used to soothe him. She would have stroked his hair and eased the ache in his lungs. As it was, he lived in a state of undeclared warfare with the servants' and the workers' children. Chucho Delgado and the herdsmen themselves were all right. They at least appreciated what it was to care for a crop, however small, whether it be of Indian corn or arnica. They saw the drought rubbing out Lucien's meagre garden, and they sympathised with his failure to resist its scourge. For them, he was growing up, as they had all had to do. As a rich man, it came later than it had for them, but it came none the less to Lucien, in that particular year of drought. There were no free men in los Llanos. Landowner and peasant alike were slaves to the vagaries of the climate and the tigers and the dysentery. So, that Lucien, at ten, should reach his second puberty seemed only right.

Before the incident of the stool and the erection of the barbed-wire fence, only Lucien had seen or heard any signs of trespassers. Afterwards, however, it became common knowledge that someone was teasing him. Twice more, patches of excrement appeared plastered over the paths and even the plants themselves, and finally Lucien found a wounded dog locked in his compound. Its two back legs were broken and its jaw was lopsided and swollen. Lucien left it where he had found it, in a patch of dried blood to one corner of the outer beds, and, locking all the padlocks behind him, he went into the cool of Misia Schmutter's room to consider what to do. He realised that the initiative had slipped away from him. He had broken his grand-mother's first rule. But someone had thrown this mongrel over his fence, and Lucien recognised this as his own chance to be decisive. That his garden must die seemed inevitable now, and he knew that, as with any teasing, if he could feign indifference, his tormentors would leave him alone. But he couldn't withdraw from the conflict with the sacrilege of the crippled dog there.

He could hear the dog whining all through the morning and on into the dead hours of the afternoon. Whenever it flagged for a moment, Misia Schmutter's own dog, the aged Thor, encouraged it with long howls of his own. The servants heard it and crossed themselves and arranged endless cloves of garlic along the window-ledges to ward off what they considered to be the returning spirit of Misia Schmutter. The workers and herdsmen heard it and tightened the faded red bandanas around their necks, instinctively covering the part of them that felt the weakest. They all knew that it was through the nape of the neck that sun-stroke came, and fever and chills, and also any treachery, and the death rattle always sounded in the throat, and they had seen how Misia Schmutter's foreign hands had long heavy thumbs—strangler's hands.

Lucien sat in the darkened room, listening to the uneven whining and touching the raised scars on his own upper arm. It was nearly three o'clock by the old downstairs clock when he finally decided what to do. He could hear the three chimes through the walls like a biblical warning. He opened the shutters and looked across to the horizon over the scorched fields and the disused cattle pens and half of his barricaded garden. The other half was out of sight but he knew that the bluebottles and the horse flies would be on it already, and the vultures would be overhead.

Misia Schmutter's belongings were packed in stitched bags of camphor and stored in her own chest of drawers. Lucien slit open one of them with his penknife and took out from among her black lace gloves her prayer book and the small revolver inlaid with mother-of-pearl. It was the same one that she had always used to shoot down vultures. Then he took a key from a ribbon around his neck and unlocked the door of his grandmother's dressing-room. It was lined as it always had been with her cures and poisons. Lucien dipped the blade of his penknife into the phial marked curí. Then he carefully resealed the phial, took a flask of rum from another shelf, relocked the door and made his way back to the wounded dog in the herb garden. As he knelt over it, he thought of how Misia Schmutter would have been able to cure the dog. She could have mended its broken bones and rearranged its flesh. She could have done that, or she could have killed it outright. She wouldn't have endured its whining for a whole day until the sound seemed to have found a place in his brain for ever. But Lucien himself felt very much a child as he knelt over the helpless body and stabbed his penknife quickly into its thin side, just piercing the skin as he might have done to a balloon. There wasn't really much of a death throe, just an end to the whining and a slight tremor of the legs. Lucien noticed that it had died with its eyes open. They were very clear brown eyes with darker speckles in them, like Niemen's. He cleaned his penknife by jabbing it through the cork of the flask of rum, then he picked the dead dog up by its good legs and carried it out of his garden and across the yards to an expanse of dried mud beyond the cattle pens. There he laid down the dog and the rum and left them as an offering to the vultures and whoever might come for them. Misia Schmutter's corrupted rum was as lethal as any cyanide, and Lucien had faith in it, as he had in her.

Back in Misia Schmutter's bedroom, with the smell of mothballs and musty leaves, he observed through her binoculars the carcass and the flask. They were clearly visible. At five o'clock he saw something move in the outer pens. They had been long disused for the cattle and none of the workers or servants would venture near them—they had a reputation for harbouring the Evil Eye. In Misia Schmutter's time, innumerable crimes had been discovered in those sheds, even though the culprits could swear by all that they held most sacred that they hadn't been witnessed. None of them understood about the binoculars. Lucien believed that whoever it was who taunted him and wished such disrespect on Misia Schmutter's garden would feel brave enough to take a risk, thinking that the power to see from afar had died with the old lady. Lucien gambled on the fact that most of the workers would still be too afraid to go near the sheds or their yards. It was a gamble, but then gambling was his creed.

At five o'clock he saw something move and freeze in the pens, and a few minutes later a flurry of stones disturbed a vulture from the carcass, and then he saw Angel Ramos creep out to the dead dog and the rum. Lucien watched him turn the dog over with his foot, look around him, and then slip the abandoned bottle into his belt. Next morning, Lucien called Chucho Delgado to him to remove the pile of bones from behind the old pens and bury them.

Chucho said, 'Angel Ramos died in his hammock last night without a sound.'

'You'd better bury him too,' Lucien replied.

'As Misia Schmutter would have done?' Chucho asked him.

'Yes, give him all the trappings.'

No more stools appeared after that, in fact nothing was ever slung over the barbed-wire fence again, not even so much as a guava pip found its way in. But the garden was dead, and Lucien knew it. Angel Ramos might have stopped killing his herbs but Lucien's revenge couldn't make it rain.

For the next many months, Lucien sat in his summerhouse and thought about himself; his strengths and his inabilities, his role and his ignorance. Nobody disturbed him as he weathered his depression. El Patrón took no more interest in his son than he did in the matters of the estate or the running of the house. After Misia Schmutter's death, el Patrón had found his new position confusing. He had grown so accustomed to having his mother tyrannise his every thought that to be forced to think for himself, suddenly at the age of fifty, was distressing. After Misia Schmutter's death, he had hoped that he might have some peace, but now it was Chucho Delgado who plagued him, pestering him with questions. All el Patrón ever asked for was a little peace and quiet to enjoy the Arco Iris to its full, but Chucho wouldn't let him, with his, 'How many cattle shall we brand today, Patrón?' and his, 'Shall I lay Ignacio Salazar off, he is drunk again?' and his, 'We need some more dynamite and there is none left in the store.'

There was no end to Chucho Delgado's demands. El Patrón didn't know why the man expected him to know the answers. He had had all his ideas taken from him as a child, he was conditioned to obey, Misia Schmutter had seen to that. He was a part of the ritual, a mere thread in the fabric. So he left Chucho Delgado as a reluctant substitute for himself, and rode off into San Fernando each morning, and each evening he would ride home drunk. But an anxious Chucho would be lying in wait for him; el Patrón could hear his voice through the muzziness, 'Shall we bring in the corn tomorrow, or shall we risk another week, Patrón?' It was easier not to come home at all. It was easier to stay at the Arco Iris, where the whores had a room for him, and never asked him questions, and were afraid of him, and took it in turns to sit on his lap and hold his glass of iced rum and lemon.

By October, when the drought had bitten so hard that again every day was a battle to survive, el Patrón had taken to saying, 'Ask the child Lucien,' whenever Chucho Delgado managed to corner him for advice and guidance. Chucho himself felt too old to make the decisions. When he was a young man he had sometimes thought that he would have liked to, but now that his mouth was broken, and the sores on his legs would never heal again, and his hands had grown gnarled and hardened by handling cows all day, he was just waiting to die. There was no more hope or ambition left in him. He had even stopped watching the cock fights, and sold his own game cock to Jacinto Alarcón. No matter how much lime juice he dipped its spurs in, it would never win. He had lost hope. His last hope had been to out-live Misia Schmutter, and now that he had done that there was a pointlessness about his own life. She had been both his scourge and his protection. Now, save for the flies and the climate, there was nothing to torture him any more, but where was his shell? How could he keep his underbelly from the sun? How could he protect his neck, his balding head, his broken mouth?

Chucho's mother had told him, years before, that God had a purpose in all He did, and the drought was just His way of rest, and then everything returned. But Chucho had learned that only hardship ever returned. Meanwhile he himself was just waiting to die. In the evenings he would sit on the fence of the cattle pens and scrabble at the dry earth

101

with his horny toes, turning over the red flecks of wings and brittle corpses. The only birds in the trees were vultures and nightjars, all the others had fled, the only plants were dead ones, and save for the odd cactus and araguaney, the only trees outside the orchard were dead ones, which proved yet again that his mother had been wrong in this as in so many other things.

El Patrón refused to assume responsibility for the estate, and Chucho Delgado didn't know how to, so he followed his master's instructions, and asked Lucien, who decided things as best he could and was horrified by his own inadequacy. There was so much he didn't know. Apart from his architecture and a smattering of botany, he was almost as uneducated as the peasants who could neither read nor write. He had read Palladio, and Vitruvius, Violet le Duc, Campbell and a string of other theorists whose views had found their way to San Fernando, and he was sure that he could recognise a Tuscan column at a glance. Studying plans of palaces and galleries made the back of his neck tingle, and the sight of a beautiful building could relax him as well as any of Misia Schmutter's balm or hibiscus tisanes. At night, by the thick-smelling spluttering of tallow lamps, he had read of the construction of some of the finest houses in Europe. He knew the exact inner dimensions of Il Duomo in Milan and endless anecdotes about building-site tragedies. But nothing that he knew was of any practical use in running the tens of thousands of acres of scorched parkland that belonged to his family. His ability to name and recognise different styles of pillars and gables, roofs and steeples, churches and turrets, couldn't stop his cows from bloating or starving, or marauding tigers from killing the calves, or the wells from drying. Misia Schmutter had fuelled his single-mindedness with new books ferried from Caracas, and Lucien had even learned a little German and a little French, a little English and a little Italian, just enough to decipher the captions under the photographs and illustrations in the foreign books. It had never dawned on him that if he learned the whole language, he could read the whole text. He built scale models of famous buildings, burned them, and built them again, perfecting his skill with each new attempt. He had felt that he was getting better, sometimes he even felt a glow of pride, so it was a hard truth to discover his terrible ignorance, and he struggled to make amends.

He scarcely noticed the Christmas of 1921. How could there be a real Christmas without Misia Schmutter? And although he had lit the customary bonfire on the preceding November 18th, it had seemed like a paltry affair, and he fancied that one of the kitchen maids had had the affrontery not to attend. He made a mental note to call a register the following year. His brothers returned for the holiday, and then went back to their respective schools after the New Year. Lucien had dusted off the old graffonola, and they had sung 'Alma Llanera' and 'Deutschland über Alles' as they always did, but his brothers were almost grown up now. Franz Wilhelm was waiting for his commission, and Detlev, the eldest, would start at the University Andrés Bello the following year. They had pale moustaches and fancy boots, and they spent most of their brief holiday in target practice or dancing in San Fernando. When Lucien asked Detlev for advice about the wells and their water supply and the ranch, his brother ruffled his hair in a way that irritated Lucien and told him not to bother about such things. 'What does it matter if the old place crumbles into the ground? It's a hellhole anyway, I'll be glad to see the end of it.'

After the new term began, the house was empty again. Lucien's brothers had asked him why he didn't go back to Caracas with them. He toyed with the idea and then rejected it. They had said that he wouldn't be able to build things there. There would be no more projects, no more gazebos and no more explosions, and when he returned, if he went, he feared that there might be no more of his past to return to. If he went away, he feared that his hellhole might crumble to dust, so he stayed, boring his way through the remains of Misia Schmutter's library just a step ahead of the book worms and the cockroaches and the termites.

Chapter 11

SOMETIMES IN FEBRUARY AND MARCH IN THE DRY SEASON
before the rains, which could also be the dry season before
the drought, depending on the year, strange winds blew
across el Llano. These winds brought a layer of dust to
settle everywhere. They came into San Fernando from
along the yellow drag of the Orinoco, and across its swamps,
blew for an hour and were gone. They were said to be the
flapping of lost souls escaped from their chains and then
returned unwillingly to the treacherous waters. These winds
were said to have strange powers: they could make holes in
the road without rain, they could twist metal and wood,
they could make flocks of scarlet ibis fly upside down like a
fringed Presidential canopy in the sky, they whispered things
to the town gossips that they could never have known.

Guillermo La Paz was said to have been struck dumb by
one, and la Vieja Angelica saw a vision once that she said
she could never describe to anyone even on pain of death.
No one believed la Vieja and her dream, which made her
so angry that it brought on her fits and she had to be
carried, frothing, over her daughter's donkey to be nursed
back to calm and reason at the other end of the town. But it
was Angelica's insistence on the 'pain of death' that did it,
because death was the one thing that had never been known
to come from the freak March winds. It was this that made
them so strange, when dying was endemic. But when the
vultures flew in formation, or the tree frogs and the cicadas
stopped singing and the town heard the first silence in

living memory, that was the March wind, the so called Alemán.

Each time someone took note of Lucien, his dress, his manner, his height, or any other part of him, there seemed to have been such changes that no other explanation but the Alemanes could be found. As he matured, Lucien acquired at once both a gentleness and a distance, and the latter rarely put the former to the test. El Patrón watched his son with growing pride, he seemed to have all the firmness of his ancestors without Misia Schmutter's eccentricity. When the other boys came home, groomed and skilled from their schools and the academy, it was Lucien who shot the straightest, Lucien, the one who had stayed home, who rode the fastest, who could leap from one horse to another and ride bareback like a true Llanero. It was Lucien who could fish and hunt the best, lasso and spear better even than his own peones, and they had it in their blood to master knives and horses.

El Patrón freely admitted that he had misjudged his youngest son. Even after Lucien had grown strong, el Patrón still disliked him and thought of him as some kind of fortified reptile. But then, in 1925, San Fernando was scourged —as occasionally happened—by a man-eating tiger, and it was Lucien who tracked and shot the beast where half the town had failed, Lucien on his own, and at almost point-blank range. El Patrón had wanted to cure and hang the head in the dining-room, to glower down over their uneasy meals as Misia Schmutter had done. Lucien, however, refused. He had thrown the whole tiger, the so called massive 'Jaguar of the plains', with its black and tawny hide and its still warm flesh, into the Apure River. Chucho Delgado said that Lucien had fired directly into the heart, killing it in seconds, and that a less perfect shot would have ended in the joint death of hunter and hunted. Not since the end of the nineteenth century and Don Wilhelm Lucien's legendary aim had there been such a shot in the family. Straight through the main artery!

El Patrón said that you had to kill a man to be a man. But when his fourteen-year-old son returned with a tiger trussed to a pole, el Patrón felt both envy and pride. A tiger wasn't like a cayman, or a sting-ray or a mad dog or a wolverine or even a snake. It was the very spirit of the plains. El Patrón and his kind lived by cattle, and the tigers took their tithe. Some were baited with poisoned meat, and some were trapped, and some were shot from afar, and some always survived to return, turned man-eater and more cunning than all the animals of the forest and el Llano together. No one who ever got near a tiger lived to tell the tale—except Lucien, who had stood almost on its talons and fired. Why had the tiger let him get so close? Why, of all men, had it failed to attack Lucien? It was a mystery.

In the still sweaty afternoons el Patrón could hear all the women of San Fernando gasping for his son. He himself basked in the reflected glory, he could see it in every woman's eye, from the wizened old market vendors who lined the town square to the star of the Arco Iris. The young girls in church blushed for him, and that made them blush a little for his father. El Patrón imagined the whole female population in a series of erotic poses as he tussled with his siesta, and all for this son of his, who looked like a film star. It was undoubtedly Lucien who had made available to his own sensual imagination both the cream and the dregs of San Fernando's society. Thanks to the boy's unprecedented attractions, there was no longer an upper age barrier to his father's thoughts. Thirteen, however, was and always would be the youngest limit to which his lascivious fancy would fly. El Patrón felt very strongly on the point. In fact, he would still, personally, drive a corkscrew through the parts of any man attempting to accost a girl of twelve or under. What was magic about thirteen? He didn't know, but had he not horsewhipped the father of a younger child who was sold to the Arco Iris? The then Madame, la Rusa, had explained in vain that the child would be worse abused left to her own devices. He had sat the good lady on his lap, or, that is, as much of her ample frame as he could gather on to his lap, and explained in his turn that he would ensure that no brick or plank remained of her brothel if the child so much as set foot in it. And so it was that thirteen remained the age of consent among would-be prostitutes in the region.

Even though girls were girls and whores were whores, it was considered that boys, to have the upper hand, should become men at twelve. Detlev and Franz Wilhelm and the other boys had all been initiated at the Arco Iris by experienced women, chosen and tried by el Patrón himself. Not much had filtered through el Patrón's bruised nervous system either as a boy or as a man. But here and there stray shreds of ritual were preserved, thin strands that he tied and kept and sometimes adapted, and this sexual education of his sons was one. Perhaps it was the machismo of los Llanos overriding the old lady's Puritan zeal, or perhaps it was a warped remnant of her zeal itself. Whatever it was, and however it originated, el Patrón believed it to be his duty.

Misia Schmutter would definitely not have approved. Detlev went in her lifetime, and Franz too. But they went in secret, and returned in disgrace. Lucien was twelve and thirteen and fourteen and he still hadn't been either to the Arco Iris with its peeling rainbow over the dance floor, or to the many other smaller establishments, some old and some new like shanty towns along the notorious Calle Vargas. Neither had he been to the regular rival place where the young men went, including his own brothers, and where there were new records sent in padded crates by muleback in a never-ending train from La Guaira, foreign songs and foreign wines and dancing.

At fifteen he would have been the laughing stock of the town, tarred and feathered by his peers maybe, for being perverted, had the continuing fact of his virginity been known. However, Lucien was a survivor, and he disguised his state of purity so well that his supposed conquests became legendary in number. None of the girls for miles in each direction dared be the one not to have shared his favours, so they invented hours of secret passion and added them to the general rumour, until his reputation as a lover became unrivalled outside the capital itself.

Lucien visited his grandmother's grave, scraping the slime from the stone with his penknife and poisoning the ants. He would climb on to the high flat top of her tomb and sit for hours and hours thinking and talking aloud. He would also spend an hour or so every day gathering weeds and roots and barks to add to the Schmutter collection. It was these frequent absences that gave credence to his fame.

During these years of Lucien's adolescence, Chucho Delgado was growing old. His was not a natural ageing from year to year, but rather a series of irreparable landslides. The townsfolk all discussed the changes in Lucien, his strength and beauty and that something about him which seemed to set him apart. They gave the Alemanes the credit for his change, but when it came to Chucho Delgado, they shrugged and said, 'What can you expect at his age.' There was no sense of wonder for them that the blood in Chucho's veins was drying up, and that his joints creaked worse than all the stiff hinges of the house together, and no graphite rubbed into the cracks could ever ease them. The bleary decay of old age would come to them all one day, if they were lucky enough to live that long, and when it did, their score of trials would be such that the final rest must seem a welcome one. While the itinerant gusts turned Lucien into a hero, Chucho, on his fence in the cattle pens, was passed by; and the only Alemán to come to him was his young master, Lucien, whose family were all Alemanes. It was they, no doubt, who had given the name to the wind itself as a tribute to their own inexplicable behaviour.

Though Lucien read and read, treaties on yucca and Indian corn on the cultivation of rice from the paddy fields of China to the banks of the Ganges, and more specific works on pest control, crop rotation, drainage and irrigation, Chucho Delgado was his main source of information. For pamphlets on cows and the tse tse fly were all very well, but they took no account of such local complaints as the Mayera. His books spoke of disinfecting cattle pens, but they offered no help when it came to dealing with the vast smitten savannahs that fell under his care. Lucien could study the diagrams of fat slug-like worms being dug out of the hides of cows, and he could read all they had to say about sterilising the knife and getting some special tool with a curve to hook out these worms, but every head of cattle that he owned had dozens of such grubs and he couldn't leave their flanks like a patchwork of lance wounds to fester and ooze in the sun. Only Chucho with his thin arms growing daily thinner could tell him to rub spat tobacco over the small hole where the grub was living and the fumes would make it drunk and it would force its own pale head through, stretching the skin from the inside without a tear, and the great fat maggot would roll out on its own, thus avoiding the humps and bumps of septic mounds made by the trapped ones. To illustrate his point, Chucho had spat on to his own fist and rubbed the dark tobacco juice on to a bump under his elbow.

'How do you know when to do it?' Lucien asked him.

108

'You just wait until you can see the lump throbbing, and that means that the gusano is ready to come out.'

'And if we washed the cattle down with creosote, wouldn't it help keep the flies away, like the books say?'

'You can try, Niño Lucien, you can try.'

Even ranching became a game of chance and decision. The creosote and the foot baths and the isolation pens and the irrigation ditches worked; and the alfalfa and most of the new grasses, the ground nuts and the sweet potato failed. The fencing fell into a category of its own, since Lucien could see neither an advantage nor a disadvantage to it. One thing was sure, the ranch was making good money again, the lean years were never as lean as they had been, and the good years were better than ever. Only Chucho hobbling round the peones and the pens chewing imaginary water and waiting to die had no faith in the prosperity. Now that his wages had doubled and his billy-can came to him daily from his hut with thick slices of mortadella and two pats of cream cheese wrapped in a leaf, he had lost his appetite. He had seen too many reverses. His only defence was to be prepared, and he was, for the worst. One day the irrigation ditches would dry out, or the water be blighted, and Niemen the fat bull who lived in el Niño Lucien's new pavilion would find his smooth haunches ravished by worms, and the horse flies would blind him and the turkey vultures would fight over his carcass.

As the months passed by and no calamity occurred to claim either the ranch or Chucho himself, and Chucho's luncheon sausage tasted no better and the small cheeses that he ate with it seemed to curdle inside him before they had even passed his throat, he decided to set his wages aside towards a gravestone. He had been infected by Lucien's architectural grandeur, by years of supervising or perhaps just by a desire to have the upper hand over the vultures when he should finally go, but he didn't want a simple cross, either in wood or stone, he wanted a tomb, something carved and vaulted, something so thick that the vultures would break their beaks against it. Each week he returned half his wages to this end, and Lucien would match the sum out of his own pocket.

From six to six Chucho Delgado toiled, supervising his men with a tenth of his attention, while the other nine-tenths tried to calculate the present state of his fund. Was there enough to buy a carved angel for his head? Could he have columns and arches? Would el Niño Lucien order some of that strange purple stone to inlay at the sides? How high would the tomb stand from the ground? Would it be two feet or three or even four? How thick would the sides be? Sometimes, on Saturdays when he got drunk, Chucho imagined a stone as wide as the horizon.

There wasn't a skill or phrase that Chucho Delgado wouldn't teach Lucien. He taught him everything he knew and more, stretching his memory to its limits, remembering things his mother and his grandparents and his greataunts had known long before the War of Independence. And Lucien repaid him with stones, as a king might repay a courtier. Chucho had moved his meagre belongings into one cramped room of his adobe hut. The small, windowless middle room was still a store hut, with sacks of black beans scraped out of the dirt and wooden boxes of grey coffee beans and sacks of yucca and corn. Chucho had felt his shins ache with hunger too many times to let any passion, new or old, reduce his stock of food. But the third room became a place to lay his blocks and slabs as they accumulated for his future tomb. No other peón had three such rooms in his home. It was a mark of privilege as capo of the estate to be able to sleep separately from his children. His eleven children had either died or grown and gone, with only la Tuerca Maria, squinting in the blackened kitchen that stood half-open to the wind at the far end of his hut, to represent them. The peones might call him chocho if they liked, to so forget himself and belittle his family in the eyes of their neighbours; he didn't care. He had slung his hammock and that of his long-suffering wife beside his daughter's, leaving their own room, papered from dirt floor to thatched ceiling with newspaper cuttings pasted over the wattle and daub and faded to indistinguishable yellow and greys, to fill with stone.

At first, it had been enough to imagine his monument, but as the months passed, Chucho wanted to feel the stone itself, particularly, he argued, since he would be unable to feel anything but the weight of it when he died. So he would meet Lucien at the place of the boy's choosing and unfurl to him the intricacies of the savannah as he knew and understood it after his long years of trial and survival under its tyranny. He told him strange things about Misia

110

Schmutter, and el Patrón, and distant cousins who lived in the cities. And he told him things about Lucien's own frail mother.

Each Saturday, after the midday pay, Chucho would hitch his heavy reward to his bald, bow-legged mule and walk beside her as she dragged her load of stone along the winding track to his home. He had slate and marble and alabaster, sandstone slabs and granite lintels. He had a gargoyle, two pilasters and yards of bevelled edging, and lastly, he had a bag of crumbling, corroded stone that Lucien told him was a broken Virgin. In his spare moments, Chucho tried without success to piece this last together. He felt that one day, when his time was really near, when all the flesh had fallen from his bones, and the fever on the nape of his neck underneath his worn bandana was about to get the better of him, and his bowels finally fell through his body and gave in to their years of holding back the dysentery and the watery flux, it would come to him, like a vision. Then he, Chucho Delgado, would have the Virgin of pain and sorrows to preside over his decomposition.

Chucho's wife had begun by viewing her husband's craze for stone with a mixture of horror and despair. She had survived Misia Schmutter and more droughts than she could remember, and the black vomit and a mapanare bite. Now that Chucho's money went on stone, sixty-five years of resignation and toil had brought her, seemingly, half-wages and half-rations and a room full of cold dead weight. However, as the months wore on, she grew to see Chucho's passion as one that she might share. God was a long way off, of that she was sure. The rituals of His faith were observed to ward off His further wrath; but she, Efigenia Delgado, had survived by her own sweat and grit. This God had not cared for her body in life, would He really care for her corpse? If she were young and pretty again, she might be an angel, but Efigenia wasn't fooled, she knew that if only the under-twelves became angels it was not just because they were innocent. (And despite all el Patrón's efforts, there was a lot of innocence lost before the age of twelve. She herself had lost hers when she was nine, gathering furze for the kitchen fire. A slap round the face and a two-minute rape, and never so much as a locha for her pains.) Whoever heard of an angel with a pockmarked face

111

and sunken cheeks and a toothless trembling grin? Angels didn't have elbows like hers, and their breasts didn't dangle at their waist in such flat pouches of yellowed skin. So perhaps Chucho was right, and it would be better to lie under a monument and not just be dug into the dry, ant-ridden ground.

One evening, as Chucho returned late from talking to el Niño Lucien, with a bar of green marble in his thin knotted hands, she called to him from the cluttered verandah of their hut, 'Señor, what a fine piece of stone you have there.'

Chucho smiled like a small child, and quickened his step. He didn't greet his wife, he never did. She was just there like the land, a part of him that he loved but barely noticed. She had grumbled at his treasures often enough, but for once she seemed ready to praise them.

'Now that you have so many, they look wonderful,' she said. 'It must be very hard for you to choose which of them you'll use.'

Chucho grunted impatiently, 'I'll use them all, woman!'

'But a plot is a plot, and the stones will topple over without a wide base; so someone will have to choose, and it may as well be you, since they are your stones.' Efigenia paused, and then added, 'I'll reheat the coffee and the beans now,' and turned quietly, leaving Chucho dashed and belittled to contemplate his loss. He ate his black beans and bird peppers in silence. Even his daughter la Tuerca could see with her imperfect eyes that her father was in no mood to be spoken to, and she checked her usual prattle and went out to feed the three hens.

Efigenia heard her husband return well into the night. She imagined that he had been to the cemetery, as indeed he had. On the following day he asked her,

'Efigenia, we've been lying together for so many years now, perhaps we should lie together when we are dead.'

Efigenia's dim eyes brightened, but she didn't allow herself to smile. 'Would I have a monument too?'

'You can share mine,' Chucho said.

'How tall will it be?'

'Misia Schmutter's is seventeen hands from the ground, Efigenia; if we could save more, maybe ours could be bigger.'

Efigenia felt her blood pulsing as it used to pulse when

112

Chucho first married her. 'I could bring damaged coconuts from the market, Chucho, and we could eat them like we do when the drought is here, and we could eat into our stores even, and the hens can go, and the good-for-nothing pig, and Maria can find work . . .'

Chucho stared at his wife in amazement. Such plans could raise their tomb by almost a hand a month. He felt as he felt when the new flowers came after the first rain. It was a sensation of happiness and foolishness at once, mixed with a kind of awe.

'You're a wonderful woman, Efigenia,' he said, paying her his first compliment in thirty years.

Chucho and Efigenia would have bartered their own fingers for stones, had somebody wanted them. But there was no use for flesh and blood, Lucien bought only memories and flowers. By a kind of osmosis he swapped obsessions with Chucho Delgado, filling the old man's thoughts with masonry while his own head filled with folklore and the means of survival against whatever odds.

Some six months after Chucho and his wife had twinned their efforts and sacrificed everything to the tomb that would cover them, they were saved from having to devise any further hardships. An epidemic of typhoid fever swept through San Fernando in May 1926, claiming victims of all ages, but mostly the children and the very old. Both Chucho and his wife succumbed. Lucien had drawn up a Will for him. It read: 'I, Chucho Delgado, of the Lucien estate, San Fernando, do wish to be buried with my wife, Efigenia Delgado, and over our joint graves for there to be a monument incorporating all the stones in my house, and all my belongings are to be sold to buy more, and the monument is to be as high as possible, with the mended statue of the Virgin of pain and sorrow to be stuck on top.'

Lucien designed the tomb himself, adding a great deal of flat stones and two more pilasters to Chucho's existing stock. El Patrón was fearful that it would seem inappropriate.

'¿Qué dirán? Lucien, ¿qué dirán?' he asked nervously from time to time while the works were taking place at the cemetery. But Lucien could do no wrong in the eyes of the town. He set the tone. If Chucho Delgado had a tomb like the Viceroy himself, it must be because there was something about the man that they didn't know about. Had he lived in hiding and in disguise? Nobody knew.

113

Lucien was only sad that Chucho couldn't see the tomb. It stood seven hands from the ground, twelve with the mended Virgin. Had he been able to see, Chucho would have appreciated the irony of his last defeat. He had starved himself to raise the height of his stones, but in the end, the man who had been driven to a mere shell of himself under the reign of Misia Schmutter was obliged to lie ostentatiously in her shadow, in death as he had in life. She would tower over him into eternity or decay. There was no beating her and no escape.

Chapter 12

LUCIEN NEVER REALLY KNEW WHY HE LEFT SAN FERNANDO and went to Caracas. In the long prison years to come, when every day gave him scope to retrace and analyse his moves, no one clear reason emerged. He could not decide whether he was fleeing from his past, his family, the climate, the landscape, the boredom, the responsibility or his own virginity. They were all important to him at the time of his departure, but none of them was new.

Sometimes he felt that he was fleeing the silence, and sometimes the noise. After Chucho Delgado's death, there was no one to talk to in the evenings. His brothers avoided the place, and his sisters seemed to get younger rather than older with each year. Even the company of his father distressed him, after the latter developed gout and never recovered enough to resume his nightly wandering. At heart, Lucien felt that el Patrón's presence did much to mar his enjoyment of the house. He could not share his father's pleasure in dominoes. Even when they gambled for heavy stakes, the game was too slow. He had tried to convert him to roulette, but el Patrón hated to be hurried, and was a bad loser, and always insisted on turning the wheel again when he lost, refusing to pay his debts and forfeits. Then there was el Patrón's 'masseuse' who played the graffonola before breakfast, and could be found in almost any room of the house manicuring her nails. After two weeks, when Lucien had managed to impress on the painted girl the rules of the household, she would leave, only to be replaced by another noisier and more vivid version of herself.

Each afternoon and evening, Lucien could hear his father through the thin partition walls of the house, grunting and groaning intermittently as his desire or his gout got the better of him.

At twilight, el Patrón would sit on the verandah with his massive swollen feet raised on cushioned rests, and shoot down passing buzzards, and chicken hawks, and any other bird rash enough to fly within his range. He was a good shot and very rarely missed. The downed birds brought more birds to the site, and el Patrón came to be such a man of habit in this meagre sport that although his mother would not have been proud of him had she been alive, she would at least have approved of his constancy. Lucien, however, was irked by the mediocrity of their life. The extremity and the challenge seemed to have gone. There were silos of grain against the drought, and stocks of hard cheese waxed away from the flies, and beef so salt it was hard as pemmican. The days when salt had been as scarce as gold were gone. Now the mule trains came in from Araya, laden with more precious salt than they could use, and the sweetness from their stews had gone, and the sweetness from their lives. Lucien felt himself trapped by his own endeavours in this land of new plenty, mosquitoes, termites and thorns. He was expected to rule for ever and to fill each clay pot with black beans and the new casks with rum. Beauty was two plates of rice and chicken and plantains baked in their skin, and withal there was resignation. Resignation to birth and death, to the slaughter of blighted cattle, to the monotony and the lethargy and the pests. When the rains came they were just water, and when the drought came it was just heat. Sometimes it seemed that the whole miraculous Llano was branded and packaged and cured.

Then Lucien wanted a woman. It was 1929, and he was eighteen and a virgin and anxious for a great romantic love. He wanted someone as wayward as Misia Schmutter to hold him, but someone who would not rupture his neck in her stranglehold as his grandmother so nearly had. And he wanted someone as haunting and strange as Katrina. Someone with grey eyes like rock pools who would soothe but not smother him. There was no one in San Fernando who would do. After his more disturbed nights he felt that he might resort to his father's trick with a cloth or a paper

116

bag, or just cover the face with a pillow slip and release the tension that was choking him. Lucien knew that he needed sex, medicinally. But he didn't know what to do. There were two or three vague areas in the process which made it impossible to take just anyone. He had heard his brothers speak of expertise, and el Patrón maintained that a gentleman didn't fumble. Lucien's reputation had turned him into the Casanova of the wasted plains, and he had to live up to it. One false move and he would lay himself open to ridicule, and he could never allow such a thing.

Had he been a free agent, he need not have bothered: he had been born with a self-assurance which helped him through such crises. But Misia Schmutter had lived and died in the rigour of her own creation; and his father and their workers looked to Lucien as a defender of the faith. And their faith was the code of honour that was like a second skin to every Llanero. So Lucien bore his share of this prickly skin, albeit reluctantly, and he staggered under the weight of it, and the heaviest of all his responsibilities was to make something of his life, to *do* something. Katrina had died a sacrifice to his own education. She had floated face-down in the rain pond so that her brother could see the true nature of power. He had been apprenticed and groomed to it, and sometimes it felt heavier than the stones for Chucho Delgado's tomb. Lucien knew that Misia Schmutter had practically invented him; and he felt that it could not have been with the intention that he fester and mould his years away filling sacks with corn in San Fernando.

For Lucien, the inner pressure to make something of himself was enormous. He learnt about power very early on, but it wasn't until much later that he learnt about the power of power. El Llano had been right for Misia Schmutter with her mixture of tyranny and healing and she had presided like a legend over the flatlands of the Orinoco, giving to its people all the great emotions but one. She had inspired fear and respect, faith and pain, hatred and despair, but not love. As a child, Lucien had wanted the world to love his grandmother. When he grew up and took over to some extent her role, he realised that love could only come naturally, no one could decree it.

Lucien had put a stop to the hatred, and in less than ten years he had tripled the average intake of food of every peasant. He had seen their poverty in terms of food and shelter, he had thought that he could brighten the dull stare in their eyes by wiping out their hunger. Gone were the days when a man could drown his sorrows in a cow's foot of rot-gut rum. Now sores and sorrows alike were swamped in massive stews of salt beef and beans: beans with cheese, cheese with eggs, eggs with meat, there was a great surfeit of protein, and every mud hut had a bin of preserved fruits in syrup with a tin tray of water underneath it to keep off the ants. Lucien could make their yucca as soft and fluffy as newly-fallen snow, and he could devise ways of making flavoured oils to dip it in, and bird peppers so hot that they made grown men see coloured stars when they ate them.

It dawned on Lucien very slowly, as slowly as thick syrup leaking from a barrel, that more workers died from his indulgences than had died under Misia Schmutter's scourge. It was not food so much as the herbs which had died in her garden that the people needed. There had been a balance in their diet before, a fine balance evolved over centuries of toil and poaching. Lucien eyed the fat corpses in their coffins, and genuinely shared their relatives' despair. Whatever it was that brought death to San Fernando, it was in the air. No one could hold it or see it, and no one could fight it; you could only breathe it, and know that it was there. It wasn't something to be defied by an extra pack of rice. The balance controlled everything.

Lucien knew that his life on San Fernando was a waste. He watched his crops thrive and his peasants bloat and die with growing distaste. Where was the point in marshalling men and cows like a second-rate circus, all to make a few tons of salt beef that the same men would gulp in deference to a lifetime's hunger? The beef would churn in their tripes like snakes and their feet would swell with the salt and the veins in their faces burst and their eyes yellow, and they would know, for the first time, about constipation in between their bouts of dysentery, and no amount of hot towels would relieve the ache. Apart from their races, which would never change—he, German and Germanic, they, Amerindian with a smattering of Guaojira Negro and Spanish—Lucien felt that there wasn't so much to choose between him and any of his workers that a reversal of his hereditary power wouldn't remove. But there was something, a nagging feeling of discontent that was more than his urge to mate.

118

It was this feeling that drove Lucien, firstly from San Fernando, but later from place to place, always in search of somewhere to excel. That was how he came to travel, he with his clear chiselled face that everyone could see, and Misia Schmutter, invisible, with her arms wrapped round his neck, piggyback, with her frail weight scarcely bowing him, and the bulge of her growth trapped between them. Some days Misia Schmutter seemed more like a presence in the air, and some days she felt like chainmail on his back to protect him from unseen enemies, but mostly she felt like her old self, a power to be reckoned with, tightening her grip at the least false step. When he set out for Caracas, Misia Schmutter's presence shrank to nothing more than the brittle inner lining of an eggshell at the nape of Lucien's neck. He packed this white parchment-like substance, as white and brittle as his grandmother's skin had been, in a rosewood box, together with some of the many poisons and trinkets that Misia Schmutter had left.

When Lucien rode away from San Fernando, the town mourned what it had never had. More girls languished of a broken heart than had ever been known before. Carmen Miranda Salazar took arsenic and died in the mansion where she lived at the end of the Plaza Bolívar (and malicious tongues claimed that she died of a failed abortion). At the convent, the senior girls went on hunger strike and even wrote to Cardinal Mendez asking him to forcibly return their idol to them. At the Arco Iris, the four-poster bed was draped with black as a mark of despair for the man who had never been there. Every tailor and seamstress in the neighbourhood was busy making dozens of suits identical to the one Lucien wore when he rode through town on his way to Caracas, and there was hardly a young man left who didn't lighten his hair, by camomile, lemon, bleach or peroxide, in imitation of the blond prodigy who had stolen all the hearts. Angel Salas tried all the methods, and went bald.

Lucien liked all the people waving. He had often ridden through these streets before, and he had seen people wave before, but they had waved then in a timid, giggling way, or in a lewd and lustful one, peering through the slatted shutters. Now there was a mournfulness in their waving that appealed to his sense of ritual, and he felt closer to them in their anticipated loss than he ever had done in their lust.

He was leaving, and none of them would be able to shame him or ridicule him in the eyes of his old grandmother on his back. He would never have to punch or shoot any of these sad girls or their brothers. He would never need to redeem his honour in their eyes and for himself. There was no threat as he rode away, just a feeling of well-being. And there would be a yet greater feeling of well-being when he reached Caracas. Arriving and leaving are always easier than staying. It is the sticking power that costs the most. Lucien was twice forced to remain somewhere: once on the flatlands of his birthplace, and once in prison: two life sentences, with his travels in between.

He had spent months arranging the estate in such a way that a foreman could step in and take over the running of it. At the point of leaving, Lucien had felt pangs of regret at the thought of turning over his herd of healthy Ceibu to the inevitable fate of worms and crackfoot and tick fever. After the years of seemingly mindless boredom, tending his cattle and fattening their sides, he felt sad to leave them; even though he knew that within weeks of his going they would be dismembered and their strong creosoted feet would be jellying in the peasants' black cauldrons, and their stocky, lump-free legs would be making a knuckle-bone soup for the cooks to ladle out to the workers. Zancocho de rés, years of his life wasted in making beef stew for a few peasants who would get indigestion from his very bounty. Would a new foreman really irrigate the rice fields? Would he know how to cheat the weevils of the corn? Would he remember to plant garlic around the yucca to keep out the snakes? Would he know what hydrophonic farming was? Lucien smiled to himself at this last thought.

Lucien told his father of his proposed departure two weeks before the event. Each evening, as they sat on the verandah, el Patrón would intersperse the popping of his shotgun with the questions,

'What will become of the lands, Lucien?'

'The foreman will care for them, Patrón.'

'But what if he doesn't, Lucien?'

'Then they will revert to slime and dirt.'

'Where will you go, Lucien?'

Lucien waited until the echo of his father's shotgun had died down, and then he would say, 'I am going to Caracas to make my name, Patrón.' At which point his father would invariably forget about his gout and stamp his foot, and then turn pale with pain.

'Your name became a name in San Fernando. It needs no making. You will never be worshipped anywhere else the way that you are worshipped here.'

'I don't want to be worshipped, father.'

Out on the scorched lawn another vulture cracked its beak as it collided with the ground. El Patrón smiled, in-voluntarily, and shouted, 'Eighteen, by Jove! That's more than usual, Lucien,' he explained, half-apologetically, as though Lucien didn't know exactly how many birds his father shot down every night, day after day, with excruciating regularity, leaving the pathetic heavy corpses to be gathered and burnt by one of the servants, or occasionally by Lucien himself, heaping up their crumpled beaks and wings.

'When I am gone, Patrón, I beg you to remember that if you shoot this many vultures, there will be so much carrion around here it will crawl up to the steps of this very house!'

'But what can I do, Lucien, these feet of mine are like carrion, they won't take me anywhere nowadays; and a man must have his sport.'

'You could bag the red cardinals, or the cora coras, or the rice birds, Patrón.'

'You'll have me shooting those wretched little colibris next, Lucien, and when I'm not blasting them you'll have me shooting wasps and mosquitoes, like a child put out to play . . . This is *my* house, you know.' El Patrón was very easily tired, and he would slump back and say half to himself, 'This is my house, but it is your will—just like my mother. Where will you go, Lucien?'

'I am going to Caracas, father, to make my name.'

'You have a name, Lucien.'

'I have your name, father, and Der Altman's name, and I am proud of it, but I want to make things happen.'

'Make what happen?'

'I am a catalyst, father, that is what I am. I make things happen.'

El Patrón picked up his gun again, strengthened by his ignorance. Lucien used such strange words, he couldn't follow the boy half the time. Years ago, he had thought that Lucien was one of Misia Schmutter's poisons, but now he was a good-looking boy with a straight eye and a good

121

aim—he had a streak of the devil in him, and that was good.

'If you can make things happen, make it rain.'

'I can't.'

'Then heal my gout.'

'I can't.'

'Well you're not much of a catalyst, are you? What is it anyway, some kind of a doctor?'

'Sort of.'

'A damned witch-doctor, no doubt, like my mother!'

Lucien left on a parched February morning of 1933. He rode ahead on his own black stallion, richly caparisoned with his father's silver stirrups and trappings. Behind him rode Luis Aguirre, Chucho Delgado's nephew, who was to be his manservant for the next four years. Luis rode his own mule and brought along in tow another mule, laden with luggage, including Misia Schmutter's enormous German bible and her roulette board; and in the rear came Niemen, the huge twelve-year-old bull, switching the flies irritably from his back at the start of this, to him, unwanted journey.

III

Niemenberg

Chapter 13

LUCIEN RODE THROUGH THE LAND OF HIS GRANDMOTHER'S fame, through one dusty village after another, along each new litter of straggling houses thrown together on the edge of a dirt track. For the first fifty miles of his journey, he could sometimes see taunts rise to the lips of men in the street, and then get swallowed, uneasily, as Lucien's blond looks jogged memories. They were dark in los Llanos, with dark hair and eyes and skin, and there were dark places in their memories where they kept count of their feuds and fears. They knew that the Luciens were famed above all others as killers, blue-eyed killers. It was not the killing itself that stayed the roadside cowboys. It was the skill and ruthlessness of the Luciens, which time had magnified. Killing was not murder in their code, and there was no capital punishment. Instead, there were men like this boy of the Luciens who could pick them off like razor-back pigs in a fever if he chose. Any one of them would have stabbed him in the back, but they had heard that Misia Schmutter's grandson had eyes in his shoulderblades, and even the tigers were afraid of his eyes.

Just as the men guessed his heritage, so the girls recognised Lucien as the great lover of the plains. Some of them, unused to such pale colouring, were put off by the sight of him; they had heard that he looked like an angel, and angels, for their money, were not transparent like a gecko, and they didn't trail bulls behind them. But most of the girls stopped what they were doing to watch him ride by, and the sound of his horse's hooves clattered through their longing.

If Lucien was protected by his ancestry of violence close to home, by the time he was a hundred miles away from San Fernando, he was on his own. He began to find the journey depressing. His brothers had often told him about their trips to the capital, to and from school, and he had an ample list of names and addresses where he could lodge for the night with well-disposed families who would feed him and his horse and not try to steal his money or his roulette wheel. But they had not warned him of the grinding poverty of the homesteads he would have to pass, where the tips of the children's hair were nearly as fair as his own, but from malnutrition. He rode down street after street full of children with great bellies of parasites and hunger, they ran out to his horse and tugged at his silver stirrups, limping along behind him from the niguas in their feet. Lucien could see the men of these villages, sharpening their machetes on whetstones, or playing dominoes squat on the dirt floors, or paring their fighting cocks' spurs, or staring red-eyed from cane liquor, barring his path. Lucien wished that he had left his father's silver tackle at home, or put it in his luggage. It taunted the peasants to see him, riding so slowly past them, with the still fat Niemen in tow. He and his bull would be worth killing for. Lucien could read the thought as it dawned on more than one of the men he passed by.

His father and his grandfather and his great-grandfather had terrorised such places, shooting alternate tiles from the roofs of the houses just for the fun of it. They had shot the ends of the peasants' bandanas from around their necks, they had shot their own names in the dust on the ground, they had shot the coconut cups of liquor clean out of the drinkers' hands. Lucien despised such senseless shooting. He particularly disliked any show of prowess for its own sake. Misia Schmutter had brought him up to be a gentleman, and gentlemen didn't shoot roofs.

Even Lucien, with his ideals and his principles, realised that he would have to shoot something before long or get shot. At best, he thought, they will hack my legs off with their machetes. From the looks that he was getting, he knew they would do it for malice. From the looks that Niemen was getting, he knew that they wanted to eat him.

He had ridden through two villages on one particular day, and each time he had doubted whether he would reach the end of the winding dusty street in one piece. It was late in the afternoon when he reached his third gathering of homesteads; it seemed even uglier than its predecessors. There was a still, unpleasant feeling in the air. Lucien looked down the road of merging yellow and greys with a wavering resolution about not shooting tiles. He noticed with a mixture of relief and annoyance that there weren't any tiles as such, only rough palmiche leaves lashed on to the huts to keep out the rains. A well-regulated stream of bullets would have been wasted on such a heap of thatch. The men were coming into the street, weaving their way through the pigs and chickens, closing in on him. The nearest of them was some twenty feet away, still coming, and already drawing his machete. Lucien noticed that there were notches on the blade. Ahead of him, in a little triangle of dust, there was a prickly pear with bleached empty eggshells decked over the thorns like budding flowers. The men were almost at his feet, one more step and they could slash his knees. Lucien drew Misia Schmutter's silver revolver—the one she used for vultures—with his right hand, and with his left he drew his own Colt. Then he fired them together at the prickly pear, and the men drew back. Lucien rode on, and as he passed the newly-battered cactus he noticed that eleven of the eggs were shot away. He was not pleased, he had missed one, he had been afraid for Niemen at his back and it had affected his aim. And then, he had waited too long; he should have fired sooner, before anyone came within striking distance of his legs.

The journey took him eleven days. Eleven days of watching the ash-coloured herons watching him. Eleven days of waiting for the reluctant and thinning Niemen to catch up, while Luis Aguirre urged and prodded him. Luis Aguirre was proud to be travelling with such a fine master, yet saddened by the presence of this recalcitrant bull. But for Niemen, he too could canter up to the villages and get his share of admiring stares. He felt no shame at being a cowboy, it was being a cowboy to this one old flabby bull that was demeaning. And then these hungry peasants that they had to pass—they looked as if they wouldn't stop at eating old Niemen's tough flanks, but would gladly get their teeth into his own pocked shanks, and el Niño Lucien's pale shins too. What a God-forsaken lot they were! He must stop thinking of el Niño Lucien as a child, he must call him 'señor' in the capital. That was very important. Almost as important as not getting stewed by these barbarians.

Luis Aguirre saw with relief that they had come to the outskirts of a proper town. It was Calabozo, a place about the size of San Fernando, but with bigger houses. He waited at the gate with his hand on his machete while el Niño Lucien asked his way and then rode up to a shady square and a tall house beside a church. He dismounted at the iron gates and rang a long bell-pull of wrought-iron flowers and leaves. He could hear the clanging of it. Lucien introduced himself to a thin woman with graceful, brushed hair swept back in a ribbon, whom he took to be the housekeeper. Presently an elderly man appeared.

'So you are the last Lucien,' he called to him, smiling and beckoning him in. Luis Aguirre took hold of his master's horse, and holding the four sets of reins he was obliged to let go of his weapon. Smiles aren't everything, he thought, as a manservant came out and helped him round to the back of the rambling old house. Luis Aguirre followed his guide, noticing a blotch of pale-pink skin on the man's dark, withered neck. It was cárete, Luis could recognise it anywhere and he spent a sleepless night silently cursing his fate for having brought him within reach of the disfiguring disease. He knew, as anyone would know, that cárete was contracted through infected blood, and he knew of the malice of the already blighted. They deliberately cut themselves and dripped their blood into a stranger's coffee or stew. Luis, himself, would rather starve than carry the pale blotches all his life. Lucien, however, spent a pleasant evening in the company of his host, who kept a coconut grove outside the town, and a hundred hectares of sugarcane, and the customary herd of cattle.

In the morning he warned Lucien, 'This is a rough road, my boy. If you'll take my advice, you'll leave that bull here, to be sent back to San Fernando. Food is scarce with all these months of drought, and the sight of that walking zancocho can make men turn nasty.'

Lucien thanked him and demurred, explaining that Niemen was a kind of mascot. He didn't go into detail, such as that he didn't trust his own workers not to eat him if he left

128

Niemen at home. There was plenty of food at San Fernando, too much perhaps, but it was the indifference and the lethargy that killed and ate into men's bones.

Lucien would have dearly liked to have changed his silver trim for something less extravagant, at least until he reached the city. But he had decided to sport the silver ones, and he felt that he would have to stick with his choice, no matter how much they glinted in the sun. Luis Aguirre would have cleaned them by now, with soap and soda, and they would be gleaming more than ever. He didn't feel that he could tell the man to let them stay tarnished.

'So you won't leave the bull?' his host urged him, adding, 'It's a big risk you are taking.'

Lucien shook his head sadly, it would take him too long to explain that risk was at the core of his upbringing, calculated risks and the manipulation of chance. Lucien wished that his host had pressed him to change his stirrups. But that would have been impossible, as personal remarks were accountable for, even between an old man and his guest.

Until the end of the journey, Lucien continued to ride ahead, shooting ten eggs of the prickly pears of the villages that he passed, and leaving two bullets, just in case. In one place, where there was no such cactus bush, he shot the thin red flowers off a hibiscus. News of his marksmanship travelled ahead of him, across the dry spiky grasslands, slowed as he was by his pet bull's pace, and no one molested him again, or even stepped out into his path. He had a clear road all the way to Caracas, he out front, and Luis Aguirre trailing behind with the baggage and the bull.

At the toll-gates, at Calabozo, Ortiz and San Juan, Lucien felt a great knot of history wrap around his throat. Particularly at Calabozo, he was aware of standing at the very barrier where Der Altman had stood a century before him, when the tollman had asked his tall ancestor to pay for his mule, and he had refused, and carried his animal through a loophole in the law across the barrier, and his stubbornness and strength had been rewarded with a fortune in gold. That was the past, Lucien thought sadly. When the tollman asked *him* to pay not only for his mule, but his bull as well, Lucien just dipped into his ample purse.

'And an extra rial for the baggage,' the tollman called to him. And Lucien paid an extra rial for his baggage with a sense of deep shame. Der Altman would have carried them all across, and Luis Aguirre too, no doubt. But there was a time and place for everything, and toll-gates were no longer the places to make a man's name. Since Der Altman had stunned them all with his feats, there had been too much wealth and too many circuses travelling through those parts. Boris and his amazing bears had come and gone on their yearly pilgrimage to the plains, and Gladstone, the ancient one-eyed tiger, had wrestled with its trainer so many times that the crowds hardly bothered to watch any more. They had all seen the human cannonballs and the three-legged ladies and Atlas, the Muscle Man from Brazil. There was oil in Maracaibo, black treacle from the sea that was worth more than gold. Lucien had heard that in Maracaibo, barrels of the stuff kept disappearing from the deposits, and his brothers claimed that the peasants stole and drank it in the belief that it had fantastic aphrodisiac powers.

No, mules could no longer compete with oil. So when the tollman called again, 'It looks to me as though you'll have to pay double for that bull', Lucien shrugged and took a small coin from his leather poke and gave it to the tollman.

'This is for you,' he said. 'For yourself. Take it, and shut up. You know as well as I do, that you pay nothing for cattle!' The tollman took the coin and looked away, embarrassed.

When Lucien left the banks of the River Guárico to climb the uplands that divided him from Caracas, he was glad. The smell of the dried swamps had got on his nerves. He was tired of the shaved fighting cocks in the cages, and tired of the worm-ridden chickens in the road, and he was tired of seeing the bare backsides of hungry children, tired of the hornets and ants and flies, tired of seeing chicken hawks trussed up and tortured alive, or left to gasp, impaled, in the sun, and he was tired of the low sheets of smoke that rose up around him where the coarse grass was being burnt, often for no better reason than that it was hot and the village boys were bored. He found the landscape monotonous, and Niemen was going lame. The bull was just footsore, he knew, but that was bad enough. Each night, Lucien prepared a mixture of lemon juice and salt, and Luis Aguirre dipped the bull's feet one by one into a tin of it. At Ortiz and Ocumare, Lucien went into the church and sat in silence for up to an hour at a time, while Luis Aguirre waited patiently outside with the beasts in the scorching sun. The churches revived Lucien's spirit. On the desolate road from his home to the capital, he had grown sick for the sight of stone. He craved carved stone to stroke, the damp abrasion and the smooth chill.

Of all the journeys that Lucien was to make, this first was perhaps the hardest. He had never felt so alien, not even when he fell from favour as a child. For eleven days he rode, and every step seemed to underline the difference between himself and his fellow men. And were they fellow, these gatherings of skin and bones who would have killed him if they dared? The children were always children, before they switched race, and their eyes at least had a flicker of interest and charm. But it was at night, in the company of the people who gave him lodging, in their comfortable houses and their semblance of learning, with the nightjars calling from their mercy trees, that he felt most alone. They were mostly white-skinned, like him, though not as blond, but they were worlds apart; and worst of all, Misia Schmutter had abandoned him. Lucien liked to think that shooting the eggshells on the prickly pears was her idea. But he couldn't be sure. She had let go her strangle hold and her gossamer weight had gone. He still kept the eggshell-lining that seemed to come when she let go. But she had never left him before like this, and Lucien was desolate. He wore a white-silk cravat wrapped round and round his neck so tightly that it flushed his face and he could hardly breathe. The cravat was as white as her hands, although there were no blue veins showing, but the cloth didn't have the skill of Misia Schmutter's fingers, and he had to keep loosening the knot.

When Lucien reached Caracas with his meagre and unusual train, he was again disappointed. This time it was by the sight of the shanty town that straddled the eroded hill slopes on the southern approach to the city. It stretched up on either side of the cobbled road that led to the old town, lining his path with a trail of debris. Lucien knew that he could not return to San Fernando for a long time, maybe never; had he come all this way to live in a squalid slum?

131

Luis Aguirre was impressed by the sheer quantity of every-thing, huts, houses, people, rubbish, he had never seen anything like it before. And now the menace of the villages had gone, there was a safety in these numbers. Urchins were throwing sticks at Niemen and the pack mule, and he could even make out some of the taunts they were shout-ing. For el Niño Lucien, it was the usual, 'Have you seen a ghost?' on account of his pallor, alternated now with allu-sions to their trade. 'Hey, cowboy,' they shouted, and then swivelled round with imaginary guns.

It took them seven hours to find the house of Detlev, Lucien's brother, who lived in the heart of the city, behind the labyrinth that flanked the enormous Plaza Bolívar, quite unlike their own Plaza Bolívar in San Fernando. None of the streets had a name on it, and to Luis Aguirre's despair, Lucien kept wandering off to admire now this house and now that, and then when he discovered the Cathedral, and the Casa Amarilla and the golden cupola of the Capitolio, there was no getting him to go anywhere. Eventually, after a door-to-door search, Detlev was located in a small green shuttered villa identical to all the other green shuttered villas in the street. Detlev hugged Lucien, while eyeing the bull with horror.

'Why did you bring that cow with you, brother?' he asked as pleasantly as he could.

'He's not a cow, it's Niemen,' Lucien explained, shocked in his turn that his own brother couldn't or didn't want to see the difference between a cow and bull. 'Here,' he said, giving Detlev a bag of coins, 'have him stabled somewhere out of your way.'

His brother pocketed the bag and then said, 'He can be stabled here. I've had a streak of bad luck on the track, actually, so my stables are damned nearly empty. Is this really your first time here?'

Lucien nodded.

'You look pretty miserable. I suppose it was a rough ride from San Fernando with that cow-bull thing. I don't know how you stuck it out there, you know, none of us did. It's quite something, your actually coming to civilisation. There's a party tonight, we can creep out after the curfew and go through the gardens to the Urdaneta.' Detlev added wistfully, 'I don't often find myself being grateful to our Großmutter for anything, but, as it happens, having survived her regime, it makes living under a dictatorship seem easy. As long as you conform to the appearances, Lucien, you'll be fine. It's like a game really, all this curfew stuff, and saluting that old baboon Gomez.' Detlev paused again, and then he mused, 'You always did play some very odd games, Lucien!'

Chapter 14

LUCIEN WAS SO NEW TO CITY LIFE, THAT IT SWALLOWED HIM whole as a boa constrictor does its prey. He felt the process begin as he wandered around dazed by the splendour of the old city centre. But he felt the process take a real grip at this first clandestine party to which Detlev took him. Not that there was anything particularly clandestine about the hundred or so guests who arrived in their bead dresses with glittering headbands or their silk brocade jackets, or about the two bands that played American or Criollan music by turn, crooning into the chorus of cicadas that sang through the night. Lucien himself had no city clothes as such, but he borrowed a dinner jacket and a cummerbund from Detlev, and he enjoyed the dressing up and the flattening of his hair.

The half-hearted curfew began at seven o'clock, and they set out for their party at seven-thirty, through a back door on to the garden.

'Why didn't we leave before the curfew?' Lucien asked.

'Well, it's half the fun, you know, the risk. It's all we get to see of the government, actually; guards on street corners and the military band on Sunday, and a sort of regal pantomime from time to time when the old man emerges from La Casona or Miraflores with half the army to escort him and the generals bent double under the weight of their medals.'

'But would they shoot you if they saw you out at night, Detlev?'

'Sí señor. And you might be like God in San Fernando, but they'd shoot you too, Lucien. They say that the President has all the lizards and mice and pests rounded up every day and that he himself passes sentence and shoots them in the garden at Miraflores, and that he can't get enough, so some poor under-secretary has to rush around gathering lizards for the dictator to execute. He likes it, just as Misia Schmutter used to.'

Lucien scrambled through a bank of rough scrubland that clung to the edge of a kind of precipice, skirting the site of a new development to the north of the fashionable parks and squares around the city centre, as he followed his brother on his perilous trail to the party in the neighbouring Avenida Urdaneta. Under the cover of darkness, with a black cravat over his starched white tuxedo, he scratched and banged himself on thorns and boulders. His hair, so recently made immaculate with agua de azahar, would no longer be smooth.

'My dinner jacket is ruined, Detlev!' he complained.

Detlev stifled a laugh. 'Oh you are so serious, Lucien, so German. It's like going out of bounds at school. Anyway, it's *my* jacket, Lucien!' Lucien was silent. He had never been to school.

A few minutes later, a faint sound of music drifted towards them, and Lucien saw below him a garden studded with lanterns. 'How will we get back?' he asked.

'Tomorrow.'

'Where will we sleep?' Lucien whispered.

'Sleep? For God's sake, Lucien, we're going to a party, we're not going to sleep . . . Now shush,' Detlev said, lowering his voice. 'The Mendezes have opened a gap in their railings and we can get in through the third window at the side of the house.'

'Who are the Mendezes?'

'It's their party.'

Fifteen hours later, Lucien was still no clearer who the Mendezes were, but he had met a great many other people, of both sexes, and they all seemed genuinely delighted to see him. Best of all he had liked a girl called Mariana. Not since Chucho Delgado's death, or maybe even Katrina's, had Lucien known anyone whose conversation interested him so much as this Mariana. She had read books that Lucien had never even heard of, and she could make him laugh, and listen and talk. The boa constrictor was squeezing and swallowing and Lucien felt, wrapped in the silvery glare of its making—with his limbs and his will-power cocooned to a standstill—a restful sense of inevitability with the startlingly beautiful Mariana beside him. Gone were the days when he would have to arrange everything, life would take its own course from now on. Back in San Fernando, his nerves had frayed, and he had often wandered angrily through the littered yards. They were rages that he could not understand. He had decided that they were not his rages at all, but Misia Schmutter's, who, in her superior wisdom, didn't wish to explain them to him. Misia Schmutter had left him now, he had been five weeks without her. Did he like Mariana because she clung to his neck, almost hung from it? Maybe. Even Misia Schmutter would have approved of the way she ate her caviare canapés.

Mariana had said to him in the early morning, when the party flagged a little, before the guests either passed out or took their second wind, 'We'll have to call you something, you know, because your brother is Lucien, not you. My brother went to school with him, and the whole world calls him that, you must have a first name or something.'

'*I* am Lucien, it is my brothers who have their other names, my grandmother confiscated mine when I was three. I am Lucien.'

Mariana raised her eyebrows in mock alarm.

'I say, what a temper, I think I'll just call you el Purísimo. I believe you would have us all slaves to that temper if you could.'

Lucien smiled. Of all the people on the littered terrace waiting for the sun to rise, he alone had elected to suppress his own will, and carried the most savage temper in the world on his back.

Mariana interrupted his reverie.

'So, Purísimo, what do you like best in the world?'

'Roulette.'

'Really?'

'Truly.'

'Tomorrow? That is, tonight?'

'Where?'

'I'll pick you up at six.'

'You'll pick me up?'

'Of course,' Mariana said archly, and Lucien noticed how like Katrina's her grey eyes were.

'What are you thinking?' Mariana asked, disturbed by the intensity of his stare.

'Your eyes,' he said.

Mariana arrived on the following evening at Detlev's villa in a slightly battered Ford.

'You are late,' Lucien told her.

'You don't want to worry about things like that, Purísimo, take my advice and forget about time, or you'll grow old for nothing. Whoever invented time was no caraqueño, of that you can be sure.'

They rode at a cautious speed to the casino.

'Ulises will meet us there,' Mariana said.

'Who is Ulises?' Lucien asked.

'My lover . . . Are you shocked, Purísimo?'

'Yes.'

There was silence and then Lucien asked, 'What about your family?'

'They disowned me when I stayed out late with him one night last year; so you could say that I don't have a family.'

'Then why don't you marry him?'

Mariana was silent and turned her head away. Lucien nodded to himself, and decided that he would build a house for himself and invite Mariana to live there with him.

They arrived at the casino just as the great bells of St Peter and St Mary the Virgin tolled the curfew. The casino was, nominally, a hotel, and to comply with the law there was an ostentatious closing and barring of its doors as the great bells chimed their stay-at-home. Ulises was there, and Lucien was struck by the man's relative coolness to Mariana, and his apparent enthusiasm for himself. Then Mariana guided him by his elbow into the gaming-room, while Ulises smiled, clearing a space for them.

From the moment of their first meeting, Mariana's lover, Ulises, had assumed a natural leadership towards Lucien, and he patronised and protected him, like a delightful green-horn come in from nowhere. He led him to the roulette wheel with a trace of guilt at leading this lamb to the slaughter. His own credit was down at the casino, and the manager was beginning to get quite unpleasant. Ulises hoped that the crumb of Lucien's fortune surrendered into the croupier's able hands would soothe the manager for another week or two. He looked at Lucien from across the table, and he was surprised to confirm what Mariana had told him that early morning. Here was the best-looking man he had ever seen—a bit short for a European, but stunning. No wonder Mariana was so keen, perhaps it would be the best thing, he mused, he was sick of having her family thrown in his face, and her dress bills were more than even true love could bear. There was a kind of mystic quality about Mariana that drove other men wild, but he, Ulises, with little sense of the mystical, found it rather unnerving—whatever it was. And now that she had got marriage engraved on her brain, his passion for her was waning. All his friends had been love-sick for her cold grey eyes and her seaweed hair with its strands of red and brown. Ulises' passion had always been more for the idea of the most attractive girl in the group than for Mariana herself.

As the wheel began to turn Ulises and Lucien switched their roles. Lucien was unaware of this sideshow, his attention was wholly on the game. It was Ulises who noticed, after the sixth or seventh spin, that watching Lucien play he felt something akin to what he had felt in church when his cousin Consuelo died. Ulises had been a child at the time, and Cousin Consuelo was staying with them; she had died of a scorpion sting after eleven hours of delirious screaming. Ulises had sat up for the wake. It had been his first all-night wake, and by the morning of her funeral he was so tired he felt sick. The choir had sung a Te Deum, and Ulises had heard their voices soar up to the vaulted roof of the great Cathedral, and seen the procession of children dressed in white satin with wings pinned to their backs like angels, and between them all, little Consuelo, draped in silk and lilies. Then he had felt as though his head had been prised open, and a feeling of great happiness had swept over him like a breaker of sweetness. He had fainted in the Cathedral. Now, in the casino, watching Lucien, he felt a similar wave of pleasure take hold of him, but this time, he steadied himself, gripping the edge of the table, and watched.

Ulises was not alone, as he watched; the whole room was mesmerised. Lucien was a great gambler, the kind of gambler who went down in history for breaking banks. Theirs was a rich city, a city of glitter and black treacly gold. Their stakes were often high. Some of them had seen men ruined, broken, bankrupt, shot, at the same wheel.

They had heard about winning streaks in the far east of the country, where people played for diamonds, and in San Felix, where gold from the Callao mines was gambled away almost before it left the vein. They had even seen winning streaks at the very table where Lucien played, but something in the room told them this was different. A strange wind blew through the half-open shutters. It made people's scalps crawl with excitement, it knocked the cocktail shaker from a waiter's hand as he was about to pour Lucien his third tequila sunrise. If they had been in San Fernando, they would have called it an Alemán. But there was no name in Caracas for this chill, so the assembled crowd blamed Lucien. He had reached the upper limit of allowed stakes. Each turn of the wheel was a new win. No other tables played, and the dull chorus of 'Faites vos jeux, from the French croupiers ceased, except for Lucien's table, where the call rolled time and again, and time and again Lucien won. Red, black, red, red, red, black, red, black, red; it was his game.

The night became legendary. The management reserved themselves the right to close down their tables at midnight. On that unusually chill night of February 27th, 1933 they used their option for the first time. Had they not done so, Lucien would certainly have broken the bank. As it was, he left the casino a celebrity and with two million Bolívares in winnings. He had arrived in Caracas with exactly one hundred gold fuertes, enough, perhaps to have lived on for two months. He had had no idea what he would have done had he not been so lucky. It was never any use asking him, he would always say, 'But I did win.'

Detlev could have wept for joy. He had been sailing so close to the gutter that he thought his fall must have been inevitable. Now Lucien returned and asked his brother what he wanted that money could buy. Detlev was quite sure, as sure as Lucien had been about his roulette.

'I want a new start: no debts, and a commission in the army.'

Both were easily arranged. Detlev had gone from the university to the military academy; besides, the size of Lucien's bribes was such that Detlev became a major in the army of the dictator Juan Vicente Gomez, President of the Republic, within a few weeks. Lucien was able to revert to his own simple name again, unchallenged and undisputed as it had been from the age of three.

Each morning, Detlev's manservant, accompanied by Lucien's own Luis Aguirre (squeezed into a bow tie and tails and leather boots that caused him constant anxiety) collected up the letters of invitation that littered the hall like flurries of autumn leaves. Lucien and his brother, Major Lucien, had invitations to breakfasts and lunches, cocktails and races, soirées and teas. There were invitations from embassies and visiting dignitaries, from government officials and to La Casona itself. The Church was interested in him, Monseñor Mejia invited him daily to dine at his home. And then, like insects drawn to a night-light, the mothers of Caracas all flocked to him, wanting him to marry their daughters.

Lucien, however, had his own programme: the building of his house, together with a magnificent stable for his long-suffering Niemen. He worked on the supervision of his house as he had on the estate and as he had on the construction of his gazebos: from six until six, he was there, on the site. Sometimes he directed the work itself, and sometimes he sat and amended his plans in a red and white palanquin. Lucien had assembled a number of objects, which he added to, almost daily. By the end of the fourth week, a marquee had to be set up beside the palanquin to take the overflow of furniture and fountains, statues and lamps that Lucien was collecting. As the house progressed on the site below, the marquees spread above, like a royal shanty town.

The house that Lucien built was a compromise between his own taste for the gothic revival of the previous century and the house at San Fernando where he was born. Thus the front was made of weathered red brick, and the back of timber and blocks. The main entrance led into a great octagonal tower, four floors high and crowned with a cupola of coloured glass. The roofscape was a forest of Jacobean-style chimneys and polygonal angle-shafts. The windows were all stone-mullioned, with real glass in their panes instead of wooden shutters. This detail so fascinated the populace that they pressed against the railings around the site to watch first the windows being made and then the thin panes of glass being puttied into them. As each massive frame was ready, the glaziers would hold it up to the crowd, who whooped and clucked their approval. This was to be a palace indeed.

The main elevation was two storeys high with twenty-seven bays built and recessed in it, and buttressed with chequered angle-shafts, each with a decorated pinnacle. Fame of the legendary Lucien's folly spread across the hills and beyond to the oilfields themselves, and back across the plains to his native Llano. A travelling chandler told el Patrón, 'Your son is building an upside-down house, with corridors on the roof and monuments climbing up the walls.'

This came as no surprise to el Patrón, he had seen the things that his son had been building in their own grounds since his boyhood, gazebos, tombs and towers.

'What do you think of that?' the chandler had asked him.

El Patrón had only said, 'Ouf, well let's hope he can keep his matches away from it.'

Lucien didn't even attempt to explain his creation to the astonished onlookers. When they asked about something, he would say flatly,

'It is like that because that looks right.'

Nobody argued. You didn't argue with a man as rich as this Lucien. The builders tried to tell him: who needs chimneys in the tropics? The temperature had an average of 68°F., and it never fell below 55°, not even on the coldest nights. They had seen immigrants wanting chimneys before, one or maybe even two so that they could stew by a wood fire in the steamy hot evenings and imagine themselves back home in Italy or France or Germany. It was not a longing that the master builder shared, having been brought up with a smoky wood fire to cook on, pouring its acrid fumes directly into the small enclosed room where his entire family slept. However, the builder was a builder and no more, and if this Señor Lucien wished to pay him double his usual wage to start and finish this mansion in record time with not one, but forty-three chimneys on the roof, well, he said, fine. You didn't argue with that kind of money. Still, he was an honest builder, or nearly, and he had taken the liberty of pointing out to el Señor Lucien that the two halves of the house didn't match. Lucien had merely said, 'That's right,' and clicked his heels in a way he had; so the builder had thought, fine. What did he mind if there was a brick monster three storeys high at the front with half of a normal wooden pillared

141

Spanish colonial house tacked on to the back? No, he lived in a shanty town himself, he was a past master at joining incongruous bits of buildings together. Fine!

Lucien bought carved wood and carved stone. He bought statues to stand in niches between each window, gargoyles for the corners of the turrets, a fountain for the main hall, and more fountains for the gardens. He bought carved wooden pillars, and carved newel posts for the stairs, balustrades, banisters, beams and brackets. He could have commissioned things, but he was impatient to see his work done. He had set himself a time limit of four months from start to finish. By the eighth week, he was employing four hundred men. He had to watch them all the time. While he was supervising the laying of the drains at one end of the house, masons would put the balustrades on the wrong way round, like rounded ladders. Later, they would put pinnacles on the chimneys, and the massive cupola was mounted upside down like a coloured pool, and it took thirty men with levers to right it again.

If Lucien encountered such paltry problems outside, it was inside where the inventiveness of the builders and plumbers threatened to baffle his plans. It was as though his own flights of creation became contagious. Everywhere, craftsmen were adding touches of their own. The most noticeable was perhaps the Italian fountain with its carved cupids all leaning out from a centre column and all spouting water in unison into an upper bowl which tipped into a lower tier which tipped into a pool at the bottom, supported on giant alcanthus leaves. Lucien was very proud of this statue, and although he hadn't told anyone of his plan, it was his intention to link the fountain to the wine room and make it flow, on occasion, with champagne.

The master plumber, however, had other ideas. He had piped the fountains to the kitchen as he had been instructed to do, but, out of a sense of real gratitude for his exorbitant wage and also for having had the honour of working on such a house, he wanted to give el Señor Lucien a surprise. He succeeded. Working by dead of night, in defiance of the curfew, with two assistants and the dimmest of candlelight, he fitted the seven lavatories, destined for the seven water closets of the house, around the fountain base, so that each lavatory bowl faced out directly under each cupid. Then, by careful drilling through the stone basin, he connected the pull-water systems to the fountain proper so that water would flush, if necessary into each of the seven simultaneously. The master plumber was astonished by the effect it made from the galleried first-floor landing, and although he himself was used to squatting over a hole in the ground or, when necessary, behind a bush, he felt that he had raised the whole art of plumbing to new heights.

On the following morning, Lucien was fascinated to see what had been done, and before dismantling the arrangement, he took detailed notes and drawings of the design and kept it in mind, through the rest of the building, so that he could incorporate the principle behind the plan into one of the less prominent parts of his house, while the master plumber himself was so incensed by Lucien's destruction of his masterpiece that he left immediately. Later, when Lucien was tried in Caracas and then imprisoned, this plumber was one of the few people who believed that it served him right. On the whole, Lucien enjoyed the participation of the citizens of Caracas in his design. Each morning, at eight o'clock, after the work was begun and before the midday sun addled the brains of his men so much that they turned from the inventive to the outrageous, Lucien picked over and bought contributions to his building. No self-respecting caraqueño ever forms a queue, so it was really he who had the sharpest elbows or the longest hatpin or the hardest punch who got through to Lucien with his wares. Lucien stood in a booth, which had at one time been a confessional box, and through the small curtain he examined the goods. When they were very large, and they often were, he would examine the cartloads at one o'clock until one-thirty. He paid entirely what his whim dictated and his customers were well pleased since they believed that they were selling him rubbish. Most of what they brought was collected from rubble heaps or dug out of old yards. Quite a lot of it was torn out of graveyards or pulled off churches, but again, the vendors were glad to take what they could get, since apart from a few pulled muscles and perhaps the occasional dislocated shoulder, these had cost them nothing either.

As the crowds became bigger and bigger, Lucien began to suspect that his trade came largely from illegal sources. Angels and Virgins were appearing more and more often with the white powder where they had been severed. And it was weeks since he had flatly refused to buy any more Christs on the Cross. So he sent out a decree. He would not buy any more statues or mouldings that showed signs of having been broken off. After this, the trade slackened for a few days, and then there was a rush of staues with weathered bases and mouldings with dull grey backs. This eased Lucien's conscience. It would not have done so had he known that a subsidiary industry had begun to flourish in the yards of the monumental masons. Now they no longer cut new stones for graves, they worked round the clock weathering the clean patches of old ones with jugs of milk and manure and goat's piss and little pomades of powdered lichen.

Chapter 15

MARIANA OFTEN VISITED LUCIEN'S PALANQUIN, WITH AND without Ulises. She was intrigued by the house, which she said resembled her mother's doll's house. Despite knowing the answer, she used to ask him over and over again,

'Is it really true that one wing of the house is to be a stable?'

'That's right.'

'I think people will laugh at it, Lucien, when they know.'

'Well, you know, and are you laughing?'

'Not laughing; but it worries me.'

'There will be worse worries than my cowsheds, Mariana.'

'Yes, but people of taste don't put their animals right next to them like peasants.'

'Who are these people of taste? Where are they?'

'You can't see them just like that, Lucien, but they are there, and they'll hold all these things against you, and when your luck changes, they'll gloat over your downfall.'

'I am my luck.'

Mariana never carried her questioning too far, realising that it was as effective asjabbing a needle into a stone wall. She had a hold over Lucien, and she didn't want to lose it. Lucien, meanwhile, had reached such a state of infatuation that he could scarcely breathe unless Mariana were near. The new house drew them together and relieved the otherwise unbearable tension. The first part of the house to be erected was the central octagonal turret, and around it came the rest of the main structure. To speed up the process each piece of the house was finished as soon as it

145

was built, so the floors and ceilings, panelling and windows, were put in one place before the rest had even risen from the ground. After the plasterers and the painters and the varnishers and the stencillers had finished with the turret rooms, Lucien moved in behind them. He worked from the fourth-floor turret downwards, furnishing and arranging the rooms with manic precision. He hung curtains and blinds and laid carpets and rugs. Each room was designed to have a small, built-in cupboard large enough to hold a barrel of powdered lime, which he had Luis Aguirre scatter and sweep every day to keep down the insects, particularly the ants and the cockroaches, which were as prevalent in the city as they had been on the plains.

The swarms of caraqueños with their carvings to sell increased, bringing now carpets and bales of cloth, chairs and beds. They were so many that Lucien had to employ an extra workforce of antique dealers to buy these goods for him. Despite their profession, however, the antique dealers seemed incapable of grasping Lucien's wide and eccentric taste. Finally, Luis Aguirre was given the job, which he carried out with ruthless efficiency, choosing instinctively such items as el Niño Lucien had loved at home and any such stones that Chucho Delgado would have wanted on his tomb. Whenever any of the vendors tried to haggle, Luis Aguirre would hit them over the head with a knotted truncheon that he made for the purpose. He paid a flat rate for what he bought, thus levelling the value of everything, whether a reredos, a tapestry, a Spanish casket or a chair, to exactly five Bolívares. Luis Aguirre was a good man in Lucien's opinion, and within a week of his appointment, two new marquees were erected round the rim of the building site.

From time to time, as the spread of marquees grew, inspectors came to see why there was such a commotion in Valle Arriba, the select and usually empty part of Caracas where Lucien had chosen to build. Twice the inspectors came to stop work on his house, and twice he bribed them away. Lucien managed to charm and bribe all the officials, their secretaries, surveyors, chauffeurs, guards and outriders, and the house rose up from Valle Arriba uninterrupted by the dictatorship of the city regulations. In the rubble and wasteland that was to be the garden, landscapers and gardeners were already at work, planning and planting what they could without interfering with the construction work. The cult of the garden had not reached Caracas in the 1930s. Perhaps this was due to an instinctive fear of snakes and scorpions that the caraqueños shared with the Llaneros; or perhaps it was just that there was a surfeit of plants with the great baskets of ferns and the cascading jasmines and passion-flowers that decked every balcony and verandah from Sabana Grande to Valle Arriba. The gardens were very definitely in the houses: trails of tradescantia twenty feet long decorated many a drawing-room, as did orchids and geraniums and the ubiquitous fern. The yards, however, were still the realm of the scrabbling chickens and the ravenous pigs; they were places where vegetables could be peeled, and coffee and corn laid out and clothes set to dry over whatever bushes grew wild enough to survive the animals. Sometimes a guava or a mango tree with perhaps an orange and a lemon would be specially planted to bring shade to the back of the house, but a good garden was rare.

Before his fine house was even half finished, Lucien's new park was beginning to look like the botanical garden itself. Tramloads of sightseers arrived, not just to stare at the rising masonry, but also to see with their own eyes the speed at which the famous Lucien could turn a wasteland into flowers. Inside a low wall, twenty feet square, a miniature replica of his grandmother's herb garden was being made. The soil was imported by the cartload from the fertile slopes of San Antonio de los Altos, where Swiss and Italian market gardeners had already begun to plant their terraces of carrots and lettuces and strawberries for the town. A new gate was put in the high iron railings around the site, and between the hours of seven and eight, immediately after the curfew ended, and before the sun came up, Lucien bought plants and roots and cuttings. Those who came to him with their tins of roses and lilies and rosemary, and those who came with more exotic offerings, found that Lucien had an uncanny knack of knowing when the plant had a root and when it did not. Unerringly, he seemed to know when to pull at the stem and draw it clean out of the ground for the rootless stick it was, and when it would be genuine. A small stream ran over the ground at the back of Lucien's property, and this he had enlarged and channelled to irrigate the newly planted beds.

Lucien made the top room of the octagonal tower Misia

Schmutter's room with a massive sixteenth-century lectern for her bible to rest on. Against each of the eight walls he stood a hardbacked chair with a shield and an iron fist carved on the seat. These chairs were extremely uncomfortable, and Lucien flattered himself that Misia Schmutter would have thoroughly approved of them. The next room down, however, Lucien kept for himself, with a fourposter bed and a clutter of statues, and very little else. He was not at all sure that his grandmother would have approved of this room, particularly since he had come to share it, on Wednesdays and Fridays, with Mariana. As with all things, routine played an important part in this affair. Mariana would arrive in her battered car, or sometimes in the chauffeur-driven Frazer-Nash that Lucien had given her in the first week of his winnings. Ulises was so taken with the car that he almost decided to continue his liaison with Mariana so as to have a share in it, but, somehow, he didn't care to cross Lucien, and Mariana moved into the luxurious Tamanaco Hotel.

Lucien was truly alarmed by his virginity. Detlev went to a charming brothel called the Carousel three times a week after lunch. There was a time when he had made only nightly visits, but the curfew had put an end to that. Much as he enjoyed flaunting the guards and crawling along the backstreets after dark, he found that the excitement had an unfortunate effect on his sexual performance. On the first day that Lucien went with him, Detlev had said, casually,

'I know you've got a tremendous reputation, so you probably think it's a cheek to tell you, but here in the city, we always douche the girls out with a bit of carbolic before, just in case, you know. It's a filthy place, really, the city.'

This piece of information did not endear the Carousel to Lucien, or indeed any other of its rival establishments. He drank at the bar, and danced paso dobles and boleros with any number of girls, and sat them on his knee one by one, with the exception of a redhead called Magdalena who was immensely fat, but he never went any further than that. He had braced himself to a possible fumble in the course of his endeavour, yet the problem of the carbolic douche struck him as insurmountable. He lay in bed at night wondering how it might be applied. Several times he came near to asking his brother for guidance, but Detlev was often at his

148

barracks, and Lucien could not trust him not to talk. Mariana would have to be the first. He would have preferred making love to her after he had gathered some expertise. He wanted to impress and please her, and return some of the solace that he felt at seeing her sad face engraved on every stone.

Mariana was far from a whore, of this Lucien was certain. Yet he was not so sure that she might not need the carbolic wash; had he not seen Ulises at the Carousel? To this end, the first-floor turret was fitted out with two matching bathtubs, each encased in white marble, with solid gold taps and giant conch shells on gilded brackets shaped like birds to hold the soap. A dazzling chandelier hung from the ceiling with eighty candles to light the room when the inner shutters were drawn, and in each corner, carved bosses held jars of exquisite oils and lotions. There were phials of frangipani and musk, and bottles of the distilled water of orange flowers, of roses, lilies and gardenias. The whole room with its patchwork marble floor was designed to be so deeply scented as to disguise the smell of carbolic that Lucien put in the bath assigned to Mariana.

Had she been asked to describe her new lover, Mariana would have said, 'He's insane!' Whenever she discovered yet another of his eccentricities, she thought to herself, 'He's completely mad.' But he was kind and beautiful and generous and very rich, and she was determined not to let Ulises see how much he had hurt her. Ulises, who had promised to marry her and had not, and who had not loved her, though she loved him. Now, with Lucien, it would be he who was not fully loved, who could not be by Mariana, because something inside her was breaking, leaving only the glittering shell around her irreparably tangled nerves.

After the ritual bath, which they took together in their separate tubs, Lucien would lead his mistress upstairs, via a spiral staircase that led directly into his bedroom, and he would make love to her from half-past four to half-past five exactly. Mariana was moved and flattered by Lucien's innocence. She found it so surprising that in later years she wondered if she had imagined it. She would gladly have dispensed with the five days of abstinence, but Lucien shared his passion for her with his passion for his building, and the last was of a much longer standing. And then, he sensed her holding back her emotions, and he held back

149

too as a kind of self-defence. None the less, Lucien found his relationship with Mariana deeply reassuring. It was not just the immediate pleasure, it was also the confirmation of his normality, his manhood restored to him, an end to all the lies that had surrounded his sex life or the lack of it for the last fourteen years.

He looked at everyone with new eyes now, in the light of his discoveries. When he bought plants at his gates, he tried to imagine all the vendors in similar positions to the ones he took with Mariana. Sometimes it was very hard. Did the pock-marked old man with the runny eyes really feel himself on the brink of an explosion that burst like hot ash in his veins? Could the fat girl who brought the fruit trees bring him the same flood of ease as Mariana? What did these weary people see in each other to quicken their blood? What had his father seen in the servants? Sometimes it was the face and sometimes not. El Patrón had covered girls' faces with cloths, and it was Mariana, with her pale Madonna-like features and her hair like burnt sand and her grey eyes that transfixed Lucien, who had made him understand why. She had unleashed cravings in him that he never knew he had, and although his immediate frustration was satisfied, he still had to live with the new restlessness that possessed him.

While his house rose and burst into a rush of pinnacles along the roof, Lucien's thoughts turned to reproduction. Every aged mother whom he saw had conceived her children in this strange new way, which was not, of course, new at all to them. Even Misia Schmutter must have lain with her husband, Don Wilhelm Lucien, and conceived her sons in the same manner. He wondered how many times she would have allowed her subservient husband to climb on to her. She had had six sons, how many times would that have been? Carmen Ivelisia de Gonzalez claimed that her husband had mounted her only four times in all the years of their marriage, and that her four daughters were the living proof. Perhaps in los Llanos conception was harder.

His thoughts twisted and turned along these lines, causing him great confusion. What seemed clearer and clearer was that if Misia Schmutter had slept with her husband, or husbands, whom she had not loved, why had she not lain with Lucien, whom she did love? He tormented himself with the thought that, had he been older when she died, he might not have needed to have waited until he was twenty-two to lose his virginity. Would she have approved, he asked himself, or did her love only run to strangulation? If he abstained from Mariana on five days out of each seven, it was only partly because of his house. The other part was because she held back and would not be the spirit of Misia Schmutter. Mariana held him tightly, but not tightly enough. She gave him a sense of power and fulfilment, but it was not the power or the fulfilment that Misia Schmutter had in her gift.

Although his house was scheduled to be finished by the end of January 1934, Lucien was having second thoughts about living there with Mariana, with their love on the unresolved basis that it was. His loneliness and sense of loss at the desertion of Misia Schmutter were growing daily harder to bear. It was now six months since he had felt the reassuring warmth of her body pressed against his back. Without her, he was like a knight without his armour or a tortoise without its shell. All his pleasures and successes could not make up for her absence. He was torn between guilt and desire. At times, when he could not bear the strain any longer, he would climb up into Misia Schmutter's room and take out the eggshell lining from its rosewood box and finger it carefully, like the relic it was. He found it hard to believe that such a powerful person could have shrunk to this mere membrane.

As a boy, Lucien had rarely masturbated. He had heard say, on numerous occasions, that it softened the brain, emptied the spine of its vital liquid, brought hair on the palms of the hands and ended in blindness, but it was not these tales that had deterred him. It was merely that he felt little pleasure in his own body, and the vague excitement that he felt each time was small compared to other excitements, and was invariably outweighed by a feeling of discontent, of missing something. All this altered with Mariana, and together with the pleasure came the discovery that one part of the true partner of his craving was always Misia Schmutter.

So, although he had occasionally masturbated as a boy and felt neither guilt nor shame, the fact that he now took to doing so in Misia Schmutter's turret filled him with both. Try as he might, he could not resist the temptation of going there at night when the house was empty and placing the brittle remains of the eggshell over him like a broken condom. Where before he had placed only his love and loyalty, he now put his seed and his desire as well.

Lucien had planned a grand opening of his house, a party for six hundred guests, and a banquet and a ball, and then a more select affair, after the curfew, for his friends, who were mostly Detlev's friends whom he had adopted. There was a tremendous amount of new wealth changing hands in Caracas, what with the oil and the booming industries that fed on it, not to mention the more traditional fortunes made by gold and diamonds, or the stabler wealth of the landed interests. Nobody's fortune, however, came as easily as Lucien's. When he ordered his banquet and the caterers told him how many thousands it would cost, he merely gambled for a few hours, and with his winnings he could pay it three times over. Even the drain of the expense of his new house could not compete with his winnings. For each hundred thousand Bolívares that it cost him to build and furnish it, he would make double at the roulette wheel. His winning streak was such that several club owners decided to cut their losses, closed down their clubs or casinos and moved to another town while they still had something left to move.

Everyone wanted to go to Lucien's ball. Those who were not invited but felt that they should have been took to their beds and pined for weeks to come. The Alarza family with their five daughters to wed were so affronted that they sailed to Europe and were abroad for five years. In later times they were to claim that they had known all along that Lucien was 'a bad lot'. They said they could see through his huge donations to charities, there was an underlying amorality about him that, they insisted, they had seen all along. What nobody realised was that this first great binge was more like the opening of a great exhibition or pleasure garden than a single event. Day after day there would be parties and banquets, the semi-circle of dining-tables would never be unlaid, and if the fountain in the great hall ever stopped flowing with champagne, the wall fountains had only to be pressed to replace it.

In deference to Lucien's passion for carving, the ice appeared in every imaginable shape, great blocks of it hewn into the likenesses of bulls and bears. There were cakes and quesillos and every kind of meat and fish, from

152

chicken to partridge, and salmon to shrimps. The bowls of oysters and chipi chipis rose four feet from the cloth, and there were pyramids of limes and such traditional dishes as escabeche and Russian salad. At regular intervals along the damask cloths there were loaves of black bread for Misia Schmutter. Along the walls there were giant coolers full of German wines. The caterers had tried to insist on French, but Lucien would not have it.

In his stable, which was the whole of the ground floor of the east wing of the house, from the long middle corridor to the row of garages, Niemen chewed his oats and hay, spilling them on to the carpets that he had in lieu of straw. It took Lucien some weeks to appreciate that Niemen did not want these floor coverings. The bull was old and irritable, and Lucien was sad to see that Niemen didn't really share his taste in anything any more, just a desultory munch at his food and a restlessness that no amount of care or exercise or herbal brews could cure.

While the party raged through his house, Lucien sat in the darkened stable, stroking his listless bull. He didn't see how the party ended, not even how the more select, post-curfew part of it went. Instead, he retired to Misia Schmutter's room and read his book on the architecture of Munich. At one stage, while he was still in the stable, he heard what sounded like stampeding cattle rampaging through the hall. Even Niemen pricked his ears and lowed at the familiar sound. Then it died down, and Lucien didn't bother to find out what it was.

On the following morning he found that there were people sleeping everywhere, under the tables, on the sofas, and in and under all his beds in all of his forty-seven bedrooms. Half of Detlev's platoon seemed to have taken over the west wing. He found a drunken ambassador asleep the gun-room, and a huddle of waiters lay in a heap under the stairs. Lucien found that he did not know most of his guests, and he guessed, rightly, that many of them were uninvited. On the whole, he thought, they were a poor exchange for his magnificent ice bears, and the sturgeons moulded out of caviare and the great barrels of escabeche. The marble floors were afloat with spilt wine and vomit and cigar butts. In future, Lucien decided, he would make his staff work in shifts, so that the food never became this mass of melting leftovers crawling with ants and flies. He would have people to clean the floors and change the cloths every few hours. Never again would he see his house buried in filth. However, the worst was yet to come. The washbasins in every closet had their blue and white hand-painted flowers smeared with excrement—the modern plumbing had obviously been too much for some of his less educated gate-crashers. And worst of all, in the garden, hundreds of bladders had been emptied over his flowers, hundreds of backsides had squatted over his herbs. Lucien sent out for the plumbers, who were so hung-over from their illicit share of the previous night's proceedings that they were unable to come, and a new batch of plumbers arrived with instructions to turn ten more rooms into water closets, each with a hand basin at chin level only. Then he went to his own room and waited for the arrival of Mariana.

She arrived, by some miracle, on time. The party had definitely not agreed with her. Even under the powder and the beetroot stains that she used for rouge, and with the lemon that she had squirted into her eyes to freshen them, she looked frail and prematurely aged. To Lucien's surprise, he liked her better like that. So much so that he dispensed with the ritual bath, and took her straight to his bed. He began to make love to her with a fervour he had never shown before. The hour of curfew came and passed and Lucien was still turning her over and over, entering her again and again. The more he moved inside her, the greater his desire became, until, as the hours wore on, his every thrust slowed down to a painful heaving. Mariana, who was exhausted and satisfied to the point of virtual unconsciousness, assumed that he was weary from his demonic exertion, but Lucien continued to pin her down for another aching hour. He had never felt so happy in his life. All his power had returned. Although he moved slowly, he felt his energy tearing at him from the inside. Misia Schmutter had returned. She was weighing him down, throttling him. Mariana moaned under the weight, and fainted. Then Lucien slept with the other half of himself safely on his back.

154

Chapter 16

AFTER THAT FIRST PARTY, LUCIEN SETTLED DOWN TO LIFE IN his new mansion, which he called Niemenberg, but which was known, irreverently, as 'The Stable' by his friends. Mariana was very upset by the disrespect implied in the nickname; Lucien was not. Mariana, perhaps on account of her rather dubious social position, suspected a snub in even the most casual remark and insults in almost every gesture. She stayed on at Niemenberg after their night of extended passion, through a casual invitation. Lucien had merely said, 'Don't go, Mariana.' He had not said, 'Please stay.'

To have become, even by side-stepping, the mistress of a great mansion should have pleased Mariana more than it did, yet her new position seemed only to exacerbate her growing bitterness. She was no longer merely a kept woman, but a courtesan. Sometimes, in the past, with Ulises, she had thought that if only she could pay her dress bill, and buy herself the occasional necklace and dance all night, every night, she could enjoy life until the day she died. She had not, however, bargained for the bitterness. It had begun as a dull ache, a numb part of her brain that screened an overwhelming sense of despair and loss. With Ulises she had always tried to control this sensation, but sometimes it got the better of her, and she would go on and on about how her family would not see her and her own sisters and even the housekeeper and the schoolteacher and her friends from school would cross the road if they saw her, partly to hurt her, and partly to avoid the contamination of a fallen woman. Ulises should have married her, she said. He was the only one who could restore her to a decent place in society. He had said that he would, admittedly when he was drunk. He had said so not once but five times.

When Ulises was present at these tirades of regret, he had been in the habit of turning an imaginary handle as though to imply that the record was going round and round. Mariana had learnt to dissimulate the rage that she felt when he did this, though she didn't forget. She had often asked him,

'Why did you dishonour me, Ulises?'

And he would reply, 'Why did you come with me?'

'I loved you.'

'That', Ulises would say, inspecting his fingernails, 'was your mistake. Never go with the man you love.'

'Do you know what love is, Ulises?'

'Yes, it's having a good time. Now don't worry so, it doesn't suit you; and anyway, you've got nothing to worry about. I look after you, don't I?'

That wasn't that, however, for Ulises' picture did not take into account the shrinking feeling that was taking over Mariana. When she met Lucien, she had thought that he would be able to protect her, while enabling her to strike a blow at Ulises' pride by leaving him. Her vanity would not have let her believe it even had she known that Ulises had long been wanting to be free of her, and was waiting only until he could afford to pay her off. So, when Lucien asked Mariana not to go, he inherited not only her charms and defects, but the whiplash of her discontent as well. Lucien, however, was eminently skilled at dealing with discontent, and he grew so bound up with Mariana that he came to love even the bitterness in her. It was a mark of his skill that, although her troubles grew, she dwelt on them little more than she had with Ulises and between her monologues of slights and offences, they still had time to discuss Gallegos and Nietzsche and Whitman.

Whenever Lucien had time to spare, he would join the chefs in their immaculate kitchens and, wearing a borrowed apron, he would concoct this or that dish on the menu, under their care. It was Mariana's lot to draw up the guest lists she desired, and she enjoyed summoning people from the far corners of the country to attend her balls and banquets. Others needed no invitation, since, like Mariana herself, they had never left Niemenberg after the excesses of the opening night. Some of these were friends of Lucien's, and one was a gambling partner, one was a fellow officer of Detlev's who had fallen from grace at the barracks and was lying low, and there was a strange man called Gaston Pierson, whom Lucien had never met in his life before, but with whom he became very friendly.

On the whole, Mariana managed the house, Luis Aguirre dealt with the servants and cared for Niemen, the solitary occupant of the magnificent stable, and Lucien managed the garden. He had his grandmother's knack of creeping up on people and catching them unawares, and although he usually spoke in the gentlest of terms—and when he admonished, he did so kindly—ever since the opening of Niemenberg, people were a little afraid of him. His very gentleness was unnerving. Despite delegating his power, Lucien liked to keep an eye on everything. He regretted that although his presence could cause dread, it didn't automatically ensure efficiency. This was particularly true of his own exclusive realm, the garden. He had two and a half acres of young orchard, flowers, vegetables and herbs to care for, and three full-time gardeners to tend them.

The initial shock of being turned into an open latrine was more than many of the frailer plants could bear. These Lucien replaced with new plants, which continued to wilt and pine, and worse still, they began to disappear. One day he would have a bank of tarragon and another of chives, and the next day there would be a bare furrow and no trace of its former occupants. The gardeners denied all knowledge of them. Lucien believed that he was employing the dregs of his former team, they were the last of the original fourteen. When the house was finished he had asked for three men to volunteer, and these three had stepped out with such alacrity that he had taken them on then and there. After a month or so of no improvement, he toyed with the idea of swapping them for some of their more capable colleagues. However, he found on inquiry that the others had all gone into premature retirement on the excessive bonuses they had earned by getting the grounds ready in time for the opening. This made him suspect that it was something more than the flowers that was attracting his three men to their job. At first he suspected some kind of liaison with the maids, but far from hanging around the house, they seemed to lock themselves away on the slightest pretext in their garden shed.

For Lucien, his garden would always be a kind of Achilles heel. Wherever he went, he would contrive to have a garden, whether it was large or small, park or allotment, window-box or pot, he would have plants to care for, and fret over. And he was prone to feel oversensitive about them. Plants, and in particular medicinal plants, were inextricably bound up with Misia Schmutter for him. He had been made to weigh and analyse life from the age of three, he had been taught his version of Nietzschean philosophy by practical lessons, and the demonstrations remained singed into his memory. All his feelings had been stretched and pressed and folded like so many strips of bandage; and they had been extracted from him and wrapped around him, mummifying his thoughts and blockading his reactions. Nothing came or went without their filter. Misia Schmutter had told him, and he knew that it was true: he wasn't a man, he was a catalyst, his life had a purpose beyond the purpose of other men's. He had been chosen to be different, and he had been born different to that end.

Although Lucien knew all this, and believed it, it was as nothing where his garden was concerned. He was simply incapable of mastering his reactions whenever it came to his plants. So when they disappeared from the terraced gardens of Niemenberg he felt only a sickening rage. As he walked around the pattern of the beds, his head grew dizzy with anger. Each day it would be some different aspect of the garden that infuriated him anew. He would lie awake for hours at night, forcing himself to be calm about his withering herbs. If one day his angelón had seemed to wilt, and he had felt his head burst at the thought of it, and the blood had raced around his troubled veins so fast he had thought that he would have a fit, then the next day he would rise determined to ignore the state of that particular bed. He would go out and wander around the low maze of paths, immune to the caprice not only of the angelón but all the pulmonary decongestants in his stock. He would walk past the drooping heads of pale-blue bells and will himself not to care. Then the sight of one of his grapevines upside down in the ground with its roots dangling miserably in the sun would be too much for him.

Each night, as he drank and danced and gambled, he

wondered why he bothered to shoulder the vexation of rearing a garden in the tropics. It wasn't a real question, though. He knew that he did it not only for himself, but for Misia Schmutter, who had come back; and Lucien felt that if she ever left him again, he would shrivel up like a crushed spider. The plants were his stumbling block. He could no more pass the obstacle of their disappearance than a small child with a soft heart can pass a beggar in the street, and must be lifted bodily past the object of its pity and shame. So Lucien, who single-handed could control the social life of the city, and who was afraid of no one, and who believed that it was his mission to realign the world, could not cope with his recalcitrant flowers. It was Mariana who helped him.

One morning, as Lucien was about to set out for his ritual and increasingly stressful morning walk, she said,

'You know, Lucien, there's something funny about those gardeners. I've been watching them, and I think they've just picked up their work from the Swiss gardeners that you had before . . . and they do something in that hut of theirs.'

'What?' Lucien asked, dully.

'They do something in their hut.'

'But what do they do?'

'Oh, I don't know. At first I thought that they just drank, but I have never seen them take any liquor in. I wonder, though, if they haven't got a still somewhere—the whole place stinks of aniseed.'

Lucien felt the tension ease in his head to such an extent that it hurt him and he had to sit down. Mariana was right, the smell in the garden was aniseed. Why hadn't he realised that before? His jasmine and the cloying dama de noche and the gardenias on the low wall all smelt subtly wrong. Now he knew that it was aniseed; and in his experience, where there was aniseed, there was always something wrong.

'Come with me,' he said to Mariana, and they went into Niemen's stable for his ritual 'good morning' and then on into the garden together, where they tracked down the first of the three gardeners kneeling over an ornamental bed. He was meticulously scratching at the earth around a border of young carnations. Lucien demanded,

'Why are you scrabbling like that, haven't you got something better to do?'

'It's the red-necked ants, señor,' the gardener replied without a moment's hesitation. 'They're something terrible this year. You have to put these little grains of salt down to get them, or they would have this garden.'

'And where are these grains of salt?' Lucien asked, leaning over to look for them.

'Why, they're so small, señor, you can hardly see them.'

'I can't see them at all!'

'Well, there you are then, señor, that shows they're working.'

The second gardener was sitting on a piece of hessian in the shade of a puma rosa tree. He had a stack of pebbles beside him which he would occasionally bang together.

'What are you doing?' Lucien asked him.

'I would get up, Señor Lucien, only this is a very delicate sort of a job. It's the stone beetles, you see, señor,' he hiccuped, 'they live under the stones and they eat the roots of a plant right at the point where it joins the stem. They're like vampires, señor, they snap right through the stalk and then they suck the vital juices. One beetle will go through no end of plants in a day; and there's nothing can kill them. But . . . if I bang these stones together, they think it's an earthquake, and they panic and bite each other.'

Lucien listened, and with each breath that the gardener took, the air filled more and more with the heavy tang of aniseed. It had been so with his colleague of the red-necked ants, and it was so with the third of the trio, who was to be found stroking orange leaves in the orchard.

This last gardener didn't wait to be questioned, greeting them hurriedly with, 'Good-morning, Señor Lucien; Señora.'

Mariana noticed that even this imbecilic, bleary-eyed liar smirked as he said, 'Señora.' Everyone, from the smallest child to the poorest retainer, knew how to say 'Señora' with just enough pause before the word to cancel its deference immediately.

'Seeing as how you know so much about flowers, Señor Lucien, you probably know what a benefit it is to an orange tree to stroke its leaves when it flowers. They're like women, trees are—begging your pardon, señora,' the man continued with a cursory nod towards Mariana, '—they like to be stroked.'

'That will do.'

'Thank you, señor.'

Then Lucien and Mariana went back to the house, she to her books and guests and bitter thoughts, and he to his octagonal tower. He waited there all day, watching from Misia Schmutter's room, through Misia Schmutter's binoculars. He touched the three scars on his arm, and he felt his old worries drain away. He no longer had to take the affront personally, the plants were ailing and disappearing because the gardeners were drunk and ignorant. They had cheated him and they would have to go. Even Misia Schmutter agreed, and eased her grip a little. What remained was to find out the mechanism of their deceit. He felt no urge for revenge, as such, just a need to set things right, and a great sense of curiosity. How did they get their liquor to the hut, and how did they tend the garden at all?

He answered the second question first. At nine o'clock, in defiance of the curfew, and Lucien's own walls and railings, a silent task force of small boys climbed into his grounds, and set to work with sickles and machetes, trowels and string, weeding and tying and cutting and hoeing for hour after hour of frenzied fumbling work. They left at about two in the morning. In the half-moonlight, Lucien could make out about eight or nine of these urchins. Through the roof of the house below him he could hear the tunes of the string band drifting into the night. One band would stop and then another play. Each seemed to have its favourite songs which would come up more and more often as the night wore on. That night, Lucien could hear the crooning of 'Entre candilejas'; it was one of the few modern tunes that he liked, but Misia Schmutter did not, and he felt a perverse pleasure at enjoying it barefacedly in the light of her disapproval. Everything, he thought, had its disadvantages, and that must be one of the bad things about death: you couldn't make the band play another tune, or turn off the graffonola. Had she been alive, she would have had the musicians horse-whipped.

The main rooms at Niemenberg had electric light, which was a wonderful novelty for Lucien and his guests. The lights themselves were switched on and off so often, however, that they fused repeatedly, plunging the great house into darkness. After the first few blackouts, Lucien had an alternative system of oil lamps fitted throughout, and the blackouts were overcome with relative ease. On the night of his vigil, somebody flashed the lights on and off, rhythmically for a full ten minutes, to the tune of 'Bye Bye Blackbird', and then there was a succession of minor explosions. Lucien thought sadly that he hadn't heard a good explosion for months, and he made a mental note to add fireworks to his regular entertainments. Although he watched through the rest of the night, nothing else happened.

The gardeners were due to start work at half-past six, and Lucien had decided to confront them then. Meanwhile, he sat and watched through the small hours, alone in his tower. One or two of his guests inquired after him, though mostly they were content to dance and revel and brawl.

Usually, Lucien saw and took toll of the pranks and the dance-floor romances. He didn't know why it pleased him so to watch his staff and his guests come and go in shifts. It was a strange business, this amusing people, at first it was easy, and then it all went uphill and they just wanted more and more, until it became a tournament of excess. Only last week, Gerardo Joroba had danced with the great ice bear—a graceful paso doble across the ballroom floor with a trail of melted ice dripping down his numbed hands and trickling from his sodden sleeves. Now Gerardo claimed that the ice bear was a bore, and he had thrown it on to the terrace. The girls grew tired of their dresses even before the new waves of guests arrived from the recuperating rooms upstairs. The fountain was getting choked up with the tiaras that the girls threw into it. The couples who danced just to be together and not for show were booed off the floor. Bouquets of orchids were given to those with the most inventive partners. A young man called Aristo de Mowbray had taken the prize one night for dancing with an alligator. There were dozens of convent girls who came with their lovers, and women who were reputed to have lived in sin for more years than they could remember, and enjoyed every minute of it. Lucien watched them all, the flappers and the stars and the hangers on; there were those who were genuinely beautiful, and those who merely behaved as though they were, and he watched Mariana struggling to survive, torn between her obsession about not being accepted, and her need to shine.

During the moments when Lucien was alone with Misia Schmutter, away from the carousing but still within earshot of it, his thoughts would often turn to San Fernando, and his Ceibu herds and his battle to tend and fatten them for the slaughter. These guests of his, who came in droves of two and three hundred at a time, were more like the worms that nestled in the hides than like the beasts themselves. They arrived, small and insignificant, but within a few hours of drinking his rum and wine, they would begin to swell and grow, they would work their own kind of fever into the bloodstream of his house, they would get fatter and fatter, throbbing on the dance floor and rolling on his sofas. If they had really been worms, these pastyfaced bloated ghosts of themselves, Lucien would have had to lure them out and kill them; instead, he fed them richer and richer foods, more and more, stuffing them with oysters and caviare and eels' livers to burst their own livers.

Lucien felt bad when the morning came. It was never a good idea to sit brooding through the night. Mariana came to see him on her way to bed.

'You look terrible,' she said.

'Thinking brings on my chest pains.'

'Perhaps you've got a growth.'

'If I have, I believe it's on my back.'

'You can't get one on your back.'

'You can if it just jumps up and clings on,' Lucien told her.

Mariana laughed and stroked his hair.

'You should see the doctor, you know, about those chest pains. Sometimes you go the colour of willow flowers.'

'Don't worry about me, Mariana, I have lungs like a scrap-metal crusher.'

'And do these metal-grinding lungs crush charlatans for breakfast?'

'Maybe,' Lucien said.

The charlatan gardeners arrived neither that day nor any other, warned, as though by some survival instinct, that they had gone far enough. So Lucien had to content himself with his usual breakfast of devilled kidneys, black bread and a tequila sunrise, while the housemaids took it in turns to stand in and water the plants.

Drink, as Mariana had so shrewdly seen, had been the key to the whole problem. The gardeners, with the connivance of one of the plumbers, had connected a pipeline to the cellar vats. Hidden behind a tray of broken crocks was a tap which served Rhine wine instead of water. Thus the men drank all day, and paid a fraction of their salary to the children who came in by night and managed the garden as best they could in their ignorance and the dark. Lucien was impressed by the ingenuity—in San Fernando, no one would bother.

There was an attaché at the German Embassy known as Captain Walter, who was a regular visitor to Lucien's house, and he suggested that his host employ some of the many German immigrants who were arriving in Venezuela, lured by tales of the black treacle and the streets of gold.

'At least when they're German, you know they'll work hard,' the attaché had said, and Lucien agreed.

Within a few days, Lucien was delighted with his three new, gangling men, whose thin Germanic features grew steadily more porcine on their diet of banquets and flowers. Hearing the familiar Teutonic names of the plants that he had grown up with, his ear became attuned once more to the guttural sounds he had learnt from Misia Schmutter, and he found himself practising his mother tongue with them while the garden flourished and blossomed and fruited.

Chapter 17

IN LUCIEN'S LATER YEARS, THE TWENTY-FIVE YEARS OF EN-
forced introspection, he saw his time in Caracas as a waste.
It was a mere lull between leaps in his memory. When he tried
to explain the extravagance and pointlessness to himself he
could find no excuse for it. Even while he was living at
Niemenberg all the days had felt like lost days. He did
make his name, as he had told his father that he would, but
he made it known as that of an extravagant buffoon. He
had arrived as a complete unknown in the city; that had
changed, anyone at the Teatro Municipal or a cinema or a
thé dansant, or even a vendor in the marketplace, would
know who Lucien was. He had become famous, even notorious, but not for the ideas that were at the core of him, the
ideals that Misia Schmutter had given him. Katrina had
worn a cruel backboard to keep her straight; even Misia
Schmutter had worn her corsets, with massive whalebone
stays and reinforcements of Saxon steel. Lucien needed no
such device; his spine was kept rigid by his will-power.

Again, in later years, his former friends and acquaint-
ances would find it impossible to connect Lucien, their
foolishly genial host, to Lucien, the man-eating monster.
He was such a generous man, as his staff and his neighbours and his guests all knew. Some of them might even
have run the gauntlet of public scandal and testified at his
trial, but for the fact that there seemed to be no link
between the two men. They mostly imagined that this second Lucien, the convict, was an impostor. It was their
privilege and their misfortune to live through a time of

great social upheaval. The oilfields and Maracaibo had put out both tendrils and tentacles, and by whichever way they could, they were taking over every aspect of caraqueñan life. The tapestry of their Criollan culture with its Spanish weft was being swept away by a plastic wave of Yankee influence. Not much could be counted on in such times of change; of one thing, though, they were sure: their Lucien was not the wanton killer whose face stared out at them from every street corner (not that killing was murder, anyone might have to kill). There was no cruelty in him, not a single drop, and they would swear by the work of Saint Gregorio Hernandez that he was incapable of revenge. It just wasn't in him. Perhaps that was why they didn't speak for him at his trial: what was the point of defending a stranger, a usurper of a good man's name?

Meanwhile, at Niemenberg, the rumba and the tango, the Charleston and the waltz continued to escort the dozens of weary partners around the floor. More and more of the food was left each night as the enteritis and the renal congestions and the jaundices felt the glut steal round them before even the first taste of the delicacies of the day. At the back of the house, away from the crenellated grandeur of the façade with its twin oriel windows, the kitchen staff dispensed the leftovers. Although the house, to a casual eye, might seem to stagger from one night to the next in a state of unplanned abandon, every step was orchestrated by Lucien himself. Although he seemed to have dedicated his life to this binge of entertainment, the basic rules of his beliefs—time and place and chance and strength—remained with him. Thus every detail was ritualised, from the spreading of the cloths to the disposal of the banquets. At six-thirty, before the sun was hot, the food was collected into numerous tin baths, which were carried by a maid at either handle to the gates, and at seven o'clock sharp, as the curfew was officially lifted, the food would be shared out, by means of a giant ladle put through the railings, and tipped into the many dishes and pots and tins that awaited it on the far side. Poor people from all the barrios came, often creeping through the night to avoid the curfew guards. Sometimes they would be faint with hunger, and the feasts of caviare and glazed duck in orange, and pavlova cake, oysters and salmon mayonnaise, would be enough not only to fill them, but to ruin their precarious health. Others would get so severely beaten and kicked in the scrummage to get near the railings that they would have to be carted away; and once a young man was pressed to death against the iron bars around Niemenberg by the hungry mob behind him, which set Lucien brooding on the mixed blessing of charity.

Had he known that in the shanty town that crawled down the hill slopes outside the city, the remains of his lavish dinners and breakfasts and the titbits of his buffet lunches were causing the havoc they were, he would have certainly stopped the custom. If Lucien changed his parting or his cologne or danced with a new partner or refused his breakfast, news of the event would carry across the valley from misquoted mouth to mouth, and by the end of the day every peasant girl pinned to her laundry and her water pots would know what had happened at Niemenberg. The wireless and the press were avid for such details of his life. Lucien, however, had no such messengers to tell him that all the local boticas from Playa Azul to El Silencio had had such a run on kaolin they had doubled their orders. And on the scarred slopes themselves families fought over the camomile and wild garlic to take home to dose the terrible diarrhoeas that his food was causing. The market stalls sold out of antispasmodics before the sun was properly up. Notwithstanding, the parents still came, lured by the free food, and they tramped back through the dust and sun with their pails of artichokes and lobster salad as reinforcements to the ptomaine poisoning and the colitis that were already reaching epidemic proportions in the slums.

At first, the hand-outs had come as a real disappointment. They would pick over the remains of the three French chefs' creations and ask each other, 'Is this food?' Times, however, were hard, despite the oil boom, and the élite and their fat Dictator Gomez didn't care, there were one or two recognisable scraps of protein in each ladleful, and gradually they came to enjoy the food. The kitchen maids could still hear words of encouragement given to newcomers, 'Just close your eyes and swallow it,' Or, 'Most of the bits aren't as slimy as that,' or, 'Don't look too closely at all the little bugs and you'll do all right.'

A few, not many, with intestines of the calibre of drain-pipes, returned day after day, week after week, with signs of positive relish as they spotted some new favourites falling into their billycans. These ones would wait at the back of the crowd after they had got their share and try to beg or barter for more. Luis Aguirre, whose job it was to supervise the sweeping of the street after the dispensary was closed, and to ensure that exactly the right number of buckets of water and creosote were swilled over the cobbles and dirt, could hear them asking, 'Could I have the little pink slugs you've got on top there?' Occasionally, an innocent, 'I wonder if you would swap my braised frogs for your fried lizards,' would cause the hapless boy or girl to drop the dish and run, leaving the entire contents to the breadline gourmets. And an 'Oh, you are lucky, you've got some of the grilled geckos,' would invariably work with the girls. The new society, the black treacle empire, mirrored itself in the microcosm of Niemenberg's human vultures: some grew fat, and some died.

The effect of Niemenberg on its visitors was to be a lasting one. None of them would forget the sumptuous excess. Some remembered one aspect better than the rest, others recalled a general impression. They would all, however, have agreed on certain things that made their mark, like the splendour of the flowers, and the geniality of their host. Mariana could occasionally be seen weeping or laughing hysterically. She had been known to have certain people ordered from the house. She had twice slapped Gerardo Joroba, and it was rumoured that she had even quarrelled with Walter, the German attaché. It was well known that Mariana had pulled Doña Alicia Valero's hair because the lady in question had refused to acknowledge her, and one night she nearly drowned Sofía Alarza in the champagne fountain after the girl had made some remark about whores being publicly branded. Nobody, though, not even Aristo Mendoza, one of the fastest scandalmongers in South America, could recall a single incident of anger or ill-will on Lucien's part. The best that the dedicated Aristo could come up with was that 'Lucien definitely wasn't normal'. Why? 'Because nobody can be that perfect.'

Many years later, when Lucien was declared a public menace and locked away, those who had visited Niemenberg would tell about it to the incredulous who had not. Fathers, upon hearing of a coming-out ball or a dance or a Liberator's birthday dinner, would say, 'It sounds very splendid, but of course, it is nothing compared to the balls at Niemenberg, my boy.' Then their sons would take out their imaginary violins, and play their silent tunes as Ulises had played to Mariana's complaints.

'At Niemenberg, the tables were never unlaid. The food came in relays. I remember counting once, and there were nineteen different kinds of meat on the table. The champagne was shipped specially from France, in sealed consignments whose bands were broken only inside the gates. The champagne came from fountains. I heard that they watered the garden with it too, but I never believed that. I just tell you what I saw with my own eyes. Three, four, five hundred guests every night, all night. I saw people die of exhaustion on the dance floor. People talk about Hollywood: huh, we had it right here.'

Nobody believed these tales twenty years after the event. They had been hard enough to believe at the time with the evidence on hand of guests flocking to the front porch and a trail of musicians and waiters and caterers and launderers and florists leaving the side door with their pockets weighed down with their wages and their heads numbed with astonishment.

When girls came down for nochebuena in their new gowns of silk and taffeta with trains of scarlet voile to twirl around them at the Christmas dance, and burst in on their parents and asked, 'What do you think?', their parents, if they forgot to check themselves, would say, 'At Niemenberg there were dresses shipped in from Rome and Paris.' Then their daughters' faces would fall, unnoticed as their parents reminisced. 'It was the only way to glitter back to Lucien. There could be no rival balls to match his. No mansion was as splendid or unique. More than one family went bankrupt trying to match his hospitality, but no one would go for long elsewhere. Everyone who was anyone was there, under the painted vaults of the great hall. The only way to stand out was by the extravagance of your dress, and your behaviour. People used to die there, trying to be different.'

No one who hadn't been there believed it, and those who had found it so incredible that they half-doubted their own memories. They all noticed that the schools and the toys and the houses and the trees that they used to know grew in their imaginations and then shrank again, sadly, when they were seen not down the telescope of the years between, but in reality. So, they persuaded themselves,

169

Niemenberg could not have been as large or as splendid as it had seemed, and it was no longer there, to be measured up. Several streets of houses had been built over its site.

Whenever Lucien had time to spare, he divided it between Mariana, who seemed to lean on him more and more, Niemen, who was old and irritable, and his German gardeners, who had come to replace Chucho Delgado, teaching Lucien all they knew of their language, their country and their craft. The gardeners were intrigued by their new job, it was no ordinary matter of skill to keep a garden going on that caraqueñan terrace; unlike anything they had known before. It was not a matter of watering and dead-heading, as it had been in Munich in the municipal gardens where two of them had worked before. The garden at Niemenberg was a matter of constant warfare. It was the gardeners versus the marauding pests and the fungi and the flies. The insects were challenging not only their livelihood but their inherent supremacy. Together with Lucien they invented new poisons with which to batter them, and they won.

Mariana, meanwhile, was growing desperate; everywhere she walked, she seemed to be sinking. Sometimes she felt that all the guests at Niemenberg were pushing her under, and sometimes she felt that they were just waiting for her to disappear under the great mud banks of her own depression. There seemed to be no choice: she would poison herself with her own bitterness; only by marrying Ulises, her old lover, could she save her name. Five years before, she would have denied even the possibility of falling into such a predicament. Now, she sat and stared dully through the stone-clad windows of the south façade, pleading with her pride for her sanity. If deep down she didn't care for the security that marriage would bring, and she hated the thought of the endless childbearing and the neglect that was the lot of so many wives around her, she still craved the acceptance it carried with it, and more, the shield it could hold up for her to keep back the scorn and the silence. There were days when Mariana felt that she could scarcely breathe under the weight of the silence.

She watched and collected the smiles that were imperceptible to other people, smiles that Lucien never saw, smiles that raised a barrier between her and her world. Every day she saw and gathered them, and she kept them

with the silences inside her head; together they were stretching her skull to such a point that her life seemed intolerable. Every day, yet more of these unspoken snubs were
crammed in with the rest, until each day seemed like the
last dregs of her endurance. For each new day, however,
she mustered just enough strength to see her through to the
moment when she could lie on her bed and weep from her
headful of tension and her aches and her pains. While
Lucien was reluctantly swaddled by good will, Mariana
caught the whiplash of the hysteria. To the ladies of
caraqueñan high society, Mariana was not just a girl from a
good family who had dishonoured her name—although that
was bad enough. No, for them she was more vile even than
that: she was the person who was keeping the most eligible
bachelor in the whole of Venezuela away from their daughters. Without Mariana's presence, they might have stabbed
each other for what would turn out to be the dubious
honour of being Lucien's mother-in-law. As it was, Mariana was there, a scapegoat for all their gall and their moth-
erly viciousness. Their daughters joined ranks with them in
a rare coalition of interests. While Lucien had eyes only for
Mariana, he failed to see their adolescent charms. They
could buy dresses by Worth or Erté, and wear them to
Niemenberg with hairstyles that had taken four hours to
create, but still Lucien would not notice. They could dip
their hands in olive oil and bathe their faces in yeast and
albumen, and polish their nails until the island of Margarita
sank into the sea: it was to no avail. Lucien would never so
much as touch their melting fingers.

In the long, restless hours from one day to the next,
Mariana would pull herself out of her growing lethargy only
to file and sort the silences. Some of the women, most
notably those of the clan Arismendi, and the Rangels, knew,
to a split second, how to reserve the discourtesy of their
stares exclusively for their victim. Their smiles were like
razors, they could lacerate as effectively from a distance as
they could close to. Mariana was herself reasonably skilled
at the art of snubbing, it was just something that girls
learnt, a secret, cruel skill.

Mariana didn't recover her confidence after losing Ulises'
love, which had been, she knew, just a pretence of love.
She had thought that by leaving him for Lucien she would
salvage some of her pride, not least in the eyes of the

world. The very women who hated her had to admit that she had been clever to have made the switch when she did. Some, who did not have marriageable daughters, and who were not looking to catch Lucien for themselves, even admired her. She had the envy and the attention she had looked for, yet she was still miserable. She had once been the most eligible bride in the city, some said, although the Arismendis, who would have suffered torture rather than say a good word for someone, hinted that the Jewish blood in Mariana's veins was not of the best there was. When Lucien and Mariana danced together, though, even the Arismendis were impressed by Mariana's grace and beauty, with her clear grey eyes that seemed almost quartz-like with their sparkling, white rimmed pupils, and her mass of hair. She seemed to Lucien like a hybrid puma, and he saw that when she chose, her presence in a room could arouse the same kind of fear and abandon as that of a wild animal, even of his jaguar of the plains. Behind her wide, sad eyes, there was a voracious suction that made people feel they were falling into her stare. He imagined, all over the city, would-be lovers lying awake at night, trying to conjure up Mariana's eyes, so that they could flounder again.

Mariana's nature was such that she would never be entirely content. However, there were certain levels of discontent below which it was impossible for her to go and still be Mariana. She reached this point after some eighteen months of living with Lucien at Niemenberg. Whenever she lay down she could feel clots forming in her blood. They were clots of hatred. The marble floors of Niemenberg and the stone flags had turned to sponge, and the panelled and stencilled walls had become like loofahs that have been left hanging on their creepers on a tree, after the rains have come and swollen them to a strange, untenable mess. Had it not been for her many enemies, Mariana would have happily died; as it was she refused to give them that pleasure. Of all that she had had in life, nothing remained but scraps of her stubbornness, and her pride, and lastly, her tenderness to Lucien, who loved her. For all her life to come, Mariana would retain this tender loyalty to him, cocooned in her own emptiness, and she would return to him time and again, to visit him in prison in San Juan, and to visit him in prison in Trujillo, to visit him in prison in Amazonas and to visit him in Cátia La Mar. She would never forget that Lucien saved her when she had felt she was dying.

One night, as Lucien and Mariana danced around the crowded floor to the slow, crooning notes of 'Falling in Love Again', Mariana went stiff in Lucien's arms. He guided her away from the prying eyes of his guests and carried her upstairs to his tower room. As he left the hall, Lucien caught a glimpse, for the first time, of the vitriolic scorn that some of their friends felt for Mariana. He had watched her fade for the past many months and never known that her palace had become a cactus carpet. The eyes that had turned on her as they left the hall had been the remorseless eyes of good citizens, the kind of eyes that watched with grim satisfaction while witches burnt. They were the good citizens who would have burnt Misia Schmutter if they could, they would burn Mariana if they could, they were burning her now, and had been behind his back for he didn't know how long. Mariana had struck most of her most virulent tormentors from the guest list at Niemenberg months ago, but the days of order were past, and it took more than a list to contain and control the flood of guests who came and went at Niemenberg.

When Mariana came round, Lucien was beside her, staring at the floor, feeling a mixture of sickness and grief and Misia Schmutter's gloating. He looked up and spoke.

'Marry me, Mariana.'

These were the words that Mariana had dreamed of, battened into the tight rituals of her upbringing, they were the words that might once have restored her to her family, her father, her sisters, and they could have taken the scorn from the stares. Ulises, though, was the only one who could save her, and Ulises had ruined her; if she married Lucien, then she might ruin him. Lucien waited quietly for an answer. He could feel the growing heaviness as Misia Schmutter took on her full weight, and he could feel her tightening her grip around his neck, jealous in her old age of Lucien's new love. Misia Schmutter was choking the words back into his throat as he struggled to say them, but she had given her strength to Lucien, so it was no wonder that he was stronger than she, and always would be now. Whenever it came to a clash of their wills, he would win, as he did then, when he said,

'I love you, Mariana. I will do anything for you.' Then it

173

was Mariana's turn to struggle, as she battled with her honour and her depression.

'It's too late,' she said dully. No matter how hard Lucien tried to persuade her, she was adamant. Finally, she relented a little, and they arranged for her to visit Curaçao, where she had spent her holidays as a child, to think it over. They seemed to be deadlocked in their mutual consideration, she for his name, and he for her reputation.

Ten days later, Mariana embarked on the *Star of the Islands* to sail to Curaçao. She travelled as the Señorita rid, with fifteen trunks of dresses and jewels and more banker's drafts than she would have time to draw. While Misia Schmutter rejoiced at her rival's departure, Lucien watched her go, and he felt so sad that his teeth and his bones ached at the sight of her. If only she had asked him to go with her, and if only she would marry him, and stay. They parted with scarcely a word on either side. Mariana leant over the railings of the upper deck, and saw Lucien scarcely able to drag himself back to his car, bent almost double by some imaginary weight.

Niemenberg was not the same without its hostess prowling through the halls and corridors in her fabulous gowns and her mass of glittering hair. However many jewels or sequins a guest might wear, the lights and strands of Mariana's hair always out-glittered what they wore; it was a kind of hybrid hair, and Lucien missed its tangle of reds and golds, its tin and bladder-wrack, russet and sand.

Every day of the six weeks for which Mariana was away, Lucien feared that she would not return. He hated being away from her, and he suspected, through his own aches and longing, that Mariana was the one woman who didn't really love him. When she returned on May 1st, 1936, Lucien was waiting for her on the rainy quay at La Guiara. He was so relieved to see her that he asked no questions. Her homecoming brought with it a sense of freedom. In the previous year the dictatorship had ended, and Juan Vicente Gomez had been ousted, after nearly thirty years of tyranny, for the benign rule of President Rómulo Gallegos, the chronicler of los Llanos and a man of reason and good sense. This change of government, though, after the fireworks and the parades and the street dances were over, had been as nothing to the freedom that filled Lucien when Mariana sailed home to him.

Two weeks later, they married at a private ceremony in St Francis's Church, then they jostled their way through the throng of uninvited guests and disappeared for a week. Some said that they had rented the entire upper floor of the gigantic Hotel Tamanaco, others claimed that they were cruising on a novelty yacht, and still others maintained that they had gone to Europe, never to return. The mystery was never solved. Not even Detlev knew about the tiny villa that Lucien had rented and arranged for his bride, and where they dined exclusively on champagne and fresh pineapples and the most exquisite escabeche fish and a pyramid of chocolate truffles. Every item in the little villa was there because it was a favourite of Mariana's. There were her favourite flowers and records, sweets and clothes. Lucien would have been content to have stayed there for months or even years, offering to send for his bull and settle there. Mariana, however, wanted to be seen, so they returned to Niemenberg.

The marriage lasted for six, to Lucien short, months, while Mariana agonised over her ever-growing obsession. Now that she was married, the Señora that she used was said more quickly than before, but there was still a scarcely perceptible pause before the word. The world still knew that Lucien was not the first, the wedding had not been white, her family had not been there. Mariana was not one of them.

Sometimes, alone in her sitting-room, she felt that she could have borne such things, but for a strange feeling that she had when she was alone with Lucien. It was as though behind his own kind eyes there was another pair staring disapprovingly at her. There always seemed to be an invisible, censorious third presence. Even in bed, she felt a kind of intense hatred boring into her. It was as though there was to be no escape from her enemies, or at least, not at Niemenberg, and not with Lucien.

During her six months of married life, the strain of her position worsened from day to day, until her only choices seemed to be to stay and go insane, or to leave and free herself from persecution. It was in the October of 1936 that she finally told Lucien of her plan to leave him. She was hurt to find that he was not surprised. Misia Schmutter was driving her out, driving her mad, just as she had done to Katrina. His sister had died in the rain pond, and he saw that Mariana would die at Niemenberg unless she escaped. He only hoped that, unlike Katrina, she would actually succeed in getting away.

Mariana sailed to Italy in November, accompanied by a train of luxurious luggage such as the Union Castle Line had not seen since the Greek Royal Family sailed with them. Ahead of her in Rome, in her newly-acquired name of Mariana de Lucien, was a bank balance of several million lire. She would buy in Italy what she had lost in Caracas, the respect of her peers. And Mariana would never want for anything in her life again, except for the passion that she herself had felt for Ulises, and the more subdued love that was all that was left to her after the first passion was spent. In Rome, where she settled on the Via Firenze in a green damask suite of the Hotel Farnese, she would be admired at the opera and on the street. Behind the brocade curtains of her hotel room, Mariana nurtured her bitterness and buried her grief. She often wondered whether she had been justified in leaving Lucien. Would she have been happier had she stayed? She often remembered the stunned look on his face as her ship weighed anchor and left the dock, and she tormented herself with the knowledge that Lucien, the gentlest man in Caracas, had been left alone with the ghostly, spiteful eyes that had driven her away from him.

IV

The Götterdämmerung of the Wounded Bull

Chapter 18

*I*T WAS *LUCIEN'S LOT IN LIFE THAT NO ONE BUT MISIA SCHMÜT*-ter should understand his motives. Not even Mariana, who brooded over and analysed his every known move, appreciated why he did what he did. Since Lucien believed that it was his duty to fulfil a mission, he merely carried out his task, he didn't explain it. It distressed him sometimes to see how wrong people were about him, but he knew that as a man set apart from other men by his ability to manipulate chance, his life necessarily must be a lonely one, and on the whole, he bore his losses with the same even good temper with which he bore his gains.

When Mariana left Niemenberg, Lucien's pleasure in the house left with her. Misia Schmutter, with unprecedented tact, reverted to a mere sensation at the nape of his neck. To most of Lucien's contemporaries, to go to Italy, or indeed anywhere half as far away, was a step so drastic it was considered as irreversible as being dead. When somebody died, his character was given a customary whitewash, no doubt from the general belief that the newly deceased would have enough to contend with, sorting out his sins with St Peter and his maker, without having any mortal gossip at his back. Even Mariana had some of the vitriol scrubbed from her name, and in 1941, when she returned briefly as Mariana la Millonaria, even the dreaded Arismendis openly welcomed her back.

Although Lucien scarcely believed a word of the praise he heard for her, he still liked to hear it. Only Luis Aguirre, who had come with him from San Fernando, and the three gardeners, and the elderly gentlemen who had formed a sort of club in the morning-room, had ever really cared for her, it seemed. Even his brother, Detlev, was secretly relieved to see her go. He knew that there had been a lot of bad talk at the barracks about the way Lucien had flaunted his relationship with the girl before their marriage. Detlev and his other brothers, who occasionally came to Niemenberg when they could get leave—two from the army and one from the navy—had lived in dread of Lucien's marrying Mariana; not, of course, that they had any old-fashioned prejudices, but there were their sisters to consider. And not, of course, that they wanted these girls to grow up to be anything other than tolerant and liberal, but they had to draw the line somewhere. The Jazz Age had come and gone in Caracas, lingering on at Niemenberg, the last stronghold of the stars and the flappers. It was a strange hotchpotch of a Jazz Age that arrived at La Guaira, a little bedraggled and bewildered from its voyage. Some of the new idea's and values came through, and others got caught up in the customs, and the tunes and the music arrived, although some of the instruments had been lost at sea. The new wave of fashion and music and speed stirred up the city, but it wasn't enough to shake the reins from the hands of the older generations; nothing, it seemed, short of an apocalypse could do that. It did, however, settle like a film of glamour, an iridescent sheen that could be seen by those who had enough time and money to look for it.

Lucien, despite having been drawn to the glitter and the excess, began to feel repelled by it after Mariana left. To keep abreast of Niemenberg was like swimming against a strong current. More and more he began to opt out, and hide from his hundreds of guests in the garden or in the stable wing, or outside the house in the city, playing roulette at one of the many clubs. Lucien had discovered that the only way to keep the clubs open and solvent, and thus able to amuse him, was to visit them by turn and gamble for a very limited time and then move on.

Once the casino managers and owners discovered that Lucien was not the devil incarnate out to bankrupt them, they sometimes saw the positive attraction of Lucien wandering in and raking off half a week's profit in half an hour. Crowds of Lucien's fans would follow him and fill the coffers that he so casually depleted.

Now that the city's curfew was finally lifted, and the dictatorship come to an end, business in the casinos was so good that one or two of them began to expand again and a few new ones unbattened their doors in the hopes that Lucien would be kind to them too. Caracas was too euphoric to take note of international events. It had its oil to spill and its profits to spend. It was a citadel of idle wealth. News was the latest antic at Niemenberg, or the latest scandal in Sabana Grande. Newspapers were used to clean car windows. It was Lucien's gardeners who kept him abreast of events. In February 1937 they told him of the party celebrations in the Munich Hofbräuhaus. Then, in the November of that year, one of them returned to Germany in order to enlist and see the new expansion to the east. The two other men gave him intermittent news of Hitler and the Third Reich, and Mariana sent him bulletins on the social and artistic life of Rome.

Nothing much changed at Niemenberg, except that the atmosphere of suppressed hysteria grew, while Lucien himself kept more and more to his private rooms, away from the feasts and the frenzied dancing and the bored decadence below. One year after Mariana sailed for Italy, he received word that his father had suffered a stroke, and he prepared to return to San Fernando. When Luis Aguirre heard that his master was going home, he begged leave to go with him. Lucien looked at Luis, in his starched day-livery with its gold braid and buttons, and his immaculate patent-leather shoes, and then he recalled him as he had been only three years before. He had worn crumpled cotton trousers then, and a loose shirt with a scarlet cloth tied round his neck like a bandit, and Luis had never worn proper shoes in his life before except for his first communion. His mother had carried them for him to the church in a paper bag and he had squeezed his feet into the borrowed monsters of leather brogue just to hobble down the aisle and back. Instead of his customary machete, Luis Aguirre now flaunted a massive bundle of keys. At night he tippled on Benedictine and Cointreau swigged from the hundreds of bottles that were in his keep. Lucien carried nine-tenths of his home on his back. Luis Aguirre had had to leave all of his behind him in el Llano.

Lucien wondered how he could repay the man for his

sacrifice and his loyalty. If he gave him money, Luis might go on such a binge that he died of alcohol poisoning. He thought for a while more, and then he said,

'What would you do, Luis, if you owned all of this?'

'I'd go back to San Fernando, Señor Lucien,' he answered simply.

'And what about all this?'

Luis shrugged as though to imply that it would just be left.

'And if you had a lot of money, what would you do with it? I mean, if you were in San Fernando.'

'I would play the game that you play with the wheel, señor.'

'Roulette?'

'Yes, señor.'

'Why?' Lucien asked him.

'I have seen how men go for it—what they do. It has power.'

'It can ruin you. Finish you.'

'I know,' Luis answered in the same monotone that he used whenever anyone tried to dissuade him from something.

'Well, if you played, and won, you'd have the money, but you said you didn't want riches, so why bother?'

'For the power. You have played and you have the power, but you always had it: Misia Schmutter chose you and she gave it to you, but I am Luis Aguirre and it is different for me—'

'But you have power here at Niemenberg, you're my deputy,' Lucien interrupted.

'I want the power that has no name, the kind that people sense and step out of the way for.'

'If you had the money, and you played roulette, and you lost it, wouldn't you kick yourself afterwards, every time you wanted something? You'd always be thinking, if I hadn't lost that money at the tables I could have what I wanted now.'

'No, Señor Lucien, if I played and failed, I would think: at least I tried. I did my best, what I wanted. Someone like me doesn't get the chance to do what he wants; sometimes it doesn't matter whether you win or lose, there is power in being able to do it.'

'And if you didn't get the chance to play, then what would you do, Luis?'

Luis shrugged. It was clear that he had enjoyed the conversation, in fact he would have happily talked all night of such things. Lucien saw his disappointment and said briskly, 'We shall be leaving for San Fernando tomorrow morning at six o'clock sharp.'

Luis shook his fingers in a way that he had when he was pleased. When he reached the door, he turned and said, 'I would buy a ploughshare and two fat oxen to hire out, and I would ask Carmen Diaz from La Cañada to marry me, señor.'

'And would she?'

'She would if I had the ploughshare and the oxen.' Luis smiled, and left Lucien while he went to make ready for the journey.

Lucien made his own preparations, packing the things that would always travel with him, such as the huge gothic German bible, and Misia Schmutter's trinkets, and some clothes for himself, and his photos of Mariana and a jade necklace she had left behind. As an afterthought, he added the passport he had had made ready to join her. He packed them all into two small leather trunks, then he emptied the contents of his safe into a third one, and made his way down to the stables, where Niemen was lying restlessly awake.

'Poor Niemen,' he said, stroking the old bull's battered nose. 'You'd probably like to go home too, though sometimes I think you don't like anything any more, not since you've got so rheumatic.' Niemen was frothing slightly at the mouth as he chewed. It was a long time since he had frisked or played with Lucien, and he no longer even answered his call with a steady lowing as he had been accustomed to. But Lucien thought that Niemen liked to hear him talk, and he would go to sit with him, breathing in the familiar smell of creosote and manure, and speak to him in a low, soothing voice for an hour or so at a time.

Now and again he thought of taking Luis Aguirre to a casino and giving him money to play with, although, for some reason, he felt a great reluctance to go out that night. Eventually, as eleven o'clock chimed, and Niemen had been asleep for nearly two hours and was snorting and blowing like a dying engine, Lucien made up his mind. He would go to a casino. He made his way through the huddles of drunken or embracing bodies that cluttered the corridors between the stable and the servants' wing. He found Luis fast asleep on a mattress on the floor; beside him lay the bed he had never used. As Lucien shook him by the shoulder he awoke like a true Llanero, springing up with a knife in his hand.

'It's me; Lucien.'

'Oh, forgive me,' Luis said sheepishly, and then added more gruffly, 'They'd slit my throat for these keys.'

Lucien took his servant to one of the smaller casinos around Sabana Grande, and he gave him one thousand dollars to gamble with. Luis Aguirre held the money in his hand and stared at it in a kind of daze. It was one thousand days of wages.

'How much of it do you want to gamble?' Lucien asked him.

'All of it.'

'It is better to keep at least half,' Lucien advised him.

'I want to use it all,' Luis insisted stubbornly.

Lucien shrugged.

'How much would you play, Señor Lucien, if it was yours?'

'All of it,' Lucien admitted with a smile. 'But I am me . . .'

'And you are the king of the tables, that is what they call you, I know, but just for one night I want to test my chance.'

There were many witnesses that night to the Llanero who lost a fortune, and Lucien who broke his own spell. No two accounts were exactly alike. The sums of money involved varied, for Luis from one to fifty thousand dollars, and for Lucien truly astronomical sums. What all the people did agree on was that the two Llaneros were two losers. Luis played first, alone, and he lost six times in a row; on the seventh turn he won, and his brown face flushed purple with excitement; then he lost five more times, and all his money was gone, his brief fortune. Lucien had no wish to play that night, but he took pity on Luis Aguirre, who was stunned and trembling, and who had already twice asked in a broken voice, 'Is that all?' That was when Lucien began to play, and for the first time since his arrival in Caracas five years before, the roulette wheel turned and he lost. Even the inscrutable croupier, who in fourteen years of service had never so much as raised an eyebrow while a game was being played, uttered a shriek. The audience gasped, Luis Aguirre swore, one of the players fell off his chair, another left the room with a sudden attack of diarrhoea, and for five minutes the room was in an uproar. Only Lucien seemed unperturbed. He hadn't wanted to play that night, after all.

The hold that Lucien had had over the city ended on that night. While he was winning, everyone was with him. Once he lost, he became no better than any other man. The fact that he had become famous by his first extraordinary win no longer mattered; that was history now. He could have stopped playing after his one astonishing loss, but something in him egged him on, whether it was boredom or daredevilry or his grandmother at his back, he didn't know, but he went on to play and play again, losing and losing and losing in a phenomenal streak of bad luck. News of it spread, and in no time the casino was packed full of onlookers, all there to see the great Lucien fall from his pinnacle. Several men crossed themselves and held their fingers up to ward off the Evil Eye. Lucien felt himself dragged down by the wheel. It was spinning his brain, turning it into thin strips and then squeezing them back together again. It would not let him down, he was dizzy, he couldn't win, he didn't care, so he couldn't win. He had to care. Misia Schmutter was whispering to him in her shrill voice, he had to win! He had lost to her over and over again. Why shouldn't he just lose now in this vortex of faces round the board? He didn't care. Misia Schmutter was screaming in his ear, in Spanish, in German, she was choking him with her spidery arms. He wouldn't listen, and she was pulling his hair.

'Lucien,' she was shouting, 'you have to care! Get back the initiative or you are lost.'

When Lucien's losses passed the million dollar mark, and he had signed his hundred and third credit slip, the manager of the casino swooned with joy and shock and had to be carried upstairs by his staff, where he remained unconscious for the rest of the night, thus failing to see the remainder of Lucien's failed bets, and the final turn of his bad luck with three successive wins at the end of his spree. Although Luis Aguirre had sustained his own loss like a true soldier, he was reduced almost to tears by Lucien's. By four-thirty of that same morning, when Lucien sent him home with two armed guards from the casino to collect his waiting suitcase of cash and bring it back there to pay his colossal debt, everyone at Niemenberg knew that Lucien had lost his winning knack. Not everyone believed it, but everyone had heard the news. Lucien paid his debt from his suitcase of bank notes, and the crowd was impressed. It even circulated a second, revised story to partly contradict the first, for some hours previously, word had been sent round that the great Lucien was bankrupt and would have to sell Niemenberg and the coat on his back to pay. Now the story was told that he had lost more than half of his fortune.

Lucien was exhausted, and he slept for an hour or so on the brocaded chaise-longue that stood opposite the chesterfield where the manager himself lay unconscious. Luis Aguirre woke his master just after six, when the city was either collapsing its way into bed or groping its way out of it, and only the peasants were out on the streets. The route to San Fernando took a third of the time it had done five years before, with no Niemen to hinder their progress and no donkeys to slow them down. Instead they had their own horses and three mules to take the luggage. Luis Aguirre had suggested taking one of the many cars that Lucien kept gleaming in the empty parts of the stables. The road, however, was mostly a dirt track, and if it rained there might be no road. Instead, they rode for seven hours a day, and within the week they were home again on the parched grass patchwork of San Fernando, scarcely having needed to fire the battery of guns that Luis had so carefully prepared for them.

El Patrón's first words were, 'You should never have left me, Lucien.' And for the ten days that Lucien remained at San Fernando, he never once swerved from the same plaintive tone of neglect.

Lucien was more distressed to see how shabby his home was, compared to the brilliance of Niemenberg, than by his father's complaints. He had come prepared to face his father's death, and he felt vaguely cheated by el Patrón's recovery. By the side of Niemenberg, the old estate house had shrunk to the size of a mere shack. The paint and lime were peeling from the walls, and the woodworm were crumbling away the gables. In some of the corners, the powdered lime that had always been swept away each day before dawn was allowed to lie three inches deep, together with its trophies of brittle wings and mandibles.

The land was still the same land, stretching out to the horizon, and the cattle still had four legs and a hide, even if his irrigation channels were silted up and his new fences broken. Then the pens were ruined where bits of them had been torn off for firewood for cooking. The garden was a wasteland compared to the garden at Niemenberg, and Misia Schmutter's disused wing of the house didn't seem grand enough for her. Each morning, the plain country food was laid on the tables, and Lucien noticed the occasional sour taste in the corn or the beans, and the flies stuck and hovered over the chipped Dresden plates. Lucien felt almost ashamed of the place, and then doubly ashamed at the feeling. He compared the servants with their makeshift cotton frocks and their eternal cloth slippers and their missing teeth to the swarms of efficient staff at Niemenberg, or indeed at any affluent city house. Such was his desperation during his stay at the dilapidated place of his birth, that he took to shooting down birds in the evening, just as his father had done before him. Out in the hinterland, Luis Aguirre told and retold his tales, fanning his master's fame to even greater heights, and also becoming something of a hero himself as the peasant who had scorned wealth for the sake of it.

El Patrón heard the shots ringing out across the plain, and the squawks of the small birds as they fell, with a kind of grim pleasure. Lucien spurned all the invitations he was sent from the neighbouring towns: he could think of nothing he wanted less than to visit more such houses as his own faded realm, and his heart sank at the thought of dancing some heavy joropo with a string of shy, chaperoned country girls all out to trick him into a proposal. He filled his days by ordering new bed linen and tablecloths, and replacing the moth-eaten hammocks for newly woven ones, and the servants' sleeping mats for fresher stock. He sent for new china and bought new pots. Then he bought each of the many maids a new length of material for a frock, and he paid the estate seamstress in advance to make them up. Lastly, he gave Luis Aguirre a ploughshare and two oxen.

Lucien spent the last of his ten-day visit at the cemetery. Both Misia Schmutter's and Chucho Delgado's graves were overgrown with trails of bindweed and ipomoea. He sat for hours on his dead sister's grave, comparing the childish Katrina to Mariana—they had had the same eyes and the same hair and the same obsessions. He saw tht on his grandmother's tomb the word 'witch' had been scratched into the slab. He felt her wince at his back. Although they didn't stone witches at San Fernando, he remembered the tales of her homeland, and he scraped the letters out of the tombstone and wondered if it was the taunts that had hardened Misia Schmutter into the scourge she became, or had it been the desolation of the plains? Lucien packed his travelling bags and took his leave of el Patrón.

'Goodbye, father,' he said, as briskly as he could.

'How can you leave me now, like this, Lucien?'

'I have to get back.'

'Back to what?'

'Back to the city. I —'

'Go then!' el Patrón said irritably. 'Nobody cares if I die here, not one of you.' El Patrón paused, and then looked at Lucien with a strange inquiring expression, then he said, 'Do you know, sometimes I could swear my mother was in the room. She seems to come and go with you.'

Lucien smiled, uneasily. 'You'll be all right, father.'

'Can you feel her in this room?' el Patrón insisted.

'It's her house,' Lucien said.

'But it should be my house now,' his father moaned. 'When will I get anything? You've brought her back with you, Lucien, that's what you've done, and I don't care now if you do go so long as you take *her* away.' Then he turned over pettishly, leaving the back of his greying head for his son to take his final leave of. Lucien touched it, and el Patrón shot away from his hand, then he turned back and stared at Lucien in alarm. 'Who are you?' he whispered.

'I am Lucien.'

But his father would not believe it, and finally Lucien left so as not to agitate him further. It was a sad ride for him, his return to Caracas, alone, with his thoughts and his uneasy guilt. The more he thought of his decaying home in San Fernando, the more he felt a kind of anger at Niemenberg: the place had come between him and his upbringing, it had blasted a hole in his beloved Llano, a hole in his hopes and dreams, and he worried what troubles might not come in through the breach now.

Chapter 19

Lucien had been away from Caracas for twenty-five days altogether, and that was a long time to be away when your luck was down. It was rumoured that he had fled in shame, and his name, so recently admired and revered, was ridiculed in his absence. Guests still came and went at Niemenberg, but they came more than ever as though it was their right to do so. Some of the old habitués even went into Lucien's private chambers, and people like the Arismendis and the Rangels, who had been banished from the house, returned and flaunted their presence. Vases and trinkets were spoiled, the door to the wine cellar was kicked in, and the wine was pillaged. As each day passed and the master of the house did not return, the last strands of restraint were broken. Major Detlev had managed to control things for the first few days, but he was very aware of the damage of a scandal, and he withdrew to his barracks before the first week was up, and washed his hands of the affair. He felt that he had salvaged at least some of his brother's more valuable possessions; what more could he do?

As more and more people came in off the streets, riffraff of every description who ate and drank and stole, the regular servants fled, armed with whatever they could load on to handcarts or donkeys. Without staff, excess became chaos. There was no one to sweep the vomit from the floors or disinfect the closets, no one to change the cloths or wash the glasses, no one to gather up the dregs or scrape away the leftover, rotting food. Mountains of putrid seafood began to melt over the tablecloths; in the kitchens, pots of stale rice and dozens of unserved chickens in aspic, sides of beef and half-stuffed tunas, formed a breeding ground for maggots. The gangrenous smell of neglected flesh began to waft over the slopes of the valley. While vultures hovered over the chimneys, drunken and unruly visitors ransacked the store-rooms and then trampled and stripped the gardens and greenhouses of their fruits. The gardeners were so angry that just before the final onslaught they sprayed the peaches and nectarines and the tomatoes and the medlars with a good coating of copper sulphate. As the mob stampeded through their maze of beautifully clipped hedges, trampling the precious herbs and falling into the fountains, they packed up their meagre belongings and prepared to leave. They would go to San Antonio de los Altos and throw in their lot with the Swiss market gardeners at El Sitio.

Lastly, the frenzied visitors rummaged through the stables in their search for food, and they came across Niemen, Lucien's tired but still magnificent bull, whom the servants had forgotten in their haste to get away. They dragged the reluctant animal into the great hall, and while some of the men broke up Lucien's priceless tables and chairs to make a fire in the hearth of the great hall, others prepared to sacrifice Niemen, the best-loved of bulls. This happened on the very day that Lucien returned to town. Had he not arrived in such a state of melancholy, he might have been able to prevent it. As it was, he rested at one of the casino hotels that he knew so well, and it was after he had rested and won back a part of the fortune that he had so recently lost, that he discovered Ulises drinking guiltily in a corner of the bar.

Ulises had been one of the most frequent guests at Niemenberg. He had been there on the first day, and he was there on the last. Even after Lucien's luck changed, Ulises was drawn there by a kind of morbid fascination. Many of the guests had given up going to Niemenberg in its last week but some, like Ulises, felt unable to tear themselves away. Although they were not the first to break down doors or ruin the garden, they followed behind as a kind of uncommitted rearguard. They suffered, along with the worst of them, the ravages of enteritis after the gardeners' revenge, and then they too were caught up in the hysteria of the wreckers.

Ulises, however, was one of the few who could see more to Lucien than his genial mask. Perhaps he did what he did out of gratitude for having been relieved of Mariana and her grievances, or perhaps he did it because he sometimes felt a shudder when he was in the same room as Lucien, a kind of inexplicable fear. Whatever his reason, and it might just have been disgust, he was the one to remonstrate with the vandals and to tell Lucien that Niemenberg had gone mad and Niemen himself had been slaughtered.

'What do you mean, slaughtered?' Lucien asked.

'They're roasting him.'

'Who are they?'

'You wouldn't know half of them; they've taken over things while you were away.'

Lucien was silent, his face was unnaturally still. Ulises watched him with alarm. There was no Latin choler, no visible wrath or grief, just the slow ticking of Lucien's brain and the hair standing out on Ulises' own neck on the gooseflesh that was creeping all over him.

'What will you do?' Ulises finally ventured to ask.

'It doesn't look as if there is anything to do,' Lucien said calmly.

'They have broken up the house, vandalised it,' Ulises said, spurring his friend on to some sort of revenge.

But Lucien was unreachable, and he said only, 'Guests are like parasites really.'

'All the servants left days ago,' Ulises continued.

'What about the gardeners?'

'They stayed until yesterday, but they went too after the garden was spoilt.'

Ulises saw the faint flush at this mention of the garden, and he felt the air tense around him.

Lucien waited a moment and then he said, 'I'll be on my way now.'

He held out his hand to Ulises and shook it warmly. Then he clicked his heels in the way he had learnt as a small child, like a Prussian officer, and he rode with his baggage to the hill over Niemenberg, past the vultures circling over the turreted roofs, past the heavy smell of decay, past the clatter and banging of drums and bands inside, and past the curl of acrid smoke that unfurled itself from the barley-twist chimney of the great hall. Lucien hardly paused beside his house; instead he spurred his weary horse on to Detlev's barracks on the outskirts of the city, and rode through the whirring twilight with his eyes half-closed in thought.

Detlev was in the second officer's mess when his brother arrived, and a steward called him out. He was amazed to find that Lucien the man was no different from Lucien the boy, the strange emotionless machine of always.

'How was father?' Detlev asked.

'He's all right.'

'I thought it might have been taps for him,' Detlev said.

'No, he's as strong as an ox.'

Detlev blushed scarlet at the mention of an ox, and he asked Lucien, 'Have you been to Niemenberg?'

'Ulises told me what happened,' he said pleasantly. Detlev was so relieved to hear this calm reply that he called for a bottle of champagne and for some of his fellow officers to join them. He had been fearing a scandal, duels and revenge. He had become very conscious of his reputation lately, and this business with the ox had threatened to ruin his chances of promotion. He would have to stand by Lucien, whatever he did. He was, after all, his own brother.

'Where will you stay?' he asked.

'I am going away,' Lucien told him.

'Where will you go?'

'Oh, just abroad.'

Detlev emptied his glass and instantly refilled it. This was wonderful news indeed. Lucien guessed his brother's thoughts, and drank up and left him. On his way out of the barracks he bribed the guard on yard duty to fetch him another bottle of liquor. Fifty Bolívars for a fifty cent drink. Then, while the guard was gone, Lucien picked the lock of the ammunition store, filled his pockets and his waistband with dynamite, locked the store-room again, and waited casually in the yard for the duty guard to reappear from Detlev's rooms with the necessary bottle of rum. 'Vaya con Dios,' the duty guard called after him. Go with God. Lucien was struck by the prophetic note of the words, for such was his intention.

Lucien was a great believer in popular myth. He liked the embellishments that were added to a tale as it passed by word of mouth from one voice to the next. Such storytellers always had a certain magic in their words, and when this ingredient was missing, they would add it themselves.

Names and numbers and times had to sound right, to add force to a story. Lucien appreciated this, and he would, when he could, accommodate this need in his work. So he chose to blow up Niemenberg, not at ten or eleven in the evening, but on the very stroke of midnight, knowing that such a precise time would put the fear of God into the populace, and also sound better in the retelling.

He planted his dynamite in seven strategic positions and then he waited for the great Cathedral clock to chime and echo through the low valley with its sumptuous mansions and its slums. Never before, and never again, would a mansion as splendid as Niemenberg raise its face on the terraced slopes. The flagstaffs and the chimneys, the turrets and the shafts and the blocks of window bays in yard upon yard of stone and brick façade, would never be repeated. No such gothic folly would rise to replace it, nor would there again be such a clearly schizophrenic house, with its northern front and its southern back. It was an old hand Lucien was playing as he waited to blow up his creation. He had destroyed his gazebos, his childhood pavilions, and now he would blow up his gothic palace. His glorious design would collapse into a massive tomb around Nieman, his symbol, the bull who had died and been cremated and eaten inside. That night, there was no need for Misia Schmutter to tell him what to do, he knew already. At ten minutes to twelve he climbed down the slope and into his own back garden, scrambling over the railings as the urchins who had first tended his grounds had done. At four minutes to twelve he lit his seven fuses, and was irritated by having to use three separate tapers for the job. At one minute to twelve he ran back through the orchard and out over the railings. He was half-way to his horse when the first explosion came.

Lucien watched and listened; there were six explosions, and with each one another part of his house leapt into the air and hurled itself back down into the ground. For some minutes the explosions drowned any other sounds. Lucien could see people running out of the side door of the house, some of them with their clothes in flames, and he could hear screams over the sound of falling masonry. He waited a while for the seventh explosion, but none came. 'That', he thought sadly, 'is the difference between army ammunition and your own.' There was always someone ready to slice off a fatter margin of profit by cheating here and there.

Niemen was dead and buried, and the fantasy skyline of Niemenberg was gone. Lucien rode along the newly-surfaced Camino Real that wound its way along the edge of the narrow escarpment to La Guaira, and the port, and whatever ship would carry him away. Behind him, for many miles of his route, he could see the column of smoke that rose up from Niemenberg for many hours afterwards as it burnt. Days later, the rubble and ashes would still be smouldering, but Lucien would be at sea by then, past the island of Trinidad and the Caribbean reefs, and he wouldn't know about the treasure hunting that would take place in the hot remains of his mansion.

Lucien's only previous contact with a ship had been when he saw off his German gardener when the man enlisted and went home, so this night-time arrival at the docks was confusing. Access to the ships seemed like a far from easy matter, and in the dark there was no knowing either what the vessels were like, or where they were bound. Lucien tethered his horse and waited for more than half an hour, simply staring at the different hulls and wondering which one to choose and how to board it once the decision was made. He began to feel a kind of prickling on his skin that he always felt as dawn was about to break. Then a group of sailors came stumbling towards him. He uncocked his pistol for safe measure, and approached the men. They were speaking some form of German.

'Entschuldigen Sie,' Lucien said in his best gardener's German, while barring their way all the while.

'What do you want?' they asked him rudely.

'I want to enlist,' Lucien explained politely. 'I need to sail home.'

'More fool you,' one of the sailors scoffed.

'Shut up,' another of the men said sharply, adding in an undertone, 'how do you know who he is?'

'It would be worth a great deal to me,' Lucien insisted.

'Like how much?'

'Like fifty dollars apiece,' Lucien told them, guessing that the ubiquitous fifty would speak where patriotism failed.

'How do we get it?' the men asked together.

'Take me on board your ship.'

'As a stowaway?'

'No, as a passenger.' Then he added, 'When do you sail?'

'At eight o'clock, to Hamburg.'

'Ist gut,' Lucien told them. 'Take me with you.'

The men had been almost convinced, but they grew suspicious again and restless.

'What if we don't?' their spokesman asked, with a hint of rudeness back in his voice.

'I'll shoot your head off.'

'There are four of us,' the spokesman pointed out warily.

'I have six bullets,' Lucien told him and showed them his gun.

'What have you done?' the sailor asked.

'Nothing yet,' Lucien replied.

By some good chance, the four men were crew members of the luxury liner *Gelria*. Thus, far from the voyage of deprivation that Lucien had envisaged might be his lot, he found himself thrown into the ordered extravagance of the *Gelria's* decks as one of her first-class passengers. From the Empire style of the dining-saloon with its ivory enamel and its Cuban mahogany and its glass dome, to the social hall and the promenade deck, or the smoking-room or the cricket pitch which was a leftover from its Anglicised Dutch days, the library or the heavy veining of the marble barber's shop, Lucien was very much in his element.

His German, polished by the three gardeners who had worked for him, was good enough to fool the Spanish-speaking members of the crew and passengers, and just fluent enough to hold the attention of the native Germans. Lucien loved the voyage. The food was excellent, and the decor, though a little faded, suited his present taste; it was not furnished in the style of the day, but carried with it a hint of the grace of his early childhood. It had a pre-Great War feel to it and seemed to sum up virtually all the periods that had gone before that terrible defeat. One room would be Louis XIV and another old Dutch style, with a Rennie Mackintosh verandah café, and an art deco suite. It was all a three-dimensional education for Lucien, from which he fled occasionally to the quiet of his own cabin, which was by no means one of the *Gelria's* best cabins, but then, he had booked a little late.

Chapter 20

L*UCIEN SPENT NINE MONTHS COMBING THROUGH HIS PAST*
along the banks of the Elbe, and the Niemen, and during
that time he did not once write to his family, nor did he
send any word to his friends. Mariana alone received a
cryptic telegram in the summer. It said, 'I am in Tilsit,
where the stones have killed witches. It is all stones. Lucien.'

Tilsit had been a great disappointment to him. He should
have known better. Misia Schmutter had described it to
him, sparing no details of its inbred savagery and its desolation. She had described the sense of humiliation that
clung to the town ever since Napoleon's treaty with Russia
there. It was a place of defeat. And yet Lucien had gone
there like a pilgrim to a shrine. It was no wonder that he
was nearly strangled every day of the nine days that he
remained in that wasteland of witchhunters and shame.

Everywhere he went, through the dry swept streets, or
past the warehouses of baled flax and hemp, or past the
shops with the food knotted and coiled into strange shapes,
the townspeople stared at him with open hostility. The
butchers with fat fists of Wurtz hung in their windows, and
long white sausages like whole guts strung over bars, and
others, bulging on dipped slabs like stuffed foreskins, glared
at him. The bakers with their weirdly plaited loaves, and
high bread bursting over its tins, marked him out for their
dislike.

They seemed to sense the presence of his aged passenger. Even the children threw stones. It was just a small
group of children who banded together to follow Lucien,

and they went no further than hurling two or three tentative pebbles, but the will was there, the instinctive urge to throw and kill, even in these bewildered urchins. Lucien would remember, well into his nine thousand days of imprisonment, counted and measured as they were to be into routine and fantasy, the children of Tilsit with their stones. And the children themselves would remember how they followed a stranger down the streets one day, before the war, having spotted him for the outsider he was by his air of detachment and his gait. He walked like a gunslinger in a film, like a man who needs a horse between his legs. These children lived in a world of silent pressure; tadpoles in a cauldron that was about to boil over. No wonder they followed the stranger, Lucien, bowed under an invisible weight, with his fingers twitching in the unaccustomed frost as though for a gun, and his eyes as vacant as the River Niemen. They threw taunts at his cold stare, stones at his strange bones. They would have thrown more, but no sooner had they begun than this man with the arctic eyes turned round and faced them, and they were afraid and stopped. Lucien said nothing, he just stared, and the light from his eyes fixed the gangling children to the spot.

These children lived in fear, it was like a winter coat to them, and like the river wind itself. It soothed and slapped by turns. It was in their mothers' rare kisses and in their more frequent threats, in their teachers' cajoling and in their foreboding, it was in their sticks. It was in the air. It blew in off the Niemen with fears of the Russian North, of Russian bears, of Cossacks whom they believed ate babies and sliced off women's breasts for fun. It came in on the railway track, in the freight trains and in the plush seats of the passenger carriages, and the wooden slats of the third class. It was on the wireless with the daily speeches and the incitement to rally and riot and march. It was part of the Third Reich that they were all fragments of, so it was part of them.

The fear they felt when Lucien turned his eyes on them was something that would last through the rise and fall of their Führer, through the war and the famine that followed. Of the seven children who taunted Lucien, three would die in the war; one as an apprentice mechanic trapped down a hole in the wake of an incendiary raid, and two in their grey uniforms, conscripted with the other adolescents towards the end of the war, shouldering rifles which they knew how to load but not how to clean. As for the others, even while the tanks rolled and the bullets whined, they felt again the terrible cold that had lodged in their shins like a crippling ache from the coldest eyes they had ever seen. They were the only people ever to see the full force of Misia Schmutter in Lucien.

Misia Schmutter had worked hard on Lucien, kneading and moulding him to the model in her mind. She had moulded his every thought even, obsessed by his and her ability to create shapes. Her compatriots all shared in this manic shaping of soft things, be they bread or meat or boys. Sometimes, from something overstrained inside herself, Misia Schmutter had overworked her material, grazing and bruising Lucien in the process. Lucien knew that it was, in turn, something specific that had made her do this: and he knew that the Tilsit witchhunt was somewhere near the core of the thing. There were stones for her learning, ridicule for her rare knowledge. If she had been a midwife, they might have torn out her hair. If she chose to be a scholar, they would beat the woman out of her: stones for her herbs, stones for her bones. So, when Lucien turned on the taunting boys, he was not turning on thoughtless urchins, but on the children who would have murdered his grandmother, and who were unrelenting even after her death. He was turning on the implacable cruelty of the Prussian polders.

Misia Schmutter had moulded him into a wunderkind, or as near to one as the thorny Llanos would allow. And she taught him that only actions speak. Words, she had told him, could not speak at all. She made of him a human grenade, and the boys in Tilsit dislodged the pin. Lucien returned to Hamburg, and then to Brazil and Caracas, not just as a man with a tiger on his back, but with his own claws drawn, and with a mission so strong, no man or law could stop him. Only death could have halted his life's work then, and Lucien knew that, together with his solitary cause, he was destined to be a survivor.

It was a dreary journey from Tilsit to Hamburg, involving two days of travel on draughty overcrowded trains. Perversely, Lucien chose not to travel first-class in comfort and some degree of privacy, but opted rather to sit squeezed between the small farmers with their sacks of produce, and the soldiers and market women and families of chilblained children being shunted from one stop to another, visiting and returning in the hope of easing the tension. But the tension was always there, it boarded the train at Tilsit with them, and it climbed out of the overcrowded carriage at Königsberg. It was there in the Polish Corridor, and it was still in the train at Elbing and Marienberg and at Neustettin and Stargard and Schönfliess and Berlin. Lucien changed trains here, but the new train, with its crowd of dull and eager faces, more uniformed than before, held the tension strained between its blackened roof and its stained swept floors just the same, and though the other passengers came and went, it was still there, at Neustadt and Wittenberge and Ludwigslust as well. Lucien travelled along this scooped-out channel of suppressed hysteria, feeling its prickle on his skin.

All the signs of the devil, he thought, conspired within him on the trains. He crossed his legs with a smile and looked through the window at the rushing countryside. Even the train had an air of suppressed excitement about it. People looked from one corner of the carriage to another surreptitiously. Lucien could feel the mixture of pride and apprehension in his fellow travellers. The most self-righteous stared about them, trying to discover any sign of subversion, or unorthodox thoughts. Lucien noticed something of himself in them. They too had a sense of purpose, but while his own was a solitary purpose for a common good that very few could see, their new German pride seemed to depend on numbers. There was no single aim, it appeared, but a mass dream, a seductive dream, that swallowed whole towns in rally after rally as Caracas had first swallowed him, like an endless boa constrictor, crushing and dribbling until the last drop of will was gone.

Lucien had listened when he could to the views and aims of the National Socialists and they sounded like good aims. They were the sort of aims, when laid out in a manifesto or heard on the wireless, that most Germans, or indeed most Venezuelans or Britons, would agree with. But why the frenzy, Lucien wondered? Such moderate views as he heard in the shops and bars, how could they produce such hysteria? Everywhere he went, Lucien could sense this over-winding of nerves and emotions, it was a land of clockwork tears and joy. They were, he suspected, not real tears like the tears of Llaneras, but crocodile tears and tears of relief. It was as though all the clock keys in all the cities had been diverted to wind up the populace. Half the people he saw were as tense as himself: millions of grenades without their pins, waiting for the signal to let themselves go.

As his train sidled into Ludwigslust, two weary days after he had left East Prussia far behind him, he reflected that if all the world were supermen, they would probably become cannibals and eat each other or there wouldn't be hands enough to bury the dead. There was a smell like offal in the air, hot offal such as he had grown up with on the plains. Through the window, as the train departed, he could see the skyscape of factory chimneys; there wasn't much to choose between hot offal and the chemical smell of industrial Germany working round the clock. Only Hamburg remained aloof, unruffled and unperturbed by the avalanche of tension that was heaping up around it. Of all the towns and cities down the line, only Hamburg didn't seem to care. In Hamburg, according to his drinking companions, the Berkenmeyers and the Rieppels, the Führer was not the Führer as elsewhere in Germany. He was just a little man whom they could not follow because, they assured Lucien, he was not 'comme il faut'.

Place, Lucien thought, was nine-tenths of action. If he had been reared in Tilsit instead of San Fernando, would he stone strangers too? Would he cheer and scream at the rallies? Would he despise the Jews as they did in Munich, and would he torment them too? If his master had been this small new man instead of his own Misia Schmutter, what would he have been like? The arrival of the train at Hamburg ended his idle conjecture. He stepped out on to the platform carrying his heavy Gladstone bag, with his massive bible and his box of eggshells and the rest of his and his grandmother's things, and he was what he was, and that was no part of the new Germany.

In Tilsit the earth was all sand, and it was a barren land that blew up and blinded its inhabitants, and between this outback of East Prussia and the great port itself on the banks of the Elbe, the sand in the hourglass that was everyone's time was being hurried through the widened waistline of the glass. Events were being precipitated, nothing would wait. Lucien had crossed the country and he knew from the violence of his own upbringing that there was blood in the air. Then, in Hamburg, there was sand as well. But it was the sand that the noble inhabitants of that free city buried their heads in.

Hamburg had known too many disasters to worry about an upstart in power. They had been razed by fire; they had suffered war and plague, and survived. In this December of 1938, whatever anxiety had found its way into the city had been squeezed out by the coming of Christmas, only four days away. The first snows had fallen, and Lucien made his way through the melting slush on the pavement to St Peter's Church, and then took a taxi to his small hotel on the Marienterrasse, to the Pension Helbig, where he lodged modestly during his stay there. It was seven o'clock, and through the darkness he could see glimpses of the armbands of the Jews, like so many darting stars in the night as they made their way home before their curfew at seven-thirty. It was the only time when many Jews could be seen on the streets, this brief half-hour of hurrying home. Lucien noticed them more and more, he stared after the hurried, banded figures, trying to see a young orange-seller from the market whom he desired. It did not surprise him that she wasn't there, he only ever saw this girl, Maria Hahns, on market days.

In the narrow hall of his hotel, a dwarfed Christmas tree had been decked for the guests and it shone with newly-dusted glass balls and glittering chains, chocolate rings and the local Benidt-Kringel and sausage made of marzipan. After his recent experience in Tilsit, Lucien found this last detail rather grotesque, but it was Christmas, and Christmas was a time of goodwill to all men, except, it seemed, to the underdogs: so the Jews in Germany, and the Negroes in America, and the Algerians in France and the Irish in Britain, all slunk home through the safest alleys that they could while the others prepared for their feast.

Lucien changed his clothes, and shaved himself and then went down to the Michelsen, the restaurant next door to his hotel. There he ordered his plate of soup and his veal and potatoes and the almost obligatory sauerkraut, and waited for his new-found friends to arrive. It was not long before Franz and Carl von Ledebur appeared, the latter whistling the opening of 'Oh Du Froliche' as a token of Christmas cheer while he pulled a chair round to Lucien's table and sat on it backwards, straddled as over a horse.

Lucien liked Carl von Ledebur best of the two. He was a member of the Luftwaffe, and his younger brother, Franz, was a very minor officer in an Artillery Corps. They were soon joined by a young houseman from the Barmbeck Hospital and a listless young man whose interest in clothing, particularly his own, far surpassed any fleeting interest he might have in an imminent war. This last arrival, Rudi Schlensog, drank with Lucien because it seemed, to him inexplicably so, the thing to do. Notwithstanding he was piqued by Lucien's rival looks and insouciance. For one so naturally idle, Rudi Schlensog devoted a great deal of time to trying to undermine Lucien.

Lucien discovered, sitting round his table at the Michelsen, that he had become more restless than he had realised with his trip to Tilsit. He could no longer sit with this crowd of dandies, listening to Carl expound on his brilliant future in the air, and Rudi drone on about his constant boredom. Lucien had returned as a machine already in motion. He stood up abruptly, took his leave of his astonished companions and went out into the Hamburg night, catching his breath in the frosted air as he stepped into the streetlight. He wished that he could see Maria Hahns, the girl from the fruit market who had eyes like Mariana's, but he didn't know where she lived. He had asked, but she wouldn't tell. Jews didn't mix with Arians, not even foreign ones, not even in Hamburg any more, too much sand had been scraped through the hour-glass for that. So he waited, and once a week he saw her, selling oranges and apples in the market, always with gloves so that she would not contaminate the fruit, and her stall was always the emptiest there, as more and more people preferred to buy elsewhere: apples from ungloved fingers sold better. Lucien would have liked to spend the night with her, and many nights more after that. He could feel that Misia Schmutter did not approve, not, he believed, from antiSemitism, but because of the peasant blood in Maria Hahns's veins. Misia Schmutter liked good blood to flow, and traced veins that went back for generation after generation, breeding morals and social codes tighter than stays. She had not approved of Mariana either, but perhaps she would forgive her a little now that Mariana had taken back the initiative and doused the scorn and put a gold frame around her bank account.

In Caracas, people were people, peasants or élite, with a

cross pattern that made up a dull tartan where new wealth had chequered the old blood with its liquid riches. Mariana had not been half-Jewish in Caracas, she had been first, before he knew her, la Niña Mariana, daughter of Don Luis Cifuentes; later she became anything from 'you know who', to 'that shameless one', and later still, just 'la Millionaria', but never a Jew. If he had married her in Germany his children would have been branded; his face bore the light, and his children would have carried the stars.

It took him half an hour to walk through the freezing night to the harbour. He could have taken the underground, but even the novelty of that miraculous steel creature couldn't lure him any more. So he walked past the huge blocks of flats with their winter balconies that made up street after street of Hamburg. They were all modern and clean and oblivious of his search, hiding in their well-regulated bowel the whereabouts of Maria Hahns. On market days she would smile at him shyly from above her gloved hands and suffer him to stand beside her stacks of oranges and overhear the obscene remarks that schoolboys shouted at her.

There was a bar that Lucien frequented down by the harbour called the Jungle. It was a sailors' bar, rough and dirty with spit and tobacco glueing the never-too-fresh sawdust to the floor. The décor was like a jungle, with pots of giant ferns surviving miraculously in the hot, foetid air, and a date palm, studded with cigarette burns, gracing one corner in a forlorn and drooping watch. The walls were painted mostly green and brown in a kind of jungle camouflage, and an occasional tropical flower crept out from the painted foliage, once startlingly red or orange, but now faded to a uniform ambery grey. There was a parrot behind the bar, chained disconsolately to a rough metal perch, and much time was spent by sailors on their leave trying to tempt the bird to speak. The parrot, however, with its meticulous if slightly balding feathers, lived in complete silence. He was the only live member of his species in the bar. Around the walls and suspended from the ceiling was a host of parrots and parakeets, macaws and mynah birds, in every hue of red and blue and green, but all stuffed by an ancient taxidermist.

Gernot Sieveking, who had come by chance to be Lucien's closest friend in Hamburg, claimed that he could tell a man's character by the way he spoke to these birds. Those who stumbled on the bar and chanced to venture in were often disconcerted by what they found inside. The interior of the Jungle was a complete contrast to the ordered routines of the port itself, it was a kind of sailors, respite, a place where the more travelled of the citizens, or strangers come to that, could sit in a simulacrum of the tropical disorder that they had learnt to live with and look forward to. Sailors were particularly bad at getting used to staying at home in Hamburg. They would set sail as young men and return only to die. Even when they had families and children to go home to, they would slip out again to the Jungle, fleeing from the regimented blocks of flats with their matching balconies and geraniums and trailing lobelias, and their lifts that never failed and their electric lights that were said to be brighter than anywhere else, and their parks that were so spotless that the keepers replaced the bits of gravel if ever they were kicked out of place. So Gernot Sieveking said that he could tell a man's nature by the way he behaved there.

'That's one of the things I noticed about you.'

'What is?'

'Well, you didn't talk to the parrots. You didn't even smile at them. And that's the first time I've ever seen someone come in new off the street and sit down and not even look at the walls, and not talk to the parrots.'

Lucien smiled.

'So,' Gernot asked, 'why didn't you?'

'Because I could see they were dead,' Lucien explained simply.

'But the one at the bar?' Gernot asked, 'what about him?'

'Well, to tell you the truth, he's so raddled I thought he was dead too.'

'But all the regulars were talking to him.'

'Yes,' Lucien agreed, 'but I thought they were drunk.'

'And the walls and the ferns and lianas, weren't you surprised to see them in Hamburg?'

'No. You see, I was brought up in the tropics, and this is the first time I have travelled abroad, so really I was surprised not to see more such scenes over here.'

Gernot was amused by these answers, and the two struck up a friendship that lasted for the five months that Lucien remained in Germany. The two men were similar in build and looks. Gernot, however, was a poor scholar who had truanted and then left school at fourteen to become a cook's assistant in a Polish restaurant in the Rubenkamp area on the outskirts of the city, in sharp contrast to Lucien's own fortune. It was a long way to go every day, up and down the stairs that led from train to train on the U-bahn, and then through the allotments that made a shortcut to the Poznan, a steamy, depressing restaurant that fed the Polish immigrants all through the week on cheap greasy soups with bits of pork and giant cabbage leaves sloshing about in the broth. On Saturday nights, the place was swept and swabbed, and a band of gypsy musicians was brought in to play while the same Poles who had stinted themselves all week lashed out on a five-course meal of meat and fish and junkety sour puddings, with coffee and vodka and cherry liqueur to follow.

'Why do you work there?' Lucien had asked him early on in their friendship.

'My sister, Vilma, was fool enough to marry a Pole. The Poznan belongs to her brother-in-law, and I was fool enough to want to learn to cook there. I could give you a discourse on washing dishes and scraping up sick. I could lecture in peeling potatoes and picking out slugs from between cabbage leaves from the crack of dawn until night, and lifting giant saucepans from that slimy basement to the clients' bowls, but I hardly ever get to cook.

'Everyone talks about the Jews, and the Poles sigh with relief because it is not they who are getting it. But when we all find that the Jews have been blamed and silenced and robbed and nothing improves, then we'll start looking for another scapegoat. That's the trouble with scapegoats, they have to grow, and then the Poles will have their turn, and then it won't do to be found in that stinking basement. I'm not even a Pole, for God's sake. It's not my problem.'

'So why don't you leave, Gernot?'

'A job is a job, Lucien. There's the job you want to do, and that isn't always the same as the job you have to do.'

'What would you do if you could choose?'

Gernot smiled, then he was silent for a while.

'What would *you* do, Lucien, if you could choose?' he replied eventually.

Now it was Lucien's turn to pause, and then he said,

'If I could choose, I would build a tower taller than any

tower that has been built before, and of such beauty and such perfect proportions that all who saw it, man or beast, would be struck by it, and I would sit on the very top with my bull Niemen beside me, and there would be nothing on my back, no roof even, not even the tiger, and I would breathe whenever I wanted to, and my only duty would be to sit on that tower and breathe and die there when I wanted to, and there would be nothing around my neck, not even a shirt.'

Gernot was puzzled and silent.

'I take it,' Lucien said, 'that you would not choose such a tower yourself.'

'Hardly. I'd be a chef on a merchant ship, and sail to Brazil and save enough money to come back here and open a restaurant on the Andreasstrasse or somewhere really smart like that, and the food would be something that people talked about days after they had eaten it. Pork, you know, Lucien, with a proper flavour and no water or any-thing in it, and steak that you could cut with a spoon if you chose to. That's what I'd do,' Gernot admitted, surprised again, but this time by his own candour.

Before Lucien set out for his visit to Tilsit, he had said to Gernot in their usual dark corner under the stencilled date palm,

'Why go to Brazil? It's hot and full of mosquitoes, and the food would be abominable, you'd be cooking grubs and slugs and ants and things.'

Gernot had become genuinely annoyed. 'You've got no business interfering with other people's dreams,' he said. 'Your bloody tower would probably fall down, but I didn't say that. Did I even comment on this bull thing on top? Did I? So who are you to tell me I wouldn't like Brazil? It's my dream.'

Lucien apologised and sat quietly staring into his Pils, more concerned, had Gernot but known it, with the thought of his imaginary tower falling down than with his friend's bad temper.

'I'll tell you what,' Gernot volunteered, 'let's go down to the Hamburg Amerika office tomorrow and see if they have a vacancy as a chef. If they have, I'll sign on. Yes,' he continued, inspired by his own idea, 'all I need is a refer-ence. Who could give me that? That mean old piece of pig's fat at the Poznan won't for sure.'

'I'll give you a reference,' Lucien said firmly.

Gernot Sieveking signed on to sail on the *Orpheus*. His sailing date was December 23rd and his destination Rio de Janeiro. Lucien found him on the night of his own return from Tilsit sitting sadly in his favourite corner of the Jungle. He didn't see Lucien arrive, so engrossed was he in staring at his beer.

'Gernot,' Lucien called to him, 'what's the matter?'

'I was thinking about the slugs, Lucien,' he said.

Lucien felt immediately cheered on seeing his friend so forlorn, and then he made every effort to reassure and comfort him, but however much he tried, there was always some detail still troubling Gernot. Lucien suggested a walk, and together they strolled through the shadowy docks, beside the ships that were there for loading or unloading with their crews scattered across the city in bars and brothels and nightclubs that could take money in twenty languages, and whose bouncers carried crowbars and chains.

'What's the matter?' Lucien asked his friend again.

'Last night my boss's niece was raped and beaten up.'

'For being a Pole?'

'No, for being a Jew, a Polish Jew. She was only sixteen, I used to fancy her myself, but she had a father who could knock my brains out with one hand, and then she was the kind of girl you wouldn't want to hurt. Marrying is definitely not for me. I'm not one of those who covets the iron cross either. If I were that sort, though, and I had the courage to marry a Jew and it hadn't been banned and all that, well I might have married her. I've heard all this stuff about killing babies at the Passover, but if you saw her selling oranges day after day, you'd know that Maria Hahns wouldn't hurt a fly. I don't know why they do it.'

The muscles in Lucien's stomach tightened and he felt his chest contract.

'Where does she live?' he asked as casually as he could.

'Ach, out at Barmbeck, near the hospital. Her father used to work there before. I don't know what he did. Now they sell oranges to keep going, but they still have their old flat opposite the morgue. It's a nice flat. I've seen it from outside with my boss, and it's the only one with a covered balcony in the block . . . You look sick, Lucien . . . This city is getting sick, really sick.'

'Where did it happen, and when?'

'On the allotments by Rubenkamp, at six o'clock. Nobody found her for hours afterwards. They say at the Poznan that it was a local gang of Hitler Youth, who have missed the army and forgotten to grow up. I think I might even have seen them hanging around the U-bahn at Barmbeck, I don't know.'

Lucien left his friend musing forlornly by the quay, while he himself caught a tram back to Marienterrasse and the Pension Helbig, where he had stayed for nine months and where he sensed that he would not stay much longer. Goebbels was broadcasting yet another rally that night, and an eloquent string of explanations rang through the Pension. Whatever rights or wrongs there were, whatever reasons, sides or faiths, Lucien no longer wanted to know. Gernot was right, Hamburg was sick, and Lucien, casting aside yet again his role as a catalyst, felt the old instinct to cure well up in him. Misia Schmutter had taught him that too, but she could no longer control him, she could take only his breath away, not his power.

Chapter 21

LUCIEN WOKE EARLY AND LAY IN BED LISTENING TO THE SPARrows making the most of the frozen morning. By special arrangement with the proprietor, he had five eiderdowns heaped into an almost insufferably heavy mass of feathers over which he could scarcely see. He wasn't used to the European winter, his life had been spent in the grip of heat and rains. In Caracas the temperature had occasionally dropped low enough to wear light woollens or tweeds at the beginning and the end of the day. This cold, though, that ate into his backbone like an icy knot at the base of his spine, with its matching tight bands of pain at head and foot, was something entirely new to Lucien. Gernot claimed that the cold was stimulating. Lucien disagreed.

At eight o'clock he drank his customary tisanes of balm and vervain, and at eight-thirty he breakfasted on fresh rolls and honey and a cup of what the proprietor called real coffee, which was a brown-coloured watery grit, brewed with a great sense of mystery in the hotel kitchen, and whose aroma was a fair imitation of the coffee Lucien drank at home. In deference to his generous tipping, and to his tropical origins, Lucien was always served two cups of this excruciating liquid with his rolls, and nothing that he did or said could be taken as a refusal. Finally, Lucien had resorted to having breakfast served in his room, so that he could at least tip this dysenteric brew down his wash hand basin.

Lucien lay in his bed, huddled away from the cold, weighed down not only by his feather covers, but by a sense of his own inadequacy as well. In nine months he had been incapable of finding a way of turning down his host's foul coffee; and in the same period he had done nothing but spend money and waste time, and grow into the morose state in which he now found himself. Nothing he did or said could alter the orchestrated chaos that was to come, all over Germany, and he too was German. Nothing he could do would un-rape Maria Hahns, or put the mocking sparkle back in her eyes. He could avenge the attack; that was all, it wouldn't help her but it would make life more bearable for himself. However many men he caught and killed, there would be more, just as there would be more Marias with frightened eyes and scarred vaginas.

He had a busy day before him, and he planned it with exemplary calm. Firstly, he packed his bags, leaving nothing in the room, then he paid his rent in advance for a further two weeks, carried his bags down, and took a taxi to Gernot Sieveking's work address in Rubenkamp, where he found that Gernot's description of the Poznan restaurant, far from exaggerating, had flattered it. Gernot, like many young men brought up with the uncertainties of a sailor father, had not given notice at the Poznan, even though his ship was due to sail on the following day. Lucien deposited his luggage in the least offensive-looking corner of the empty restaurant, explained to Gernot's boss that he was an old school friend of Gernot's, and that he had come to take his leave of him. Then he took Gernot by the elbow and dragged him outside, while the startled proprietor looked on in fear and disbelief.

'Gernot,' Lucien said. 'How much do you want to go to Brazil?'

'Why?' Gernot asked, suspiciously.

'Because I want to go instead.'

'Want to, or need to?' Gernot asked, looking back towards the restaurant and Lucien's luggage.

'Today, I want to, tomorrow . . . well—I might need to.'

'Now you've seen it, Lucien, and smelt it. I hope you know what you're asking me to do. I've thought about the slugs in Brazil, and I don't know if I even believe you, but any day now slugs are going to start crawling out of those soup pots, and Brazil is romantic and hot, and I hate this place, and I hate this too,' he said, waving his arms out to

211

the bare allotments that fanned out in rows of winter cabbages and muddy weeds.

'I can repay you for your trouble, not enough I know for what I would take from you, but enough maybe to start your restaurant on the Andreasstrasse and to stock up with that steak you can cut with a spoon,' Lucien told him.

'How much?' Gernot asked, looking sideways at Lucien.

'Ten thousand Marks.'

Gernot whistled and then laughed. 'Do you mean that you've been sitting in the Jungle all these months, surrounded by that bunch of cut-throats and muggers, with that kind of money around you?'

'Not in my pocket, Gernot.'

'Even so, I might have kidnapped you and held you to ransom.'

'It would have been a long long ransom, Gernot; who would you have written to?'

'Well, maybe I would have just punched your head in for the price of a bottle of schnapps.'

'Is it a deal, then?'

'Would you want my papers?'

'Of course.'

'And how would I get more? The National Socialists are not such fools as everyone here would have you believe.'

'You keep half your papers, and I'll keep the other half, then in six weeks, just apply for replacements.'

'Done.'

'Done?' Lucien echoed in surprise. He had expected a longer battle. They made their way back to the steaming Poznan restaurant, discussing the finer details of their plan as they walked along the uneven, dustbin-lined street.

'Meet me at the Jungle tonight at six o'clock.'

'You know I can't get there by six. Old pork fat in there won't let me go.

'Then meet me at nine.'

They walked on in silence until the restaurant was once more in sight.

'Why, anyway?' Gernot insisted.

'Just because,' Lucien said firmly.

They walked on a few more paces, and then it was Gernot who took Lucien firmly by the elbow and pulled him round to the direction of the allotments once more.

'Are you Jewish?' Gernot demanded sharply. 'Because if

you are, and we swap papers even for six weeks, and you're in trouble and I get my dick chopped off and everything else branded from my hands to my house . . . arschloch! Not for you, and not for anybody, do you hear?'

Lucien smiled patiently. 'I'm not Jewish. You can relax.'

'How the hell can I *know?*'

'I give you my word,'

'You're a gentleman, Lucien, the only one I've ever known at that; but I wasn't brought up with these codes of honour, so I'm afraid it will have to be something else you give me.'

'I swear on whatever you choose, on the Bible, on my dead sister, on what you will.'

'Look, Lucien, if I were a Jew and I were in trouble, I would swear on my mother, dead or alive or roasted.'

They stood together in silence once more, on the fringe of the drab allotments. Some fifty yards from them was a derelict iron hut with a leafless elder tree growing over it. Gernot pointed to the tree and said, 'Come with me, behind that tree, and show me your dick. That's how I'll know.' This was what they were doing when Gernot's boss, exasperated by his assistant's long absence, called to them from across the allotments to return. They emerged sheepishly, Gernot first, shielding Lucien while the latter did up his buttons.

'I'm sorry, Lucien,' Gernot whispered.

'That's all right. Forget it, Gernot. You're helping me and I am very grateful.'

'We were such good friends! I'll tell you what, I'll do it for half your price.'

They were joined now by the irate restaurateur, whose mouth was set, twisting slightly to meet a sabre scar on his right cheek. Lucien addressed him.

'I have not yet finished with your young man,' he said. 'Go back to the restaurant and wait for him there.' To Gernot's astonishment, his fat, frightened boss did exactly that, leaving them alone again to exchange their documents, and for Lucien to memorise some details of Gernot's ship.

On leaving the Poznan, he made his way to the harbour where Gernot's ship, the *Orpheus*, was docked and bustling. Lucien eyed the vessel with dismay. It was a ship that not only had seen better days, but had seen them in such a distant past that Lucien wondered if there was really anything left of her hull under the many layers of grey paint that covered her fragile skeleton. Notwithstanding, he paid a porter a lavish but plausible tip to carry his baggage aboard. Although it was eccentric to sail to Brazil, Misia Schmutter seemed to urge him to leave by this circuitous method. At least, it was very good timing to leave by Gernot's ship, and Brazil was en route for San Fernando. He could, once he got to Rio, travel round the coast to his home. All he needed now was more funds. So he sought out his drinking companion, Carl von Ledebur, and together they telephoned Captain Berkenmeyer, a mutual friend and a dedicated gambler. Berkenmeyer turned up armed with a fourth player, and they sat down to an hour of schnapps and poker. Lucien won. Lucien always won, unless he made a tremendous effort not to. Sometimes he had to dissemble his gambling luck in this way, if only so that he continued to have opponents to play against. That afternoon, though, Lucien was playing to win, to replenish his coffers, to repay Gernot and finance his own voyage, and to leave behind him all that he could rake off that card table to the newly-battered hands of Maria Hahns.

At three o'clock precisely, he left the bar where he had been playing, and made his way into the town centre. The pockets of his fur-lined greatcoat were stuffed with his afternoon's winnings. Carl von Ledebur ran after him and followed him down the road.

'Don't go, old man,' he said. 'The game was just getting good.'

'I have an appointment to keep,' Lucien told him.

'And I have debts to pay,' Carl whispered sadly as he walked away.

'I can help you out,' Lucien called after him.

'Thanks, but I'd rather win it back from some poor sucker.'

At three twenty-five, Lucien went into Kollmar's the stationer's, and pushing his way past the Christmas cards, he bought a packet of large envelopes, a pad of writing paper, a shopping bag, a rubber stamp and an ink pad. The stamp read 'sub-standard'.

At three-fifty, Lucien passed the church of Saint Jacobi and looked up automatically, as he always did, to admire the spire. Then he went into the tea rooms that were in the same block, and ordered a cup of coffee. He took out his writing paper and his fountain pen, and wrote in his wide, childish copperplate something that he had read and remembered for Maria Hahns as a homage to her clear grey eyes and her beauty and her gloved hands. 'That which breaks others must not break you,' he wrote. Then he put the paper with these words into one of his new envelopes, together with five thousand Deutschmarks, and stuck it down. He would have liked to have taken Maria Hahns away, but she was not Mariana, and, besides, she probably had a man of her own, and he suspected that she regarded his vigil by her stall as a subtle form of torment. So he contented himself with his note and the money, and gulped down his cold coffee, grimacing at the taste. Then he transferred his money and two black objects to the bag, and left the tea room at exactly four-fifteen.

In the market where Maria Hahns had kept her stall, a man whom Lucien took to be her father stood in her place. This man's face was darker and more ravaged than Maria's, but there was a definite resemblance between the two, and the grey eyes were the same. Lucien approached his orange stall. All around people were crowding to buy dates and nuts and mandarins, oranges and polished apples. There were only two more days to Christmas, and the prices had tripled. Only Herr Hahns's orange stall was empty of customers. Lucien asked for three oranges. Herr Hahns invited him to choose them himself.

'I have a letter for your daughter, Maria, Herr Hahns. I know what has happened,' Lucien added hurriedly, 'and I want to help her. I, too, am a foreigner . . . sometimes it is better to go home.' Maria's father stared at him suspiciously. 'Say it is from a well-wisher, she doesn't know my name. I have often seen her in the market here.' Lucien seemed to be getting nowhere with Maria's father, or rather he was leading him to draw inaccurate conclusions, so he thrust his note in the envelope over the barrow and into the crates behind it.

At four fifty-five, Lucien found himself changing trains at Sierichstrasse, en route for Barmbeck. At Barmbeck itself he bought three packets of razorblades and a bicycle chain, and then he made his way, on foot, through a maze of drab terraced houses, until he found a semi-deserted one. An old slow-footed Jew was coming towards him, dragging his slippered feet all the while. Lucien accosted him, threatened him with a cut throat if he so much as spoke, and stole his starred armband and the prayer cap from his head.

At five-thirty, Lucien was standing propped against an empty shack on a derelict part of Barmbeck suburb. He hoped that he was very close to the spot where Maria Hahns had been beaten and raped, and he hoped that the same gang of Hitler Youth who had attacked her would be lured to attack him. Lucien had been unable to get the Jude Armband on over his greatcoat, so this last lay on the frosty ground beside him. He wore the old man's prayer cap on his head, having carefully shaken out the dandruff, and he was smoking a long cigar as provocatively as he could. Slowly, and then faster, people began to return home laden with shopping and tinsel and sometimes struggling with a Christmas tree. Only the Jews shuffled by, embarrassed and frightened by his presence there, with his smart suit and his fashionable tie, and his cold blue eyes staring out with a mocking expression from under his thick fringe of blond hair and his jaunty, dirty prayer cap. All the Arians stared at him, the good Hamburg citizens with their liebekuchen in their baskets and their sense of decorum. This lounging stranger, they thought, had no right to be there, or to be so blond and Jewish, no right to be beautiful, no right to wear such expensive clothes. It was his type that had ruined Germany before, and his type that gave their Jews a bad name.

News travelled fast around the straggling suburb that someone not a mile from Barmbeck Hospital was waiting to be put inside the casualty wing. By six, two young men had come to check him out. They were dressed in the uniform of the Hitler Youth, and they were both carrying wooden clubs.

'Get off that shack, Jew,' one of them said to Lucien.

Lucien slid his elbow nonchalantly from the corrugated iron, and dusted his sleeve.

'Get out of our neighbourhood, you pig!' the same one said. 'Or there won't be anything left of you to go.'

Lucien raised his eyes in mock horror, lit another cigar, and proceeded to smoke it. The second of the two young men lunged at Lucien's feet, took his overcoat and trampled its fine honey-coloured fur into the slush and crushed ice of the street.

'It wasn't mine, actually,' Lucien told him. 'Somebody just left it here.' Then, looking down the street, he pointed to an elegant fellow sporting a mac and a stick, and said, 'That's him, there.'

The two young men walked away, and Lucien, who was feeling almost frostbitten, walked across the wasteland, and putting his armband and prayer cap into his shopping bag, together with his purchases, he made his way to a small café, where he ordered yet another cup of the watery sludge that in Hamburg passed for coffee.

At seven-fifteen, he emerged into the cold dark night once more to reposition himself by the derelict shack. This time he stood without the stolen Jewish insignia. It was only a few minutes to the curfew, and he didn't want his plan spoilt by the police. He left his shopping bag under a heap of sodden swept leaves half-way between the shack and the café, having transferred the money to his waistband, and his collection of weaponry, knives, razors and the chain to various parts of his clothing.

At seven thirty-five, to Lucien's intense relief, since without his trampled overcoat he felt himself shrivelling with cold, he saw two groups of men converging on him from opposite ends of the street. They were all wearing their Hitler Youth bands and some of them wore the uniform as well. Lucien began to move backwards into the wasteland, luring them away from the lamplight and into the dark. He had counted seven men, but only six followed him on to the derelict plots, so he taunted the seventh, to lure them all even farther into the uneven ground where no one could see them and no one could escape. Lucien picked his way across the muddy allotments and the gang of young Nazis followed him. Then Lucien crept silently among the gang, who had spread out in readiness to attack, and one after another he cut their throats. Three of them had fallen before anyone realised what was happening. There was no one else on the street, and no houses from which they could be seen, but still Lucien wasted no time.

'Come on then, pretty boy, after we've finished you won't ever want to show your face again,' the leader of the gang told him, talking blindly into the total darkness of the allotments.

'Jan, you get behind him. Willi, cut him off to his right,' the gang leader told his group.

'All right, Leo, but where is he?'

'Willi!' Silence. 'Where is Willi?'

The four would-be attackers stumbled and turned in the dark. One of them found something on the ground, and cried out. It was just a short cry, no more than that of a screech owl, for Lucien's hands had found him too, and taken his knife to the man's throat, swiftly, as Chucho Delgado had taught him to do.

Now Lucien and the gang of Nazis were three to one, and the three were still confident of getting their man. They didn't know that Lucien's gambling odds were the highest ever known, or that their would-be victim could see in the dark and strike at two places at a time, or that he never hesitated before the kill, just chose his moment and struck ruthlessly like the tyrant he carried on his back.

So Lucien took his fifth man and his sixth; and was surprised to see that this last was the young houseman from the Barmbeck Hospital with whom he had played cards and drunk schnapps on so many evenings at his own Pension Helbig, and who had always been such good company. Then there was only one man left, one man and Lucien, out on the wasteland with six dead bodies at their feet and not a single witness to the retaliatory deaths.

'I'm going to get you, you Jewish pig,' his last attacker shouted.

'I'm not Jewish,' Lucien told him calmly.

'Then what are you, you lump of shit.'

'I am Lucien.'

'What?'

Lucien slashed out at him with his chain, catching him around the ear and then once again. The man crumpled up in pain.

'Why?' he croaked.

Lucien was silent.

'Why?'

'Just because,' Lucien said, and sunk his knife into the man's chest.

'Mein lieber Gott, why?'

Lucien pulled out his knife and sunk it again and then slit the boy's throat too for good measure. He checked over his seven corpses to make sure they were dead, and then he stamped 'sub-standard' on their foreheads.

Although Lucien felt the cold hunching his spine, he didn't feel disturbed as he examined the corpses in the straggling cabbage patch. He covered up every scrap of evidence and left the allotment in a leisurely way. He was confident that the attack would look like a gangland killing. There had been a great deal of tightening up of late, even in the Hitler Youth, and Lucien didn't imagine that a few dead bodies in a slum allotment would cause much excitement, not after the Anschluss and the rallies. He travelled back to the city as he had come, on foot and by train, passing late Christmas shoppers on his way. Nobody noticed him much. It was a widespread habit in Hamburg to walk around with imaginary blinkers down. Near the harbour, Lucien dropped his sodden overcoat and the stolen cap and armband deep into the River Elbe, and watched them for a moment in the dark as they flowed out to sea.

At nine o'clock, when he met Gernot Sieveking at the Jungle, Lucien could hardly breathe for cold. He drank a double brandy, which revived him sufficiently to deliver Gernot's money to him and to take his leave. Then he boarded Gernot's ship and registered with the purser, and spent his first night on the elderly *Orpheus*, reading through his list of duties and a collection of previous menus. He didn't go ashore again, at least not on German soil, so he never knew how the bodies were found, or when. He learnt from the waif-like boy who peeled potatoes and washed up for him that seven men had died in a gangland razor fight near the Barmbeck Hospital by the canal.

V

Our
Lady
of
Bitterness

Chapter 22

*T*HE VOYAGE TO RIO DE JANEIRO, WITH ITS LOADING AND unloading at Lisbon and Tenerife, Bahia and Rio itself, took twenty-nine slow days through wind and rain and then through stifling tropical calm, and Lucien enjoyed every one of them. He enjoyed the hierarchy of the ship, and his own relative anonymity in it. For the first time in his life he was not Lucien, he was merely the ship's cook, and the ship's cook was infinitely more important there than Lucien himself could ever have been. There was no place on this creaking cargo vessel for passengers and their whims; there was no place for a man with a mission; there were just old decks to be scrubbed and engines oiled and meals served and all with a precision that delighted Lucien.

He could lie in bed at night, on his tight bunk, directly over his assistant, and so close to the man's stomach that he could hear the occasional gurgling of his guts as he rolled over and adjusted his load of sauté potatoes or spiced red cabbage, and listen to the machinery of the engine churning while the ship slept. Lucien had been down once to the engine room and, in return for providing the chief engineer with a saltless diet, he had been allowed to wander through the maze of polished pipes and pistons and to see the oil-fuelled furnaces at work with their wonder of cogs and dials.

In Hamburg, Lucien had often been to the four o'clock concerts at the Musikhalle. One afternoon he had heard Hans Erich Rubensahn play all the Beethoven sonatas by heart, and Lucien had been so lost in admiration that he

223

had thought that if he were not what he was, he would have liked to have been a pianist. Now, in the bowels of the *Orpheus*, he thought that he would like to have been an engineer.

It had never occurred to him that he would have liked to be a ship's cook. Not even while he cooked and invented at Niemenberg had he thought of doing so professionally; as it was, though, he took enormous pleasure in his work. He found satisfaction in the physical contact with the food he prepared: the kneading of the daily dough for bread, and the rolling of pastry and the shaping of rissoles and croquettes. From Hamburg to Lisbon he perfected his new trade. Despite his previous apprenticeship under his own chefs at Niemenberg, he still slaved for eighteen hours a day to keep up with his work. By the time the *Orpheus* had rounded the Bay of Biscay, Lucien had found a rhythm and routine to his job, and from merely meeting the deadlines with his rows of pies and his massive cauldrons of potatoes, he carried his cooking to a new area of creation. His soups became the talk of the ship. Each new day jogged his memory a little more, and the finer details of his old banquets and exquisite dinners for hundreds of guests, when he had watched and helped the French chefs in his vaulted kitchens concocting and decorating such wonderful dishes, came back to him.

Within days of setting sail, Lucien converted the menus from heavy wholesome fillers to delicacies of every kind and description. He cooked by trial and error, and he was delighted to find that his errors were very few, and getting fewer. Around the coastal waters of England and Scotland, the local fish had followed the ship in swarms, bloating themselves on Lucien's aborted stews and sauces, but by Lisbon, it was rare to see an unsalvageable dish being tipped overboard.

While perfecting his craft, Lucien was aware of having squandered a great deal of the kitchen's future resources, and at Lisbon he replaced such smaller items as he could out of his own pocket. While making these necessary purchases he discovered dozens of tempting further ones, and before his day of shore leave was out, he had stocked up on vast quantities of herbs and spices, wines and garnishes, oils and vegetables, nuts and fruits of every description.

The ship's purser watched in astonishment as crates of cherries in maraschino, and tins of anchovies, boxes of vanilla pods and strings of shallots were carried aboard. He soon became convinced that Lucien was smuggling, and on such a large scale that he would have to be stopped and punished before the voyage was out. However, as a man of much experience in the ways of the sea, the purser knew that a ship without a cook was as bad as a ship becalmed, and so he said nothing as he made his close notes of the size and contents of Lucien's private cargo. This Gernot Sieveking, for such was Lucien's name throughout the voyage, was as brash a smuggler as the purser had ever seen.

Five hours later, after a dinner of creamed leek soup and a succulent peppered steak, pineapple and apples in a cream and maraschino sauce, camembert and Bath Olivers, coffee, and almond torten, the purser decided that this new cook had been judged a little harshly, and throughout the voyage, as the ship sliced her way through the North African current and the North Equatorial current and the South Equatorial current, past Cabo San Boque and Pernambuco, Bahia and finally Rio itself, his opinion of the new cook rose and soared, until he pressed Lucien to accept tenure on the *Orpheus*. When Lucien declined, the purser said, 'Herr Sieveking, I will double your wages.' Lucien promised to think it over. Over the years, as he prepared his solitary meals and cooked delicacies to accompany the lavish cocktails for his prison cell-mates, he thought over the purser's offer with real regret. To know that, instead of twenty-five years in an airless brick cell, he could have been sailing the seas, criss-crossing the Atlantic as cook to a crew of ecstatic gourmets, was one of the few things that could truly sadden Lucien's heart.

Neither the old prison at San Juan de los Morros nor the tall stone pile at Trujillo could destroy his culinary drive. But it was not the same crouching over his two-ring Primus stove with its stink of paraffin and its rebellious flame. Aboard the *Orpheus* there had been four bread ovens, while in prison Lucien made do with a series of cake tins with wire grids inside them. The sailors and officers had so enjoyed their meals that they had cheered him as he went ashore at Rio, and they had come, shyly, in ones and twos to his scrubbed kitchens to give him trinkets and schnapps and whittled toys that they had made for him as tokens of gratitude. In prison, his customers would be much less appreciative. Perhaps, he thought, because life was scarcely life in prison, or food, food. There was little appetite to be gained from regret.

There was always something musty about the food itself by the time it reached his cell. It was as though it had been dragged through dust, or rolled in cobwebs. So, although Lucien had the money to buy fresh provisions, and his loyal manservant ferried them to him, they never seemed fresh. Poor doddering Molinas always ate his dish of whatever casserole or brew Lucien had made, and thanked him profusely in his lurching stammering way. Lucien doubted whether Molinas could have told the difference between his own fine sauces and a ladleful of boiled slops from the latrines. Molinas, who shared a cell with Lucien for seven years in Trujillo's penitentiary, was lucky to be alive, if it were luck to survive the torture that he had been through and be reduced to a dribbling stuttering wreck of a man whose nerves could never rest, but shuddered and jerked in a permanent state of what looked like delirium tremens. Molinas was a lesson to Lucien and a source of continual strength. He himself was always better off than Molinas; however hard new warders might try to humiliate him, or however hard they kicked, or however often they put weevils in his flour and mouldy crusts in with his new bread and tore out pages from his books and killed his plants, he was always better off than Molinas.

Lucien had seen how men recovered before their last death throe. Even Misia Schmutter with her terrible growth had brightened before her end, which was not her end, since she continued to travel with Lucien, but it was the end of her agony at San Fernando. Thinking of this, he often wondered whether his time aboard the *Orpheus,* and later trekking through Brazil en route for home, had been so easy and pleasurable because it was to be virtually his last taste of freedom before his trial. It was strange, Lucien always thought, that he had no sense of his impending captivity. Misia Schmutter certainly urged him on. When he stayed for more than a day at any of the Macumba-steeped villages, sifting through their magic herbs and medicines, she would tighten her stranglehold until he got going again.

Everywhere he went he travelled by train, for the first many weeks at least, until he lost count of the days. And the trains all rattled as they cut through the noisy plateaux and plains, humming with flurries of laden passengers who flocked to the crowded train to haggle and barter with the passengers. The locals came like flocks of rice birds over a ripening crop, and then the whistle would blow time and again, until eventually enough clinging boys had been shaken from the doors and steps. Then the great articulated metal snake would continue northwards, always north, through Leopoldina and Caravelas and all the other stops and towns that lay on the dusty route that Lucien rattled through in the dusty trains that were taking him homewards to Venezuela. He travelled with the chicken feathers and melting iced lemonade and the rust-coloured shutters that were opened and closed as the series of trains tracked through the landscape of luscious plains studded with ibis and ospreys and macaws.

At Caravelas, Lucien hired a porter and took a banana boat to Bahia, at which Misia Schmutter became heavy with rage: they were retracing the course of the *Orpheus*. Lucien might be sightseeing as he meandered back towards Venezuela, for all his hurry, but Misia Schmutter was anxious to get home and away from the unfamiliar hills of Minas Gerais and the Brazilian coast. It seemed like a failure in her grandson's education that he should stop and barter for a gate and bits of carved rubbish in wood and stone.

His luggage, which from the start had been cumbersome, had now reached such a size and proportion that a permanent porter was needed to chaperone it on and off the trains. In Caravelas, Lucien had taken on a young boy called Cruz for this purpose, and although each day of travel took him further from his home, Cruz begged to be allowed to stay with him. All round the coast of Bahia, with its towns that had grown and died with the rubber boom, leaving a trail of crumbling palaces and towns that had either flourished or been reclaimed by the swamp, depending how trade had been there, the boy Cruz tagged along. After several attempts to turn him away, Lucien

227

gave in. The further north he travelled in that vast, straggling territory of trading posts and scattered Indian villages with a rare town locked in its history, the harder it became for Lucien to communicate his needs to the people. The boy Cruz, however, with a natural sharpness that poverty had enhanced, had a dozen words in as many dialects, and he steered the two of them effortlessly forward.

By rail and sea they hopped from port to port like migrating egrets in search of their nesting site, with Lucien forging northwards to the Amazon and the jungle and the three Guianas, because these all lay in the approximate direction of his home. Cruz fussed round him with help and advice and food, and beads to ward off the Evil Eye. On the rough slatted ferries that carried the coffee and hemp and balata rubber and fruit from town to town, Lucien and Cruz shared a cabin, sleeping side by side on plantain mats on the crawling floors. Lucien showed him how to sprinkle lime under and around the mats and to anoint his skin with oil of citronella and thus sleep undisturbed by the hordes of tiny predators which would otherwise have feasted on their new blood.

Cruz was impressed by Lucien's skill with insects and poisons and guns, but he was also afraid for him. He could sense that there was something very close to this new master of his, something that would smother and destroy him. He knew from his own experience during his short and unusually violent life that pale men were wont to be blind and pig-headed. It was an inherent weakness in them and Dom Lucien was no exception. Cruz had first spotted him across the bustling market square at Caravelas, buying roots at old Piniños' stall. Lucien spoke in slow Spanish, while Piniños answered back in his slurred surly Portuguese. Piniños, as a rule, never answered anyone, civilly or uncivilly. So for this stranger to have broken the old man's habitual silence was noteworthy in itself. Then, the pickpockets and muggers and the choke-and-rob gangs let him walk through the market unmolested, and lastly Cruz felt himself drawn irresistibly towards the man. It was an instinctive urge as strong as that of steering clear of the militia in all its manifestations in the town.

The glow of pride at his discovery of this new master was tainted by his second vision of the threat that hung over Dom Lucien's head. It seemed as obvious as a flood to Cruz that Lucien was in danger, and the danger was very close, so close it seemed at times that it was already around his master's neck; yet still Lucien chose to ignore it. Cruz, however, having found someone who came as near, he suspected, as anyone would ever come to giving life a sense of purpose, was determined to hold on to his find. If Lucien would not protect himself, then Cruz would do it for him. So he stuck to Lucien like a grass tick, from Caravelas to Bahia in the creaking fruit boat. When Lucien manoeuvred his way out of the quays and customs to the town itself, wandering over the chipped paving bricks into the city itself, Cruz was close behind him, with a handcart of luggage in tow. He waited silently while Lucien visited one building after another, pausing for precisely fifteen minutes in front of each. Not even the Saldanha Palace or the São Domaso Seminary could draw his master in. Much as Lucien would have liked to enter every church that he saw, Misia Schmutter was desperate to move on, and he was anxious to appease her, so he contented himself with the brilliant façades: white stuccoes and blue tiles, and the domes and bells. On the steep downhill journey back to the harbour, Cruz was too busy trying to keep the cartload of luggage steady to notice that Lucien moved again with relative freedom, as Misia Schmutter relaxed in gratitude for being taken away from the unruly splendour of the Portuguese forts and convents. She had nothing but scorn for such haphazard displays of wealth and fervour. It distressed her that Lucien should wade through the stinking, littered streets admiring such disorder.

From Bahia they took the train to Aracaju, and then continued by sea again through the turbid coastal waters to Maceió. There followed an awkward stretch by train and mule to Pernambuco, which was a great metropolis that swallowed them up and spewed them out at a place called Nazareth, to nurse their dysentery and recover from the revelry in which Lucien had participated on a scale that Cruz, who had witnessed much, had never seen before. Cruz had nearly gone mad with worry at Pernambuco: Lucien had left him at the station to disentangle their luggage and book into the hotel, and had then disappeared for a week. For the first four days Cruz searched the town,

229

asking at every bar and church and square, and for the next three days he wept. When Lucien finally returned, haggard and unrepentant, to scoop him up and make him a witness to the last days of his spree, Cruz was too debilitated to enjoy anything.

Then it was the train again, first-class now for reasons Cruz neither knew nor asked, with himself travelling in the rear wagon with the luggage. It was some two hundred miles from Nazareth to Natal, their destination, and Cruz travelled them squatting suspiciously over his master's cumbersome collection of luggage. He eyed his fellow travellers with open disdain, for which impertinence he had his ears boxed by a cotton picker at a place called Flor. After the train had begun to leave the station, the cotton picker in question having disembarked, Cruz, who was small for his ten or eleven years, leaned out of the window and waved his curved knife, shouting a string of abuse so long and so eloquent that Lucien, from the oppressive heat of his first-class carriage, heard him and went to investigate.

Two hours later, Cruz was installed in the plush relative comfort of the first-class end of the train, having carried the baggage with his master from wagon to wagon across the menacing moving links. The guard, who had waited until the last piece of luggage had been gathered into their compartment, then announced that not only had the baggage to move once more, but that 'parasites' like Cruz were not allowed to mix with the 'gente fina'.

'He's my son,' Lucien told him shortly, and the guard retired unconvinced. When the train finally dragged its tail into the station at Natal, after hours of uneven rattling through the damp marshy heat of that interminable afternoon, Cruz had to be shaken out of a kind of trance.

'Vamos, Cruz!' Lucien admonished him. But the boy was nearly comatose, slumped into the corner of his wide tartan seat. '¿Qué hubo, Cruz?' Lucien chided him again, more roughly now, and the boy surfaced from his dream. It had been a dream of pleasure and of pride. For as long as Cruz could remember he had been called a son of a bitch and a son of a whore, son of a cheat and son of a nobody, he had been called fatherless scum, but never before had he been somebody's son. And then the pleasure began to cloud over with regret. If only the whole marketplace at Caravelas could have heard Dom Lucien's announcement, if only the boys from the quay could have been there too. And if only the words could have been captured and kept and repeated, not in Cruz's voice, but in Dom Lucien's own. But these regrets were soon gone, and Cruz was left with the lingering sound of the words themselves, merged into the scraps of religion that he had acquired, more as parts of elaborate obscenities than through the Church, but religion just the same. It was all made up of the stone and the effigies and the magic that was sung on the beaches and the backwards litanies that kept the devil at bay by calling him to you, and the men who knew how to control all the forces of evil, men like Lucien, who had called him his son. They were now, it seemed to Cruz, like the Trinity itself, untouchable and complete, for Lucien was the ghost and the magic, and that was holy, and now he was the father and Cruz himself the son.

'Cruz, for the love of God, get up!' Lucien told him, and Cruz obeyed, as he would always obey, and he followed Lucien, as he would always follow him, from that day until the day of his death. All the way back to Venezuela he would be there, trailing in his master's wake with love and gratitude. And in San Fernando, where the men all bowed down to Lucien, as Cruz believed they should do, he was there. And in the villa by the Botanical Gardens in Caracas, where everything was strange and cool and clean, he was there. And when the militia came and surrounded their villa, apologetically, but with guns, he was there, watering the camomile and the geraniums and the hibiscus trees. And in their tiled kitchen he was there to pass Dom Lucien his lids and skewers as he cooked, day and night it seemed: veal in coconut and escabeche fish in lime and strawberry meringues. Cruz was there to eat them, and he was there when the great heaps of leftovers were offered to the stray dogs each evening in the caraqueñan twilight. He was also there when the militia pounded on their door and arrested Dom Lucien—they didn't drag him away as the newspapers said, because Lucien offered no resistance. Cruz wanted to fight, but Dom Lucien had gone like a guest in their escort, and the only fighting was for Cruz as he tried to accompany him. But Dom Lucien alone could open doors for him, and without him they slammed as they had always slammed before. So he had to content himself with remaining a shadow, and he carried pans of food to Lucien at the barracks where he was imprisoned while he awaited his trial. Cruz had seen the market children carrying their billycans of feijoada to their fathers on the stalls, and he had looked in those faraway days with envy at these children who were so tied to their daily errand that they had hardly any time to play, unlike himself who had had all the time in the world but no family and no friends.

It had never seemed possible to Cruz that Lucien should be found guilty—guilty of what, he asked himself. And who were these strange men in black to judge him anyway? It was, Cruz thought, unnatural to decide such things as guilt and innocence. Children under a certain age were innocent, angels were innocent, and certain faces on the ceiling of the Church of Our Lady in Caravelas were innocent, or so he had once been told. But that men and women should be called either one or the other was a strange notion whose logic escaped him. No one could be entirely one thing or the other. Some men, it was true, veered more towards one state, thus el Viejo Piniños with his stall of roots was definitely more guilty than most men and of most things, but what grown man could be innocent? The answer that came to Cruz's mind was always the same: if any man could aspire to such a state, then surely that man was Dom Lucien.

The judge in Caracas, however, thought otherwise, and Lucien was found guilty. Guilty of a crime against the Republic, they said, of killing three members of the militia, of plotting, of treason. Cruz knew that the charge was a false one, but the court still found him guilty, and sentenced him to twelve years in prison. And twelve years, as every scandalmonger in the country knew, was an insanely long time. Cruz himself stayed, ferrying food and plants from the marketplaces of the several towns in which Lucien was imprisoned to his cell for the first ten of those years, right up to the time of Lucien's escape. Then his master had disappeared into the depths of unknown prisons for two long years more, emerging only as an aged and battered version of his former self. After that, Cruz had continued to ferry things to him for the thirteen years that followed as a penance for having tried to escape. That made twenty-five years in all of errands and of waiting for his strange pale Messiah to return to the freedom and the chaos and to his own adult care. And in all the days of those years—nine thousand days and more—Cruz only once regretted his self-inflicted purgatory, and that was when Lucien escaped, escaped and retraced their route through the jungle of the Orinoco to Guiana, and didn't wait for him. That was the one time that Cruz resented an action of Lucien's. 'Once,' Lucien would have said, 'once is to know you're alive.'

Chapter 23

CRUZ NEVER KNEW WHAT DICTATED HIS MASTER'S TRAVELS in that period before the arrest, except that they were wending their way slowly northwards. He just followed him and waited for his reasons to reveal themselves bit by bit. Behind all Lucien's movements was the knowledge that eventually he would go home, and all his steps were in the direction of Venezuela. Although he enjoyed sightseeing, Misia Schmutter urged him to hurry on with an impatience unprecedented even within the bounds of her usual tyranny. Occasionally, even Misia Schmutter would relent. Thus, at Cayenne, Lucien got no more of the city than a burst of patois at the docks, and a glimpse of the pushiest vendors hawking their wares at the very boatside, waving fruit and cloth and foul-smelling sticks of tallow at his chest and demanding a sale and immediate payment. He had stared through the host of urgent black faces and at the hint of the quay beyond with its customs houses leading into town, and he had wanted to go ashore and explore. Misia Schmutter, meanwhile, had grown apoplectic with rage, kicking and flaying her grandson so that he could scarcely keep his feet.

'What is it, Dom Lucien?' Cruz had asked.

But Lucien was struggling too hard for his breath to reply, so he just held on to the deck rail, wrestling with his tormentor, and choking as quietly as he could. Eventually he whispered, 'I'm all right, Cruz, I'm fine.'

To which Cruz replied his customary, 'Muito bem,' which he pronounced in a kind of sing-song. All of life, according

234

to Cruz, was 'muito bem'. He had said it so many times that it was meaningless, just a form of words brushed over everything good or bad or disastrous, all things came under that one loose phrase, like a Brazilian balm. Of all Cruz's habits, this one of pronouncing his 'muito bem' like an unfelt amen was the only one that really irritated Lucien. He had tried to rid him of it, but to no avail, no matter how many times he explained that it was not only annoying but rude to repeat constantly the same words, and that when somebody died it was not good, and when Lucien lost half his luggage at Belém it was not all right, and that there was no point in agreeing to do something if you were incapable of doing it, and lastly, and perhaps most importantly, that it would infuriate Lucien to hear those two words again: in short, that they were banned. Cruz had drooped his shoulders until they were almost flat against his sides, and he had jerked the tears from his eyes, and shuffled from the room, and when Lucien had added, in Spanish, which was the language that they had come to speak to one another, 'Now don't forget, Cruz,' Cruz had answered, in Portuguese, 'Muito bem,' not even noticing the repetition of his sin.

So, through his shortened breath and the pain in his back, Lucien could hear his boy champion reassuring the puzzled crowd.

'What's the matter with him, what's he doing? Is it a fit? Is it epilepsy? He hasn't been bitten by a dog, has he? Is he all right?' the passengers were saying as they jostled their way to the gangplank to disembark, and to each query, Cruz gave the same, 'Está muito bem, muito bem.' And his high crowing voice was all that drifted through from Cayenne, that and the blur of black faces selling their wares, and a forty-yard walk after the decks were clear to another boat, laden this time not with curious passengers but with bananas covered with joined sacks to keep the sun off them.

What might have been a simple process, this boarding of a ferry-boat to Surinam, turned out to be so complex an affair that not one but six French-speaking officials were called down to haggle with Lucien and his wide-eyed child porter. Lucien's knowledge of French was limited to a few architectural phrases, culinary names and expletives learnt from his former chefs, and the names of cakes that he had admired in a pâtisserie in Hamburg, and noted down for future reference. He had, however, been warned that on reaching French Guiana he would be met by the full force of French bureaucracy, or its colonial and more officious version. So he had taken the precaution of coming armed with visas in duplicate and letters of recommendation, these last bought from his adviser in Belém, and also a passport for Cruz, which was purchased from the same source. In the absence of any name to put on this passport after the solitary 'Cruz', Lucien added his own. So the Cayenne officials found Haydn Lucien Schmutter travelling in the company of Cruz Lucien, his unprepossessing and under-sized son and heir.

The immigration officials admitted reluctantly that the papers and passports and visas all seemed to be in order. But, they explained gleefully, no one was allowed to leave French Guiana on the same day that he arrived. So, with all due respect, the two of them would have to stay. Cruz, with his new clothes bought from a shed with swing doors, like a cowboy shop in a film, was armed with his answer. 'Muito bem,' he smiled. And Lucien understood the tech-nicality of the hitch, and although it annoyed him, he was prepared and even pleased to spend a day touring buildings in what promised to be a style of architecture hitherto unknown to him. Misia Schmutter, however, would not understand; she refused to wait. Lucien cursed her impatie-ence. Why couldn't the dead wait like the mortal, why couldn't they join a queue or suffer a setback without these tantrums on his back?

It was no use, Misia Schmutter would not settle for the official word, and Lucien's compromise was to wait at the quayside all afternoon in the throbbing sun, and then to sit on the ferry deck for the evening, and wrestle with the grey cotton sheet in his hot tin cabin all night until the sailing time came in the morning. There was to be no pleasure in Cayenne, and no peace. When the battered banana boat weighed anchor on the following morning, and slipped past the pillared villas that lined the coast, Lucien was so tired he could see black dots on the surface of the sea, and black dots on the sun.

Misia Schmutter was successful in her despotism, not least because she knew when to relent. She rewarded her grandson's loyalty and obedience with her consent to stay in the Dutch Guianese capital of Paramaribo, his next port of call, for as long as he liked. Lucien was touched by her generosity, but not entirely taken in by it. Paramaribo in the rainy season was not the most alluring place he had known.

Even Cruz found the local vernacular quite unintelligible. Lucien, however, discovered that the barman at the Hotel Krasnapolski, where he was staying, spoke German, and seemed to be the only person able to throw any light on the townscaped jungle in which he had come to land. For the rest, life was a series of silent gestures. Each evening, Lucien drank with a man who appeared to be the chief of police. Theirs was a casual bar acquaintanceship, but they looked for each other from among the would-be diners in the hotel bar on the Domineestraat, and smiled and sat down together for tumbler after tumbler of iced rum and coconut, and although they never passed their initial exchange of names, Ernst, as his new friend was called, was not in the least perturbed by this arrangement.

Lucien, on the other hand, found the silence tiring. It was not as though any pleasure could be derived from contemplating Ernst's weatherbeaten Dutch-Creole face, pitted and pock-marked by the tropics as it was. Even his uniform, weighed down by its clusters of stripes and medals, could not hold Lucien's attention beyond the first few days. What did fascinate him was Ernst's genius for pronunciation. He could take any word and repeat it in so many ways that it stood alone more eloquently than a whole language often could. Thus Lucien's own name was taken and played with and Lucien felt that from its simple utterance a barrage of things was being asked of him and said to him, to which his replies must always be inadequate since he spoke neither the Taki Taki which was the local tongue, nor the Dutch that the barman intimated would serve as well to reach the inner ear of the chief of police.

As the days passed, Lucien found that the highlight of each one was his ritual meeting with Ernst in the bar. He would watch him manipulate whole stratas of the town with single names. He conveyed orders and disapproval, disappointment and praise all by a twist of a vowel and the occasional lowering of his eyes. Something in his voice bullied people into understanding him, with his mixture of menace and charm. Every time he threw out a name he dragged something back in his net, or someone, and the whole town seemed to move to his unspoken commands. Ernst's power lay in his ability to stop things from happening. His role was almost entirely preventive, and since nobody knew in that right-angled, green-shuttered wooden town what would have happened had Ernst—the marionette master—released his strings and put them down, there was an air of hush and awe around him, as though one loud noise and the sea wall would crumble. By selecting Lucien as his drinking companion, Ernst drew him in to his charmed circle, and soothed him for a while with his aura of complicity. So for three weeks Lucien hovered in the lull around Ernst's refusal to speak, while Misia Schmutter bided her time and Cruz went shopping day after day through the gushing rain-filled streets.

Cruz took an almost perverse pleasure in getting wet. He could have bought any number of things right where they were on the Domineestraat, but it gave him a rush of excitement to cross the flooding streets to the other side of town and buy jade and ivory and glass from the Chinese vendors who spoke to him so fast they were like human hummingbirds. Lucien had given him money for these purchases, since Cruz, for the first time, had asked for it. Cruz never knew what it was in Paramaribo of all places that started him on this buying spree, he had never done it before, or wanted to. Soon, he had bought so many things, carved in wood and bamboo, or clay, that there was no more room for them in their shared rooms on the fourth floor of the rambling Hotel Krasnapolski, so they took another room, and Cruz began to buy trunks in which to store his new treasures.

Each afternoon as Cruz returned, bedraggled from the rain, clutching his sodden paper parasols and his painted gourds and mats and trays to him, Lucien could hear the rustle of Misia Schmutter pulling at her lace cuffs in irritation. And each morning when he woke and lay awake in his high iron bed listening to the rain drops beating against the closed shutters of his room, and imagined the rivulets running down the maroon and white paint of the hotel, which was like a giant matchbox hotel with its millions of tiny planks, he could feel Misia Schmutter crowing, 'Stay as long as you like,' in her high-pitched gloating voice.

When they finally left Paramaribo, three and a half weeks after they arrived there, they had so much baggage that

Lucien had to hire a second porter to help carry it, since, despite Cruz's protests, his thin childish arms were quite incapable of lugging his own hoard of bric-à-brac on to the boat that would take them to Georgetown on the next stage of their journey. This new porter, Mr Jackson, spoke English, which was a language that Lucien could understand and speak a little, and unlike the silent Ernst, Mr Jackson spoke all the time, except when he was actually swallowing his food, and managed to convey a mass of information in his steady flow of talk. He was a man who veered constantly between reticence and indiscretion. Mr Jackson always referred to British Guiana as B.G., and during the three days that it took them to navigate the Guianese coast to Georgetown, Lucien learned a great deal about it.

Lucien set his standards of travelling very low, and Cruz, used as he was to sleeping on sacks in the gutter of the market square in his native Caravelas, found everything that Lucien chose to travel in 'muito bem'. Nevertheless, the boat that took them to Georgetown was so unspeakably hot and dirty that, rather than brave the fleas and the lice and the cockroaches below, Lucien and his party slung their hammocks on the grimy decks with the crew, and watched the dolphins following their wake as they chugged uneasily towards the Caribbean.

'What's B.G. like, Mr Jackson?' Lucien asked, and Mr Jackson smiled, displaying a set of enormous and imperfect teeth, capped with rare red gold.

'It's just like what it is, it's just like that. You see, it depends how you look at it. The way I look at it, it's home to me, so I see it as the best. And it is the best; it's got the best gold, and the best meanest pork-knockers panning for it, and I can tell you that because I was one,' here Mr Jackson flashed his teeth to illustrate the point, 'and B.G.,' he continued, 'it's got the biggest mosquitoes, that's in New Amsterdam where my aunt Maud comes from, well there has to be something in that Godforsaken pit and it isn't charity, but the mosquitoes there, well they're just the best; and the best rum and girls and the very best star apples in the world.'

Lucien soon realised that Mr Jackson was like a piece of machinery from the engine room of the *Orpheus*, once set in motion it could not stop easily. Now the boat could lurch from side to side as it rocked around the hemline of the

Courantyne, and it could almost keel over to join the hundreds of wrecks of pirate ships that had keeled over on that same coast before, but Mr Jackson was in mid-tale and he was determined to have his say.

'Well, *my* girl, Mr Lucien, was not the best girl. I used to say to her, "Girl, why did you make those big eyes at me, 'cos eyes was the one good thing you got." But I already got her then, and her ma was the curse of Stabroek. Her ma kept a stall there selling somebody's gold. Don't ask me whose, maybe she didn't know either, but she had plenty gold, and that daughter of hers with the cow eyes, she just followed me around that market with her cow eyes all soft and sweet, and me, a jackass back from the Essequibo with my nuggets of gold after four rotten months of prospecting, I get tricked once by the ma—she changed the nuggets, I know it—and then she offers me the daughter all draped round with gold bangles. What happens?' Mr Jackson inquired of the bewildered Cruz, who spoke no English and could not, therefore, follow his monologue. But even had he been able to reply, Mr Jackson was too zealous a raconteur to allow a mere lad to interrupt his flow, so he chimed in again himself, only seconds after his question, with, 'I'll tell you what happened. I get my money for my gold, and then I take the money to the rum shop, and who got to the rum shop first?' Again Mr Jackson paused, but this time only for breath before he continued, 'The damn woman with her cow-eye girl is there. I drink the rum, I buy the girl. Her mother swears to me by her own mother that this girl is pure. Pure fantasy! That was what that was! "You will be the first," she tells me. The first fool man to pay four months' gold-digging for a week of nagging and a dose of the clap. I was a young man then. Now, nobody comes between me and my money. I spent plenty time with the ladies, and guilders and dollars on bracelets and frocks, and star apples, too. Now, Mr Lucien, I spend my money on cards and rum. There's a rum shop I know . . .'

But Lucien had dozed off, propped against the roped crates of cargo, some of which he recognised as his own luggage, wondering what a star apple was.

Chapter 24

*T*HEY SPENT THE THIRD DAY OF THEIR SHORT VOYAGE CRAWL-ing around the Courantyne coast with shoals of flying fish leaping like oily puddles into the sun, and the heat making a haze around people's faces. From time to time, Lucien would get up from his hammock over a makeshift nest of folded tarpaulins and walk around the desk to stretch his legs. Each time he did this, Cruz would follow him like an anxious shadow picking his way through the ship's debris as he hurried to keep up. They were pushed between the still swelter of the Atlantic and the lazy swamps of Berbice. There was a cloud over the mainland like a black cloud of flies, and an uneasiness in the air as of beating insects' wings. The only insects on their squalid boat were crawling vermin, although Mr Jackson's interminable sing-song drone made up for the customary whirring of mosquitoes. Lucien could stroll or day-dream or sleep and still pick up the threads of Mr Jackson's patter.

'If you ever go to Berbice,' he was saying as Lucien resumed his seat beside him, 'you should see the old ruined castle at East Lothian. That was the plantation's name, to tell you true, but we called the old house East Lothian too, where the Campbells lived, and old Mr Campbell was a mean, mean man, the sort of man you wouldn't trust be-hind a biscuit.' Mr Jackson paused and sucked his priceless teeth. 'Now this Mr Campbell, he had a daughter, a long time ago must be, 'cos her girl is like my own grandma, but the old one, the mother, she fell in love with a man who come to visit the estate. A man is a fool, I tell you, to visit

Berbice, there is nothing but trouble there, and plenty of trouble.'

Lucien shifted restlessly, he was very hungry, and the food that was served on board was like stewed rubbish. He would have given anything for a rainbow trout or a lightly grilled chop.

'So the man came to East Lothian, a big man with a big smile, they called him Diamond Jim. I don't know why, because everyone knows his name was Walter, but he wore a diamond as big as a child's fist for a tie-pin. He used to sit under a silk cotton tree on the edge of East Lothian, under the big house, and play his guitar at night in the moonlight. And when there wasn't a moon, the piccaninnies used to say that the diamond at his throat was like the moon itself.'

Lucien sat and listened, watching the underside of the deck rails where the sea salt had rusted away the iron, and occasionally a slant of sunlight would glint on a lingering crystal, and he could see this Diamond Jim in his mind's eye, smiling under the silk cotton tree.

'Money can buy you a diamond pin, Mr Lucien, but it can't wash the blackness out of your skin, and Diamond Jim, he was so black if he fell in a tar pit you wouldn't know where to start looking. But prissy Miss Campbell, she liked him. She just got up one day and saw him under the silk cotton tree and she liked him. When her daddy found out, he locked her up in the stone tower at East Lothian, and she went mad there, mad with the heat and the rain and nobody else there but the whisperings of the stone and Diamond Jim, just off the property singing to her under the moon. They say Old Man Campbell cut him down with a bush knife and that it was his ghost that sat under the silk cotton tree. Even now, fifty years on, the piccaninnies say you can see that tie-pin shining like a moon; but some people say that it's Diamond Jim's smile and that the light is his big teeth flashing; and some people say that it's Diamond Jim's child that Missy Campbell had in that tower all alone, but other people say that she come to that child by his dead gost and that was why the chiley was born like she was, not of this world or the next, just in between, like Diamond Jim himself, too big and too bright for real life people, only fit for the dreams of East Lothian and those Berbice people. Now Demerara, that's different, Demerara . . .'

Lucien felt his legs contract with cramp, and he left Mr Jackson to recount the past scandals of Demerara to himself and the flying fish, while he, Lucien, walked around the littered deck again, straining his eyes towards Georgetown with a sudden longing.

As the short voyage progressed, more and more of the crew emerged from below, driven out no doubt by the stench and the smotheringly cruel heat. Each time Lucien went round the deck, he seemed to find a larger and larger gathering of sailors and fishermen lying together in a huddle of heads and arms and bottles of rum. For the first two days they seemed content to croon snatches of soft Caribbean songs, but by the third day, driven perhaps by the inexorable heat to make a bid for freedom, they began to play cards. Lucien watched them with interest as he passed. They were playing a version of poker interspersed with long draughts of neat rum and strings of curses. The players eyed him suspiciously at first, with the wiry Cruz in tow, and then, as they grew more accustomed to his circuits, and he even came once on his own, they invited him to play.

'Come an' try your luck, Mister,' one of them called out. Lucien agreed and smiled. 'We ant playing for smiles though. But if you put your money down, you can play.'

Lucien took out a modest handful of Surinam guilders, and two or three of the Amerindian sailors sucked their teeth in unison. Lucien could not help but notice the series of elaborate winks and whispers that passed between the men as they arranged to cheat him out of these proffered stakes.

'You don't look like a gambling man, Mister, did you ever play before?'

'Uh huh,' Lucien said, settling down beside them on their heap of sacks.

The boat crawled along past the flat divided coast with its pale-green fields bordered by woodlands and black sage, and old wooden Dutch dykes and locks punctuating the landscape like so many primitive guillotines in the grass. They passed Mahaica with its planted stilted houses and its row of bare-legged boys along the quay, and as they neared Georgetown itself, the atmosphere among the cardplayers changed from one of apathy to anger. Even Mr Jackson, from the depths of his narrative, sensed that something was amiss, and Cruz, who had been pinned to his stack of tarpaulins ever since Lucien had left, regaled with Mr Jackson's anecdotes, was desperate to get away and see what was happening.

The stack of money and oiled bills and packets of Woodbine and half-empty bottles of rum had all drifted across the circle to sit beside Lucien. Even though he realised that he ought to lose to let the sailors take back these things that he had no desire to keep, he couldn't do so. No matter what card he chose to take or throw away, Misia Schmutter was hellbent, for reasons that Lucien could not understand, on annihilating his fellow players. For the past three games, he had been trying to disguise his luck, throwing away kings and aces, but Misia Schmutter guided his hand with her special grip, the one that no one could resist, and he kept on winning. Lucien was sweating now, not just with the heat, but from the silent battle with his wayward grandmother. Making one supreme effort, he bet his entire stakes and then managed to bungle his hand. All around the circle of his game, hands loosened on their knives and wires, and there was such a sound of sucking teeth and exultation that the Captain himself was roused from his drunken slumber below the deck and staggered up to investigate. Lucien took his leave, and rejoined a relieved Mr Jackson and the still captive Cruz.

'Even though you lose, Mister Lucien, you're a lucky man today. I know this because I'm a mean man myself, so I tell you, never take the rum from a mean man's hand. Those sailors are Indian men, Caribs. You know, and the Caribs never lose. One more win and you would have been swimming to Georgetown—inside a shark.' Mr Jackson paused to contemplate this vision, but on seeing that Cruz was about to escape, he began again, 'Does the name Governor Hillhouse mean anything to you?'

Lucien shook his head, and Cruz followed suit, glad to be able to make an intelligible sign at last.

'Well he was the English Governor who came to take over the whole of Guiana, and the tribes and the settlers he put them all in his power and he treated them all bad. And the Carib chief—who was a woman, because they always take a woman for chief, you see to go through the blood line, and they say if a woman has a baby then that is her baby, but if a man says he has a baby, you don't know whose goddam baby it is—that makes sense.' Mr Jackson added, 'That makes a lot of sense. Well the Carib queen, she had a son, called Kietur, and she sent her son to watch this Governor Hillhouse, and he sent a messenger to the Englishman saying, "We Caribs cannot be servants to anyone, but we will make peace with you and be partners." Well Governor Hillhouse, he had his English warships right behind him, and he laughed. But the messenger said, "You laugh now, but come and see the numbers of our men and then you will not laugh any more." So the Governor sailed with his ships all along this coast of Berbice like you and me today, and where we see those fields of sugar-cane, Governor Hillhouse he saw the whole coastline lined with Carib warriors: all strong men, all armed, mile upon mile of them. And after a whole day and still the warriors went on, he made a treaty with the Caribs. And do you know how many men they had?' Lucien shook his head, and Cruz, again, copied him.

'They had about two hundred men or maybe less. But every time the English ship went by, the man at the end of the line, he run like fury to the front, and the English passed the same men all day long. They never lose; I tell you, if they are clever enough to take on Governor Hillhouse, they can handle a game of cards with a blond boy like you. Why, I expect you ant ever even killed a pussy cat, have you?'

'No,' Lucien answered him, 'I've never killed a cat.'

Mr Jackson smiled and nodded indulgently, while Lucien remembered the day in San Fernando when Chucho Delgado and he and a handful of men had tracked down the tiger by the rain pool at La Cañada and Chucho and the others had stood rigid with fright while he, in his fourteenth year, had shot the marauding beast straight through the heart as it faced him, ready to leap. He remembered how it had died, convulsed in the air, wanting to leap, too late, pouncing for its last kill almost after death. And he remembered the look in el tigre's eye as it lay in a magnificent heap on the caked ground. It was a strange look almost of surprise and he felt those great yellow eyes reproach him then, and he felt the same yellow eyes reproach him now. Chucho and his men had rallied and trussed up the dead feline deity of whom they were all so afraid that they felt driven to a kind of sacrilege, flaying at its inert stripes and pulling at its bloodstained jaw for a tooth as a trophy.

'What a shot!' Chucho had said. 'Well done—a split second more and it would have mauled you. That must have been the only shot that could have killed it clean. I think it was afraid of you, Niño Lucien.'

Lucien had looked down at the open eye of his victim, and the dead eye seemed to say, 'I live by my own law, and I have a right to hunt and destroy; your cattle are my cattle. I am the tiger, and you are a mere boy, but I had a truce with you, and you have betrayed it.'

'Well done!' Chucho had said again. And Lucien had been physically sick.

Mr Jackson was so struck by the intensity of Lucien's silence that he finally asked, 'What you thinking on, man?,

'I'm thinking about the tiger,' Lucien told him.

'Oho,' Mr Jackson whispered. 'Well, mark my word, the less you think about the tiger, the better it is, because before you know where you are, one minute you thinking about that tiger, and the next minute he jumped up on your back.'

Lucien nodded and then sank back into his reverie.

'Georgetown, Mr Lucien.'

'Dom Lucien, Dom Lucien!'

The voices drifted through the blur of sea and sun and day-dreams that held Lucien pinned to his squalid hammock, and he felt the boat heave and lurch as it rammed against its dock, and a clanking of chains and cranes and pulleys brought home to him that the last of his sea voyages was over. Both he and Cruz disembarked reeling from the heat and hunger and the sheer volume of Mr Jackson's running commentary. Arriving in Georgetown was almost like being home, the very name, Guiana, was like his own Venezuelan Guyana with its swamps and its deltas.

Lucien had insisted on taking a jug of the thick, amoebic drinking water and washing and shaving and combing down his hair. This last was no easy job, since he had been rash enough to have his hair cut in Paramaribo, where a Javanese barber had strapped him to a swivel chair and virtually shaved his head. That was three weeks before, and the stubble had again begun to lie flat in the short back and sides he was used to, but he still had the air of a U.S. Marine about him, which sat incongruously with the crumpled but still obviously well-cut cream linen suit. No sooner had he stepped off the boat on to the raised quay than two uniformed Englishmen in sun helmets and shorts approached him; one of them stepped forward.

'Mr Schmutter?' he asked.

'Lucien. My name is Lucien,' he replied in his halting English.

'Yes, well come this way, please.'

So Lucien followed the men into the cool peeling customs house, and he sat down in the chair they offered him opposite a broad teak desk. One of the men sat down while the other paced the room passing continually round and behind Lucien, flicking a straw fly-switch now and then.

'We don't know why you've come here, but you may as well know that every step you take in British Guiana will be followed by one of our men. You are not a German citizen, so we cannot legally intern you, but we can make it clear, as I hope we are doing now, and as I am afraid we shall go on doing, that we do not want you here. We don't like it, and we don't want it. If you'll take my advice, Mr Schmutter—'Here Lucien broke in for the first time.

'Lucien, my name is Lucien.'

'Mmm, well, Mr Schmutter, if you'll take my advice you'll go back to Venezuela by the next boat. We are holding your luggage, as a precaution—'

'But why?' Lucien asked them. 'What have I done?'

'It is not what you've done, it's what you are. You are a German, Mr Schmutter, and we are at war.'

'War?'

'Come come, don't tell me you didn't know. We might be colonials, but we can think for ourselves, even out here.'

Everywhere he went, the news of his status seemed to have travelled before him. He was an 'undesirable alien', a potential traitor, a man whose loyalties were elsewhere and in active opposition to their own. And every day, as the papers came out on the hoardings, Lucien bought his copy of the *Georgetown Times* and read about the enemy action, and he too was the enemy. He could have moved on then and there, to Venezuela which was neutral and where truckloads of coastguard militia would not be manning the guns in shifts and fanning the popular hysteria in the town. He could have left after the first day when one dilapidated boarding house after another turned him down. He could have left when the Park Hotel on Main Street not only refused him a room but even refused to serve him a cocktail on the first sweltering afternoon of his arrival. He had stood under the giant cupola listening to the whispering of the other guests as they eyed him with the same expression that in Germany was reserved for the Jews, and the whispered censure had mixed with the rustling of tugged lace on Misia Schmutter's withered wrists.

And all for a name, he thought. If his passport had said Lucien, the average Englishman would have let him be, but the Venezuelan custom of using the mother's name after the surname and then the grandmothers' maiden names made Lucien seem like a simple Christian name before the unfurling of a string of German titles. He could have left and saved himself the scorn and the irritation, but the situation was so new to him that he seemed unable to take it in. Whatever evidence accumulated to corroborate this apparent anti-German feeling directed against him, however many pear-shaped matrons crossed Main Street or Anira to avoid him, and however much abuse was whitewashed on to the wall of his boarding house, Lucien refused to believe in it. He thought, when they realise it's me, they'll change. At home, in San Fernando, he had never cared that his brothers had thought him peculiar, and he had not dwelt on the esteem or lack of it that he might rouse in the neighbourhood; but now, in the wide streets and the wooden symmetry of Georgetown, it mattered to him what other people thought. Even in prison he was to be a loner, kept apart from other men by the intensity of his dreams. He had wanted to change the world, to increase aesthetic awareness, to build the highest and most beautiful tower in the world, to make his life a shrine and much much more, but in Georgetown, he just wanted to be accepted, and then, later still, just not to be shunned.

Cruz's age was fixed by his bought passport at twelve, although he could have been anything from ten to a stunted fourteen. Whatever his age, he was definitely still a child, but even he suffered the taunts and the stones of a political outcast. And despite his brown skin and his almost black hair which spoke more eloquently of his Amerindian blood

248

than any papers could, he was branded a German, and had even come home once bruised and bloody-nosed with the clothes torn from his back after a trip to buy star apples at the Stabroek market had ended in a chase and a fight.

'Why do they hate us, Dom Lucien?' he had asked tearfully.

'Because they have stuck a label to our backs, and they hate the label.'

Whenever he could, Lucien escorted Cruz around the town, showing him the planked Georgian buildings, the Cathedral and municipal buildings, and Queenstown with its residential villas built on stilts, beneath which servants and their families camped while colonial families fanned themselves on the wide verandahs, discussing the war and the heat, and the Tower Hotel, where Lucien might have stayed but for the war.

Mr Jackson, meanwhile, had proved a loyal friend, and despite the growing hostility to Lucien and his Brazilian son, and the swastikas chalked up on the wall of their lodging, he kept turning up with his encyclopaedia of anecdotes to show them the sights and drive them to the Botanical Gardens or a rum shop or a cock fight out at Mackenzie. Of all the inhabitants, only the Amerindians and the Chinese seemed unimpressed by Lucien's supposed nationality. For them, he could have been a Martian. As for the rest, they monitored the progress of the war in Europe, and paraded their troops and their Union Jacks, while Lucien also followed the war, and wrote of his new sadness and rejection to Mariana in Italy. She of all people, Lucien felt, would understand.

Although it was to her, Mariana, that he addressed his letters, it was the official censor of the Guianese Postal Service who read his missives, and forwarded them to Jamaica for decoding. Lucien was unaware of this, and continued to pour out his thoughts and feelings to his estranged wife, to the delight of a certain Pedro Rincón who was paid liberally for translating these letters from Spanish into English. Then he had the unheard-of honour of going to the censor's splendid residence on Almond Street, in the select Queenstown with its jacarandas and ilex palms shading the wide swept streets, and being ushered through the polished mahogany hall to the censor's study. There, he sat in a great wicker chair and read out the letters and sipped iced lemonade with mint leaves in it and ate a special kind of oatcake that the censor had shipped in from his native Scotland. Pedro Rincón would have preferred not to have had these oatcakes, which he found unpleasantly gritty and tasteless, but he never quite had the courage to refuse them.

The censor himself grew so used to this ritual, that he quite missed the daily instalments of Lucien's thoughts when the visitor finally took off one night into the Interior, guided by Mr Jackson and a group of Amerindians he had bribed. All through the war, when anything went wrong, it was the censor's firm belief that it was 'that damned Schmutter', working against them from the depths of the jungle, who was responsible. He could kick himself for not getting the man interned sooner. It was quite clear that he was spying. The censor even wondered if he had got wind of the warrant they had for him. At least, the censor told himself, Schmutter and his boy wouldn't ever see their luggage again: not unless they went deep-sea-diving. Twenty-four more hours and they would have had him, and with the emergency powers they could have had him shot.

Chapter 25

CRUZ WAS TO ASK LUCIEN NOT ONCE BUT MANY TIMES IN years to come, 'Why did we go through the jungle, Dom Lucien?' His master's reply was always the same.

'Because of Misia Schmutter.'

'And who is Misia Schmutter?'

'She is everything to me.'

Cruz never did understand the logic of this; he had just followed, as he felt destined to follow, through the thick dark tangle of the Interior. It was a time of trial for him that began as a personal test of his fortitude under the strain of the plaited undergrowth and the incessant cuts and stings. The trek through the clinging uncut paths that led towards the Orinoco basin ended as a test of endurance. At first Cruz had wanted to act like a man and hold himself well, and not complain; later, it was simply a matter of whether he could get to wherever they were going alive, and whether he could keep putting one foot in front of the other behind the heels of the seemingly tireless, silent Indian who cut through the fronds and the lianas unscathed. For Cruz however, the sores and scratches grew daily worse, and his bites became infected and his arms and legs were full of needling grubs that were exacerbated by the sheer impenetrability of the bejucales. Then, as though that were not enough, there were snakes lying on the ground like twigs, and wound around branches, and snakes whose pale eyes met his as he pushed aside leaves, and there were those so swift and deadly that they kept no disguise, and Cruz was afraid of all of them. He was even afraid of the twigs that were only twigs, lest they transformed themselves and came alive.

When Mr Jackson turned back after the first day, Cruz was desperate to go with him, but he stayed on, sick with fear and stooping so low he felt his back would break. For although Cruz carried no luggage as such, having passed long since from porter to surrogate son, he was weighed down by the amulets and the good luck charms and the lucky beans and the pepas de San Pedro that he wore around his neck and wrists and waist and feet, and the smell of garlic that he carried in cloves tucked into his pockets, and stuck in his hair like a white pomander, kept him bowed. Cruz would carry anything to escape from the powers of darkness, and these powers lived, it was well known, in the bush. Exú, the god of caprice and evil-doing, was in the dull white of every snake's eye. Only the blessed Virgin could save Cruz now, he thought, as he trudged through the sinking, leaf mould behind his Indian guide, who walked, in his turn, behind Lucien, who followed his own guide out in front. Yes, the Santísima Virgen ruled the rivers and the waters, and always to one side of them was the yellow Orinoco, surely Our Lady must remember them. Cruz knew that, in that place, to be remembered from time to time was not enough, they needed watching over night and day, and to this end, he said his lucky beads like a rosary, telling the orange and grey seeds, interspersed with a number of extravagant promises.

Lucien could hear the drone of Cruz's tearful prayers underscoring the rustle of their progress. As the days passed into weeks, and they were still making their way painfully from one camp to the next, and one Amerindian village to the next, sleeping in hammocks and swathed in nets, with circles of rubber burning around their rough clearings to keep back snakes and a bright fire to keep the tigers at bay, Cruz's pleading became louder and louder, and little that Lucien could do or say seemed to comfort the boy. Cruz had offered all of his worldly possessions to Iemanja, who was also the Blessed Virgin and the goddess of all good things. Lucien could hear him running through his recent purchases.

'Hail Mary, full of grace, the Lord is with thee, can you still hear me? Blessed art thou among women, and you shall have the blue shirt I bought in Paramaribo with the white edging if you will only see us through this patch of bog . . . and little Mother in Heaven ask the Father to have mercy upon us miserable sinners, particularly myself and the good Dom Lucien . . . Ai ai ai ai, Virgen! If we reach San Fernando, you shall have my ivory figure and the stand as well, but spare us good Lady from all evil and mischief; from sin, from the crafts and assaults of the Devil; from the anacondas and the mapanare and the alarcranes and the black widows whom I cannot see, spare him, Virgencita, and spare me.'

So Lucien promised to Cruz one thing after another, to be given to him when they arrived, and Cruz, in his turn, gave them to his Blessed Lady, again on credit until their return. The boy's fears brought out his old instinctive talent for haggling. He bargained for his salvation in a constant, moaning patter, very much as he had bargained for damaged fruit at the old market in Caravelas. He had learned to fend for himself there from his earliest childhood to the day when Dom Lucien had saved him by allowing him to stay and carry his battered leather bags across the continent, and all had been well until they came to the dark forest. Now, it seemed, not even the old magic would save them from dying in the dark dripping undergrowth.

The jungle was a predatory place, so predatory that its habits became contagious, and the gentle Cruz made himself a catapult; whenever birds came within his range, with their glistening coloured feathers and their cocked beaks and brilliant crests, he felled them or sent them flying, maimed and squawking, through the middle trees. Those that he killed, toucans and parakeets, finches, cardinales and macaws, Cruz hung around his neck like pagan trophies, which he plucked at night and laid their feathers, and dried their already festered blood, at the altar of his would-be saviour, the Blessed Lady who would shield him from the Powers of Darkness.

What Cruz did not know, and Lucien could not explain to him, was that it was the Powers of Bitterness that dogged and threatened their trip. And the Lady who needed to be appeased was not Cruz's Lady, but the one whom Lucien carried on his back, Misia Schmutter, Our Lady of Bitterness. When Cruz slew the vibrant birds which came down to accompany him in his journey through the lower tier of the forest, and tore the feathers from their warm twitching breasts, Lucien remonstrated with him, saying, 'Cruz you must not be so cruel. This forest belongs to the birds and the plants and the beasts, we are only visitors here. It is not our business to damage a single feather or leaf in this place.'

And Cruz would answer him sullenly, with his eyes turned to the ground and his head bowed, 'No puedo más, Dom Lucien.' And those three words of defeat were all that he could be brought to say in defence of his seemingly senseless slaughter.

Lucien watched over him as they eased their way through the trees, following their Wapishiana guide as he wove his way in an intricate pattern through the forest until even Lucien could no longer distinguish the greenheart from the purpleheart from the mahogany, jacaranda, or grey ceiba trees. Lucien washed Cruz's sores and healed his cuts and stings and bites with many of the plants that he recognised from his childhood studies. Between caring for the bemused boy and keeping up his own pace, he even had time to collect specimens of the rarer plants that he found en route. Where Cruz wore dead birds around his neck, Lucien wore garlands of little known flowers which he pressed and examined each evening while the fireflies and the yellow swamp gnats circled around them.

By the fourth week, most of their journey was by woodskin canoes, being paddled down the dirty, lethal waters of the Orinoco that spread out like a Llano of water as far as the eye could see, with only the overhanging undergrowth on one side to stop the travellers from falling into the horizon. Lucien never questioned the Indians who guided them through the great rain forest, and they never explained where they were leading him and why they shifted from boat to foot and foot to boat again when they did, or why they sometimes waited in thatched shelters for up to two days at a time, prey to the insects and the dark spirit of the forest.

The Indians usually numbered seven, three of whom had come all the way from Georgetown, and four of whom changed from village to hidden village, surrendering their unenviable job to new porters. Their heads were permanently drooped to the ground, as if listening for the heartbeat of the forest, which they both feared and worshipped. Wherever Lucien went in that exotic underworld, he was paid a certain homage. The porters seemed to recognise the contradictory nature of their new employer and sense the invisible presence of his aged burden. If he wished to be taken to Venezuela, they would take him there, and although he had paid them liberally, they would have taken him for nothing but their food had he so asked. The forest sheltered only its own, and their people were the chosen few who had survived there for generation after generation. They knew of her secrets and her poisons and her traps, and somehow, the man Lucien knew too. This Lucien followed them, although they suspected that they could have followed him and still got through. He was like the god of the top layer come down to observe them with his eyes like the sky that they rarely saw, and his yellow hair like the sun that could not penetrate to the lower tier where they lived and died. He could catch fish for their supper with his hands as only their best fishermen could, and he could spear meat for them whenever he chose, as only their best hunters could. He knew where to put his feet and how not to provoke the snakes and how to appease them once they were disturbed, and he knew which leaves to pluck and rub on his stings so that they would disappear without a trace. And when the boy Cruz had toothache, he gave him the right leaves to chew, and when he had the shivers the man Lucien had warmed him with flowers, and when the boy Cruz wept and moaned, Lucien alone could calm him.

Yet for all his gentleness they could see the demon through it. They could see the outline of Misia Schmutter riding her grandson with her relentless rage. At other times when they had escorted traders through the forest, these Indians had always felt afraid; now, under the protection of the man Lucien, they felt a kind of hope and relief. The water didn't seem as deep with him, or the rapids as fast, or the piranhas as vicious, or the nights as dark. They were truly sorry when their days of shouldering Lucien's canoes were over, and he and his boy arrived at a place called Soledad, from whence Lucien assured them that he knew his way home. For although he had never before been that far down river, he knew from his maps that after Soledad there was Altagracia and after Altagracia it was just Caicara. Then, Lucien knew that he would leave behind the Orinoco and follow in its stead the more familiar muddy waters of the River Apure.

255

When Cruz reached Soledad, he was so relieved that he broke down and wept for hours, until his face was so puffed and red that Lucien had to apply cold compresses and arnica leaves.

'I never thought we would see daylight again, Dom Lucien,' he explained through his tears.

Lucien reassured him. 'We shall travel by steamboat from Angosturas, across the water, to my homelands, and then to Caracas.'

'Oh yes, Dom Lucien, now it is muito bem, but when I was in the jungle I felt as though something was strangling me, and then I had to do everything I could to stay alive. I am sorry, Dom Lucien, but things change when you come within sight of your own death. I will stay with you until the day you die, but I beg you, never take me into the dark forest again. Everyone has a weak place in them, and that is mine, I never knew it until now, even Our Lady of the Waters was unable to help me there. No one should ever be so alone.'

Lucien booked their passage on the next steamboat out of Angosturas, following the thin path from the quay to the ticket office through a straggling herd of razor-back pigs. His days of trekking were over, and Cruz recovered as their upriver voyage progressed. However, Lucien remembered his words long after Cruz himself had forgotten them. He remembered when, after ten years in jail, he escaped from the forest stronghold of San Juan de los Morros and took off to the jungle again, making his way through the same swamps and mudlands. He left Cruz behind that time rather than submit him to a second torture. And rather than remind Cruz all those years later of his former weakness, he remained silent, though he knew that Cruz would hold it against him. Lucien couldn't take the risk of seeing Cruz again reduced to a trembling wreck hung with amulets and mangled half-dead birds.

Chapter 26

ALL LUCIEN'S THOUGHTS SEEMED TO RETURN TO TIME AND place, as though these two factors were the keys to life itself. The place of his thoughts was a more fixed point than the time. Place was like a root to be dragged up and moved around, so that only one place could be of paramount importance. Time was different, it was fluid and required more attention since it was always there, demanding to be taken into consideration. Even at roulette, Lucien knew that the time was far more crucial than the place.

Within his own life, the place must certainly be el Llano, and more precisely, San Fernando itself. The German in him, and his blood, at least, was all German, seemed to clamour for a continued link with Tilsit and the Black Forest. Despite this, his trip to Hamburg and to Tilsit had been wasted, he felt, except perhaps to discard a myth. So why he continued to ache for Germany he never knew. He suspected that it was really Misia Schmutter who still missed her homeland. While still considering place, Lucien brought in the Orinoco, which was both like a water deity and an oversized boa constrictor in his thoughts. El Llano and the Orinoco, though they battled and chafed, were one. So place became San Fernando and a longing for Germany.

Time, on the other hand, defied any reduction. Certain times had been more important than others: and one above all, his third birthday, when Misia Schmutter had come like a great bird of prey into the nursery and taken him from the arms of his terrified nurse, and his life had never been his own again. He tried to remember what it had been like before, but there was little left except for a hazy memory of his mother, and once of his brother Detlev, giving him a piggy-back ride and then dropping him suddenly on the verandah.

During his first ten years in prison and the last ten years in prison, when he shared a cell with a number of other inmates, and he allowed himself to indulge in idle chatter with them, Lucien asked about their earliest childhoods. He hoped to discover what they were like before they were three, and thus perhaps what he himself might have been like before that crucial age.

Time was always something that had to be mastered, and he turned the full force of his intellect to this task. As the years passed, he saw more and more clearly that it was a matter of what Misia Schmutter had taught him in his earliest years. It was about keeping the initiative. He could hear her shrill voice echoing through his cell whenever he closed his eyes and tried to recall it, 'If you ever lose the initiative, Lucien, get it back.' At times it seemed singularly pointless to Lucien that life with all its pain and suffering, its hopes and failures, should be a simple matter of 'getting it back'. And somewhere, defying all definition, there was Mariana, who had promised to return and never did. From Rio to Soledad Lucien had written to her, and he had always called at the Venezuelan Consulates of the cities he passed through to collect letters from his wife. None had come, though, not to the Consulates or to the postes restantes. Lucien had consoled himself by blaming the post for her silence.

At night, when seven o'clock brought darkness to his cell and there was nothing to do until five-thirty the following morning but think and flex his muscles and sleep, Lucien grew saddest. He had even wondered, years before, as he lay in his cell with his corner of pot plants and his trough of herbs scenting the air on one side, and the cloying stale smell of the other men masturbating on the other, with nothing but a thin line of books dividing him from them, whether Misia Schmutter had played a trick on him. Was it possible, he wondered, that she had forced him along his perilous track for no better reason than a kind of practical joke? What was his mission? How was he to be a catalyst? It was only Misia Schmutter's total lack of humour that made him doubt the likelihood of it. Misia Schmutter was incapable of a jest. Every move she made was in earnest, her clinging to his back, her clawing out his life, her leading him into the trap that led to his imprisonment, twenty-five years of incarceration—it was all for a purpose, of that he was sure. All that he needed to know, when his doubts beset him, was what that purpose was.

The more Lucien thought about time and place, the easier he became. Whole days passed and he did nothing but go over his life chronologically, or as near to chronologically as he could. For it was a strange fact that events in his life seemed to change their order, and occasionally something would drop out of the picture altogether and it was only with great difficulty that Lucien managed to fit it in again. Thus his trial, which might have been expected to figure as a major event in his life, barely had a place in his memory at all.

Lucien noticed that although for him personally the most important part of his life was and always would be what he was going to do in the future, for others, it was always what he had done in the past. So Cruz, who took a morbid interest in his master's past, asked him over and over again, the shifting details of this or that period and Lucien would tell him, not all, but some of what had happened then. Cruz returned as constantly as a magnet to its North, with his questions about the trial, and his doubts about the verdict. While Lucien himself could scarcely remember anything of the event, not the first or the last day or the many months in between. Not the first trial when he had merely been sent to his proper trial, and not the second trial when he had been convicted, ironically, of a killing that he had not done.

Six months later, Cruz wrote to Mariana in Rome and told her about the second trial, and of the conviction. Together they plotted and schemed, incensed by the injustice of the sentence: twelve years' imprisonment with no right to appeal. Twelve years for a crime that Cruz knew for certain Lucien had not committed. He and Lucien had been together at the time, nowhere near the scene. However, Cruz was a Brazilian orphan with an imperfect knowledge of Spanish, and no match for the witty counsel for the prosecution who confused and ridiculed him. Although Mariana heard of the trial only when it was over, after her return to Venezuela, she too began to amass all that had happened during those two months of questioning and cross-questioning.

Mariana left Italy in 1941 after she had become a kind of Mediterranean staff annexe for German officers. At first nights and dinners and openings she had heard so many declarations of Jew-hating and love that she found her own position quite intolerable. She had never thought of herself as Jewish until the outbreak of the war. Then the revelation that threats, and the slogans and abuse that she heard daily heaped on to all Jews and their offspring, would also apply to herself, were her origins but known, brought out the suppressed Sephardi in her. She had once been on the verge of being an outcast, in Caracas, and she was determined not to be one again, so she packed her bags, freighted her most valuable objects to La Guaira, and determined to abandon Rome once and for all, and return to Lucien, the most patient of husbands. She decided to wait for his next letter and then set sail. When no such letter arrived, she telegraphed to Hamburg and San Fernando and Caracas and filled her time by replenishing the contents of the apartment she had shipped ahead to Venezuela. She was in the throes of this interior decoration when Cruz's letter came. She sailed, within the week, from Genoa, arriving on a sultry mid-September day in 1941, too late to free Lucien and too late to save their marriage.

As the liner that carried Mariana home sliced through the kingfisher sea, calling at neither Barbados nor Trinidad as it might have done in peacetime, she had had thoughts only for Lucien. The possibilities that stretched out before them seemed as limitless as the Caribbean that slapped the ship in a continual frill of white spume. It was nearly three years since she had received Lucien's telegram from Tilsit, and over a year since his last garbled message from Brazil. This did not worry her overmuch, since letters were so unreliable; what disturbed her was his silence about the trial. How long would he have waited before telling her? Would he ever have done so?

When her ship docked, she knew she was home, not so much by the familiar sights and smells as by the chaos of the port, culminating, in lieu of proper customs, in a kind of legalised armed robbery at the customs desk. Mariana, for all her Italian papers and airs, was as Criollan as any of the officers who had conspired to steal her goods, and she managed to escape with a large part of her luggage intact, having had to forfeit only a quarter, which she knew was a good bargain under the circumstances, and she was pleased with herself. All of the statues and paintings and boxes that she had brought for Lucien were there, and they were all things that she knew would give him pleasure.

She was driven from La Guaira at breakneck speed in a battered but gleaming Rover. The driver, who on closer inspection looked barely fourteen, kept up a commentary on his progress as he swerved in and out of the oncoming traffic, whistling and tapping his feet. He was singing a particularly lively Colombian song, the rhythm of which Mariana could scarcely recognise, and from time to time he picked out the beat by playing a foot percussion on the accelerator pedal. Mariana sat in the back seat, gripping the armrest as the car lurched from one verse to the next of its driver's song. She was so taken off her guard by the tremendous changes that had taken place in the city, and by the impertinence and speed of her chauffeur, that she was rash enough to admit to understanding Spanish, or cristiano, as her incorrigible guide called it. The next half-hour was interspersed with facts and figures.

'Where are you going to stay, vale?' the driver asked, addressing her with the over-familiar term, and, before she had time to think, he added, 'Rich people stay at the Tamanaco—it's got six hundred and twenty rooms and they say some people have gone in and never come out again, it's so big. How about it, vale?'

'Vale,' it seemed, pronounced valley, was all that this young boy was going to call Mariana. She studied the back of his neck, and frequently, as he left the car spinning on its own, his face as well, and she felt vaguely afraid of his easy insolence, so she limited her replies to his varied questions with such mild protests as, 'Please keep your hands on the wheel.'

'I don't need to, vale, this car is so smooth it can run itself.' The latter accompanied by a demonstration of the car racing headlong and unchauffeured down the busy road.

'Then just pretend to keep your hands there, for me,' she said.

'Do you want to see how fast she can go round the next bend?' he volunteered.

'No I do not!'

It had taken Mariana all of the five years that she had been absent from Venezuela to restore her nerves to some condition of stability. By the time they arrived at the Tamanaco, after two hours at the mercy of her maniac driver, she was in such a state of nervous collapse that she had to be helped from the car.

'If you need a taxi again, vale, just call me.'

'What's your name?' she whispered, determined to remember it so that she could avoid him at all costs.

'General Electric Picón.'

She stared in disbelief.

The driver, not in the least abashed, repeated his name proudly and smiled, giving the ashen Mariana the full flash of his gold-studded teeth.

'Thank you,' she told him, and was escorted into the massive hall of the Tamanaco Hotel, where she had the presence of mind to count her pieces of luggage before she ordered herself a suite with a terrace and a bathroom, and retired for an early night.

That was her first day in Caracas; her second day was spent in looking for Cruz. First, she went in one of the hotel taxis, driven by the most staid and elderly-looking chauffeur she could find, to visit Niemenberg. Lucien had told her that the house was no longer there, but remembering the size of it, she felt that something must remain. When the taxi took her to the familiar site, all that was left was the orchard and the brick wall of the garden, which now housed a green-shuttered villa, and down by the lower road, where the great gates had been, there was a hummock of rubble that stretched over the land where the house had stood, like a turfed mound over which the willow herb and the elder trees had taken root.

Mariana went back to the taxi and slumped into her seat. 'Do you remember the house that was there?' she asked the ancient driver.

'Well, I'm an Andino myself, but I'm told there was a palace there with over a thousand rooms and when the oil was found in Maracaibo, fifty years ago almost today, the palace burst into flames and was consumed by fire and hundreds of people died inside there, señora, and they say there's a cemetery at San Bernardino with just the bodies from that fire. I can't read myself, so I don't know about the cemetery; but I've got a nephew who worked near the oilfield and he says that when they find oil it does burst into flames and burns for weeks on end, so it must be true, about the palace here, I mean.'

Mariana nodded and instructed him to drive on, this time to the barracks where Detlev Lucien was quartered. It was he who told her the first details of his brother's trial and imprisonment, and who gave her the address of the prison where Lucien had been for nearly a year. She asked Detlev so many questions that finally he had to send her away.

'Who spoke for him at the trial?' she demanded.

'Well, I did, and this Cruz boy he adopted in Brazil, though frankly, I would have paid that boy not to talk.'

'And who else?'

'No one much.'

'But what about all his friends, all your friends?'

'His friends all seem to have disappeared, or forgotten him; quite a few have told me since that they didn't believe it could be the same Lucien, or they would have gone. You see, it was just so unlike him, I mean, this treason charge, that I can well understand people thinking it was someone else.'

'But couldn't you have helped him?'

'I did what I could, Mariana. I bribed so many people my wrist ached from all the dipping into my pocket, and we were doing fine, but then when Lucien took the stand, he seemed to damn himself.'

'What do you mean, "damn himself"?'

'He refused to defend himself, and instead of just keeping quiet, he went on and on about right and wrong, accusing the judge and the jury and all the rest of us of every crime under the sun. The judge had begun by being very apologetic and reluctant to have to try someone of our class, but by the time he had finished, I swear he hated Lucien. Each day was worse than the last: the judge just used to forget about the court and jump right in with the questioning himself; when the counsels complained he just used to say, "Shut up or I'll have you arrested." Anyway, Lucien stayed as cool as he always is, while the judge got more and more angry. He worked himself into a terrible rage for the first half of the trial and then harangued the jury for the second half.'

'But why?' Mariana asked.

'I don't know really. I suppose Lucien just made him feel

uneasy, the way he can, and then the judge got it into his head that Lucien was an impostor.'

'Detlev, you must have defended him.'

'I tried, and do you know what he said? "Young man, although you are undoubtedly Colonel Lucien of the Armed Forces of the Republic of Venezuela, I feel that I am more able to detect this snake in the grass than you are. You have been duped, and I feel that it is my duty to save you." '

'But that's absurd.'

'I know, but we must just do what we can for him and hope.'

'No, Detlev, tell me again, what was it he said?'

Mariana returned to the Tamanaco Hotel where she spent two whole days in the steambaths, leaving them only to sleep each evening, and all the time that she sat in the blistering mineral water, she planned how to release Lucien from jail. When she finally recovered enough to visit him, she was shocked to find how contented he seemed. During her first visit she was so sorry for him that she could hardly speak, and the burden of small talk fell on Lucien.

'I'm so glad you are safely out of Europe and the war,' he told her.

'Yes,' she agreed, and brightened, and then grew silent again.

'Do you have somewhere nice to stay, Mariana?' he asked, and she nodded.

'What do you do all day?' Mariana asked, looking around her furtively at the various other inmates of the cell who were lined up behind the barred visiting room, listening to the sporadic conversation.

'I read a lot, and I have my plants, and I cook now too.'

'Cook? Who for?'

'For the cell.'

'Why?'

'I like it. I was a ship's cook once.'

Mariana, like all the other people to whom he had told this, was unimpressed.

'I'm all right, Mariana. You just look after yourself, and tell me if there's anything you need; and if you have a moment, then look after my boy Cruz.'

'You're in prison for something you didn't do!' Mariana shouted, infuriated by his resignation.

'It was going to happen, Mariana, I felt it a long time ago, whether I did it or not, and to tell you the truth, it feels fractionally better to be here for something I didn't do than something I did. You see I can keep a sort of self-righteousness about me. If I had done it and got caught, I think I would feel like a failure in some way. I have done what I have done, Mariana, and now I am here, for no better reason than I am what I am.'

'Lucien!' she said in exasperation, and then more calmly, 'Do you still feel the weight on your back?'

'We all have a weight to carry at some time, that is mine.'

Mariana stared down at the dull red tiles on the floor and then turned and kissed him with a parting, 'Shall I bring you some flowers next time?'

'Bring a book,' Lucien told her, 'on architecture, please.'

Chapter 27

*A*FTER HIS INITIAL CONVICTION *LUCIEN ENJOYED A CERTAIN* degree of comfort in his prison life, as the sympathies of the public outside and the guards inside were all with him. He was believed to be the victim of a mad judge. There was scarcely anybody better qualified to belong to the country's élite, privileged as he was by birth and wealth, and if someone like him could be thrown into jail on a trumped-up charge, then what hope was there for the millions of peasants and peones and slum-dwellers and soldiers with no money to bribe and no great names to wave or estates to flaunt.

The public had seen photographs of Lucien in the papers, double-page spreads in the smaller ones and a sort of studio portrait in *El Nacional*, and not only did he not look like a vagrant or a malandro, he was incredibly handsome. Caraqueñan housewives and their daughters kept cuttings of Lucien's face under their pillows. Market girls tucked his picture into their bodices and washerwomen into their high sleeves. Primary school children slipped into the lavatories between lessons to giggle over him, and in convents all over the country, supplies of sal volatile had to be requisitioned to restore the girls, and occasionally a wistful nun, to their senses. Along the wooden benches of Parque Central, and under the flocked leaf ceiling of Los Caobos, elderly ladies relived their youth, dreaming of Lucien and the eroticism that emanated from his suppressed smile.

Earlier, in Georgetown, abusive slogans with swastikas had appeared all over the neighbourhood where Lucien and his loyal Cruz were staying. While he was held at the cuartel in San Antonio de los Altos, ten miles from Caracas, slogans of support and encouragement were painted up on the barracks walls every night, and no amount of vigilance could prevent them from reappearing. The locals swore that they painted the signs with the connivance of Lucien's very prison guards. Whatever it was, the guards themselves vied with each other in acts of courtesy they didn't know they had in them when dealing with their new and splendid prisoner. They were as pleased as he was to see him dressed immaculately each morning, and gladly smuggled in his Italian barber and a manicurist and even his tailor whenever they could. And his dreary grey cell which had housed in its time more cut-throats and thieves and rapists and revolutionaries than many of them were numerate enough to count, and had always seemed degrading and squalid, turned under Lucien's expert hand into a kind of exquisite bower. Where previously there had been four bare expanses of damp wall, Lucien hung orchids and ferns trailing over his boxes and jardinières of herbs and flowers.

Even the furnishing, which officially could not be changed except by a few personal belongings, took on a luxurious appearance. The floor was coated liberally with powdered lime and covered with a Persian carpet and then a rug and cushions with silk tassels, and the bed was covered with tapestry and braid, and Lucien's books and his statues and boxes gave the cell an air of a royal palanquin. Some of the prisoners that the guards had dealt with, such as those who were in for fraud or debt, had been known to provide a swig of rum or Scotch in return for favours. Lucien even had his own style here. At half-past four exactly—a notion that was utterly confusing to most of his wardens, who had survived until then without any clear idea of time and its divisions—cocktails were served. Most of the guards and inmates had limited their drinking to rough aguardiente, distilled illicitly in hillside slums, or rum, or, when they were showing off, whisky, and lager for the heat and for hangovers. Lucien, however, served cocktails only, and he mixed them with a skill and delicacy that amazed everyone. Within weeks of his arrest, Lucien's prison cell had become not so much a place of punishment, as the most desirable bar in town. All over Caracas people were scheming how to get access to Lucien's most exclusive cocktail hour. For the first time in their memory, guards were bribed to allow people into the prison rather than to let them out. Ambitious conscripts from the guardia civil were applying for transfers to the cuartel at San Antonio in such numbers that a new department had to be opened up temporarily to deal with them.

Some of those who shared Lucien's alcoholic concoctions continued to merely for the cachet of doing so. Others came genuinely for the drinks themselves with their blends of liqueurs and tropical fruits. Yet others came for the plates of delicious snacks that Lucien prepared each afternoon expressly to tempt the palates of his guests. Some days he merely served caviare with a drop of lemon on wafer-thin biscuits which Cruz had brought, and a selection of French and Italian cheeses on slivers of fresh toast. On his best days, though, Lucien curled anchovies around the eggs of guinea-fowl and shaped the whole to simulate a living fish, or he made shellfish pâté in a variety of beautifully coloured shells, or he carved palm hearts or pineapples or ham into models of things he hardly knew, indulging his own taste and the Tilsit blood that shaped whatever it touched.

At first, when the guards and prisoners saw what Lucien was doing, they laughed, then gradually, they began to take the food—pasa palos, they called it. Although rather than use it as they normally would, to ballast their drinks, they took it home, or if they were fellow prisoners, they took it to bed and admired it more closely. The ants and the heat often spoilt this for them, and they soon turned to nibbling at Lucien's creations. Then the taste for sculpted food became almost addictive. No sooner had a warden eaten a celery boat than he wanted another, and then fish and birds and fleshy papaya orchids to follow. Hardened criminals, more used to putting the food into their faces with their fists, developed absolute passions for peeled and flayed grapes.

When Mariana questioned Cruz retrospectively about the different aspects of the trial and the period prior to it, it was the social details that came to him, rather than the courtroom itself. Of the courtroom, Cruz could remember virtually nothing, and Lucien told her only of the stone tub of geraniums in its outer hall, and the feeling almost of hysteria that reached him from the public gallery where crowds of women pushed and strained and poked each other for a better view of him. Then, he remembered the look in the old judge's eye whenever he turned it on him. Members of the press, talking the case over in the Chicken Bar on Sabana Grande, had described the look as one of hatred, but it wasn't quite that, it combined all the elements of cruelty. Lucien knew the look; he had seen it before: in Hamburg it was reserved for the Jews; in Georgetown for himself; in Brazil for Cruz; in San Fernando for the weak. It was an international look, and from the first time Lucien saw it in the judge's eyes he prepared for the worst.

So Lucien was sentenced in the summer of 1940 for a crime that he did not commit, by a judge who loathed and despised him because he believed that he was not the man he said he was.

'It is not enough', the judge had told the court during his sentencing, 'to send this man to prison. He must be stripped of what he has. He must have no name, no identity, and no future. If the law of this Republic were a different one, then he should be destroyed. You see before you a dangerous man. May his name and memory be wiped from every record in the land.' After a lifetime of practising in the courts, of looking for a cause to uphold, and then finding it in the guise of an easy life and working diligently to protect it, the judge had never spoken as eloquently as he did in the subsequent passages of his closing speech.

After ten years, and long before, the judge's wishes, which were practically decrees, came true. The name of Lucien and his memory passed out of popular myth. He became a has-been, the relic of a craze. Occasionally, someone would remember him indeterminately; was he a dandy, or a former dictator, a palace, a traitor, a ship? Ten years was a long time in a country spread as thickly with black oil as Venezuela for the masses to remember someone as slight and gentle as Lucien. So he existed within the limited context of his prison life, serving cocktails to a dwindling few who took them for granted and would have been quite shocked had they ceased to appear. And the food in his pasa palos lost its novelty and became, it seemed, with its familiarity, more tasteless. Although Lucien's corner of the shared cell still looked like a museum, the wardens grew used to seeing it thus, and it aroused no comment. Only Cruz and Mariana, who visited regularly, found Lucien much more than a generous and amusing raconteur.

Occasionally, prisoners who were serving shorter sentences than his own left and were replaced by other, brasher men who challenged Lucien's supremacy within the cell. Lucien never fought them. One man hammered on the iron door all night pleading to be let out after going for Lucien with a knife. He claimed that the knife had flown from his hand, and at the same moment, a terrible pain had filled his bowel and had been there ever since.

'He's got the Evil Eye,' the prisoner had screamed. 'Let me out of here.'

The guards had eventually dragged the prostrate man outside, beaten him senseless for making such a racket, and then thrown him back in. That man had spent fifteen more months in Lucien's cell and had never spoken again, not, as one of the wardens described it, 'so much as pío'. Another time, a new guard had held Lucien's shoulder roughly one morning while escorting him to the visiting-room. He claimed that Lucien never moved his hands from behind his back, but another invisible hand took hold of his own wrist and squeezed it so hard he wet himself. It was also rumoured that if you baited Lucien, he snarled in a way that was scarcely human; he could wither limbs they said, and get out any time he chose, but that for some mysterious reason he wanted to stay.

In 1951, when Lucien was transferred to the prison at San Juan de los Morros, and then broke out, he was just two years away from completing his sentence. Not Cruz, or Mariana, or his brother Detlev, or anybody else, could understand why he did it. It was one thing to escape, to use his money and his friends to fly clean away from Venezuela; going to the jungle was quite another, and it disturbed them. According to Detlev, it was the behaviour of a wild beast and not of a man. Lucien himself might have been said to have kept his public over the escape itself, even though a prison guard was killed: prison guards were not well liked and most people thought they deserved what they got. It was the episode in the jungle, his capture and the sinister shadow of his return that caused the same crowds who had chanted and cheered for him ten years

270

before to call for his blood. The old judge from Lucien's first trial had died, but no doubt it would have done him good to have heard the cries of 'Kill him, kill him' that rang through the streets on the day after Lucien's recapture.

It always seemed to Cruz a miracle that they didn't kill his master. Lucien would have welcomed death at any moment during his long torment after they brought him back from the Orinoco trussed and flayed like an animal. He had grown up in pain and fear, so their torture as such could not break him. Misia Schmutter had broken him all those years before in San Fernando, and there could only ever be one breaking point. By comparison, their crude beatings and mutilations were but amateur attempts at a skilled job. He suspected that his captors didn't hurt him more because they didn't dare: had he died, he felt sure that they would have committed atrocities with his body, alive they were afraid of his power.

It was in 1952, after the torture ended, that Cruz had been allowed to visit him again. Then Cruz, who had grown into a shy, wiry young man, had found not his usual Lucien but a prematurely old man shackled to a wall. Shocked at seeing his master and father figure reduced to a grey shadow, Cruz had blamed Lucien for leaving him behind at the time of the escape.

'What good would it have done either of us, Cruz, to have fed you to the caymans or the snakes?'

'I would have been strong for you,' Cruz said reproachfully.

'I know that, but it wasn't strength we needed, it was power, and my powers have gone.'

'No, Dom Lucien,' Cruz insisted, appalled by the very thought of it, 'they cannot go.'

Lucien shrugged.

'I read about your capture in the paper. Every day for many days you were there in the headlines of *El Nacional* . . . You would not believe the things they said!'

'Oh, I would believe them.'

'But why has this all happened to you, why?'

Lucien thought a while, huddled against the sheen of green mould on the wall to which he was chained by one hand and one foot, and he shifted the manacle on the raw patch of scabby skin on his wrist, and then he said,

'It is because I am different.'

271

'And is that a crime?' Cruz burst in.

'Yes,' Lucien told him soothingly, 'that is a crime and a terrible one, worse than any other crime there is. Some animals kill the likes of me at birth, and others wait and harass them to death. Even pigeons destroy the ones who transgress. Only we humans pride ourselves on our individuality: we admire and follow leaders.'

'Then why the hate, Dom Lucien?'

'Perhaps because they used to love me, Cruz, and because I didn't stop when they expected me to.'

'Who are they?'

'You and I, Cruz, and everyone else.'

'Not I, Dom Lucien, I would never hurt you.'

'So they all say, after every atrocity and every mistake, but who can they be if they are not all of us.'

'Not I, though,' Cruz repeated stubbornly.

'I am not afraid of what they say or what they might do, I have acted alone with no regard for the consensus, I have done what I feel to be right and I feel justified in it—that is what they cannot forgive. But at the same time, they are afraid to put an end to me. They could have killed me twelve years ago when they first took me into their prisons. They could have killed me two years ago when they next caught me by the Orinoco. They could have killed me any time during these last two years of torture. They didn't, though, Cruz; and do you know why?'

'No, Dom Lucien.'

'Because they didn't dare. You see, there is a tremendous power in taking the initiative. It is the ultimate weapon, the trump card; if you have it, you win. I always made the first move, and they are afraid to touch me now, so they prod and poke and kick and that is all they dare to do, Cruz.'

Cruz listened sadly, saying nothing now, while he weighed with one half of his mind the differences between the beautiful young man whom he had first seen enter the prison twelve years before and the scarred haggard shell crouching opposite him with his clothes in rags and his once immaculate hands torn and battered and nailless.

'In prisons everywhere there are the likes of me, I am not unique. Some call us monsters, and some killers, and some outlaws and some martyrs. Mostly, though, the people try to forget us. Only those who come near us cannot forget, cannot for the most part oblige their fellows by disposing of me and these other stubborn men who walk their own paths. And every day that we stay alive is a day of significance.'

'But why?'

'I don't know why. I've been here for twelve years, and I can feel myself growing old, and I think about it and I search my brain for an explanation—for some reason for what I do and have done—and none comes: I just know that I am right, I just know that I have to go on. It is my mission.'

Cruz felt uneasy with this kind of talk. Had he not heard it many times before in Georgetown and Caracas, and then in the prison again and again during the first ten years of Lucien's sentence, he might have thought that his master's recent torment had unhinged his brain. As it was, he found Lucien battered and gaunt almost beyond recognition, but behind the maltreated façade, he was unchanged. So much so that Cruz ventured to ask, 'Shall I bring you a trough?'

'Yes, and cuttings and compost.'

'What shall you start with? It is so dark in here.'

'Bring me ñongué and garden mint, and maidenhair fern and one or two violets and some garlic to plant and a clump of mimosa.'

Cruz, who had tried hard to study Lucien's medicinal plants and their various uses, had spent many hours at home in the big empty villa tucked away behind the Botanical Gardens poring over Lucien's herb lists and manuals. In twelve years he had become fairly expert, and although he saw the reason for each of his master's new requests, he could not immediately see why he should want to have the mimosa, commonly and wrongly known as adormidera. So he asked, 'Why the mimosa?'

And Lucien said, 'Because I like to touch its leaves, and it pleases me to see them curl up and recover. That's all.'

Then Cruz was called by the guard, who pushed him roughly out of the cell, saying, 'It's a wonder you're not afraid to go in.'

Only the basement of this prison was dungeon-like, the rest was a converted barracks with cells and corridors and gardens, and, as he left, Cruz noticed a group of prisoners wearing their own khaki trousers and checked or plain shirts, sweeping out the main hall or leaning on their wide

273

brooms and smoking. He was struck by the difference between the relative comfort of the captivity of these easy-going prisoners and the humiliation and squalor of his own good Lucien. It was like the difference between the old sleepy violence of the cities—this one and Caracas—and the brash new tinny speed of the modern wave that was sweeping through Venezuela. Everywhere, skyscrapers and crystal towers were rising, and highways, the likes of which he had never seen before, or even dreamt of. Cruz himself always travelled by tram and train, but all around him he saw the sleek lines of American cars. These cars had invaded Caracas, they were coming down the valley day after day, like hordes of hungry red ants. Food came in tins now, and drinks shot up your nose instead of going down your throat. Life had changed, and only in Dom Lucien's ancient cell had time stood still. He might have been on Devil's Island itself or in any dungeon of any jail centuries ago in the days of the buccaneers. There were no drive-in cinemas for him, there was no bubble gum nor the ubiquitous chiclet, the chewing gum which symbolised the young generation in Venezuela like an elastic and tasteless James Dean.

On the slow train from Valencia to Caracas, Cruz found himself looking out sadly over the crossfire of cultures through which he rode. And he became almost tearful at the thought that Dom Lucien might have been chained to the wall for the twenty-one months since his escape to the Orinoco. However, he was gradually lulled by the train churning through the barren expanses of cactus and araguaney interrupted from time to time by gullies, with an occasional tin and mud shack set up to shelter a family of goatherds or Indian weavers.

Cruz returned the following week, as he would return every week until Lucien was moved to the vast white edifice of Cátia La Mar with its rows of cells like cages, one on top of the other, and the seagulls circling over its acres of roof. On this, his second visit since Lucien's recapture, Cruz came armed with food and compost, a trough and the plants to go in it. He had little to do each day but care for the books and cuttings that he kept in the green shuttered villa where he lived in the hopes of his master's return.

It had been an easy task to take a root or scion of each of

Lucien's requested plants and bring them wrapped in wet cotton wool in black plastic bags of peat. He carried his cuttings and topsoil back through the sandy bare waste of the State of Lara where nothing grew but scrubland and prickly pears that could sink their roots dozens of feet into the ground, not only to get water but to hide from the searching rays of the Laran sun. There were dogs whose ribs rocked on their haunches and whose eyes stared out through their mange. And there were chickens scrabbling in the dust and goats eating anything they could get down their gullets, from thorns to stones, and there were vultures waiting for any or all of these to die, and only the vultures thrived. Outside the mud huts that dotted the hilly wasteland, bits of goat were hung out to the flies. Cruz supposed they were really put there to dry in the sun, having been duly salted, but it was the flies that caught his attention, and the rows of metal pipes that glinted in the sun as they swung from the thatched roofs. The pipes were put between the skin and the flesh of a live goat and blown until the startled goat puffed up and died from the pressure; with the help of a knife slash, they released its skin, intact, to be sold to the chairmakers and flask coverers and also the tourists who flocked to buy native crafts in the shops in Caracas.

He found Lucien much as he had found him before, still in his underworld, still manacled, still scarred.

'Ai, Cruz,' he said. 'How good to see you.'

Cruz smiled and resented his cheerfulness, just as Lucien's jailers and interrogators and trackers had resented it.

'This is not good, Dom Lucien,' Cruz told him bluntly, spreading his arms to take in the grey-green walls of Lucien's stinking cell.

'I don't mind it, Cruz, so why should you?'

Cruz shrugged and murmured, 'Muito bem.' He then proceeded to unload his bags. They had all been tipped out and prodded and damaged at the searching post outside, and he apologised for their condition.

'They look fine to me,' Lucien reassured him, reaching across to hold a fragile, wilting mint plant in his one free hand. Together, they arranged a window box, although there was no window to place it by, and Cruz watered it from a plastic flask he had brought specially for that purpose.

'How will you manage?' he asked.

'I'll manage,' Lucien told him.

Cruz had no sooner settled down to draw Lucien into talking than the same guard as before hammered on the reinforced door and shouted, 'Time's up, little scum.'

Cruz rose to go, reluctantly.

'Have you been chained like that all this time?' he asked, as he gathered his empty bags together.

'No,' Lucien said.

'Are you sure?' Cruz insisted.

'I'm sure,' Lucien smiled.

Then Cruz left him again, relieved by this last reply. Lucien had sounded very sure as he said it, as well he might, for what Cruz did not know, and never would, was that Lucien had spent the previous eighteen months chained not by one hand and foot, but splayed out on the floor of an even deeper cell elsewhere, with every limb immobilised, pinned to the ground like a great dead frog. And the food he had eaten was what food he could suck into his mouth from that which was thrown on top of him to waste and rot. Even Misia Schmutter had shrivelled there. By some strange irony, he had flourished on that killing floor, and although Cruz found him haggard, he was stronger within than he had ever been before.

Mariana visited Lucien twice in Valencia: once to see him and once to tell him that she would not come again. She had visited him faithfully for twelve years. She loathed his prisons, and the sight of Lucien in his cell seemed to silence the words in her mouth. Even after she had nothing to share but her taciturn depression, she had still gone, every Monday and Friday, to sit and stare in what she believed to be a penance for her desertion. On Fridays, as man and wife, they had access to a curtained cubicle for half an hour, but even there Mariana kept her silence.

She was like a clock whose movement is subtly wrong. Time had passed through her, exacerbating the mismatching of her threads. Her very presence disturbed. She disturbed herself, and it seemed only natural that she should disturb others. When she moved, the people around her stood still. And on the rare occasions when she danced, her partners became so exhilarated they were sometimes physically sick. It was as though her steps were so perfect, they

276

were wrong. Her gaze and her thoughts were so intense that they wore down her admirers and they wore her down too. In the long years of waiting for Lucien's freedom, she had chafed and grated on her own nerves until the internal corrosion was such that there was scarcely any emotion left to grind.

By 1952, of the strange, volatile love she had felt for Lucien, there seemed to be nothing left but the shell. The years had passed, and Mariana had felt that shell crumble. The frailer she became, the harder she found it to bear the sight of Lucien in his jail.

She used to feel that she would have changed places with him to save him from the insanity of his grey cell. There were days when Lucien could hardly breathe, and days when she wanted to weep. It was after Lucien's recapture and his return from his long months of solitary confinement that Mariana felt her clock break down. The springs and coils, hammers and wires, had seen her through for so many years that it came as a shock when her whole inner mechanism snapped. Mariana knew from the scars on Lucien's hands and face that she couldn't bear to share his pain any longer. She would have liked to have stood by him for ever, but she was always out of step. She had been like the striking of phosphorus, and then, after twelve years of prison visits, she had become a mere pile of ash.

In Valencia Cruz had asked Lucien about the charge of cannibalism which was the talk of all Caracas, and which alone had caused Lucien's former fans to hate him. It was not that Cruz believed in the charge; apart from the ethics of the case, it was quite impossible that Lucien would have eaten the fat and pock-marked carcass of his former inmate and fellow escapee. What bothered Cruz was why Lucien had confessed to the deed. Even before there had been enough time to torture him as they must eventually have done, *El Nacional* reported that Dom Lucien was asked about the case: what became of the remainder of the man, one Mazamorra, parts of whose dismembered body he and Nelson Rojas, who escaped with him, were found to be carrying over their shoulders at Caricoa? Lucien was reported to have said, 'I ate him.' Those three words were enough.

'But why, Dom Lucien?' Cruz asked, when he had finally plucked up the courage to do so. 'Why did you say it?'

And Lucien had replied, 'You probably won't understand this, even if I tell you. They were questioning, questioning, questioning, until I couldn't bear the wheedling of their voices any more. So when they said for the thousandth time, "What did you do with the rest of the third man, Mazamorra?", I just said, "I ate him". It was supposed to be a joke, Cruz.'

Cruz was silent for a while, and then Lucien asked, 'Well, are you satisfied?'

Cruz whispered, 'Muito bem,' without raising his eyes from the ground, and he left shortly afterwards. On the train home from Valencia to Caracas, he brooded, and wondered if he dared ask Lucien why he was carrying Mazamorra's leg over his shoulder at all. Perhaps, Cruz thought, as he unloaded his many empty bags at Caracas, that is something that I will understand later. Cruz never did ask this other question, and Lucien never gave him the answer. Just as Cruz never asked him why he never bared his back again. He assumed that it was to hide yet more scars, which in a way it was: the huge blue letters branded into his flesh reading CANNIBAL. Lucien was not ashamed of the name so much as the brand that had been singed through poor Misia Schmutter's already shrivelled flesh. It hurt him more than his own pain, this desecration of her remains.

As for Mazamorra, the supposedly eaten man, he had wanted to be famous. All his life he had stolen and mugged and lied to that end. Would it, Lucien wondered, have satisfied his pride to be known as one of the most celebrated victims in Venezuelan criminal history? Of all the people who had heard of Lucien's 'joke' and taken it seriously and accused him of cannibalism and marked him down as a monster, perhaps Mazamorra alone would have appreciated the jest. If he could have made a choice between dying as he did, mauled and half-eaten by a cayman in the jungle, with no one to grieve for him for more than a few minutes, and no one to miss him ever again, and this invented death, in a blaze of publicity with colour photographs of his bloody remains in every newspaper and mugshots of his wayward hair and his slightly squinting eyes and his huge stomach that gave him his name, Lucien was sure he would have chosen the latter.

Of all the people he had known in his life, and of all the things he had done, only the cannibalism and Mazamorra would stick and still keep him famous when he emerged from prison after twenty-five years inside. Misia Schmutter, and Niemenberg, his plants and his gazebos, San Fernando, and the tiger, were all forgotten. One fat convict and his dismembered body must stand for them all.

VI

The
Tower
of
Oblivion

Chapter 28

*T*HE DAY OF LUCIEN'S RELEASE IN 1965 BEGAN LIKE ALL the other days in his prison routine in Trujillo, the mountain fortress where he had been held for the last ten years of his sentence. The only cellmate he would regret leaving was Molinas. Molinas was the one prisoner who had been with him for every day of the last ten years. Nobody could remember what Molinas was in for, let alone Molinas himself. Lucien held the record for the longest surviving prisoner, but Molinas must surely come second. Where Lucien had had the strength to resist his torture, battered but unbroken, Molinas was one of seven men who had been selected for a new kind of prison treatment. He had been injected with a massive dose of equine encephalitis. The other six had died more or less immediately, while Molinas had staggered on, and survived, a trembling, shuddering, human wreck.

At the beginning, Lucien had cared for him out of pity, but over the years, after he had learned to decipher Molinas's speech, he came to admire the man and his spirit, which was, in its way, as unbending as his own. Molinas had one great virtue left in life: he was the prison champion at tapas. Tapas was a game of shuffling lids, and it depended on the swiftness and skill with which these bottle lids, or tapas, could be switched. Molinas, for all his disability, could still move them faster than anyone else, and it was this skill that most endeared him to Lucien.

So when he rose on his last day of captivity, after he had shaved but before he had lit his Primus stove to cook his

283

breakfast, Lucien asked Molinas to play a game of tapas with him. Molinas's furrowed and anguished face lit up, and he stammered a reply. Then he sat down on the floor with three beer-bottle tops in front of him, and placed a tiny ball of silver foil under the middle one. He shuffled the lids and asked in his almost unintelligible way, 'Which one?' Lucien had watched him play the trick a thousand times, and never caught him out. Molinas kept this unbroken record to the end, since Lucien could not locate the lid that hid the silver ball.

By the time that Cruz arrived to escort him home to Caracas, all his belongings were packed. Apart from a few guards there was no one to say goodbye to after all the years he had spent there. Of his friends, Mazamorra was dead and gone in an ignominious blaze of glory, and Nelson Rojas, who had escaped with him, had died under torture at San Juan de los Morros, and Diego Beltrán, who had been with him in Trujillo for a year as a political prisoner, had long since gone home to his sugar plantation. Diego had been the only other literate person ever to share his cell, and they had in common an interest in agriculture and architecture, poetry and philosophy. Mostly, though, Diego had kept himself to himself, crouched in a kind of brooding intensity in his corner of their communal cell, with his own books around him and his gramophone with its Linguaphone French and his rival Primus stove.

At times when Diego had been too absorbed in his own thoughts, Lucien had taken one of his many 'holidays'. These so-called holidays were of the utmost importance to him. But for them, he would have found the monotony of his imprisonment intolerable. It was an accepted fact of the cell's routine that when Lucien's books were turned with their spines facing outwards, and his Primus was covered with a cloth like a sleeping canary, and his plants were draped with elaborate strings and bits of wool dripping out of buckets, and Lucien himself was turned with his face to the wall, then he was 'away'. Everyone who ever saw him doing this thought it peculiar, but no one was brave enough to say so. A prison needed its own routine, and what other prisoners did or didn't do was their own business. No one really questioned another's sanity, they just got through their time as best they could. If Lucien, who was so generous and strange, chose to unwind by turning his back for two days and then getting up and claiming he had been to the Mediterranean or to a Pension Helbig on the Marienterrasse in Hamburg which he often claimed he visited, that was up to him. And if he turned back towards his cellmates with tales of a battered old hotel in Surinam called the Krasnapolski that he described to them in minute and nostalgic detail, and from which he claimed he had just returned, well, that was his business too. Diego had never been to Europe, but he sometimes felt that he could find his way through Hamburg or Berlin by the backstreets and alleyways that Lucien described.

By 1965 Diego had long since gone back to his workers and his sugar-cane, and one day, Lucien thought as he bolted his steel-edged trunks, he would visit him there. Meanwhile, Cruz had come to ferry his master away from Trujillo's Bastille, with his luggage and his scars and his middle age. There was no train from Trujillo to take them from the bright sunlight of the winding cobbled streets of the Andean capital to a place where Lucien could adjust to his new circumstances, but Cruz had come prepared with a rusty red Dodge pick-up truck which he had bought years before when Lucien was moved to Trujillo, since the Cadillacs and the mavericks of Caracas couldn't manage the pock-marked cobbles of Andean tracks.

Lucien looked around him as he stepped outside, and he registered no surprise at the changes that he saw. He looked as though he were returning from a visit to a business acquaintance, rather than from a twenty-five-year term. Lucien looked down the slope of variegated leaves that dropped away on one side of the road, and his eyes scanned the scrubby growth and the unravelling town behind him and the vultures circling in the sky between the hills. He was looking for Mariana. Again, he was not surprised that he did not see her there, but he was vaguely disappointed; he would have liked to have been greeted by her face with its shadow of his dead sister Katrina.

Lucien knew that it was Misia Schmutter who had driven Mariana away, just as she had done to Katrina. As he left the prison, Mariana was in Italy, and he had not seen Katrina's grave since his journey from Guiana through the jungle with Cruz. He was ten years away from his wife and twenty-five years away from his sister's grave, let alone his sister. Misia Schmutter's weakening touch at his throat was all that was left of the Orinoco as he stood beside Cruz's rusty truck, dizzy with the bright light and the memories of San Fernando and the cemetery where the towering tomb of Misia Schmutter and the almost equally towering tomb of Chucho Delgado overshadowed Katrina.

Cruz had told him of el Patrón's death, shortly after Lucien's first conviction. Once a year, Cruz went to clear the family graves for him. Whether or not he actually went to San Fernando as he claimed, or just went once and then delegated his mission, Lucien couldn't tell. He knew that Cruz hated the Orinoco and the Apure Rivers, and he hated the jungle and el Llano. Even so, Lucien was sure that Cruz had been, at least once, because he told him that el Patrón's grave was marked simply with his name and the date of his death, and carved into the stone was a sun with an arc of rays like a rainbow, and he had described the mended angel on Chucho's tomb, and the graffiti on Misia Schmutter's. Lucien was always grateful to whatever mason had chiselled the rainbow on to his father's stone, for el Patrón had spent most of his life at the Arco Iris, the Rainbow brothel in San Fernando town.

On his first day of freedom, Lucien could have gone to the old estate itself. He was deterred by the memory of his last brief visit there on his return from his travels in 1939. All his work had been gradually undone, like the unpicking of a darn. His canals and drains had silted up or crumbled to dust, and his fruit trees had wilted and his prize stock died, often he suspected to fill a pot. The pipes that he had so laboriously laid had been ripped out and sold for scrap. His dipping pens had been turned upside down and now housed several families. Where he had planted rotating crops, all the land was back under the hoof of the lumpy Ceibu cows, uncrossed again gradually from the foreign stock he had brought in, and around their horns there was a halo of flies. And in the sky, the vultures were waiting for them to drop. Everything, in fact, was as it had been in the beginning, in his childhood, before he had tried to change the ways of the plains, and when the only tigers were the jaguars that roamed the mud flats attacking the stray cattle. That was before Misia Schmutter, the tyrant of San Fernando, who it was said could rule the very Orinoco, had eaten his heart away and climbed on his back.

'Shall I drive, Dom Lucien?' Cruz asked him, and Lucien

nodded. So Cruz drove along the thin road to Valera with its varying shades of green and its ruined sugar plantations, half built over with housing estates or occasionally turned into car dumps, and everywhere he went the hoardings told him 'buy this' or 'buy that', 'do this' or 'do that'; it was as though Misia Schmutter herself had invested her power in advertising. Lucien just looked out of the window as Cruz drove him to the smallholding outside Mendoza Fría which had been his home for the past many years, and was all that he had to offer Lucien. There were circles of charred hill slopes where the forest fires had taken their toll, and there were piles of rubbish by the roadside and cardboard tin-roofed huts, and he wondered if all the world had changed while he was in prison and become this strange patchwork place with which he seemed to have nothing in common.

After Betijoque with its blue and white church and its prim white houses, and its kite's tail of straggling slums, they drove around the curves of Valera on the wide new road that had been built by the dictator Pérez Jiménez while Lucien had been inside.

Whenever a crash or accident had taken place, a wooden cross was staked into the ground, and Lucien noticed how sometimes the stakes seemed to almost join tips like a fence of blunt white fingers. For mile after mile of curving empty road they travelled through the half-wooded, half-desert landscape, passing clumps of balloon-like cacti and knots of araguaney and half-starved goats and children scrabbling in the dust for whatever earth or roots there they might eat. Lucien watched, as they passed, the background of lush woods with their fringe of burnt hillocks of dust, and it was, to his eye, a desolate landscape, not like el Llano with its endless horizon. In the prison there had been despair, outside there was lethargy.

When they finally reached Mendoza Fría, two hours later, Lucien decided to stay there, not because he particularly liked what he saw, but because he could not bring himself to see any more of the ravaged countryside. La Cañada de Mendoza was proud of its eccentricity, and like anywhere else that housed such violent disparities, it offered a reasonable asylum for himself and his bizarre tastes.

Lucien felt that he had lived for so long he had no idea how old he actually was. Misia Schmutter's memory had imprinted itself on his own, and her cares were his cares, and though her physical presence had dwindled until it was scarcely a burden at all, there was all the complexity of her mind and her bitterness to deal with and carry around.

Cruz had planted a thriving and exotic garden on the four hectares around the ramshackle wattle and daub house with its tiled floors and its pantiled roof held together with weeds and wires and blobs of cement where the leaks were most persistent. Cruz had bought the old house many years before from a desiccated coffee-grower and his wife, and for thirteen years he had nursed and extended its garden. By the time that Lucien came to see it, there was hardly another garden in Trujillo as full or as flourishing, except, perhaps, for Doña Delia's in Tempé.

Lucien spent the weeks immediately after his release pacing the crumbling rooms of Cruz's house and wandering restlessly in and out of the garden. Even Cruz, who had waited for so long for Lucien's freedom, found his presence disconcerting. He became aware of the flimsiness of the walls, and of a kind of wildness in Lucien that seemed to need something stronger than wasp-ridden wattle and daub to contain it. In the evenings, when Lucien used to sit on the verandah staring into the night through a haze of gnats and flying ants, Cruz would try to tempt him to play. Lucien, however, seemed to have lost his taste for roulette. It was as though his wheel had spun so many times that it had worn out its pivot, and red and black were no longer enough to fire what was left.

On Wednesdays and Saturdays, Lucien relented and played dominoes with Cruz by candlelight on the buzzing verandah. And every night he would cook elaborate and beautifully served meals for him, which he ate in silence, speaking only to himself to suggest minor, and to Cruz incomprehensible, changes in the recipes. Part of each day would be spent in cooking, and another in preparing medicinal herbs as salves and tinctures, and another in staring. He wrote regularly to the blank silence of Mariana in Rome, filling long pages with philosophy and nostalgia. There were no letter-boxes in Mendoza Fría or La Caldera, and that was how the locals came to know that the old recluse with the blue eyes at Mendoza was called Lucien. For them he was strange because he sent letters at all, let alone received them, and stranger still because his letters went to a place called Italia, which la Nena Bertoni said she had heard of but nobody else had. This tenuous connection with la Nena Bertoni ensured a measure of protection to Lucien. Cruz had been tending his garden on the hill for years with his 'muito bem' and his otherwise impenetrable silence. The village and the town had bristled with curiosity when Lucien arrived, but the commandant at the barracks had announced that Don Diego Beltrán thought this new man, Lucien, 'all right'—so he must be, and they left him alone.

Nobody got to know Lucien properly, until he began work on his tower, and that was, some said, weeks, and some said months, after his sudden arrival in Mendoza. This tower became the source of endless wrangling, with no two people agreeing on its height, age, purpose, or inner measurements. Even those labourers and masons who assisted in its construction varied their descriptions of it so widely that it was impossible to tell whether or not they were all talking about the same building. Even Cruz, had he been asked to, could not have sworn when the tower was begun. It just seemed to materialise in the orchard, rising from the ground in the middle of the garden. One day it was a low wall of stone, and the next, whole rooms had begun to grow on to it in a way that Cruz could never understand. Only Lucien himself, with his plans and diagrams, knew how the tower should be, and how it was.

At Niemenberg, Lucien's dreams and fantasies had spread out on a palatial scale; at Mendoza, however, they just rose upwards. There had never been a tower in the valley of the Momboy. Carmania, the House of the Libertador, had narrow third-floor balconies, and Don Diego Beltrán's father had built a turret on his roof to house his library, and churches had spires, but Lucien's tower grew higher and higher, far outreaching any comparison with these places. There was no speed in the building of it, no race to finish by a certain date. This time, there was no Mariana to impress, and no city squashed against his gates to monitor his rate of progress. Neither did he need to lure Misia Schmutter back to him, as he had when he built his palace. All that was left of his grandmother was with him already. The old days of his choking were over; and her presence was reduced to an occasional wheeze or catch in his breath.

Sometimes, when he dosed one of his masons or their families, he would be advised to slow-cook a sting-ray in an earthenware pot, and take the oil from it and drink it night and morning. 'It's very good for asthma,' they told him, and on the way out of his bare grey dispensary, they would repeat the recipe to Cruz, in the hopes that he could ease his master's breathing. But Cruz knew better than to try. He had been a party to the worries of the prison doctors. As early as 1942, they had found Lucien to be tubercular. They had X-rayed his lungs and discovered a black spot of such sinister proportions that they and their colleagues called in from the military hospital declared it a miracle that Lucien was still alive. After six months of streptomycin and subsidiary drugs, the black spot was still there, and Lucien still choked and gasped in his art deco cell. He was shunted back and forth between the hospital wing and his cell, and injected and dosed and rested and X-rayed, but the black spot remained, immune to their best endeavours. After one and two and three years, Lucien's black spot still came out on the photos of his lungs; and after five years it was there, and after ten. Then, long after all treatment had ceased, it almost disappeared. That was when Lucien escaped and was caught and held in San Juan de los Morros, and tortured and branded with the word CANNIBAL singed, into his back: it was after his solitary confinement, and on his return to the comparatively civilised routine of an orthodox prison.

The doctors never understood this phenomenon of Lucien's black spot. They were sure that he had T.B., he had the haggard look of a man close to death. Even the other inmates knew. They used to say that Lucien had 'el tigre encaramado', which was their way of saying that he had terminal T.B. Cruz knew that there was nothing terminal about Lucien's lack of breath. He knew that it was his master's mysterious power that wrestled with his lungs. And only Lucien knew that it was Misia Schmutter, who had ridden him for all the years of his life, from the time he was three when she took him from his nursery, and only he knew that she had shrivelled in humiliation when they branded her grandson's back.

So Lucien built his tower in Tempé, the low hill on the outskirts of the chill mountain village of Mendoza Fría, and it rose up through the dry weather and the rains. And from the ground floor he dispensed his drugs and remedies, on Wednesdays and Saturdays from sunrise until noon. At first, it was only his builders and their wives and children

who came to be cured by the blue-eyed man. As word of
his cures fanned through the hills, more and more people
made the pilgrimage to his unfinished tower. There was a
man outside Carmania who could diagnose any disease by
holding up a sample of a sick person's urine to the sun, and
there were sobanderas on the hills who could massage
away anything from colitis to a broken bone, but Lucien
did more. He made people feel at peace with themselves,
and whether they lived or died, they did so with a kind of
inner strength which they attributed directly to his influence. They discussed the feeling with Cruz, and they marvelled how Don Lucien had driven the bitternss away from
Mendoza Fría. And when they were gone, Cruz discussed
the merits of his master, who still pretended that he was
Cruz's father, with his girlfriend of many years who came
from nearby San Isidro and was called Teresa and was
soon to be married to Cruz and move into the rambling
house on the hill.

Periodically, Lucien would order all the scaffolding to be
taken away from his tower, and he would live in the lower
rooms and sit staring out at the wooded hills that barred his
view across the valley. Even when the building work was
halted, he still saw patients in his dispensary, but he alone
would add to the tower then, carving and chipping away at
the stone to embellish this or that lintel. It was, by his
standards, a very plain tower, although plainness was always ornamented for Lucien, it was just a matter of degree. Only Cruz, who made annual visits to San Fernando
to tend the graves of el Patrón and Katrina and Chucho
Delgado and Misia Schmutter herself, realised that Lucien
was building his own mausoleum. So while the local people
inquired, 'When will it be finished?', and while they argued
and fought among themselves over the time of its comple-
tion, and eyed the massive tower with impatience, only
Cruz hoped that it would never be done, since he could not
envisage life without Lucien. Not even Teresa, not even
after they were married, could replace the feeling of mystic
allegiance that he felt for Lucien.

Meanwhile, Lucien himself carved his stones, making
crude spearheads and angels to adorn this unusual tomb
that he was designing for Misia Schmutter and himself to
lie in. Except on Wednesdays and Saturdays, he saw no
one but Cruz and occasionally Teresa. He would have liked

291

to have entertained his friends, but his friends were gone. He recalled how he had once told Gernot Sieveking in Hamburg that his idea of bliss was to build the tallest tower in the world and live on its battlemented roof. Now it seemed that the tower was taking shape, although everything else had gone. Even the sight of the contented villagers served to remind him of Mariana, steeped in her inner bitterness, far away in Italy and immune then as she always had been to his powers. He kept a certain room of the house furnished and ready to receive a friend. He would have liked particularly to see Diego Beltrán again, but he never invited him, and Diego never came. Instead, Diego's wife, la Musiua, visited him from time to time, and it was her whom he told of his sense of failure.

'I have been waiting sixty years', he said, 'to know what my mission in life would be, and now it seems that I have somehow missed the point. My grandmother wanted so much for me, you see, and it saddens me to know that she lived and died as unloved as she did, having sacrificed everything for me.'

'But you seem to have done so much,' la Musiua would protest.

'No, I have waited, and done nothing. When I die there will be nothing left but this tower. I have failed her. And you cannot know, it is a terrible thing to fail Misia Schmutter.'

'Perhaps you expected too much, Lucien.'

'Perhaps I did. But behind all her hopes and her power there was the dread of being stoned as a witch. Even the word hurt her. In San Fernando where she is buried, someone always scratches the word on to her tomb. Cruz goes every year and has it sanded away, but each year it returns. There is nobody left in the town, I am told, old enough to remember her tyranny. All the local people have moved or died, and the cattle ranches are tended by Colombians, and yet they still scratch WITCH into her stone year after year.'

La Musiua looked around at the faded roulette wheel that always stood uncovered in the room, and a huge wormeaten German bible, and a tray of trinkets, and the folders of architectural engravings, and she could think of nothing to say. Lucien looked around him in the silence, letting his eyes rest on the plates of millefeuilles and éclairs that he always served la Musiua when she came, and he wondered whether she came to see him or for the tea, and decided that it was probably both.

'What do you think rules life, Musiua?' he asked after a while.

'I don't know,' his visitor replied.

'Well, Misia Schmutter thought she did, and she taught me to control chance so that I would too. So I could say chance, and self-control, but then there is waiting. She told me about beauty and science and chance, and she forgot to warn me about waiting. She waited all those years on el Llano and they broke her in the end. The life is in the waiting. It's just a matter of balance, like this tower of stone, with time balancing one year on top of another.'

'Why always stone?' la Musiua interrupted him.

'Chucho Delgado used to say that stone was the best thing there was because the vultures broke their beaks against it.'

'Why did you pick this place?'

'Why did you?'

La Musiua shrugged and smiled.

Lucien thought, and then he too was silent: when it came to love, his feelings were so intense that he could not express them by any means other than his building. His tower would have to speak for him just as his pavilions had done before. La Musiua asked him why he used stone, but she was young and full of enthusiasms that he could not share, and he had not wanted to tell her that he used it in memory of the hard reality of el Llano, and of the bare horizons. And he used it as a homage to the ungiving tyranny of Misia Schmutter and his love for her, and as a reminder of Katrina's backboard and of the hardness at the core of Mariana that kept her away from him, and of the stone that had obsessed Chucho Delgado, and of the stone that had given him his hope and his pleasure for every day of his strange life as an example to, and an outcast from, the world.

La Musiua had risen from her seat and she was fingering the windowsill restlessly. Lucien looked up, and she said, 'And when the tower is finished, and it is taller even than my own mill chimney, taller than anything else in the Andes, and years have passed, and you are dead, what do you want people to think when they see it?'

'Nothing.'

'What do you mean, nothing? They'll have to think something.'

'Yes, but let them think what they will. By then, the tower will have nothing to do with it; because when I am dead the tower must be demolished.'

'But I thought it was a tomb.'

'A tomb of stones, let them arrange themselves as they will, and people will hear the legend and maybe know the site, but their thoughts must be their own.'

'How do you know they won't forget you?'

'Legends are rarely forgotten, and that's just a chance I have to take.'

Through the floods and droughts of the succeeding years Lucien remained in the memories of the people, not as a legend but as a living man with a tower. And the tower grew until it was higher than Don Diego's chimney on the Hacienda La Bebella, and higher by far than the spires of the churches of Saint Peter and Saint Paul, and more than three times the height, some said, of the tower at El Niño Jesús de Escuque, and it was higher than any ceiba or silk cotton tree, and higher than the royal palms that grew in a kind of arrogant exile and whose tops could be seen on a clear day from Mendoza. Some people went to see the tower, and some to seek a cure, and some, like la Musiua, went to see Lucien himself. Gradually, the small Andean world that he had moved to began to revolve around Lucien. There was scarcely a woman in the whole of Trujillo who didn't want to soothe the sadness out of his deep-blue eyes. The very wrinkles in his face merely stood to remind them how smooth his skin must once have been, before whatever cares had sapped his smiles of their almost godlike power. So while the women dreamt of him, the men drew strength from his sense of calm.

The tower was at the core of his endeavours, and he was in the tower, and near to him were Cruz and his wife Teresa, like a protective filter against the world which spread out on all sides with its patchwork of dead or dying sugar-cane where the drought had dug in its thumbs and squeezed out the last drop of sticky guarapo. He saw the valley of the Momboy decay, and after many years, when the rains returned, he helped to build it again, always from his tower on his hill in Tempé. Drought and tyranny were in his blood, they couldn't shake his faith which was a faith in the order and beauty of things and, above all, in Misia Schmutter.

Cruz saw the people coming time after time with their troubles and worries, and he saw them leaving with some of the same hope and relief that he himself had found in the presence of Lucien so many years before in the marketplace at Caravelas. And Cruz and Teresa had three sons and the sons grew and became the tacit would-be heirs of the strange old man who lived in the tower with his mysterious wealth and power. And not even Cruz knew how or where the wealth came from, now that Lucien had relinquished his wheel. Apart from his dominoes on Wednesdays and Saturdays, Dom Lucien no longer played games, except to play tapas with his former cellmate, the decrepit and trembling Molinas, on his rare visits to the tower.

In La Cañada it was said that the sound of Lucien's wheezing echoed through the valley at nights in the familiar rhythm of the sugar mills from the days before they were ruined. And it was said that Lucien could defy vultures and the Evil Eye. And though their sons were press-ganged and dragged from the fields, and crops failed, the people of Mendoza kept their pride. And Lucien symbolised their dignity with his tower that grew higher and higher, defying even the laws of nature with its height.

About the Author

LISA ST. AUBIN DE TURAN is the winner of the 1983 Somerset Maugham Award for her first novel, KEEPERS OF THE HOUSE, and the John Llewellyn Rys Memorial Prize for THE SLOW TRAIN TO MILAN. She is also the author of THE BAY OF SILENCE. For seven years she ran a plantation in Venezuela and her first three books drew on that experience. She lives with her husband, poet George MacBeth, and their two children in Norfolk, England.